Traitor's Legacy

No.1 *Sunday Times* bestseller S. J. Parris is the pseudonym of the author and journalist Stephanie Merritt. She is the author of fourteen books, including her bestselling Giordano Bruno series, set during the 1580s, which has sold over a million copies in the UK.

Stephanie has worked as a critic and feature writer for a variety of newspapers and magazines, as well as radio and television, and currently writes for the *Observer*. Under her own name, she has also written the contemporary psychological thrillers *While You Sleep* and *Storm*. She lives in Surrey.

www.sjparris.com

@sjmerrittbooks

S.J. PARRIS

Traitor's Legacy

HEMLOCK
PRESS

Hemlock Press,
an imprint of HarperCollins*Publishers* Ltd
1 London Bridge Street
London SE1 9GF

www.harpercollins.co.uk

HarperCollins*Publishers*
Macken House,
39/40 Mayor Street Upper,
Dublin 1
D01 C9W8, Ireland

First published by HarperCollins*Publishers* Ltd 2025
1

A catalogue record for this book is available from the British Library.

ISBN: 978-0-00-859579-1 (HB)
ISBN: 978-0-00-859580-7 (TPB)

Set in Sabon LT Std by HarperCollins*Publishers* India

Printed and bound in the UK using 100% Renewable
Electricity at CPI Group (UK) Ltd

MIX
Paper | Supporting
responsible forestry
FSC
www.fsc.org
FSC™ C007454

This book contains FSC™ certified paper and other controlled
sources to ensure responsible forest management.

For more information visit: www.harpercollins.co.uk/green

Dramatis Personae

The de Wolfe household:
Sophia de Wolfe, widow of Humphrey de Wolfe
Hilary Mabey, steward
Jasper de Wolfe, son of Humphrey de Wolfe
Lina, a maid
Mick, a manservant

The Lord Chamberlain's Men:
Richard Burbage, principal actor
Will Shakespeare, writer and actor
Tobie Strange, actor and musician
Doug, actor
Jo Goodchild, costume maker

The court:
Sir Robert Cecil, Master Secretary to Queen Elizabeth, and also her spymaster
Thomas Phelippes, his cryptographer
Robert Devereux, Earl of Essex
Frances Devereux, Countess of Essex
Lizzie Sidney, Frances's daughter by her first husband, Sir Philip Sidney

The North household:
Sir Thomas North, diplomat, soldier, translator
Lady Judith North, his wife
Edmund North, his son
Agnes Lovell, his ward
Fred, a stable boy

The Admiral's Men:
Philip Henslowe, theatre impresario
Ned Alleyn, principal actor
Anthony Munday, writer and former spy
John Singer, a clown

Sundry characters:
Leila Humeya, midwife and physician
Beth Munday, Anthony's wife
Nat Leman, a soldier
Dan Hammett, proprietor of the Saracen's Head
Ben Hammett, his son
Badger, a street child
Roger Manners, Earl of Rutland
Grace Perry, a nursemaid

PROLOGUE

28th December 1598

The armed men come at first light, a dozen in all, boots churning up the fresh snow. On their shoulders they carry swords, bills, axes; their faces are set grim against the cold. At their head strides a broad-chested man of some thirty or so winters, with the bearing of a Roman general, or perhaps an English prince; he calls encouragement to his fellows as they march through the dawn streets. They make a curious regiment: grey-bearded men in step with skinny youths; weather-worn faces that speak of outdoor labour next to the pale complexions and ink-stained hands of scholars. Shutters creak open as they pass, bleary-eyed neighbours squinting to glimpse the strange procession.

A street boy, feet wrapped in sacking, dances beside the men, seeming oblivious to the weather.

'Where are you going?'

'To war,' says their leader, not breaking his pace.

'In Ireland?' The boy's eyes widen. He has a white streak through his brown hair that makes him look like an inquisitive badger.

'In Shoreditch. Will you join us?'

'How much?'

The man laughs. 'Fourpence if you keep lookout. Can you whistle?'

The boy puts two fingers in his mouth and produces an alarum that could carry all the way across the frozen Thames to Bankside. The few passers-by stop in their tracks and stare.

'No, really, draw everyone's attention to our business, why don't you,' mutters one of the company, the one with the high forehead and serious eyes.

'Go home to your writing table, if this is too much adventure for you,' calls the leader cheerfully. His companion responds with something inaudible, trudging sullenly in his wake.

Two girls of the town – face-paint smudged after a busy night – watch the motley band as they round the corner on to Holywell Lane.

'I know him,' says one, nodding to the man at the front.

'Be a rarity to find a man in London you haven't known,' says her friend, pulling her shawl tighter.

'No, I mean' – the first girl smiles and shakes her head – 'I've seen him before. I can't place his name though. Come on, let's see what this is about.'

'Just call them all "sweetheart", that way you don't have to remember,' sniffs the other, though she follows in the hope of some diversion. Where can they be heading, at this hour?

The men stop in front of a shuttered building on Curtain Road. The snow falls thicker, settling on hat brims and sleeves, making white waves of the rutted street. The facade before them has a forlorn and neglected air; two years now since its timbers shook to the laughter or gasps of a crowd, on account of the leasehold dispute.

'Well, then, gentlemen,' says the broad-chested man, planting the handle of his pikestaff in the snow. Now that they are here, he seems less certain of how to proceed. 'You,' he says, snapping his fingers at the boy, who is still skipping at his side. 'Stand on that corner, whistle if anyone comes.' He flicks a coin in the air; it spins through the whirling flakes and the boy catches it deftly.

'Like who?'

'Constables. Magistrates.' The man thinks. 'Lawyers especially. You know what a lawyer's robes look like?'

'Course.' The boy glances up at the building. 'Are you robbing, then?'

'No indeed. You can't steal your own property. Am I right, gentlemen?' He turns to his fellows; they murmur doubtful assent.

'God's teeth,' says a big man as he pushes to the front. He wears a rabbit-skin hat and the apron of a master builder over his jacket. 'Stop your jawing and let's get this done while the light lasts, before we freeze our bollocks off.' And he raises a mallet and smashes it into the plaster between two joists.

'*Romeo!*' says the painted girl suddenly, pointing as the men begin to dismantle the structure before their eyes. '*That's who he is. He's Romeo.*'

'Oh yes! And Prince Hal,' exclaims her friend, delighted. They work the playhouses sometimes.

'Richard the Third!'

'Tamburlaine!'

The man who led the company hears them and turns, sweeping off his hat in a low bow to reveal a thatch of curly hair, receding only a little.

'Ladies. Richard Burbage, player, at your service.'

'You're tearing down The Theatre?'

'Not at all. Merely carrying out a few necessary refurbishments.' He offers a charming smile as a beam falls at his back.

'Christ's sake, Burbage,' one of the men shouts from the doorway, dust billowing around him, 'this was your damnable idea. Are you going to leave the rest of us to do the hard part?'

'Do excuse me, dear ladies.' And Romeo retreats to pull down a supporting wall, humming a plaintive song of love as he goes.

By the time dusk falls, the snow is ankle-deep and all the timbers have been loaded on to waiting wagons, the horses straining and slipping under the load. The site of The Theatre is now a patch of torn-up earth, scarred with trenches where the foundations once stood, like the wounds left by pulled teeth. Over the course of the day, an audience has gathered, scuffles and arguments breaking out between supporters of the men stripping the building and those who call them thieves and scoundrels, but as it grows dark and the last posts are tethered to a cart, even the most dedicated onlookers drift away.

'What will you do with it?' asks the badger-haired boy, eyeing the wagons.

'Ship it across the river and rebuild it,' says the man called Burbage. His face is streaked with sweat, despite the cold, but he looks triumphant.

'Won't they come after you? For stealing it, I mean?'

'This is all bought and paid for, lad.' Burbage slaps his palm against a pile of beams. 'The Theatre was my father's life's work. Just not the land it stood on, unfortunately. But now we have new land, and we'll raise the finest playhouse London has ever seen. Here' – he tosses the boy a sixpence – 'buy yourself some boots.'

The child magics the coin away and watches as the convoy struggles south, towards the city. When the last cart has swung precariously around the corner, wraiths begin to appear from the gaps between buildings. London's poor, the dispossessed, the hungry, scouring the churned ground for anything the players might have left behind: any scraps of timber, half-bricks, iron nails, a glove or even a ring dropped in haste, anything that can be sold. Crows and magpies loudly announce

4

themselves, descending on the fresh-turned earth in search of food before falling snow covers it again. The boy observes all this dispassionately from his vantage point in the street. Even after the scavengers have left, he finds himself reluctant to abandon his post. He was appointed watchman, after all; if the curly-haired man should return and find him still on duty, there might be another coin in it.

Along the southern wall is a row of outbuildings that the players have not bothered to dismantle. These are padlocked, but the boy is skinny enough to work his way in through a broken window. He finds the place empty, but it will do for shelter; he pulls the sacking from the casement, wraps himself in it and settles in for the night.

He dozes, loses track of the passing hours measured out by church bells, so that when he catches the sound of voices outside – hushed, urgent – he has no idea what time it might be. He presses his face to the gap in the shutters and peers out.

People are approaching from the far side of the empty plot. He can't see how many; there's a faint glimmer of moon between the clouds and their breath steams in the raw air. Two, he thinks: swaddled in hooded cloaks and carrying something large and awkward between them. Wordlessly, they lower it into one of the trenches where the foundations stood. They re-emerge; there is a sharp, whispered exchange, then a sudden curse. One of the figures is casting around as if he has lost something; he even hops back into the hole, but his fellow – the boy is sure they are both men – is growing impatient, hissing at him to hurry. The one in the ground asks for a light; 'Are you mad?' the other snaps back. Another terse back-and-forth, ending with the second man stalking away. The one in the trench remains, his head and shoulders outlined against the snow.

Slowly, the boy bends to pick up a stone from the floor; reaching his arm through the window, he pitches it as hard as he can at the wall of a garden abutting the plot. As a strategy it's not without risk; they might come in search of him. But he has gambled correctly. At the clatter, the man starts and scrambles up, cursing again as he hastens after his companion into the night.

When he is certain they have gone, the boy climbs out and inches forward to peer over the edge of the hole. The snow lends a pale glow to the darkness; he can just make out the shape at the bottom.

It's a body, wrapped tight in a shroud. He'd guessed as much from the way they were carrying it, and evidently one that is not getting Christian burial. After a moment's pause, the boy jumps down into the trench that is now a grave; he knows from experience that the dead make no fuss about being robbed, and this body might have trappings – buttons, buckles, maybe an earring – worth a few pence. Even teeth can be sold if they're sound and you know the right people, though the boy lacks the implements to remove them. He is not afraid of death; he's seen it often enough in his years on the streets.

But as he pulls back a corner of the winding cloth – one hand over his mouth and nose, you never know if it's plague that took them – he jumps back in shock. Here is the face of a girl – beautiful, young, serene and unmoving as a marble tomb. Not much older than himself, perhaps (he thinks he is twelve, it's hard to keep track). He lifts the shroud back as far as her shoulders, but can see no obvious signs of violence. You might almost think she was sleeping, the way her dark lashes lie on her white cheeks. But then, if she died naturally, why has she been left here, for the crows and dogs to find? She is wearing no jewellery, at any rate, and appears to be dressed only in a plain wool gown. The boy considers whether to unwrap her further when his finely honed instincts prickle and he freezes, alert to the slightest disturbance of the air. Was that a scuffle along the boundary wall? Maybe no more than a fox, but if he should be found here, with her, he'll be taken for a killer. He decides to cut his losses. Snowflakes are falling on her face and this bothers him somehow; he moves to cover her again, but wait – what's this? Tucked inside her bodice is a folded paper with writing on it.

The boy breathes on his frozen fingers and debates whether to take it. He can't read, but he knows a woman who can; maybe this says something about who the girl is and why she died. But if he has to give account of himself, of how he came to find it, chances are the magistrates won't believe he didn't touch her. Let someone else deal with the consequences. He whispers an apology and covers her face.

The clink of a bridle cuts through the snow-muffled air, out on Curtain Road; the horse's snorting breath alarmingly close. The boy starts and topples back, landing on his backside next to the body; as he puts out a hand to steady himself he feels a sharp pain in his palm and closes his fingers around a small, hard object. Before the rider has passed, he levers himself nimbly out of the hole and bolts over the boundary wall, crouching in the shadows on the other side. There, he unfolds his fist and smiles to himself; he can just make out the gleam of a jewelled brooch lying on his palm, the kind gentlemen wear on their caps, worth a good deal more than the pennies he had from the players. All in all, a good day's work.

ONE

29th December 1598

Thrust in tierce. Counter parry; riposte in tierce over the arm. Engage, attack, advance, retreat. Circular parry in seconde, disengage. Lunge in quarte; riposte. *Good; again.*

The clash of foils and the quick breathing of the combatants is the only sound in the gallery. Candles have been lit against the scant midday light, casting an amber glow over the wood panelling and tapestries of hunting scenes. The fencing master feints, engages, but hesitates imperceptibly, less than the space between heartbeats, as a bead of sweat trickles into his eye; his pupil spots the opening and seizes on it, lunging forward over the arm, too fast for the fencing master, who finds himself backed up with the point of a foil at his throat.

'A palpable hit,' he concedes, glad of the chance for respite.

'Consider yourself dead.' His pupil's expression is unreadable behind the thin leather mask. Only a pair of bright tawny eyes are visible, missing nothing.

'Will we rest a moment?' the master asks hopefully.

'If you need to. I'll send for something to drink.' His pupil unties the ribbons holding the mask in place and shakes loose a cascade of chestnut hair, briefly releasing a scent of rosewater into the close air, before catching the locks and winding them into a coil, which she secures with a comb at the back of her head. Her face is flushed with the exertion and the triumph of winning a bout, making her seem younger than her thirty-five years. The fencing master, who is ten years older, wonders how much longer he will be able to keep up with her.

She lays her foil in its case, crosses the gallery and takes a linen cloth proffered by the young maid who waits unobtrusively in a window embrasure, ostensibly to fetch and carry but also for the sake of propriety; not that this is something Sophia de Wolfe cares about overmuch, but her steward insists on it.

'Lina, would you bring us a jug of small beer and some elderflower cordial?' she says, wiping her face.

The maid bobs a curtsy but, before she can obey, the doors at the far end of the gallery open to admit a tall woman in a severe black dress. She ignores the fencing master entirely and casts a disapproving glance at her mistress's attire, though she manages to compose her expression before speaking.

'Madam. Forgive the interruption, but there is a man at the gate demanding to see you.'

'Really? What manner of man?' Her tone is casual, but there was a flicker of tension and she knows Hilary caught it. Her steward has never asked about her past – she is well versed in discretion – but she misses nothing.

'One with few manners.' Hilary sniffs. 'Somewhat unkempt. Forties, if I had to guess. Fading yellow hair and a face marked with pox scars.'

Sophia is careful to betray nothing. 'And what does he want?'

'He won't say. But he insists that it's urgent.' A moment's hesitation before the steward hands over a folded slip of paper. 'He sent this.'

Sophia opens it, takes in the symbol marked there, nods and refolds it, pressing the crease sharp between her fingertips.

'Show him to the library,' she says. Her voice conveys neither pleasure nor apprehension.

'Madam—'

'You are reprieved, Maître Jules,' Sophia says, turning to the fencing master with a half-smile. 'Until the same time tomorrow, anyway. Lina, you can bring those drinks to the library, but you won't need to stay.'

'Madam.' Hilary steps into her path as the fencing master packs his weapons into their case. 'You cannot receive a stranger alone. Nor dressed like that.'

Sophia glances across and considers the distorted outline of her reflection in the window glass. For her fencing practice she wears close-fitting black breeches, tailored to her own design by a seamstress who has no qualms about the propriety of such garments for a woman; grey silk hose and soft-soled velvet slippers that allow her to remain nimble on her toes; a loose white shirt beneath which she binds her small breasts with linen, for comfort. If she had her way, she would dress like this always, dispensing with stays and petticoats and hoops and bodices for good. There was a time, many years ago – she smiles to think of it – when she was obliged to present herself as a boy, and she resented having to give up that freedom of movement when the danger was past and she was restored to herself. Although, she reflects as she follows her steward out of the gallery and along a panelled corridor, she is not sure that she has ever really been herself; not since she was nineteen years old, at least. All the names she has had since then, including the one she uses now, have belonged to someone else.

'He's not a stranger,' she says, to Hilary's back. 'Besides, I could be wearing a pair of antlers on my head and he wouldn't notice. He's not a man who pays attention to such things.'

'What is he to you, then?'

'An associate. From years back. The master knew him,' she adds, as if invoking her late husband will legitimise such a meeting. At this, Hilary turns and gives her a sharp look.

'So why is he here now?'

Sophia shakes her head. 'I imagine I'm about to find out.'

Hilary doesn't reply, but the set of her shoulders is eloquent. Sophia smiles to herself. It's not as if her steward didn't know what went on in this house, with its secret rooms, its midnight comings and goings, though she probably thought those days were over. Sophia had thought so too. She is surprised to find her palms tingling.

'Bring him in through the back, though,' she says as they reach the entrance hall. Hilary nods and turns towards the kitchens, while Sophia continues along the ground-floor corridor and pushes open the door to the library. Here she breathes deeply, inhaling the scent of old books and polished wood, beeswax and leather. This room always reminds her of her father. Another thing few people know about her: that she grew up in an Oxford college, surrounded by academics, that at twelve years old she could read Greek and Latin better than her brother and almost as well as the scholars who passed through her father's tuition. But today the library fails to calm her; she paces, agitated, not so much by the prospect of the visitor himself but by what he represents, as signified by the astrological symbol for Venus hastily scribbled on the note he gave Hilary as proof of his intent.

When the door opens she forces herself to stand composed, hands clasped together. Hilary hovers behind the man with a coiled air, as if she is poised to tackle him to the floor at any sudden move.

'Thank you, Hilary. You can leave us now,' she says. Her steward hesitates, but does as she is bid, parting with a warning look.

'I need you to look at this,' the man says without preamble, thrusting a piece of paper at her.

Sophia laughs. 'I'm very well, thank you, Thomas, and how are you?'

11

He frowns, perplexed, and she remembers this about him; that he is as oblivious to sarcasm as he is to social niceties. He has come with a specific purpose and does not see the point of wasting time on anything else. She studies him as the thin December light falls on his pocked face. The years have not been kind to him, but then he is not a man to take care of himself. As predicted, he has neither noticed nor cared that her fencing clothes show off her long legs and slender hips. And yet, behind those mild eyes that swerve away from hers, one of the most remarkable minds in England is ticking away ceaselessly. This man's abilities have saved the queen's life more than once, though you wouldn't know it to look at his patched jacket and worn boots.

'Thomas Phelippes. How long has it been – five years?' She holds out her arms before remembering that he does not like to be touched, and lets them fall to her side. 'No "How do you, Mistress de Wolfe, condolences on the death of your husband"?'

'Humphrey de Wolfe died two years and three months ago. The eighteenth of September 1596.'

'That's true, he did. But I miss him still.'

At this, he shows a flicker of interest. 'The marriage was arranged for you by Sir Francis Walsingham. To provide for you financially after you left his service.'

'Again, true. And as you see, I am well provided for.' She gestures to the walls of books, the expensive carpet. 'That doesn't mean I didn't care for my husband. Humphrey was a good man.'

'He was extremely efficient,' says Thomas Phelippes, which is possibly the highest compliment he can imagine. 'I need you to look at this.'

Sophia steps forward and takes the page he holds out; she has exhausted his capacity for small talk. The paper is covered in water stains and when she opens it, she sees that the ink has run in places, blurring characters here and there, but what she reads causes her a quick intake of breath – not on account of the message, which is still hidden, but the form.

'What is this?'

'Your cipher.' He frowns. 'You don't remember?'

'Of course, but – I haven't seen these signs in nearly a decade. Where did it come from?'

'A corpse.'

'*What?* Whose?'

He shakes his head. 'Outside my brief. I was sent first to see if it meant anything to you, and second, to fetch you.'

'Fetch me where? Sent by whom? *Oh.*' She looks at him, spinning the paper between her fingers, and for a moment he meets her eye. 'You are back in harness. Government work, I mean,' she adds, when he doesn't reply.

'If you like.' His gaze slides away again. 'He's expecting us.'

Sophia glances around the room – the books, the good beeswax candles, the antique statue of the goddess Artemis on her plinth by the window, shipped from a temple in Crete – and draws breath. It's true that she has a comfortable life now, as the widow of a wealthy cloth merchant, in this handsome house he left her, with its discreet and loyal servants. The paper in her hand, this threadbare man in front of her and what he is proposing, could undo it all – what's more, it could threaten the one thing in her life more precious to her than all this material comfort. Would she really risk that, after so long spent searching? But she notices her heart is beating faster. Fear or excitement? She has always found it hard to distinguish between the two.

Eventually she nods. 'Give me a moment to change.'

Phelippes looks impatient. 'I was urged to hurry.'

'Thomas, I am dressed for a sword fight.'

'Oh.' He tilts his head to one side as if seeing her for the first time. 'I suppose you are. Well, best to be prepared.'

TWO

The house they approach is nondescript, neither grand nor ramshackle, off Monkwell Street, close by the Barbers' Hall. Sophia is familiar with the kind of place; she met Thomas Phelippes in many such forgettable locations, back when she was working closely with him. There are few people abroad in the snow-bound streets; those they pass are huddled into hoods and caps, and pay little attention to the riders, only muttering an oath if they are forced to step out of the horses' way into drifts of snow banked up along the gutters. If they glance up, they will suppose they see a fine lady wrapped in a fur-lined cloak and riding a black mare, followed by some shabby bare-headed retainer whose coat is too thin for the weather.

They pass through a gate and into a yard where the snow has been cleared; wordlessly a boy with downcast eyes takes the horses. Sophia removes her glove and slips him a coin; still he does not raise his head to look at her. Trained not to notice who comes and goes here, she guesses.

A narrow-faced man relieves them of their coats and beckons them to follow, also without speaking. Sophia tries to catch a glimpse of her reflection in a window as they pass; she has dressed hastily in a gown of dark red silk which, now that she glances down, looks peculiar with snow-damp riding boots. Despite Hilary's protestations, she had not waited to have her hair properly arranged or apply cosmetics; in consequence, her cheeks are pinked by the cold and tendrils of hair have escaped their combs; she hears her father's voice telling her she looks like a wild peasant girl, the way he used to when she would bowl in, skirts flying, breathless from racing through the Oxford meadows with her brother. Both long dead, she reflects, though the thought is interrupted by the sight of a forbidding oak door at the end of the hall. The narrow-faced man opens it and steps back.

Sophia follows Phelippes into a receiving room of middling size, dominated by a wide hearth where a fire blazes. The small casements face north and let in little light. Beneath them is a desk with fat candles in glass holders; seated behind it, a figure she feels she half-knows, though they have never met.

He is bent over a pile of papers and makes no acknowledgement of their arrival, continuing intently with his writing. It's an old trick, designed to show where the balance of power lies in the room, and Sophia has no patience for it. She clears her throat purposefully; his quill pauses. She takes five paces across the room until she is standing before the desk, and picks up a round polished lump of obsidian he is using to weigh down letters.

'Master Secretary. You sent for me.'

With a remarkably controlled lack of urgency he looks up and meets her gaze. For a long moment, they appraise one another. So this is Robert Cecil, whose late father, Lord Burghley, was Queen Elizabeth's most trusted adviser from her youth. Sophia runs through the bare facts she knows about the newly appointed principal secretary: thirty-six, Burghley's second son (his intellectual if not his official heir), raised to statecraft and its shadowy counterpart from boyhood. Distinguished enough in his looks: dark hair swept up from a wide forehead, reddish pointed beard, shrewd eyes that don't waver from hers. He wears a black wool doublet and a neat starched ruff, unshowy but expensively tailored. She observes that he doesn't rise from the desk to greet her; this, too, is a reminder of who is doing the summoning here, but she suspects it is also to divert attention from the most notable aspect of his appearance – the fact that he is unusually short. It is said that the queen calls him 'my pygmy' and that Cecil detests the nickname, which follows him in whispers through the corridors of Whitehall, undermining his political stature. In the penny broadsheets and slanderous pamphlets that circulate around the booksellers' stalls in St Paul's churchyard, anonymous detractors paint Sir Robert as a malformed hunchback, crooked as his character, but all Sophia can see – though she is careful not to let her gaze rest too long on his person – is a slight curvature of the spine, his left shoulder a little higher than the right.

He lays his pen carefully in its stand and cocks his head.

'Mistress de Wolfe.' No smile. Perhaps he noted her looking. 'How good of you to take the time.'

'I had the impression it was not optional.'

At this his lips curl thinly. 'Oh, one always has a choice, I think. Thomas, offer Mistress de Wolfe a seat.'

Phelippes draws up a chair for her, across the desk. She smooths her skirts carefully and perches on the edge. It is lower than Cecil's; this, too, is deliberate, and she dislikes it, though she determines not to let him see.

'So. Thomas has explained the situation?'

'Partially. Something about a message found with a corpse?'

Cecil steeples his fingers.

'I understand you have connections with the playing companies?'

Sophia draws on all her experience to keep her expression neutral. She fights the temptation to exchange a glance with Phelippes.

'From time to time I have donated small sums to support them with production costs. Printing of playbills, costumes, and so on. My late husband and I were great aficionados of the theatre. What has that to do with this business?'

'Why the Lord Chamberlain's Men?'

'Why not?'

'Well.' He leans back and his focus shifts to a corner of the ceiling, as if he is searching for the most diplomatic form of expression. 'The playing companies attract scandal, Mistress de Wolfe, without even trying. It seems they cannot help it. And I would have thought that, with your history, you would want to avoid any prospect of your current name being associated with the slightest whiff of notoriety.'

'My history.' Her voice is steely now; she leans forward and grips the edge of the desk, daring him to say what he means. Her current name; that was clever. A little hint of what he knows.

That pinched smile again. 'My predecessor Sir Francis Walsingham was a meticulous keeper of records, Mistress de Wolfe. I'm aware of your valuable contribution to the security of the realm in the last years of the Eighties.' He pauses, piqued at her expression. 'Something amusing?'

Only your pomposity, she wants to say. 'You make it sound so heroic, Master Secretary. As if I had led a force to war. When in fact I was a governess and ladies' companion in Catholic households. All I did was listen at doors, steal letters and lie to people for money.'

'We *were* at war,' he says, with surprising vehemence. 'Against the forces that seek to make us vassals of the Pope again. And you, with others like you, have been our foot soldiers – Walsingham knew that well enough, though he struggled to convince my father and Her Majesty to open the Treasury for his efforts. You would be surprised to know how many attempts on the queen's life were foiled by people listening at doors and stealing letters. Then again, perhaps you would not.' He picks up his quill and turns it between his fingers. 'I ask about the playing companies because yesterday the Chamberlain's Men dismantled The Theatre and carried away all the timbers while the leaseholder, Master Allen, was out of London for the holidays.'

'In this weather?' Sophia can't help but laugh at the audacity; that will have been Richard Burbage's idea, no question. Even Cecil allows a smile – the first genuine one she has seen since she arrived – though his face grows quickly sombre again.

'They are nothing if not determined. And at dawn this morning, a corpse was found in one of the foundation trenches on the empty site. That paper Thomas showed you was inside her clothing.'

'Her?' Sophia's throat constricts. Someone she knows?

'Agnes Lovell. Thirteen years of age. Daughter of the late Sir John Lovell of Suffolk, ward of Sir Thomas North. Any connection to you?'

Sophia shakes her head; the name means nothing, and a wave of relief courses through her. She flexes her hands where she had clenched them tight.

'Yet this message,' he continues, 'which was clearly meant to be found, is written in a cipher that was unique to you during your time working for Walsingham. And the body was placed in a location particular to the Lord Chamberlain's Men, with whom you also have links. Someone wishes to suggest a connection, it seems.' He waits, dark eyes fixed on her, as if that might provoke a confession.

'But who would know about that cipher? Thomas created it for me and I understood it was retired at the same time I was.' She gestures at Phelippes; he gives a terse nod. 'Only someone with access to Walsingham's papers could know of its existence, and even there I would have been referred to by an alias. As for the players – half London must have known by the end of yesterday that the site of The Theatre would be a focus of attention. Perhaps the killing was intended to incriminate them? This poor child was murdered, I take it?'

'She's being examined, but I think we may safely assume

foul play. Did you ever cross paths with Sir Thomas North?'

'No.'

'What about your husband?'

'I don't recall Humphrey mentioning him. But then I expect you would have a better idea of my husband's connections than I, Master Secretary, since you have read Walsingham's papers.' Belatedly, it occurs to her that she has not yet asked the obvious question. 'What did the message say?'

'Did you not read it?'

She laughs again. 'It's nearly ten years since I last looked at that cipher. I don't have Thomas's memory for codes – it would take time and patience to unlock its meaning.'

'We have neither,' Cecil says, in a tone that reinforces the point. 'Fortunately, we do have Thomas. Tell her.'

Phelippes clears his throat.

'Those who build their house on stolen ground

Must needs beware, lest all their sins be found.'

It's doggerel, though it sounds oddly sinister in his flat, affectless voice.

'Well?' Cecil leans forward; he looks as if he is about to snap his fingers at her.

'Stolen ground,' she muses. 'That seems obvious, doesn't it? The Theatre, I mean. The argument between the Burbages and Giles Allen over who owns it.'

He appears to weigh this. 'So you think it *is* about the playing companies?'

'I think it extreme to use a young woman's body to deliver a grievance over a leasehold dispute. But what else should it mean, if she was found at The Theatre?'

Cecil leaves a pregnant space before speaking.

'Sir Thomas North served recently in the Irish war.'

'Ah. So you think it's political?'

Cecil sighs and replaces his quill in its stand. 'Everything is political, Mistress de Wolfe. There are those who believe Ireland is stolen ground.'

'The Irish, for a start.'

'Well, quite. And since the Earl of Essex is about to launch a fresh campaign against the rebels there, with the consequent need for another round of taxes and conscription, it is in the national interest to keep morale up and the populace firmly behind our brave troops. Do you see?'

She sits back in her chair. 'I can see that a death which may reference the less than admirable actions of the English army in Ireland would be awkward for the government, Master Secretary, yes. What I don't understand is what you expect me to do about it.'

He presses his lips together as if she is being deliberately obstructive. 'You are already entangled in this matter, Mistress de Wolfe, whether you like it or no. Somebody chose to use your cipher. Surely you see the relevance of that? Assuming that you yourself are not party to the girl's death, it means that someone who knows your most secret history is involved in this business.' He exhales in frustration. 'What I mean to say is that I need your help.'

There is a kind of satisfaction in seeing his discomfort in asking; she wonders if this is because she is a woman, or simply because he is the type of man who must be in control of everything.

'In what capacity do you propose I help?' she asks. The balance of power between them has subtly shifted.

'Make enquiries. Speak to your acquaintance from the old days, discover whether anyone could have learned your cipher. Look through your husband's correspondence to see if he had any business with Sir Thomas North or Sir John Lovell. Sound out your contacts at the playhouses in case some buried matter there might offer a connection. Report your findings to me. We have not made the girl's identity public yet. I want to resolve this before the broadsheet writers and pamphleteers learn about it and use it to turn the city against the Irish campaign.'

'What if I were to tell you I have no love for the Irish campaign?'

'Then I would have to pretend I misheard you,' he says, not troubling to hide his impatience, 'because that would be a foolish opinion for a loyal citizen to express to a minister of the crown. What say you, Mistress de Wolfe – will you assist in this matter?'

She tilts her head and smiles. 'Are you asking me to work for you, Master Secretary?'

He huffs again; he is not enjoying being a supplicant. 'I am asking you to lend England such skills as you have, as you did before, to avert a crisis.'

Such skills as you have; it might be a compliment, or the reverse. Reluctantly, she is beginning to admire him. But she won't make it too easy.

'My skills, as you call them, were deemed superfluous to requirements by your father after Sir Francis Walsingham died,' she says, with a degree of hauteur.

'I regret that,' he says, and she is surprised to find his sincerity convincing. 'My father's priority was cutting costs, and in pursuit of that end he pared the Service to the bone. But my lord father is no longer with us' – here the briefest glimmer of emotion touches his eyes, before he masters it – 'and it is my intention to rebuild Walsingham's network to its former glory. You would be properly remunerated.'

'God rest my lord Burghley,' she says, and means it. When did Burghley die? Was it only this past August, still labouring day and night for England at the age of seventy-seven? She remembers the funeral procession, the horses with their black plumes, the crowds bowing heads as the cortège passed. The end of the old order; a sharp reminder that Her Majesty's reign was drawing towards its final act, with the country's future unresolved.

Cecil inclines his head with a rueful smile. 'I'm not sure even God could persuade him to rest,' he says. He presses his lips together, businesslike again. 'Well?'

'You know I have no need of your money?'

'I'm well aware that Humphrey de Wolfe left you a considerable fortune. But it was never really about the coin for you, was it? Was it not more of a *quid pro quo* arrangement, shall we say?'

'I'm not sure I take your meaning, Master Secretary.' She is tiring of this game now; she would like him to set his cards on the table. 'Please speak frankly, so that we can both go about our day.'

'Very well, Mistress de Wolfe. Or shall I call you Sophia Underhill? Or Kit? Mary Gifford? Or Kate Kingsley?' He smiles, pleased with himself. A palpable hit, she thinks. 'I see that last one is the name that makes you flinch, though you hide it well. Hardly surprising – no one was ever brought to justice for the murder of your first husband, Sir Edward Kingsley, were they?'

She holds his gaze, defiant.

'I merely observe that your arrangement with Walsingham offered a degree of protection, lest anyone ever associate you with the woman who called herself Kate Kingsley fifteen years ago. Canterbury is not so far away, after all.' He allows her a moment to digest this, before continuing, 'I would like to give you my solemn assurance that such protection would be ongoing. I hope that would set your mind at rest.'

She lets out a dry laugh. Having dangled before her the prospect of blowing her life up, he would now like to set her mind at rest, as long as she does what he asks.

'If nothing else,' he adds carefully, before she can reply, 'think of the boy. Consider the potential repercussions for him. Do you imagine the queen would receive at court any playing company that employed him, knowing who his father was? The Chamberlain's Men would have to look to their own interests first.'

She stares at him; her hands in her lap have turned cold and numb.

'I will do what I can.' Recovering herself, she stands and

brushes out her skirts. She doesn't wait for instructions; she wants to have the last word and leave before her face betrays her rising fury. Any shred of admiration has evaporated. Walsingham would never have relied on such petty threats.

'Lying to people for money,' Cecil says musingly, as she reaches the door, quoting her own words back to her. 'A pithy description of an espial's work, I like it. Perhaps more flattering to say you are a professional dissembler, Mistress de Wolfe. Clearly it runs in the family.'

She doesn't look back. She is out of the door and into the yard so fast that she almost forgets her cloak; the thin-faced retainer has to run after her, holding it out. There are almost certainly penalties for cursing at the queen's principal secretary, even in a meeting that has not officially happened; she has no wish to find out what they are by losing control.

She has mounted before the stable boy can even bring a block; she wrenches her horse around (too savagely, poor beast) and urges it on, feeling its hooves skidding on the icy cobbles. Even when Phelippes manages to catch her up at the corner of Silver Street it takes some time before she can speak; when she does, she rounds on him with all the force of her anger.

'You told him, I suppose?'

Phelippes shrinks back in his saddle; she remembers how he dislikes raised voices.

'I didn't have to – he knew already. I only confirmed my part in it.'

'Then, who—' Understanding dawns before the words are out of her mouth. 'Anthony. Damn him.' She turns the black mare and kicks her onwards. Snow has begun to fall around them again.

'Where are you going?' Phelippes calls after her.

'To The Rose,' she shouts over her shoulder, her voice carrying through the tumbling flakes.

THREE

At the Rose Theatre on Bankside, the Admiral's Men are supposed to be rehearsing, but they can talk of nothing except their rivals' daring raid on The Theatre. Philip Henslowe, the manager, a man with a comfortable girth and permanently fraught expression, walks in tight circles around the pit like a bear on a chain, too agitated to notice the snow settling on his shoulders. Leaning against a pillar in the covered seats, Anthony Munday lets out a quiet sigh and watches his breath cloud around his face in the freezing air. It is his play they are making little progress on; he should be working on the next one, but Ned Alleyn likes him to be available for last-minute changes, and they are due to perform the current work at court in a week's time. The afternoon light is fading and the best part of his day is already wasted listening to Henslowe make the same complaint over and over with a fusillade of curses. Anthony crosses his arms over his chest and tucks his hands into his armpits until he can vaguely feel his fingers again.

'Those *fuckers*,' Henslowe spits again, midway through someone's speech. 'They're planning to rebuild the whole bloody thing down here, right next door, I know it. There's a piece of land leased the other side of Maiden Lane, I'll wager that arch-fucker Burbage is behind it. Come spring, the

Chamberlain's Men will be stealing our audiences from under our noses – when we've barely got them back after the plague years.'

Ned strides to the edge of the stage and glares down at his father-in-law.

'Then we shall just have to make sure we offer better fare than them,' he says. 'Which we cannot hope to do if you keep interrupting our process.'

'*How?*' says Henslowe, throwing his hands in the air. 'They have Will Shakespeare! What do we have – Anthony Munday?' He laughs as if even the name is preposterous. 'How are we supposed to compete?'

'I'm still here, you know,' Anthony says mildly from his corner.

'Ignore him, Ant,' Ned says, throwing a grimace his way. 'You're that Stratford bumpkin's equal in every respect.'

Anthony smiles, though he knows Ned is being kind.

'Can we get on with this, I'm freezing my knackers off here?' calls John Singer, the clown, dancing a little jig to make the point.

'Stop moaning, you've got braziers, haven't you?' Henslowe says, pointing at the two burning either side of the stage before resuming his pacing. 'Costing me a fortune, and for what? Who's going to come out in this weather?'

'God's teeth – we perform before the queen on Twelfth Night! If you don't hold your tongue and let us continue,' Ned declaims, hands on his hips, 'I swear to God I'll—'

But they will never know the reach of his threat, because at that moment the doors to the pit open and a woman in a long blue cloak sweeps in, followed by a tall, muscular young man who looks as if he carries at least one knife tucked somewhere on his person and would know how to use it. In fact, Anthony knows this to be the case; he recognises them both, and his heart jolts a little at the sight of her. Silently, he chides himself.

'Well, this is all we need,' Henslowe says. 'Mistress de Wolfe – come to gloat, have you? I suppose it was your doing?'

Sophia stops short and pulls her hood back. 'What?'

'Why, this business at The Theatre, of course. I should have suspected your hand in it.'

Anthony expects Sophia to cut Henslowe down with a withering remark – she has no time for his petty resentments – so he is surprised to see that she looks appalled, the colour drained from her face.

'*My* hand? How do you mean, Master Henslowe?'

'You understand me well enough. Burbage would not feel emboldened to make such grand gestures if he didn't have the promise of your money to cushion his landing when he falls on his arse. All these men here' – he gestures to the company on stage – 'have families to feed, you know. If the Chamberlain's Men rebuild south of the river and take our audiences, their children will be on the street and you can have that on your conscience.'

Sophia stares at him for a moment, then bursts out laughing; Anthony hears a note of relief in it. 'You seem to have mistaken me for Lord Hunsdon, Master Henslowe,' she says lightly. 'I have no influence over the Chamberlain's Men – the clue is in the name. You should speak to their patron if you have a grievance.'

'But how will you sleep at night, Mistress de Wolfe, when you have put us out of business and I am forced to sell myself to sailors at Tilbury dock?' Ned says, grinning at her with his hips thrust forward, to ribald laughter from the company.

'Oh, I would not let you fall so far, Master Alleyn,' Sophia says, her composure recovered. 'I'm sure I could find a respectable position for you in my household. How are you at washing pots?'

Ned laughs; there's a chorus of murmurs from the men behind him, to the effect that they could think of positions they'd like her to offer them, until Ned snaps his fingers and they fall silent. 'I had rather be a potwasher in your house than to dwell in the tents of the wicked, Mistress de Wolfe, though I think you did not come south of the river to offer me a job in your kitchen?'

'I came to speak to Anthony,' Sophia says, her gaze raking the tiered benches until it lights on him. Again, that foolish surge of feeling as their eyes meet; he tamps it down and nods soberly, hoping she can't read his face.

'Poaching my writers as well as my audiences now?' Henslowe cuts in. 'We can't spare him, you'll have to come back.' This, even though Henslowe's only acknowledgement of his existence today has been to insult him.

'Of course we can,' Ned says gallantly. 'We've barely tackled the first scene. Well, Munday – don't keep a beautiful woman waiting.' He extends a leg and offers Sophia a sweeping bow. Perhaps he thinks that, if he is charming enough, he might win her allegiance, and the funds that come with it, from his rivals. Only Anthony knows why this will never happen, and it has nothing to do with the man from Stratford and his highfalutin verse. He grabs up his hat and follows her into the snowy yard.

'I need to speak to you,' Sophia says, whipping around and fixing him with a flinty glare. In his experience, no good has ever come of a woman saying those words in that tone. He waits. The young man, her minder, stands a few feet off and folds his arms across his chest, apparently as impervious to the weather as an oak trunk. Anthony gives him a nod; the young man returns it, unsmiling.

'Sir Robert Cecil sent for me today.' She hisses it like an accusation.

'Oh?' Whatever he had expected, it was not this. 'What did he want?'

'He knows about Tobie, and he's using it to bend me to his will. The only person who could have told him is you.'

A sharp gust of wind lifts her hood; her hair is coming loose from her jewelled hairnet beneath, her cheeks are flushed by the cold, her eyes shining. The thought occurs to Anthony, unbidden, that this is what she would look in the throes of passion (except, one hopes, less angry), and he does his best to banish it immediately.

'Could we talk somewhere warmer?'

After a moment she sighs impatiently and strides out of the gates. Bankside is full of taverns, most of which are also brothels, though this would not trouble Sophia. He follows her up the street towards the river and into the Swan. Sophia tucks herself into a corner table furthest from the fire, drawing admiring stares from the other drinkers, though any ideas they may have of approaching are quickly quashed by a glare from her young companion, who sits at a neighbouring table, hackles up like a guard dog.

'I've never spoken to Cecil about Tobie, I promise you,' Anthony says in a low voice, when Sophia has called for hot wine. 'He has access to all Walsingham's papers, don't forget. We have to get used to the idea that there's probably nothing he doesn't know about us.'

She looks at him without speaking, and there is an understanding in her expression that only those who worked for Francis Walsingham can share. Anthony still remembers the thrill of his first missions to France and Rome some twenty years ago, as a youth of barely eighteen, disguised as the son of a prominent English Catholic. Such service as he provides to the realm is less exciting these days, but it did at least bring Sophia into his life. He thinks of the day Thomas Phelippes charged him with tracing a twelve-year-old boy as the Admiral's Men toured Kent after the playhouses shut down, that plague summer of '96.

'If anyone is going to tell Tobie the truth about who he is, it should be me,' Sophia whispers, as if Anthony is the one threatening to expose her secret.

'And . . .' He hesitates to ask, it's a sensitive topic. 'Do you have plans to do so?'

She sighs. 'When the time is right.'

'Sophia, it's been two and a half years.' Two and a half years since he had found Tobie Strange in Canterbury: almost thirteen, a scrivener's son and a chorister at the cathedral school, whose future looked uncertain after his parents had died of plague within a month of one another. A conversation with an elderly servant in the scrivener's household had led him to the woman who had once been the infant's wet nurse and convinced him that this was the boy he was looking for; a child of such delicate beauty and enchanting voice that Ned Alleyn had needed little persuasion to take him into the company immediately for the women's parts.

'Exactly,' Sophia says. 'He was fifteen in November, he thrives. But it's a tender age. I have to tread carefully or I mar everything. How would you have felt, at fifteen, to learn that your parents were not your parents?'

Anthony shrugs. 'I was orphaned and made a ward of the City at eleven, I know how that feels. I might have been glad to learn that I had a mother still living.' Especially a wealthy one, he doesn't say aloud.

She drops her voice so that he can barely hear her. 'And to know that she was never married to your father, who was an executed traitor?'

'Perhaps not that.'

'Well, then. Tobie believes himself to be the legitimate son of respectable people. The truth is a hard burden to lay on young shoulders. It may be that I can never tell him, for his sake.' A flash of pain crosses her face at this, and she turns her face away. 'But I certainly don't want bloody Robert Cecil forcing my hand.'

'What does Cecil want from you?'

'This girl,' she says, when the wine has been brought and the serving boy has withdrawn. 'The one discovered in the foundations of The Theatre today. You must have heard?'

'I heard only that there was a body. A street girl, I assumed, died of cold overnight. There are bodies found every morning since the freeze came, to the city's shame. Henslowe is more exercised by Burbage's plan to move south of the river, all the talk at The Rose is of that. Why is Cecil involved?'

'She was not a street girl. She was the ward of Sir Thomas North, and they think she was murdered.'

'Good God. The Lovell heiress?' He feels his jaw slacken. He pictures North, a pompous arsehole whose greed and bad judgement had brought suffering to a great many people. 'But – what has she to do with you?'

'Good question. I never heard her name before today, poor child. But Cecil does not believe me when I say I have no connection to her, and he's using Tobie to press me into giving up what I know. Which is fruitless, since I have nothing to give.' She folds her hand into a fist and flexes it open. She hasn't touched her wine. 'What do you know of North? He's a writer, isn't he?'

'Of sorts.' He catches her smiling at his dismissive tone.

'You men of letters. What would you have to talk about, if not your rivals' lack of talent and the monstrous injustice of their success?'

He laughs, but in the back of his mind he hears Henslowe again: *They have Will Shakespeare – what do we have . . . ?*

'North has published translations of Plutarch's Great Lives of the Greeks and Romans,' he says. 'He's tried to adapt them for the stage, but has found no takers, as far as I know. So he's hardly a rival. He is a man with enemies, I can tell you that much.'

'In the theatre?'

'I was thinking more of his military career. You know he led a force in Ireland two years ago?'

'Is there any nobleman who hasn't?' Sophia rolls her eyes.

He doesn't blame her; the war to suppress the Irish rebels has gone on so long that most Londoners barely give it a thought, except when they are inconvenienced by unexpected taxes to fund it, or yet another spate of conscription – though that only affects poor men and their families. For the nobility, it's an opportunity to win the queen's favour and reward, if you're willing to take the risk.

'It's said by returning soldiers that North was among the most corrupt of commanders out there – which is an achievement, considering the competition,' he says.

'What kind of corruption?' She sits forward, interested.

'The usual. Taking of bribes to allow men to desert, keeping dead men on his muster roll so he could pocket the pay of non-existent troops, cutting corners with rations and equipment to skim off the difference. They say more of his company died from hunger or disease due to lack of provision than died in combat. And for that, the queen gave him a pension of forty pounds a year.'

Sophia acknowledges this with a wry twist of her mouth. 'I wish I could profess to be surprised when men of good birth fail catastrophically in high office and are rewarded for it, but that is how we do things in England, it seems. So you're saying any number of people might want revenge on North for the death of their brother or father or son in Ireland?' She is glaring at him as if this is his fault.

'Hundreds, potentially. He's not liked by the common man.'

'But the common man would not know about—' She stops, with a pre-emptive glance around the tap-room. The drinkers by the fire sneak furtive looks at her from time to time, but there is no indication that anyone is trying to eavesdrop.

'About what?'

She leans closer and speaks in French – not that this is any greater guarantee of security in London, Anthony reflects, especially not in Bankside, where all the foreign sailors congregate.

'The dead girl was found with a note in her clothes, written in cipher. *My* cipher,' she clarifies, watching his reaction closely. 'This is why Cecil thinks it must have some connection to my work for Walsingham. I can't explain it, but it could only have been written by someone with intimate knowledge of Walsingham's methods of communication. That rules out the average conscripted soldier, surely?'

'Walsingham had informers in the army and navy, naturally,' he says, considering. 'Perhaps some ciphers were reused?'

'Thomas Phelippes says not. That one was mine alone. He thinks it's more likely someone went through Walsingham's papers after his death, when security was less than scrupulous. If that's the case, it could be pure chance they chose mine.'

'Or not. You'll have made enemies too, during your years in Catholic households.'

She bristles. 'Only if someone suspected me. Which they did not. I was very good at what I did.'

Anthony says nothing; in his experience, when you work undercover people often suspect you on some deep level, even if they can't articulate what it is that doesn't feel right. He would wager that there are figures from Sophia's past who guessed she was not what she seemed, and if one of them is a killer of young women, this could signify danger to her. But she is right; only a handful of people would have the means to access Phelippes's ciphers, and they all belong to the highest echalons of government. He feels a chill along his arms.

'What did it say, this message?' he asks, in English.

She takes a sip of wine before intoning: '"Those who build their house on stolen ground, must needs beware, lest all their sins be found."'

He cocks an eyebrow. 'Iambic pentameter. Bit plodding. Sounds like the sort of thing Shakespeare trots out when he can't think how to end a scene.' He says this partly to amuse her, but she is frowning in concentration.

'I thought at first it was a reference to the playhouses,

because of where she was found, and Burbage not owning the land The Theatre stood on,' she says. 'But if the murder is a direct attack on Thomas North, then the message would seem to be political.'

'The English in Ireland,' he says, nodding. 'Those sins it mentions could be an allusion to North's corruption during the last campaign.'

'True, but if his general corruption is common knowledge, why warn him to beware lest it be found out? It sounds as if the writer means something more specific, something North thinks he has kept secret. Can you make enquiries?'

'Me?' He hadn't meant to yelp it quite so forcefully.

'Yes. You frequent low taverns, don't you? The kind where returning soldiers might gather to air their grievances?'

'Only when I can't avoid it,' he says, with an attempt at dignity. 'It's useful for observing people.' But it's true, he thinks; there are too many nights when he chooses to follow the players to some insalubrious tap-room after the show rather than go home.

'Like the one where Falstaff and Pistol drink in Shakespeare's play of Prince Hal,' she adds, a mischievous smile hovering at her lips.

'Did you like that scene? I found the comedy a bit heavy-handed.'

'The groundlings loved it.' She is grinning openly now. 'Oh, stop it, Anthony – petty jealousy is beneath you. London is big enough for more than one playwright. Ask around in the taverns, will you? See if any soldiers from the Irish campaigns can tell you stories about Sir Thomas North that might explain that note. If I understood its meaning, I might have a hope of working out its connection to me.'

He sighs. 'Sophia, if you will take my advice' – he already knows she won't, he wonders why he's even bothering to say it – 'we're talking about someone who has killed a young girl. Surely Robert Cecil doesn't expect you to undertake the investigation yourself? It could be dangerous. Sophia?' he nudges, when she appears lost in thought.

'Yes, that's curious, isn't it? Does Thomas North have children? By blood, I mean?'

'A grown son and daughter, I believe. What's curious?'

'The girl. Agnes Lovell. If this is someone wanting revenge on North for what he did in Ireland, wouldn't they seek to punish him by going after his own children, not a girl who was merely his ward?'

'Perhaps she was an easier target. Or perhaps it was a different kind of punishment. I would imagine the wardship was lucrative – Sir John Lovell was a wealthy man. Owned a large coastal estate in Suffolk. Agnes's death would be a financial blow to North, even if there was no affection involved.'

'That poor child.' She shakes her head. 'Used like a chess piece by men. She was only thirteen, Anthony. And that note – I don't know, it's made me feel in some obscure way responsible. Say you'll help me?'

'You can't take it upon yourself,' he begins, then stops as a thought occurs. 'Wait – you said *thirteen*?'

'So Cecil told me. Is that significant?'

He wraps his hands around his mug, considering. 'Well, when a girl is orphaned and her care signed over to a guardian through the Court of Wards, the wardship ends at fourteen, when she can legally inherit and marry. For boys it's twenty-one. But if Agnes stood to gain her father's estate, and North was managing her lands to his own profit, that arrangement would be due to end at her next birthday.'

He can see Sophia's quick mind working as she looks at him, her brows knit together.

'Not much of a punishment, then, if he was about to lose the wardship in a matter of months anyway. Or do you think someone wanted to stop her inheriting?'

'I've no idea. Just thought her age might have a bearing on it.'

'Good point.' She stands and picks up her gloves. 'That's something to pursue. Thank you, Anthony. You'll make enquiries for me about Ireland, then?'

He sighs. 'I'll try my contacts. But, Sophia, I don't think—'

'I will keep your advice in mind.' She smiles to soften the blow. 'But I have to show Cecil that I am doing as he asked, so that he will leave Tobie alone. Besides, I am already implicated by the cipher, and I want to know who's done that, and why. It's a part of my life I thought I had left behind.'

He catches the wistful note. 'And you miss it.'

'Don't you?'

He nods. He understands: once you have lived with that spike in the blood, the constant nervous energy of living on your wits and balancing on a knife's edge that comes with living a double life, the everyday can seem flat by comparison. Perhaps that's why they are both drawn to the playhouses.

'I haven't said a word to anyone about Tobie,' he repeats, as they walk back to The Rose. 'I wouldn't. You can trust me, I hope you know that.'

'Forgive me.' She lays a hand on his arm; he tenses, watching snowflakes settle on the fur trim of her glove. 'I wasn't thinking clearly – Cecil threw me with his threats. You've always been a true friend, Anthony – I do know that.'

He smiles wanly; it's the best he can hope for.

'Come to supper soon,' she says, as she turns to leave. 'Beth too, if she'd like.'

He experiences an odd jarring, as if he has missed a stair. It feels wrong, somehow, to hear his wife's name in Sophia's mouth; he likes to imagine that they belong to two entirely separate universes. Whenever Sophia acknowledges the reality of Beth's existence, that harmless little fantasy is shattered.

'Thank you,' he manages. 'I'll ask her, see how she feels.'

'How is she?' She puts her head on one side to express sympathy.

He pauses. Beth has been sick for so long with her

unexplained condition that it has become a part of everyday life; he sometimes forgets that other people regard it as cause for concern.

'Stoical,' he says. Then, since Sophia appears to be waiting for him to elaborate, he adds, 'She has good days and bad. She'll be glad of the invitation, though, I'm sure.' He is not sure of this at all; he tries to avoid mentioning Sophia at home. Beth is very sharp. Fortunately, the conversation is cut short by the arrival of Sophia's minder with their horses.

'If you learn anything, come and tell me straight away, won't you?' she says, mounting easily and wheeling the animal around towards the river without looking back. The young man raises a hand in farewell and follows her.

Anthony stands outside the playhouse for a few moments, watching the snow fall around him, and wonders how he might shake this feeling of dissatisfaction that lately dogs him. At thirty-eight, by anyone's standards he has all the trappings of a successful life. He has worked as pursuivant-at-arms and Messenger to the Queen's Chamber, and been rewarded with land grants that provide him with a good income; he has published respected translations of literary works and travelled through Europe on undercover missions; he has a comfortable house in Cripplegate, a wife and family, and now he is a regular writer on the payroll of the Admiral's Men – a fair tally for a draper's son orphaned and left a ward of the City at eleven. He may not have the flair of the man from Stratford – though it smarts to have Henslowe point that out in public – but at least, unlike Will, he still has all his hair. What he doesn't have, and never will, is Sophia de Wolfe, and he feels guilty for even thinking it.

FOUR

'Do you need to hurry home, Ben?' Sophia asks her young companion as they ride past the church of St Mary Overy, the horses' breath steaming in the raw air. Dusk is falling, though the bells have only just rung four o'clock.

'No rush,' Ben says, sitting back easily in his saddle. 'Where are we going?'

'Leila's.' She sees his face brighten and smiles to herself.

The streets of Southwark are all but deserted in this weather; she would be perfectly safe here without a bodyservant, she thinks, not that Ben is exactly her servant. She feels a twinge of guilt at keeping him from helping his father at the Saracen's Head, their family tavern in Holborn. But Ben Hammett has always done extra work on the side; when he was a skinny, fleet-footed boy, he ran errands and carried messages for Thomas Phelippes all over London, slipping in and out of shadows unnoticed. As he grew older and stronger, Walsingham found other uses for him; Sophia does not enquire too closely about these. After Walsingham's death, Humphrey de Wolfe employed Ben to deliver his most confidential messages around town; the boy became a regular fixture at their house in Broad Street. Now Sophia pays him to accompany her when she visits parts of the city where it would be unseemly for her to travel alone. She may be an accomplished swordswoman, but a respectable merchant's widow can hardly ride around town with a weapon openly strapped to her belt, and she feels safer with Ben at her side; he is handy with his fists and a knife, and his presence is a useful deterrent. At twenty-six, he is also a talented archer, she recalls, and the thought is sobering; if there is to be another Irish campaign, the army will be looking for young men like him.

'You don't want to go to war, do you, Ben?' she asks, pulling her scarf over her mouth to mask the smell as they cross Battle Bridge, passing over a tributary of the Thames that carries run-off from the Southwark tanneries.

'God, no. Why, has someone said I should?'

'I was only thinking that there will likely be more conscription for Ireland in the new year. Are you not worried about being called up?'

'Friends in high places.' He laughs, but she hears a forced note in it. 'It's not that I'm unwilling, Mistress de Wolfe,' he adds, as if she has called his virility into question. 'I would defend my county if I had to. But what we're doing in Ireland, that's not defence, that's—' He shakes his head, as if he could say more but has thought better of it. 'Besides, Dad needs me at the Saracen's. His back's not so good these days, he can't be hauling barrels off carts like he used to. I'm no coward.'

'Of course not,' Sophia says, because she has no wish to antagonise him. Privately, she wonders whose word in high places has kept him out of the army in recent years, since Walsingham's death. She reflects that there is much about Ben she doesn't know. She could ask, but if she sensed he was evading the truth, it would damage the delicate trust between them.

'Did you have much to do with Thomas Phelippes these past few years?' she says instead, as they turn into Kent Street. 'Since Walsingham died, I mean?'

Is it her imagination, or does Ben look shifty?

'Not much. But I did visit him in prison.'

'Prison?' She reins her horse to a halt and lowers her voice. 'When was Thomas in prison? What for?'

'Debt,' Ben says bluntly. 'Last year. Not the first time since the old master died, either.'

'How did I not know? I could have helped him.'

Ben shakes his head. 'He didn't want anyone knowing. Not people whose good opinion mattered to him. Besides, you were long out of that world.'

She glances sidelong at him, searching for signs that this is meant as an accusation or a reproach.

'I would still have helped,' she says quietly. 'Who paid his debts, in the end?'

Ben shrugs. 'He wrote letters to a few people from gaol – I carried them for him. But I couldn't tell you which of them got him out. You'd have to ask him.' He vaults down from his horse and takes the reins of her mare so that she can dismount. Ben appears uninterested in discussing Phelippes's history further, but the revelation leaves Sophia uneasy. With the cryptographer languishing in a debtors' prison, who knows who might have had the opportunity to search through his effects, or press him for information? She has never had cause to doubt Thomas's integrity before, but a desperate man may surprise even himself with what he is prepared to sacrifice. Either way, any number of people might have had access to his papers, with or without his cooperation. She can't work out if that makes it more or less likely that the use of her cipher in connection with the murdered girl is deliberate. She wonders how much Robert Cecil knows of this. Presumably it was he who settled Thomas's debts, since Thomas is working for the government again, but she knows better than to presume; there are others who might consider it useful to have the cryptographer beholden to them. The Earl of Essex, for one.

They leave the horses at the beer house on the corner and

pick their way through the snow. Kent Street is a broad road of whitewashed cottages on the fringes of Southwark, cleaner and sweeter-smelling than the rest of the borough, where the city limits give way to open countryside. In the well-kept front garden of one, lengths of sacking have been wrapped around the plants and shrubs to protect them from the frost, and the path to the front door has been neatly cleared.

At Sophia's knock, a girl in a white cap cracks the door an inch with a guarded expression, though her face relaxes when she recognises her visitors. Sophia understands the need for caution: things take place in this house that warrant suspicion of unannounced callers. The Liberty of Southwark may be outside the reach of the London authorities, but it is not necessarily as careless with the law as its reputation would have you believe, especially when it comes to the behaviour of foreigners, and women. Leila Humeya is both, and in addition she is a herbalist, versed in the skills of midwifery and other medical knowledge particular to female concerns, so naturally there are those who whisper of witchery as she passes (though out of her hearing, just in case).

'Good day, Moll. Can I see her?'

The girl, Moll, nods Sophia inside and points through to the back of the house, which Sophia understands to mean Leila is alone; if her friend were with a patient, Moll would gesture for her to wait in the parlour, which is why Sophia always makes a point of calling at the front door. Moll doesn't speak, but Leila communicates with her through a complex system of signs; Sophia has to rely on much more basic mimes and always feels slightly embarrassed by this, as if she is insulting the girl's intelligence. She smiles her thanks and hurries through the modest kitchen and across the yard to a one-storey outbuilding that, according to Leila, was used by the previous owner as a chandler's workshop, and now serves a very different purpose. The windows are blacked out, for a start. Ben has quietly slipped away to another part of the house.

When she opens the door, she is surprised to find that Leila has company, though it's not her usual clientele – the girls from the Southwark stews who come to consult her on everything from love philtres to the pox to unwanted pregnancies or a customer who turned violent. In the dim lantern light, she sees Leila talking quietly to a scrappy boy with a white streak through the front of his hair; both have their heads bent intently over Leila's workbench examining some small object. At the sound of the door, the boy swipes it into his fist and his eyes skitter around the room as if searching for an escape route.

Leila smiles. 'It's all right, Badger – this is my friend, Mistress de Wolfe. This is a surprise,' she says to Sophia, and though her tone is warm, Sophia thinks she hears a reproach in it, as if Leila would have preferred a prior warning. Despite spending more than half her fifty-three years in London, her accent still holds the lilt of her early life in Moorish Spain.

'I had business at The Rose – I thought to call in and see how you are,' Sophia says lightly. 'But you're busy – I'll come back.'

'Not at all. We were just—'

Before she can offer any explanation, the boy mutters a brusque word and slips past Sophia through the open door as if he is running from the constables.

'Badger! Do nothing yet, do you hear me?' Leila calls after him, but there is no reply, only a flurry of snow swirling in at the doorway. Leila huffs through pursed lips.

'Don't let all the heat out, then,' she says.

Sophia shuts the door and takes off her cloak; the workshop is warmed by a fire stoked high in the small hearth, and smells of the dried herbs suspended in bunches along the walls and from the roof beams. A pot bubbles conversationally over the flames, giving off a pungent, grassy steam, and all these medicinal odours never quite cover the ferric tang of old blood that runs beneath them, so that you can't forget what women go through in here, lying on the long oak table that dominates the room.

'So – what brings you?' Leila says, forcing her attention to Sophia, though her eyes flicker to the door where the boy disappeared.

'Who was that child?' Sophia asks, following her glance.

Leila sighs. 'People call him Badger, on account of his hair. Says he's a foundling – he grew up around the stews and some of the madams give him odd jobs, so I'm guessing his mother worked in one. Either way, she's dead or scarpered.' She reaches up and tucks an escaped lock of dark hair into her scarf. 'He fetches and carries for me sometimes, and in return I let him sit by the fire.'

'Is he living on the streets? In *this*?' Sophia feels a pang in her chest; a different spin of Fortune's wheel and Tobie might have ended up the same way.

'I don't know where he sleeps, he won't say. But his fingers and toes haven't fallen off yet, so it can't be outside.'

'No wonder you're worried about him.'

'It's not that.' Leila shakes her head. 'He brought something to show me just now. A brooch – says he found it on the shoreline at low tide, but the child's a terrible liar. The river's half-frozen and that thing had never been near Thames mud – it was bright as the day it was made. Red and white stones in a gold setting – garnets and white topaz, I'd say, though he thinks it's rubies and diamonds. He wanted my view on what would be a fair price for it.'

Sophia watches her. Leila's eyes are almost black; it's hard to read her expression. In this low light, her complexion appears barely lined; if it weren't for the streaks of grey through her abundant curls, you would take her for ten years younger.

'You think he stole it?' Sophia is not especially interested in the boy's trinket – he would not be the first light-fingered street child to pocket something shiny that didn't belong to him – but she can see that she won't have Leila's full attention until her friend has stopped turning this matter over in her mind.

'For certain. Normally I'd look the other way, but this brooch . . . The stones were set in a distinct pattern, an insignia,' Leila muses.

'Did you recognise it?'

'As if I'd know one coat of arms from another. But someone's likely to, and if the boy goes running around the inns flashing it at the highest bidder, I fear it'll bring him more than he bargained for. I don't have a good feeling about it. You understand.'

She gives Sophia a meaningful look. Leila's intuition is uncannily accurate, which is why she only mentions it to people she trusts – no sense in adding fuel to those rumours of unnatural powers, though Leila always says it's nothing to do with second sight and everything to do with knowing how to take the measure of people.

'Well,' Leila says, more brightly, wiping her hands on her apron, 'you're not here to talk about brooches. Mint tea? I'll put some water on and you can tell me what's on your mind.'

'You've heard about the girl that was found up at The Theatre, I suppose.' It's not a question; there's not a sparrow falls in London without Leila knowing about it.

Leila nods as she shifts the simmering pot along its spit to make room for a kettle of water over the fire. 'My neighbour down the street, her husband's a carpenter. He went up there at first light today imagining there'd still be planks of wood lying around for the taking, the fool.' She straightens, pressing a hand to the small of her back. 'Course, there was nothing left of it – your Chamberlain's boys stripped the place bare, down to the last nail. They've some *cojones* on them, I'll give them that. I heard they're planning to rebuild it down here, is that right?'

'So they say. What about the girl?'

'I'm coming to that. Giles Allen's lawyer turned up early this morning to see the damage.' She takes down a bunch of dried mint leaves from a beam and begins to tear them. 'Master Allen is still in the country for the holidays, they say, at least a day's ride away. So this lawyer has a walk around the site and at first he thinks they've left a stage prop in one of the foundation trenches, some kind of effigy. He jumps down to brush the snow away and would you believe – it's the frozen corpse of a girl. So he sends for the constables and the constables take one look and send for the coroner, and naturally a crowd has gathered to see the spectacle, including my neighbour, but the moment the coroner arrives he turns white as the snow on the ground, the constables are instructed to disperse everyone, with a beating if need be, and the place is closed off. So the speculation is that she was no beggar or street girl who fell in drunk and died of the cold. Or got thrown in when a tryst turned ugly, which is how it usually happens,' she adds, with feeling. Years of tending to the girls of Southwark have left Leila with a low opinion of men, which Sophia can understand.

'Her name was Agnes Lovell. Ward of Sir Thomas North.' Sophia pauses in case of a reaction, but Leila's face is blank. 'That's not common knowledge yet. Do you know anything about her?'

'Should I?'

'I wondered if you'd heard anything through your connections.'

'My *connections*.' Leila lifts her chin with a hint of a smile. 'You know I can't talk about those, any more than you can talk about yours.'

There are plenty in Southwark and beyond who wonder how Leila Humeya went from living in a rented tenement room in one of the most insalubrious parts of the borough, near the Cross Bones graveyard, to owning a smart cottage on Kent Street with its own gardens (she draws the line at moving north of the river, though she could afford to). Naturally, rumours of djinns, alchemy and devil's gold abound. Sophia knows the truth is more prosaic: more than a decade ago, around the same time she herself began working for Master Secretary Walsingham, Leila made the acquaintance of Walsingham's daughter, Lady Frances Sidney as she was then. So when a friend of Lady Sidney's became gravely ill with complications in late pregnancy and the physicians told her husband to prepare for the worst, Lady Sidney suggested in his ear that Leila's knowledge might prevail where the gentlemen physicians had failed. In their desperation, Leila was secretly summoned, mother and child were saved, and along the underground pathways of information that women maintain among themselves, Leila's reputation took root and grew. Now, when ladies of the higher classes have problems with their monthly curse, the ravages of midlife, a maid (or, God forbid, a daughter) in trouble, unexplained pain or any of the manifold afflictions that women's bodies fall prey to, they know where to turn. Leila's discretion is prized as highly as her skill; Sophia has no idea who among the nobility might have benefitted from her care, but she suspects that Leila is quite a rich woman by now.

'Agnes Lovell,' Leila says, relenting. 'I didn't know the girl, though I do know something of the North household. Between us, the wife has consulted me.'

Sophia feels her spine straighten. 'The mother of his children?'

'No. She died. This is the second Lady North, Judith. Who would like a child, but—' she spreads her hands wide. 'No luck so far. Not that I think it would make that marriage any happier. Why, what is your interest?'

Sophia hesitates, though only briefly; Leila is less likely to share a confidence than any of Master Secretary's agents. 'Robert Cecil thinks the girl's murder is political, and that it was committed by someone with a connection to me.'

Leila raises an eyebrow, but she doesn't ask for details. 'And is that possible?'

'It makes no sense. Unless I can find out something about Agnes and why anyone would want to kill her, I can't begin to guess.'

'Cecil doesn't think you're involved, surely?'

Sophia gives a dry laugh. 'I don't think he suspects me of putting her in the ground with my own hands. But if I don't bring him some answers, he may decide to make my life difficult. And Tobie's,' she adds, in a lower voice.

Leila's expression sharpens. 'Well, maybe this is the time for you to have that conversation with Tobie yourself,' she says as she lifts the boiling kettle from the fire. 'Then Cecil has nothing to hold over you.'

'Anthony told me the same thing. But you know my feelings.' Sophia hears her pitch rise. 'I risk losing him altogether if I mistime it. Besides, Cecil is threatening to tell the players about his father. It would be the end of Tobie's career – no company would touch him if they knew he was the son of a Jesuit priest executed for treason. They'd be too afraid the queen wouldn't have them at court, and the theatre is his whole life. It would destroy him.' She breaks off, a catch in her voice. 'So I must make an effort to find out anything I can about this girl, to keep Cecil on my side.'

Leila pours the water into a stoneware pot over the mint leaves and nods. 'I'll see what I can do. Was Tobie there yesterday, when they took The Theatre down?'

'I don't know.' Sophia feels stricken; she has been so caught up with Cecil and the cipher, it hasn't occurred to her to wonder. 'Was Jo?'

Leila laughs. 'What use would Jo be for lugging timbers around?' She strains the tea through a cloth and hands Sophia a cup of pale green steaming water. 'Besides, Jo's got more sense. They could all have been arrested.'

Sophia's heart squeezes at the thought. 'I might pay a visit to Master Burbage, on the pretext of concern over my investment, and remind him that he has a responsibility to the younger members of the company not to drag them into his law-breaking.' She could press Burbage on what he knows of the Lovell and North families too; in her heart, she still hopes the reference to stolen ground will turn out to be about the playhouse dispute, rather than the vastly more problematic subject of the war in Ireland.

'Don't sound too concerned, or he'll wonder at your interest,' Leila says, warming her hands around her cup.

'He'll think I'm being an interfering woman.'

'As long as he doesn't think you sound like a fretting mother,' Leila says, breaking off as the workshop door opens to let in a blast of freezing air and a willowy crop-haired youth in a wool jacket and dark breeches.

'Mistress de Wolfe, how do you?' The youth dumps a bundle wrapped in oiled leather on the table and performs an elaborate bow for Sophia.

'Well, Jo, and you?'

'Freezing my tits off out there. As you see.'

Sophia arches an eyebrow, with a glance at Jo's flat chest, and Jo lets out a bawdy laugh.

At first glance, you would take Jo Goodchild for a boy of sixteen or seventeen, and many do; she doesn't correct them. She has her brown skin and dark eyes from Leila, and her wiry build and London accent from her long-dead English father; a lucky mix, Sophia always thinks, for if she'd inherited her mother's curves she would never be able to pass as this androgynous sprite. All through her childhood, Leila dressed her daughter in boy's clothes as a measure of protection against the kind of men who come to Southwark on the hunt for little girls, and by the time Josefina was old enough to decide for herself, she found she preferred breeches to petticoats, her hair shorn close instead of dressed and piled under a hood. Now, at twenty-four, she appears entirely at ease with her boyish manner. Sophia envies her this freedom to choose, but it's easier to get away with if you work in the playhouses, as Jo does, where she is usually assumed to be one of the boy actors, though in fact she designs and sews costumes for the players. Not that her choice is without risk; there have been instances of girls from the Southwark brothels set in the pillory for dressing as boys at their clients' request.

'Taking these to Blackfriars for a fitting.' Jo pats the bundle on the table. 'Ben says I can ride with him over the bridge, as it's on your way, if Mistress de Wolfe doesn't mind? The boats are struggling to cross with the river half-frozen.'

'Are those costumes for the Chamberlain's Men?' Sophia asks, trying not to betray too much interest. 'I'd have thought they'd be lying low after yesterday's escapade.'

Jo grins. 'I don't think Master Burbage knows the meaning of lying low. He's the toast of the town today, or at least the nine-tenths of it that's ever had an unjust landlord, and he's enjoying every minute.'

'He'd better make the most of it, before Giles Allen catches up with him,' Leila remarks. 'You keep well out of the way when he does.'

'I'll come with you,' Sophia says, setting down her tea. 'I'd like a word with Master Burbage myself. Ask Ben to fetch the horses, would you?'

Leila watches the door pensively for a moment after Jo has closed it behind her.

'Poor Ben,' she murmurs. 'He ought to find himself a nice young woman who can help him run that tavern and give him a brood of boisterous children.'

'Leila, you know he's in love with Jo.'

'That's the problem. He's steering a course for a broken heart. Jo cares for him as her childhood friend, but no more. She's no intention of marrying – not Ben nor any other man.

Perhaps you could talk to him. Let him down gently, so Jo doesn't have to.'

'Me?' Sophia looks surprised.

'He respects you. And you understand the situation from the other side.'

'I don't know what you mean,' Sophia says stiffly, fastening her cloak.

'Yes you do.' Leila takes a sip of tea and gives Jo a sidelong look. 'Anthony Munday, pining for you like a knight in a French romance.'

'Don't be ridiculous. Besides, he has a wife and children.'

Leila twists her mouth. 'Since when was that an obstacle to falling in love?'

'Are you so starved of incident down here that you must invent intrigue where none exists?' Sophia says, pulling on her gloves and trying to make light of the conversation, though the subject leaves her uncomfortable. 'I'm going, before you talk any more nonsense. Let me know what you learn of Agnes Lovell.'

She says this as the door opens and Jo stands in the doorway, wrapped in a thick travelling coat.

'Ben's gone for the horses. Did you say Agnes Lovell?'

'Why, do you know her?'

Jo hesitates. 'She came to the playhouse once with her guardian, Sir Thomas. He had some business with Master Burbage and she waited in the tiring house for him while they talked. That's all I know.' From the way her eyes flit sideways, it is plainly not all she knows.

Sophia follows her into the snowy yard, wondering how she can press the matter further without alarming the girl into silence.

FIVE

The new indoor theatre at Blackfriars is a work of art, although unfortunately it is not a theatre. Not in a commercial sense, anyway. Two years ago, James Burbage, owner of The Theatre in Shoreditch (if not the land it stood on), purchased what had been the old Parliament Hall in the precinct of the Black Friars for the eye-watering sum of £700, and spent a further small fortune knocking through partitions and constructing two tiers of galleries and a stage with boxes at either side, so that the Chamberlain's Men would have a place to perform through the winter. But before the work was finished, the precinct's wealthy inhabitants – those who had bought the fine monastic buildings when the Dominican friary was dissolved – grew alarmed at the prospect of a public playhouse in their midst, and organised a petition to the Privy Council expressing their fears over the hordes of vagrants and lewd persons such a theatre would inevitably attract. The Privy Council, seeing so many influential names gathered in protest, bowed to pressure and banned public performances within the liberty of the Blackfriars. James Burbage died a year later without ever seeing a penny from his investment, and his son, Master Richard Burbage, has been left with a lavishly decorated and extremely expensive rehearsal room, into which he cannot put a paying audience.

It's not yet four, and the sky already darkening when they arrive. Ben heads off to wait at a tavern as Sophia climbs the winding stone staircase outside the building to the first floor and slips in behind Jo, who disappears to the tiring house with her creations. Sophia takes a seat in the shadows at the back of the auditorium. The sight takes her breath away for a moment, as it always does. Dozens of candles blaze in three branched candelabra over the stage, while more burn in bronze wall sconces affixed to the pillars supporting the upper gallery. Lanterns have been set along the front edge of the stage, and all this light catches the gilt paint on the back wall with its three embellished doors, picking out geometric patterns in black and gold. The polished wood of the benches and boards still smells new. At one side of the pit, a man of Italian appearance plucks at a lute while a boy of eleven or twelve years sings a lament in a clear, fluting voice, stumbling on the same note each time and beginning again. Facing them, two older men practice a jig, colliding and bickering over their missteps. At the foot of the stage, another man is painting trees on a flat wooden panel set on trestles.

There is Richard Burbage, striding about the stage and huffing, while a skinny red-haired youth whirls a wooden sword beside him, testing its weight. In one of the boxes, she sees the man from Stratford resting his forearms on the ledge, his eyes following Burbage and the boy distractedly, his lips moving silently as if in prayer – she guesses he is revising lines in his head and thinks with a private smile how his solemnity would annoy Anthony.

She leans back against a wooden pillar and watches the bustle of a rehearsal with pleasure. She has always loved spectacle and performance, even as a child in Oxford, when she would beg her father to let her see the travelling companies put on their shows in the inn yards. In a different life (one in which she had been born a man, she supposes), she would

51

have loved to have been a player. But then, she thinks wryly, hasn't she been acting various parts her whole life? She is so wrapped in these thoughts that it only gradually dawns on her that the atmosphere in the playhouse feels oddly muted, as if a note has been struck out of key.

Burbage claps his hands sharply and the room falls silent.

'Master Strange, might you see your way to gracing us with your presence before the end of winter?' he bellows at one of the doors to the tiring house, and moments later a boy hurtles on to the stage, breathlessly apologising – 'Sorry, sorry – the sword was in the wrong trunk' – and Sophia sits up straighter, her heart catching in her throat.

She thinks he has grown again since she last saw him; is that possible? He is almost as tall as Burbage now, near six foot, and shows no sign of stopping. The childish softness of his face has fallen away in the past year; he is all planes and angles, and with the dark blond hair that falls in a sweep across his brow, he looks so like his father that she forgets to breathe. Sixteen years shrink to nothing, and she sees herself walking under the trees in an Oxford college garden with the brilliant young scholar whose reticence had only fanned the flames of her desire, and whose secrets she had guarded with all the intensity of her youthful passion. But she had not been able to prevent what happened to him, though at the time she felt she would gladly have sacrificed herself to save him. Nor, in the wake of his death, had she been in any state to fight her father when he sent her away for her confinement to his sister in Kent, nor to resist when her baby was taken from her arms and they would not tell her where he had gone. It was for the best, they said, the child would have a Christian family and not have to live his life stained by her shame. She remembers little about the months that came after, only that she had existed in a limbo between living and dying, lacking the impetus to turn towards either. She had been barely nineteen years old – not much more than Tobie is now.

'From the top,' says Burbage, giving Tobie an affectionate cuff around the head, and the boy takes his position, wooden sword at arm's length, to begin a bout of duelling with the skinny youth. Each time they clash, or trip, or fail to coordinate their steps, Burbage patiently takes them through the routine again; the fight is as carefully timed as a dance. Sophia watches them. Tobie moves with grace (though his fencing technique leaves much to be desired; she can almost hear Maître Jules's pained sighs); he is long-limbed and athletic, although he too seems infected with the listlessness that hangs over the company today, and she notices that he is limping slightly on his left foot. At one point, he mistimes a thrust and catches the red-haired boy a blow to the stomach; immediately, Tobie rushes to his colleague, apologising and checking he is not hurt. He is kind, Sophia thinks with a rush of pride; he is a kind person, and she wonders if that is to the credit of the people who raised him, or something native to Tobie himself. How strange it is to be learning the character of your own child in glimpses like this, when he is almost a man. She speculates, not for the first time, on how she would have felt if he had turned out to be arrogant or spoiled or brattish (naturally, she would have blamed his adoptive parents). But Tobie – to her relief – seems wholly at ease with himself and the world. What's more, he is thriving among the players; with a ferocity long dormant, she finds herself primed to fight with every fibre of her being against anyone who threatens his happiness – yes, even Robert Cecil. When the boys make it through the duel with no errors, she can't hold back from standing up in her seat and applauding.

The sound startles the company, who turn to see the source of the interruption; the lute player stops, and she thinks she detects a trace of fear in their expressions, before a delayed ripple of greeting reaches her. Sophia does not delude herself; she is not one of them, and she is careful never to outstay her welcome, but the warmth she receives from the playing company is unequalled anywhere else she goes in London. Burbage flings his arms wide, as if he has been awaiting her arrival from a long voyage, and vaults heavily down from the stage. Tobie raises a hand briefly before turning his attention back to the other boy, and she feels the sting of his indifference; to him, she is just some wealthy widow who must be humoured on account of her generous purse.

She walks down the stairs between the banks of seating and meets Burbage at the edge of the pit.

'Mistress de Wolfe – what an unexpected honour!' He drops to one knee and kisses her hand. 'Look, I know why you're here, and I can assure you—'

'I'm surprised to find you still at liberty, Master Burbage,' she says, smiling. 'I'd have thought you'd be clapped in irons in Newgate after yesterday.'

She meant it as a joke, but Burbage looks stricken. He takes her by the elbow and leads her to a bench.

'It's hardly a laughing matter, Mistress de Wolfe.'

'Oh – I was speaking of Giles Allen, who I hear is even now haring back from the country with an army of lawyers to rescue his stolen theatre.'

'Not stolen,' Burbage says, with mock reproach. His face falls serious again. 'Forgive me, I thought you meant—'

'The girl?'

He lowers his eyes. 'News has spread, then. Shocking business. We've lost half the day being questioned by the coroner, who refuses to believe that we know nothing about it. They say she was murdered. We were all giddy with triumph after yesterday – we never expected . . .' He rubs a hand across his beard. 'No one's in the mood to play a comedy after that.'

'They questioned all of you?' Her gaze flicks instinctively to the stage, where the sword fight has recommenced.

'All who took part in our manual labours yesterday. Which is to say, every able-bodied man in the company. The coroner is convinced that there must be a connection – why else would this girl have been left on our site, he says.'

'And what do you think?' She watches him closely, but he knits his hands together between his knees and she sees only distress and confusion in his face. She wonders if he has been told the victim's identity, and waits to see what details he offers.

'I can't fathom it, Mistress de Wolfe, truly. If you ask me, the most likely explanation is that whoever killed that poor girl heard The Theatre was down and thought it would be a useful place to dispose of the body.' He shakes his head at the state of a world where such things can happen.

'There are easier places,' Sophia says. 'Unless she was intended to be found, and an association made with the Chamberlain's Men.'

'So the coroner says. But to what end?' Burbage spreads his hands, palms up. 'Lord knows there are plenty of people with grievances against us – most of the other playing companies, for a start – but to kill a young girl with the aim of . . . I don't know, tainting our reputation? I can't fathom it,' he says again, and his eyes are pained. 'In any case, Mistress de Wolfe, I want to assure you that this unfortunate event is no fault of ours. And while I understand that it must be profoundly distressing for a lady of your standing and sensibility to have even a tangential connection to such a terrible crime, I hope you know how much we value your loyal support—'

'Did you really see nothing?' she says, cutting him off in full flow. 'Yesterday, when you'd cleared the site – not one of you saw them come? It must have taken two people at least to carry a body over rough ground in this weather.'

Burbage passes a hand over his beard again. 'We were gone shortly after dusk,' he says. 'We had to take the carts straight to Peter Street's warehouse at Bridewell to store the timbers – we spent half the night unloading them. Whoever put the girl in that trench must have done it when the site was abandoned – she wasn't discovered until dawn. The only person who might have seen anything was our little watchman, and I doubt we'll ever find him again.'

'What watchman?'

He gives a muted laugh. 'Just a street boy who was hanging around asking questions. I liked his mettle, so I gave him fourpence to keep a lookout for constables while we dismantled the place. He was still loitering when we left – probably hoping to find any nails or broken bricks we'd missed. I mentioned him to the coroner because he could at least vouch for the fact that my men were packed up and gone by six – although in my experience, any street child would run like Mercury in the opposite direction if an officer of the law tried to question him. No doubt they'll track him down eventually – he was a distinctive lad, white streak through his hair here.' He taps his exuberant curls above his right temple. 'I did wonder if I should attempt to find him, offer some incentive to speak up for us – but then I'd be accused of bribing a witness . . .'

'A white streak?' Sophia sits up.

'Yes – like a little feral badger.' He reaches across and takes her hand between both of his. 'Let us not dwell on this unhappy business, Mistress de Wolfe. I don't have a great deal of faith in the machinery of the law, but I dare say the culprit will be found in due course and it will be clear to all of London that there is nothing to link the girl's death to the Chamberlain's Men. In the meantime, I am glad you're here, because I wanted to talk to you about our new enterprise—'

His prepared speech is interrupted by the thunder of several pairs of feet on the steps outside; the door is thrown open, hitting the wall with a crash and juddering on its hinges; all the candles flicker in the sudden draught as six armed men erupt into the auditorium carrying the crisp scent of snow on their clothes, drawn swords reflecting the wavering candles in a thousand scattered points of light. The music and

56

conversation stops abruptly, the actors freeze in their dance. For a moment, the whole company appears turned to stone, staring wordlessly while the swordsmen now gathered in the pit cast around, as if uncertain of their cue.

In their wake, a man in a black fur-lined cloak and hat appears in the doorway and strides down the steps between the benches, pausing halfway to point dramatically at the stage, for all the world as if he is making his entrance in the part of a vengeful villain. He is tall and broad-shouldered, neat grey beard trimmed to a point concealing a pursed mouth that gives him a look of permanent disapproval. At his shoulder is a stocky man in the livery of a City constable, who holds out a rolled document and, as an afterthought, hurriedly closes the door behind them, causing the lights to stutter once again.

'That's him,' the man in the cloak pronounces, in a voice well suited to the space, pulling off a fur glove to stab his pointing finger at the air. Sophia follows the direction of his gaze and realises with horror that he appears to be indicating the boys on the stage. 'The one with yellow hair. Arrest him.'

As if in some waking dream where she is powerless to move, Sophia watches uncomprehending as four of the armed men mount the stage and take hold of Tobie, bending his arms behind his back as he cries out, his face blank with shock.

SIX

Anthony rides past the Aldgate Bars, the posts marking the eastern boundary of the City, silently thanking whichever version of God is listening these days that he is of neither the class to be conscripted as a foot soldier nor commissioned as an officer. He darts a glance at the man beside him, who has seen sights on the battlefield that Anthony prays never to witness. Nat Leman is a tall, broad-shouldered Kentishman in his early forties, still with the upright bearing of the soldier he was in his youth. Anthony knows him from his time working as a pursuivant; while Anthony carried the warrants, Nat was one of the armed men employed to accompany him, in case the Catholics he was sent to arrest didn't want to leave their safehouses willingly. Over the years, Nat has become a valued and trusted source of information, and his contacts among the soldiery are unrivalled.

'So you think this Grinkin knows something?' he says, raising his voice so that Nat can hear him through the thick fur cap he wears pulled over his ears. Nat is economical with words; he has said only that he knows of a man who fought under Sir Thomas North in Ireland and might be willing to talk, but Anthony would like to be reassured that he is not riding out to Whitechapel for nothing.

Although, what else would you call this, if not a fool's errand? What is he doing on the road, in this weather, when he has revisions to make on the script the Admiral's Men will perform at court in a week? The answer, of course, is Sophia de Wolfe. He tells himself he wishes merely to be of service to her, as a loyal friend, in her words, or a former comrade in Walsingham's invisible army. He also scoffs at himself for even imagining this might be convincing to anyone.

'I think if you want someone to tell the truth about North, George Grinkin's your man,' Nat replies, his face set grimly into the oncoming wind.

'I heard Sir Thomas left his troops without proper rations or equipment.'

Nat lets out a bitter laugh. 'That's a gentle way of putting it. I've seen men come back whose feet and legs rotted off for want of shoes. Some of his company starved to death while they waited at the Dublin garrison for orders. And the money that was given for the troops' wages and provisions – where did that go?' He makes a face. 'Even so, I suppose you'd call Sir Thomas a success compared to his son. Better negligent than reckless.'

Anthony sits up straighter in his saddle. 'Tell me about his son.'

'Sir Thomas barely stayed three months in Dublin,' Nat says, bringing his horse closer so he doesn't have to shout. 'Never even saw combat. He sailed back to England in December, handing the company – what was left of them – to the command of his son. Edmund North lacked the experience to lead men into battle, but then most of the gentlemen captains do.' His mouth twists in contempt. 'He got lucky at first – there was a ceasefire with the Irish rebels, but it didn't hold. Some months later they were up in Carrickfergus, defending the garrison there, when the Irish leaders closed in with a small force. Did you hear about it?'

Embarrassed, Anthony shakes head. He, too, is guilty of

glossing over news from Ireland; all the losses begin to blur together.

Nat grunts. 'Not surprised. They kept it quiet. I heard this from one of the few foot soldiers who made it back. As he tells it, the governor of the garrison, with Captain North and the other officers, requested a parley with the enemy, and the troops were made to march out with them. The men thought they were there to make a show of strength, back up the talks. But at a certain point, as they approached, there was a signal between the governor and the captains, who gave the order to attack. Our boys drove the Irish back a way, but it was a trap. They had reinforcements hidden in the hills with muskets. Cut through our soldiers like hail flattening stalks of wheat. Maybe two dozen survived, out of near three hundred men.'

Anthony looks at him in dismay. 'And Captain North?'

'Oh, he made it all right.' Nat's voice is tight with anger. 'Fled after his horse was shot from under him. Two of the other captains survived too, by turning on their heels after they led their men unprepared into that skirmish like lambs to slaughter. How any commander could do that and live with himself is beyond me.'

Anthony tries to imagine it: the betrayal of trust, the arrogance of the English officers, three hundred souls lost for an ill-judged gamble.

'And what about this George Grinkin? He was there?'

'He was Edmund North's lieutenant at Carrickfergus. If you're looking for someone with a grudge against the Norths, start there.'

'A particular grudge, beyond North leading the company into an ambush, you mean?'

Nat nods. 'Captain North's horse was shot from under him, as I say. The man who told me saw it with his own eyes. North was injured – not badly, but Grinkin went back for him, dismounted and pulled him to his feet, trying to help him out of the line of fire. They'd made it back to Grinkin's horse – the lieutenant meant for them to ride together. But North shoved Grinkin aside, hauled himself up and turned tail, leaving his men behind. A moment later, Grinkin was hit in the leg. That was his reward for saving his commanding officer.'

'Jesus.' Anthony can't think of an adequate response. 'Did he not report Edmund North for desertion?'

Nat laughs aloud, fogging the air. 'If he tried, nothing came of it. Meanwhile, Sir Thomas North got a pension of £40 a year from the queen for his services, did you know that? A fucking pension. While the men whose lives he wrecked now depend on almshouses.'

They fall silent as they approach Whitechapel. Smoke from the chimneys of the bell foundry thickens the air, and the few snowflakes drifting around them are tainted black with smuts. Anthony thinks of all the ruined men that the Irish wars have left in their wake over the past five years, on both sides, and despairs at the waste of it. But Queen Elizabeth is caught in a bind; she has to keep pouring men and money into suppressing the rebellion, because it's not just about the island of Ireland. The Irish are allies of their co-religionists the Spanish, and if the Earl of Tyrone and his rebel forces succeed in ending English rule there, it would give the Spanish a staging post on England's doorstep, the better to retake the kingdom for the Catholic Church. It may be a decade since their great Armada failed, but they have attempted two more in the past couple of years, and even the death of Elizabeth's implacable enemy, the Spanish king Philip II, this past September has brought no respite; his son, Philip III, seems just as determined to succeed where his father failed in bringing England to heel. Hence this latest campaign to quell the Irish rebels, planned for the coming spring and led by the queen's sometime favourite, Robert Devereux, the handsome and charismatic young Earl of Essex. Anthony has his own views on Essex, which he keeps to himself because the earl and his friends are influential in the literary and intellectual circles at court, and he doesn't want to sabotage any chance of future patronage, but he finds it hard to believe that an Irish campaign with Essex at its helm would be any less catastrophic than all those that have preceded it. And yet, he thinks, the war is far enough away that most Londoners have managed to close their eyes to the broken husks of soldiers begging and dying in the streets. Could someone have felt that the murder of a thirteen-year-old girl was a useful way to remind them? It seems unthinkable, but he has seen how the horrors of war can warp or destroy a man's humanity.

'I'll wait for you here,' Nat says, slowing as they approach the sign of the Hoop and Grapes. 'You want Three Bowl Alley, third house.'

Anthony passes him the agreed shilling and leaves him at the tavern, continuing on to a narrow street of six modest houses and workshops. He knocks at the third and the door is opened by a large woman of indeterminate middle age, made larger by the many layers of wool wrapped around her. At her back, he sees that the ground floor of the cottage is one long room with another door at the far end.

'Give you good day, Goodwife. I'm looking for George Grinkin,' he says.

The woman narrows her eyes. 'Who wants him?'

'My name is Munday. I've come on a matter of business.'

She sizes him up, and a faint recognition dawns. 'Are you from St Botolph's, about them screens?'

'That's right,' Anthony says, with his most winning smile and barely a hesitation. One advantage of his years in Walsingham's service is the ability to say whatever is most convenient and sound plausible.

'Wait there.' The woman leaves him on the threshold while she crosses to the back door and yells, 'Georgie! Feller from St Botolph's to see you!' An indistinct call answers, and she returns to the step. 'You can tie your horse under the porch,

I'll keep an eye on him,' she says, and nods him through. Anthony notices that there is no fire in the grate, and ice inside the windows.

At the back of the house is a yard and a workshop; he opens the door to find a young man with a gaunt, stubbled face seated behind a bench, sanding down a small object cupped in the palm of one hand. The place smells of freshly cut wood and sawdust. The walls are stacked with carved linenfold panels of varying patterns, and a brazier burns in one corner, giving off a feeble warmth.

George Grinkin greets him with a smile, but his eyes are wary. He is probably still in his twenties, but looks older.

'I wasn't expecting anyone,' he says pleasantly. 'I thought we'd agreed the end of next month?'

Anthony approaches the bench and sees that Grinkin is making a set of chess pieces from ebony and boxwood. Some are still awaiting a final polish, but the detail is exquisite. He picks up a black knight about two inches high and runs his thumb over the smooth grain where the horse's mane falls in ripples.

'This is beautiful,' he says, feeling the weight of it in his hand.

'Thank you.' Grinkin inclines his head to accept the praise, but his wariness has only increased. 'You wanted to talk about the rood screen?'

'No.' Anthony sets down the knight and looks the man in the eye. 'Lieutenant Grinkin. I'm not from the church. I want to talk to you about Carrickfergus.'

Grinkin goes very still. 'One moment,' he says, as he bends and rummages in the shelves beneath his workbench.

Anthony waits. When Grinkin straightens, he is holding a pistol aimed at Anthony's chest.

'Get out,' he says, his voice low and charged. 'Turn around, and keep walking. Tell him I've been as good as my word and kept my mouth shut. Now he needs to do the same and leave us alone.'

Anthony raises his hands slowly, though his heart is hammering and his thoughts racing too fast to make sense of the man's words. 'Tell who?'

Grinkin snorts. 'That's how we're playing it now, is it? He wants to pretend this is nothing to do with him? You were just going to come in here, smash a few things, threaten to burn us out, and act like you have no idea who sent you? Well, not this time.' He cocks the pistol. 'Tell him I'm better prepared these days. I ever see you in Whitechapel again, whoever you are, I'll shoot you in your fucking face and dump you in the river. Tell him that.'

'Grinkin, I'm not here to smash anything,' Anthony says, as calmly as he can manage. 'My name is Anthony Munday, I'm a writer. I'm working on a pamphlet telling the truth about the Irish wars and I heard a story about you rescuing Edmund North at the battle of Carrickfergus. I was hoping you would tell it in your own words.'

Grinkin stares at him. He lowers the pistol a fraction. 'Where did you hear that?'

'From a survivor. An infantryman who saw you dismount to save your captain.'

'What, he witnessed it? He saw North desert?'

'So he says.'

The lieutenant's eyes widen. 'Would he testify?' His desperation is painful to watch.

'I don't know. I can ask him, if you put that down.'

Grinkin glances at the gun as if he has forgotten he was holding it. He sets it carefully on the bench and clasps his hands together to stop them shaking. 'All right, then. What do you want to know?'

'Tell me about Carrickfergus.'

Anthony listens patiently while Grinkin repeats the story he has heard from Nat Leman. Grinkin tells it dispassionately, concentrating on the facts, but Anthony can see his knuckles pressed white with contained emotion.

'Did you report it?' he asks, when Grinkin has finished.

The lieutenant looks at him as if he's an idiot. 'I tried. Believe me, I petitioned every senior English commander who'd been out in Ireland, trying to bring it to a court martial. But there were so few survivors, it was only my word against North's. He claimed I was slandering him out of malice. And who would listen to me, when his uncle's on the Privy Council?' He pauses, spreads his palms flat on the table. 'But if you say there's a witness—'

'So who's been smashing your place up and threatening you?' Anthony asks, with a glance around the workshop. 'Edmund North?'

Grinkin picks at a loose splinter on the tabletop and doesn't meet his eye. He shifts in his seat.

'When I got nowhere with the court martial, I—' He bites his lip. 'I lost myself a bit. I believed in justice, you see. There are rules in the army, and I trusted in the rules to hold. But I learned the hard way that those rules don't apply to men like Edmund North.'

'So what happened?'

Grinkin still won't look at him. 'I took to hanging around outside the North house. I was drinking a lot last year, see, and I wasn't always thinking straight. I would shout curses at him when he came out the gate, calling him a murderer and a coward. One time I threw a bucket of pig's blood at his door, to signify he had blood on his hands. Don't put that in your pamphlet, will you?' He darts a furtive glance at Anthony.

'Did you ever attack him physically? Threaten him, or his family?' Anthony gestures to the pistol.

'Not as such. They go everywhere with bodyservants. But I thought about it. Thought about lying in wait for the brave captain and putting a shot through his brain. I'd hang for it, but I was past caring at that point.'

'What made you stop?'

Grinkin heaves a sigh that rattles his thin frame. 'I had a visit. Six months back, it must be. Two big fellers, kerchiefs round their faces. Smashed up my workshop with mallets, broke every piece I'd been working on. They said if I didn't back off and stop my slanders, the next time they'd rape my mother and burn the house down with her in it. So.' He lifts one narrow shoulder. 'I stopped talking about Carrickfergus. When you mentioned it, I thought he'd sent you to make sure I hadn't forgotten.'

Anthony shakes his head. 'Did you ever make threats to the North women? Sir Thomas's wife or his daughter? His ward?'

Grinkin gives him a long, cold look. He pushes his stool back slowly and stands, the fingers of his right hand creeping nearer the gun. 'Go fuck yourself,' he says, with quiet menace. 'I'm a soldier – least, I was. If I have a quarrel with a man, I don't go at it by hurting his women. You broadsheet writers, you disgust me. You're not interested in the real story – you only want some lurid lie to sell more copies. Go on, get out.'

Anthony can't help but agree with his assessment of pamphleteers.

'Where were you last night?' he asks.

For a moment, he thinks Grinkin is going for the pistol, but instead he regards Anthony with a puzzled frown.

'At the Hoop and Grapes with my brother-in-law and some of his workmates from the foundry. Why?'

'Till what time?'

He shrugs. 'Around midnight. I'd had a few drinks so I went back to my sister's to sleep it off so's I didn't wake Ma. Who are you, the constable? What's all this about?'

'Sir Thomas North's ward was murdered last night.' Anthony recalls that Sophia had said this wasn't common knowledge yet, but he reasons it will get out soon enough, and he wants to see the man's reaction.

All the colour drains from Grinkin's face; he grips the workbench to hold himself steady.

'And you reckon I did it? So he *did* send you?'

'No. I'm nothing to do with the Norths. I'm just making enquiries on behalf of an interested party.'

'Christ. They'll pin this on me.' The soldier gives Anthony a pleading look, and there is genuine fear in his voice. 'I never touched her. She's just a child.'

'You knew the girl, then?'

'Well, I've seen her. I told you, I used to wait outside the house. I'm not proud of myself, though I wasn't in my right senses. But even at my lowest, that's a thing I'd never do. I'm not the one that likes to hurt young girls.'

'What do you mean?'

Grinkin moves out from behind the workbench with a lurching step, and Anthony sees for the first time that his right leg ends mid-thigh. Strapped to the stump is a polished wooden post, finely turned with a curlicued pattern carved into the grain. The lieutenant leans one hand on the bench.

'When we were kicking our heels at Carrickfergus, while the ceasefire held, there were local girls that used to come to the garrison. Happens everywhere you've got a fort full of soldiers, they know there's money to be made. One night, I was outside the officers' quarters and a young lass came rushing out, crying, with blood all over her face. I offered to get a physician but she just wanted to leave. She said the man she'd been with was too drunk to perform, and when she'd failed to rouse him, he'd got into a fury and thrown her across the room. She couldn't have been more than fourteen or fifteen, that one.'

'Let me guess – Edmund North.'

He grimaces. 'I'm not afraid of death. I dragged four men off the field that day, not just Captain North – went back for them while we were shot at from all sides. But I'm damned if I'll die at the end of a rope and be remembered for killing a child. I didn't do it.'

'As long as your brother-in-law can vouch for you . . .'

Grinkin lets out a hollow laugh. 'You think that'll make a difference, if the Norths have decided to put it on me?' He limps to the door and holds it open. 'Listen, I'm sorry for what I said about writers. Not all of you are liars. If I'm arrested for this, print what I just told you. That's my only chance of having my story heard.'

'I'll do what I can,' Anthony says. 'But you know, if there's no evidence against you, then—'

'*Evidence*. Sure.' The lieutenant shakes his head bitterly. 'I have no faith in justice any more, Master Munday, and you're a fool if you do. It's bought and sold like everything else in London.'

Anthony takes his leave, and doesn't contradict him.

SEVEN

The Blackfriars falls silent; every person in the theatre remains rooted to the spot in disbelief. After a moment, Burbage recovers himself sufficiently to leap up and confront the man in the cloak.

'Good God, Sir Thomas – what is the meaning of this?'

The intruder rounds on him, pale eyes flashing beneath arched black brows.

'You're a thief and a scoundrel, Burbage, and you preside over a den of thieves and *murderers*.' He allows his gaze to sweep the room; he is so taut with rage, his voice shakes.

Burbage looks as bewildered as Tobie. 'Can we not discuss this like gentlemen, sir? Only let the boy go, for pity's sake, what harm has he done? He has nothing to do with our quarrel.'

This only seems to make Sir Thomas angrier. He tears off his hat, revealing a mane of thick grey hair.

'What harm, you ask me? This man here' – he jerks a thumb at the constable – 'on behalf of the City of London, has a warrant to arrest Tobie Strange for the murder of my ward, Mistress Agnes Lovell, who was discovered this morning on your site.'

A cry escapes Sophia before she can press her hand to her mouth.

'If you prevent him from doing his job,' he continues imperiously, 'I will see that you are arrested as well, and any man who interferes, for disturbance of the peace.'

'Your *ward*?' Burbage manages. He is staring at the older man as if he might have lost his wits. 'What—'

'Murder?' Tobie says, in a wavering voice. 'You mean to say, it was *Agnes* . . . ?' Words appear to fail him; his knees buckle, one of the armed men twists his arm harder and he yelps in pain.

The sound snaps Sophia from her state of shock. She pushes past Burbage and plants herself in the path of the grey-haired man, hands on hips.

'On what evidence do you arrest this boy?' she demands.

Sir Thomas blinks at her as if a dog had jumped up and addressed him.

'Who is this impertinent harridan shouting at me?' he asks, looking past her in expectation that one of the men will bring her to heel. 'Do you know to whom you speak, woman?'

'I deduce you are Sir Thomas North,' she says, not moving. 'My name is Sophia de Wolfe, and I'm asking you what grounds you have for accusing a boy of murder.'

'De Wolfe?' He angles his head to assess her. 'Humphrey's widow, I suppose?' When she doesn't answer, he nods, and his mouth draws tighter. 'Our boys were at Gray's Inn together. I hear he disinherited his son for you.'

She stares back, unflinching; she will not be disconcerted by him. 'To obtain an arrest warrant, you must have compelling proof of guilt. So where is your proof?'

Sir Thomas's nostrils flare briefly and she sees the flash of anger in his eyes; in the same instant, she sees him calculate his possible moves and their outcomes. Unexpectedly, he laughs.

'Gentlemen, Mistress de Wolfe appears to believe we are in a court of law, and she the presiding judge.' Only the constable rewards him with a sycophantic chuckle. Sir Thomas presses on: 'Well, though you have no authority to ask such questions, I will indulge you, madam. You ask for evidence – I have it here. You know what I'm talking about, don't you, boy?'

This last is addressed in the direction of the stage; Sophia turns to see that Tobie, white as a corpse, is shaking his head in fear.

Sir Thomas reaches into his doublet and withdraws a bundle of papers tied in a red ribbon. 'You recognise these, eh, lad? Shall I read a portion to your colleagues?'

Tobie strains against the men holding him, on the verge of tears. 'No – please—'

Sir Thomas allows a wolfish smile. 'Very well, I will spare the company your childish verse. Suffice to say these are letters, found in my ward's bedchamber, written by Master Strange to Agnes, who – as this boy must be well aware – was pre-contracted to marry my son Edmund when she came of age. Letters swearing Master Strange's undying love for her. In one – dated the eighteenth day of December – he says he would do anything to prevent her marriage.' He taps the papers against the flat of his left hand. 'Well, it seems he found the means to do that. If you could not have her yourself, Strange, you would put her beyond anyone's reach, isn't that so? You've as good as confessed it here.'

'No – I didn't mean – I would never hurt her.' Tobie writhes against the guards; one kicks him behind the knees and he falls to the boards with a cry.

'Don't say any more, Tobie – not without a lawyer.' At this new voice, a stillness falls. Will Shakespeare has emerged from the box; he does not speak loudly, but there is authority in his words.

Sir Thomas looks needled. 'Master Shakespeare talks sense, for once. It will go worse for you if you resist arrest.'

The guards haul Tobie to his feet and push him across the pit. With a half-swallowed sob, he submits, and Sophia feels her heart wrenched out of her as they shove him roughly towards the steps.

'We will make sure you have a good lawyer, Tobie,' she says, trying to sound calm, as they draw level.

'I did write letters to Agnes, Mistress de Wolfe, but that was all. I never harmed her, I never would—' He fixes her with an imploring look, his eyes threatening to spill with tears, and she sees – not for the first time – that his eyes are hers, the same tawny-golden that his father once told her belonged to a lioness. She grips her hands together tightly to prevent her from running to him and prising the guards off by force.

'Now, look here, don't worry, Tobie – there's been a bit of a misunderstanding, that's all. We'll get it straightened in no time,' says Burbage, and Sophia – who has always considered him too much of a showman to be wholly reliable – feels a sudden flood of gratitude.

'Help me, Burbage, please,' Tobie says, and he sounds like a child. It strikes her that, as far as he knows, he is alone in the world; the Chamberlain's Men are the nearest thing he has to a family now. For the first time, she concedes that Anthony and Leila may have been right: would Sir Thomas North feel at liberty to treat the boy in this way if he knew Tobie had a wealthy parent to speak up for him? Or would his illegitimacy count against both of them? Well, too late to worry about that now. She will have to work with things as they are.

'Where are you taking him?' she demands.

'Newgate,' says the constable, who is already at the door, holding it open.

Sir Thomas turns and gives her a look that suggests he thinks he has won. 'I'm sure your husband's money will buy the boy an extra blanket for his cell if you wish to show your charity, Mistress de Wolfe,' he says, jamming his hat back on his head. 'Though I would advise discretion – you don't want people speculating about why you would support a common murderer. There's enough talk about you as it is.'

Before she can think of a suitable response, the whole entourage has swept out of the building, leaving the players staring in their wake.

'Good God,' Burbage says, clutching at his hair with both hands. 'What just happened? The dead girl was Agnes Lovell? I had no idea Tobie even knew her. How on earth did she come to be in a trench at The Theatre?' He sits heavily. All the ebullience has leaked from him like air from a punctured pig's bladder.

'He met her at The Curtain,' says a soft voice at their shoulder. Sophia turns to see Jo behind them, turning a broad-brimmed hat trimmed with peacock feathers between her hands. 'September, it must have been – remember, Burbage, when Sir Thomas came to see you about your dispute after the show? Agnes grew bored with waiting and came into the tiring house to see the players. She was a sweet girl. I saw her speaking with Tobie then.'

'And they had some kind of – dalliance?' Burbage stares at her, incredulous. 'He confided in you?'

Jo pulls gently at the feather and doesn't quite meet his eye. 'It was letters only, as far as I understand. But he was besotted. Romeo and Juliet stuff.' She smiles ruefully at the hat. 'I just can't believe he would hurt her.'

'Of course not.' Burbage draws himself up, decisive again. 'Mistress de Wolfe, I realise how this looks, but I would stake my life on that boy's honesty – from what I know of him, he wouldn't harm a mouse. Sir Thomas North is a man of influence, and the coroner will have been pressed to make a quick arrest to give the appearance of doing something. Did you notice – those armed men were not wearing City livery? I'd bet they were in North's pocket. But please, pay no heed to his words – he spoke in grief, and in any case he is disposed to think badly of this company—'

'Christ alive, Burbage – is that all you care about – that I might take my money away?' She rounds on him; he recoils, startled. 'We have to *do* something. He's just a boy. God knows what they'll do to him in Newgate.'

Her voice cracks a little; she digs her nails into her palms, forcing her emotions under control, furious that she almost gave herself away.

Burbage looks at her curiously. 'Your tender heart does you credit, Mistress de Wolfe, and I'm sorry for what must appear crassness on my part. But' – he lowers his voice – 'if you understood how precariously things stand with us. I've staked everything on this new playhouse on Bankside, and I was braced for a lawsuit from Giles Allen, but this killing . . .' He shakes his head. 'Thomas North is in good favour with the queen at the moment, and if she should see this business as cause to close down the Chamberlain's Men, as she has done with other companies who displease her—' He bites at a hangnail on his thumb and looks around at the players, who watch him in silence, waiting for his lead.

Sophia pities him then; she can never forget the chill of poverty, the dread of ruin, though she has never had, as Burbage does, the responsibility of other people's families depending on her to make the right decision.

'I will undertake to pay Master Strange's legal costs,' she says, reaching for the purse that hangs discreetly at her belt. 'And take this' – she withdraws a sovereign – 'to buy him food and blankets for his cell and make sure he's well treated. I will go home immediately and write letters on his behalf. Will I find you here tomorrow?'

'If the Master of the Revels hasn't shut us down by then,' Burbage says gloomily, then shakes himself like an ungainly dog and enfolds her in a sudden embrace. 'God bless you, Mistress de Wolfe. Thank you for your faith in us. I have often said to the men that you are an angel sent by heaven in our time of need—'

'Let's concentrate on Master Strange and proving his innocence,' she says, extricating herself and patting him on the arm, but he insists on walking her to the door. At the top of the steps, she turns to him. 'You mentioned a quarrel with Sir Thomas. Has that any bearing on this matter?'

'On the murder of his ward? Good God, no. Impossible.' He pauses. 'Thomas North likes to imagine himself a writer. Plenty at court do. He's a competent translator, but that's the limit of it. He's sent scripts to me before, and I believe he's also tried the Admiral's Men, and there's not a chance any of his works will see the light of day, they're as wooden as this post.' He slaps the nearest pillar. 'But in recent months, Sir Thomas had become fixated on the notion that our Will had taken one of his plays and passed it off as his own. He was threatening us with a lawsuit.'

Stolen ground, Sophia thinks. But that makes no sense; if Thomas North believed he was the victim of literary theft, he would hardly kill his own ward to make the point. She glances back to the stage, but Will has disappeared.

'And what does Master Shakespeare say?'

'He says the idea's laughable.' Burbage waves a hand in dismissal. 'It is, of course. But if the coroner believes there's an existing grievance between Sir Thomas and the Chamberlain's Men, it could add fuel to the accusations against Tobie.' His brow furrows again.

'I'll come back tomorrow with a lawyer,' Sophia says, pulling on her gloves. 'In the meantime, make sure Master Strange is warm and fed tonight.' She knows there is no guarantee that, even if the gaoler accepts a bribe, it will translate into blankets and food for Tobie; the authorities may have given instructions for him to be treated harshly, and Newgate is infamous as the worst of all the London prisons. Her jaw aches from the pressure of trying to contain her feelings, and suddenly she fears she might cry.

Burbage is still speaking as she rushes out, slipping on the treacherous steps. She heads blindly away from the river through the dark precinct, passing outbuildings converted into artisans' workshops, and when she is far enough from the theatre she ducks into the shadow of the former cloister and leans against the wall, doubled over, snatching shallow gulps of cold air. Her chest constricts and she struggles to breathe; she thinks she might vomit or pass out. A huge sob forces its way up from her gut, shaking her whole frame. Seeing Tobie dragged away has dredged up memories of his father's arrest – how could it not? – and of what came after. It's not the same, she tells herself; Tobie has done nothing wrong, no jury could find him guilty. But there is plenty that could be done to him in prison while he awaits trial, and if Thomas North has a grudge against the Chamberlain's Men, who is to say that proof can't be fabricated or juries bought? It was rumoured that Phelippes embellished the evidence that sent Mary Stuart to the block, on Walsingham's orders, and if that can be done to the queen's own cousin, then Burbage is right – who can trust the machinery of the law?

She steels herself; she can't fall apart now, Tobie needs her to think clearly. She must hurry home and beg every person of influence she knows to help her remedy this situation, without betraying the reason for her desperation.

Snow is falling again, light but steady. She brushes flakes from her lashes, heaves another ragged breath and catches, suddenly, the creak of footsteps through the powdery drifts underfoot. Her hand moves to her hip and she presses against the wall as the wavering beam of a lantern swings across the path; in an instant Sophia reacts, springing around the corner, a blade drawn to the throat of the approaching figure.

'Jesus, easy, it's only me.' Jo draws down her hood with a nervous laugh. 'I might have regretted sewing that dress for you, eh.'

Sophia stares at the weapon in her hand as if she can't remember how it came to be there. It's a slender quill-knife, a three-inch blade with a pearl handle, not much to look at, but forged from Toledo steel and honed to a point that could take out an eye, possibly even cut a throat if need be, though she has not yet had occasion to test that. She keeps it in a special pocket sewn into the seam of her skirts by her right hip, a trick Jo learned from Leila, who never goes out unarmed. Sophia tucks the knife away and realises her hands are trembling.

'Sorry. I – I was shaken, I thought someone was coming to rob me.'

'You shouldn't walk through the precinct on your own after dark. Where's Ben?'

'I told him to wait at the tavern on Crede Lane.' Sophia works to steady her breathing.

'I wanted to see if you were all right, you seemed upset. That was dreadful, what happened back there. Everyone's in shock.' Jo gives her a long look. Sophia is never sure how much Jo knows about Tobie; she trusts Leila not to have told her outright, but Jo is sharp enough to make her own deductions. 'They can't hold him though, can they? If they have no evidence.'

'If Tobie really wrote those letters, they might be enough to keep him in prison until trial,' Sophia says, and that rush of fear threatens to overwhelm her again; she lays a palm against the wall to support herself.

'But they were harmless – just boyish love poems,' Jo protests.

'You saw them?'

Jo lowers her gaze, scuffing a pile of snow with the toe of her boot. 'Only one verse. He wanted someone to hear it, and I happened to be backstage. It was all very innocent – nothing lewd.'

'Even so,' Sophia says, feeling her jaw clench. 'The ward of a knight of the realm, and he a player – what was he thinking?'

'I told him to be careful,' Jo says, pulling her coat tighter with her free hand. 'I said he shouldn't sign them – Sir Thomas has reason enough to make trouble for this company as it is. But that only made Tobie more determined.' She gives a faint smile. 'He thought he was Romeo.'

'And look how well that ended,' Sophia says.

'I should have stopped him.' Jo bites her lip. 'But he was smitten with her, Sophia – I watched them when they first met. He could never have done this. And surely he couldn't be charged with murder on the strength of a few love letters?'

'I suppose it will depend on whether the letters can be twisted to mean whatever suits Sir Thomas. And in the absence of any other proof—' Sophia stops, mouth agape. She had been so shaken by what followed with the armed men that Burbage's words had barely registered; now they come back to her like a slap. 'What am I saying – there *is* proof. Jo – that boy who helps your mother sometimes, the one they call Badger – where can I find him?'

'No idea – he comes and goes when it suits him. I can ask around, though – what has he to do with it?'

'Burbage said he was keeping watch for them yesterday while they took The Theatre down, and he stayed on at the site. And this morning Badger was showing Leila a brooch he said had washed up from the river, but she didn't believe him. What if he found that brooch where the body was left? Leila said it had a distinctive insignia – if it wasn't the girl's, it could have belonged to whoever dumped her body there. We have to find him.'

Jo lets out a small sound, and Sophia realises she is shaking the girl's arm hard in her urgency. She releases her grip with a murmured apology.

'Mama would know how to track him down – I'll ask her tonight. But he could have got that brooch anywhere, you know. He picks pockets.'

'I need to ask him, before he sells it on. If he found it at The Theatre, and we can identify the crest on it, we'd have proof that someone else was there that night. He might even have seen them with the girl. It's worth a try, anyway.' The weight lifts from her chest a little at this prospect of reprieve.

'Agnes,' Jo says softly.

'What?'

'You keep saying "the girl". Her name was Agnes.'

'I'm sorry.' Sophia looks down, chastened. All her concern has been for Tobie; she has barely spared a thought for the dead child, who had no mother to worry about her – only a guardian who did not seem exactly grief-stricken over her murder, despite what Burbage said. 'Did you know her?'

'I only spoke to her that one time. She picked up a pair of swan-feather wings and wanted to know how I had made them. A sweet girl, like I said, but there was a sadness hanging over her. I saw the way she lit up when she talked to Tobie. As if for a moment she'd seen the sun come out.'

'Did she write back to him?' Sophia asks, as a thought occurs.

'Yeah. He never showed me those letters, but sometimes I'd see him tucked away in a corner, reading, and he'd be all smiles, like he was glowing from inside.'

'How did she get them to him? She wasn't running around London delivering love notes.' She recalls Leila saying she had visited the North household, but she can't picture Leila taking that risk.

'Must have had a go-between,' Jo says, with a shrug. Her dark eyes are glimmers in the lamplight. Jo is quick at thinking on her feet, but Sophia is quicker at spotting an evasion.

'Jo, if you—'

Before she can ask, Jo tenses and holds up a hand in warning.

Sophia strains to listen, and can faintly make out the soft tread of boots in snow, moving slowly and deliberately. Her hand slides towards her knife. Once again she lunges out from the shadow of the wall, blade drawn, but her eyes have grown used to the lantern, and she can see nothing.

'Who's there?' she calls, forcing herself to sound firm. Nothing, then a patter of feet; she can just make out a denser patch of black detach itself from the shadows and vanish around the corner of an outbuilding. Sophia hoists her skirt with her free hand and runs after them, but there are too many places to hide here in the dark. By the time she reaches the narrow lane by the workshops, there is no sign of anyone. Jo appears at her shoulder with the lantern, blinding them to anything beyond its small bright circle.

'Did you see them?' she asks.

'No. They moved too fast.' Sophia crouches to examine the ground; there is a trail of footprints, but the snow is too soft and new to give them any distinction.

Jo lowers the lantern to give her more light. 'Were they following you?'

'I don't know. Whoever it was clearly didn't want to be seen. Probably just an opportunist thief – you're right, it's not safe to walk alone here after dark.' She straightens with a glance over her shoulder.

'I'll come with you to Crede Lane,' Jo says, tucking her arm through Sophia's as they set off towards the boundary wall. This time Sophia keeps her knife in her hand.

EIGHT

'One more job for you, Ben, before I let you go,' Sophia says, as they mount their horses in the tavern yard. 'I need you to help me break into a house.'

Ben gives her a quizzical look, and when no more information is forthcoming, he simply nods. 'Right,' he says. 'Lead on.'

Sophia knows where Tobie lives, of course; she has made it her business to know. When he first came to London, he lodged with Ned Alleyn's family, an arrangement she approved of, confident that he would be well fed and looked after. After he moved out, last year, to share rooms with two of the other boys from the company, she had asked Anthony to go round on some pretext, to make sure the place was hygienic, that it didn't have rats, that the landlord wasn't fleecing them and they weren't surrounded by bawds and criminals. He had reported back that he wouldn't object to his own son living there, and she'd had to be satisfied with that.

On the way, she tells Ben about the arrest. He is suitably outraged on Tobie's behalf.

'You reckon those letters will be enough for them to hold him?' he asks, as they ride up Threadneedle Street.

'Depends what's in them.' She raises her voice to be heard

over the gusting wind. 'But I imagine those men will be occupied for the moment in getting him to gaol, before they think to search his lodgings. If there's anything potentially incriminating there, I want to find it first.'

'Like what?'

'Letters from Agnes. Or anything they could use against him.'

Ben nods. He doesn't ask why she feels this is her responsibility, though sometimes she suspects that he, like Jo, could take a shrewd guess at her interest in Tobie.

The lodging house in the small square of St Helen's, Bishopsgate, is respectable enough; a large, timber-framed building listing queasily to the left, divided into multiple rented rooms on each floor. It's a neighbourhood popular with actors, being close to The Curtain and The Theatre in Shoreditch, and Sophia keeps her hood pulled up close around her face as they cross the square after leaving the horses, in case they run into anyone who might know her, but it seems the residents of St Helen's are keeping sensibly indoors.

The front door is left on the latch, but there is no one on the stairs as she and Ben climb to the top floor under the eaves; all the same, she finds herself unexpectedly nervous. She holds the lantern steady as Ben unhooks an implement from the leather case at his belt and kneels to work the lock. This is a skill that Sophia possesses herself; Thomas Phelippes taught her when she first started in Walsingham's service, for all the times when a locked cupboard or casket of letters needed to be examined. With her slim fingers and steady hand she had picked it up quickly, but it's a long time since she has practised, and she doesn't trust herself to do the job right tonight; there is too much riding on it.

Ben has the lock open in a matter of minutes. 'Do you want me to wait out here?' he says. She nods, and closes the door behind her.

Inside, the room smells thickly of boy: sweat, feet and

crusted sheets. Sophia winces and looks around, breathing through her mouth. The attic floor is divided into two connecting chambers; the outer one containing a truckle bed and a table, with two further beds in the inner room. In here, dirty clothes are strewn all across the mattresses and the floor. But the bed in the outer room is neatly made, blankets folded back, and she recognises the wool jacket laid on top as Tobie's Sunday best.

At the bed's foot is a wooden chest with no lock. She rummages inside and finds a couple of shirts, four pairs of hose, a broken quill and a sheaf of papers, which she draws out with anticipation, only to find they are annotated pages of play scripts. Nothing else in the chest; the only other place that is his alone is the bed.

She pulls back the blanket and kneels on the rough straw mattress, wondering how she could discreetly provide him with a better one, as she feels around the edges; this, too, is something she did often when she was resident in Catholic households, in search of secret communications. At the head of the bed, tucked between the frame and the wall, she finds a worn leather portfolio, the kind used for carrying papers.

She unties the fastening; inside is a packet of letters. When she opens this, a handful of dried rose petals fall out. The notes are written in a cultivated hand, given to girlish flourishes. Turning one sheet, she sees the signature AL; confident that this is what she came for, she tucks the pages inside the leather bag that hangs at her waist, and is about to replace the portfolio when she notices another item inside it. A silver picture frame, hinged, the size of a small prayer book. With a quick glance at the door, she flicks open the catch to see a pair of portraits. On the left, a sandy-haired man in his middle years, with a round red face and prominent eyebrows; facing him, a woman in a white coif who looks out of the frame with an air of suspicion. Sophia realises she is holding her breath. This must be Christopher and Hannah Strange, the couple who adopted Tobie (*bought him*, says the implacable voice in her head; she knows her aunt took money for the transaction). All she knows of Christopher Strange is that he was a scrivener employed by the cathedral in Canterbury. From the few conversations she has had with Tobie on the subject of his family, it seems that Christopher was a decent enough father, though she wishes – absurdly – that she could have met the man, to judge for herself. Of his adoptive mother, Hannah, Tobie has said very little, and Sophia has not wanted to push. This is the first time she has had any idea what they looked like. The fact that he keeps their pictures under his bed suggests affection, and it moves her; she wants desperately to believe that his childhood was happy. To learn otherwise would break her.

She is lost in these thoughts when Ben slips into the room, holding a finger to his lips.

'People outside,' he hisses.

Sophia looks at him; there is no exit except the staircase, and no innocent way to explain their presence in the room. Ben points to the dormer window in the sloping ceiling. She watches as he jumps on to the table and pushes it open, leaning his head and shoulders through. After a moment, he nods and beckons to her. She stuffs the portfolio and picture behind the bed; without hesitation, she raises her skirt to her thighs and ties it before climbing on to the table and hoisting herself through the casement, thanking Providence that she has not worn a wide-hooped dress.

The window gives on to a gulley between two pointed gables, now piled thick with snow after the day's fall. Sophia shifts along through the drift, careful not to slip on the icy tiles, to make room for Ben, who pulls himself up after her and closes the window. As he does so, he knocks a lump of snow through to the room below, and curses softly. Moments later, the door beneath them slams open, followed by the sound of heavy footsteps across the boards.

The wind is stronger here, three storeys up; it moans around the angles of the roof, making it hard to catch the exchanges from below, but it sounds to Sophia as if there are only two men. She and Ben remain as still as possible, shivering as the snow soaks through their clothes, listening to the thuds and crashes of the search below. Whoever the men are, they clearly have no interest in discretion. A sudden lull in the gusts allows the voices to carry. Both speak with London accents.

'Fucking nothing,' says one. 'He won't be happy.'

'If they were here, we'd have found them.'

'You reckon he gave them to a mate for safekeeping?'

'Or else someone got here before us. Did it look like the place had been turned over?'

The first man lets out a bark of a laugh. 'Three boys live here. How would you tell the difference?'

'That door was unlocked. Don't like that.'

'Maybe they don't bother. They've got nothing worth robbing, have they?'

'Wait, look at this.' The men fall silent; Sophia exchanges a look with Ben. She knows his thoughts are running the same way as hers: the men have noticed the melted snow from the window. The wind makes a long, drawn-out skirl through the gulley between the roofs, drowning out the next few words. She watches as Ben reaches slowly into his boot and withdraws a slim blade.

'Out there?' one is saying, when the wind drops again. 'In this weather? Nah. Old building like this, roof's bound to leak.'

His companion says something Sophia doesn't catch; the first man laughs.

'You have a look if you want, mate. I'm going back. If you ask me, quickest way to find those letters is to hang the little fucker by his wrists – he'll bleat in less than a minute.'

Sophia lurches upright; Ben puts out a hand to stay her. The wind buffets them from all sides, throwing handfuls of snow into their faces. There is a further muttered exchange from below, indecipherable; she can feel Ben braced for an attack, all his muscles taut. But the window remains closed. After more banging of furniture beneath them, a door slams and there is silence. They wait another few minutes before Ben edges forward far enough to peer through the glass. Turning back to her, he nods and tucks his knife back into his boot.

By the time they drop down into the room, Sophia is frozen to the bone, her skirt and hose soaking. She can't feel her feet. Half-dazed, she casts around to see the damage. The place has been torn apart: mattresses ripped, chairs broken, drinking mugs flung from shelves. The men have even prised up a couple of floorboards. Part of her wants to stay and put it right for Tobie and his friends, but she has more urgent tasks.

'Did you get a look at them?' she whispers. Her teeth are chattering so hard she can barely form the words.

Ben shakes his head. 'But I'd guess they're North's men, like the ones you said picked Tobie up from the theatre. Those letters must be important.'

He is too tactful to ask for information, but he leaves a space for her to elaborate if she chooses.

'Maybe North thinks there'd be something he could use to incriminate Tobie further. Or the opposite – he could be worried that the letters point to someone else. Him or his son, for example. If Agnes confided anything to Tobie in writing, North wouldn't want that in the wrong hands.' She presses her palms to her face. 'Shit, Ben. I thought this was the right thing to do – keep North from getting hold of the letters. But now they'll torture Tobie to find out where they are. I should have just handed them over.' She feels the ache of tears again at the back of her throat.

Ben gives her a long, unreadable look, as if he is weighing up what to say. 'You should probably have a read of them first,' he suggests eventually. 'Just in case.'

'In case of what?' She fixes him with an indignant stare. 'Surely you don't think Tobie killed her?'

'No. But you may as well check there's nothing in there that could make things go worse for him before anyone else gets a look at them. After that, well – you've got friends in high places too. You know people who could step in, make sure no one lays a finger on him in Newgate.'

Sophia leans against the wall, hit by a sudden wave of exhaustion. He's right: she's fussing with money for food and blankets, when she should be summoning all her resources to get Tobie out of prison altogether.

'But first you need to get warm,' Ben says firmly. 'You'll be no use to anyone if you take a fever.' At the door, he turns to her. 'That young lad's lucky to have you looking out for him, Mistress de Wolfe.'

'The Chamberlain's Men were a refuge for me after Humphrey died,' she says, forcing herself to meet his enquiring gaze. 'They're my friends, I'd do the same for any of them. But Tobie's only fifteen, and he's got no family in London.'

'Like I say, he's lucky. Maybe one day he'll realise how fortunate he is.'

There is nothing to read in Ben's tone, but she hears an undercurrent all the same. She thinks of the portrait of the Stranges under his bed, and wonders whether Tobie would regard the truth about his parentage as a stroke of good fortune, or if it would drive him away. The thing she has never said to Anthony, or to Leila, is that keeping the truth from him these past two years has been an act of pure cowardice, less about protecting him than herself. Because after so many years of shaping her life around his absence, the risk of losing him a second time terrifies her. If he should blame her or reject her, she would have nothing left.

'Come on, I'll see you home,' Ben says. Numbly she allows herself to be led.

NINE

Anthony finds Nat in the tap-room of the Hoop and Grapes, deep in conversation with the landlord.

'Do you know a former soldier, name of George Grinkin?' Anthony asks, as he orders a hot cider and another for Nat.

The man shoots him a suspicious look, and Anthony wonders if the Norths have sent people to Whitechapel in search of information that would discredit the lieutenant.

'Course. Everyone knows George, poor lad. He drinks here.'

'Was he in last night?'

The man rolls his eyes. 'Oh yes. I gave him and his mates a lock-in, till well after curfew, more fool me. I was still clearing up at one o'clock. But I suppose it's only Christmas once a year, God be thanked.'

He disappears into the kitchen and Anthony pulls up a stool opposite Nat. He didn't really need the landlord's confirmation to persuade him that Grinkin is unlikely to be the killer; while the lieutenant certainly harbours justified resentments against the Norths, a man with a wooden leg would struggle to carry a dead body over rough ground in the snow, even if the brother-in-law or some other friend helped him.

'Useful visit?' Nat asks.

'Well, I've learned some things about Edmund North that

haven't improved my opinion of him.' Anthony grimaces. A man with a taste for young girls and a violent temper, who has a history of doing whatever is necessary to save his own skin; is this the man Sophia is pitting herself against? He leans in. 'Nat, do me one more favour, will you? If you hear news that George Grinkin has been arrested, can you let me know immediately?'

'Arrested?' Nat raises an eyebrow. 'All right, I will. But, look – what's this Irish business about, Munday? Only, if you're going after the Norths, you need to watch yourself.' He lowers his voice. 'Thomas North is not someone you want to cross if you can help it. His family's got influence, and if he learns you're digging up his misdeeds, or his son's, he might be inclined to put obstacles in your path. Especially since he's just been rewarded by the queen for his good service.'

Anthony hesitates. He and Nat know things about one another that neither want coming to light; Nat can be trusted.

'Did you hear about the body found up at the site of The Theatre this morning?'

'I did. Young girl, they're saying.'

'Thomas North's ward. That's why I'm looking for anyone with a grudge against him for Ireland. Keep that to yourself for now.'

Nat's eyes widen. 'They think it's a revenge killing, then?' He frowns. 'Hold on – does that mean you're working for *North*?' He sits back, evidently worrying that he's been led into a trap.

'God, no. I'm making enquiries on behalf of someone who wants the killer found as quickly as possible, for reasons I can't go into. So if you can think of anyone besides Grinkin with a motive to attack the Norths, let me know.'

Nat considers. 'From what I've heard of Grinkin, he's an honourable man – I can't picture him killing a child, and I wouldn't like to see him take the blame. I'll ask around. Discreetly,' he adds, with a knowing smile. He has assumed

Anthony is working for the government, which is not too far wide of the mark.

The landlord brings their drinks, and when he leaves, Nat leans forward, his brow creased again.

'Wait, though – are you sure this is about Ireland?'

'Why, what else would it be?'

'I'm just thinking – North's ward was the Lovell girl, right?'

'Agnes, yes. Do you know the family?'

Nat drops his voice further as two men push past their table to the door. 'I arrested her uncle once.'

'I don't remember that.'

'After your time. Must be five years back now. You know the Lovells are Catholic?'

Anthony absorbs the implications of this. 'I don't know much about them, except the girl's father, Sir John, had land in Suffolk.'

Nat wraps his hands around his mug. 'That's right. Sir John was canny, though – he loved his estate and his income more than the pope, and after the first time he was fined for recusancy, he rolled over for the queen, kept his head down and worshipped like a good loyal Englishman. But his younger brother, Vincent – he stayed ardent for the old faith.'

That would explain why Agnes Lovell's uncle had not been made her legal guardian on her father's death, Anthony thinks. 'What was he arrested for?'

'He was part of a network bringing missionary priests into the country from France. Had houses rented in his name in Essex and London where they stayed after they landed.'

'How was he caught?'

'There was a raid on the Colchester house. Four priests had come in by boat, they'd only been there a couple of hours, hadn't even had a chance to disguise themselves. Someone had tipped off the magistrate, and the pursuivants broke the door down. Vincent Lovell wasn't there – I got orders to pick him up in London. He claimed he knew nothing about it, of course, but they threw him in gaol anyway.'

'I suppose the priests were executed?'

'Oh yes. One of them confessed he was part of a mission to kill the queen. Mind you, he said it after a session on the wall, so who knows.'

They both fall silent. The wall was a form of interrogation where the suspect was put in manacles and suspended by his wrists from iron brackets with his toes barely touching the floor, often for hours at a time. Anthony never saw this part of the process, but he couldn't pretend he didn't know exactly what he was delivering his prisoners to. When you have heard the sounds made by a man hanged, cut down alive and disembowelled, you don't forget it in a hurry. When you had a hand in sending him to the scaffold, you hear it in your sleep. You see his face when you close your eyes. It's why Anthony gave up being a pursuivant, even though at the time he had told himself over and over that he was doing the job to protect England.

'Here's the thing,' Nat says, keeping an eye on the drinkers around them, 'there were plenty of people who thought it was Sir John Lovell that told the authorities where to find them that night.'

'He betrayed his own brother?'

'It's possible. I heard Sir John was worried about Vincent's activities bringing the whole family under suspicion of Catholic allegiance. But he died a year after Vincent was arrested, so I suppose we'll never know.'

'So you're saying a disgruntled Catholic might have killed Agnes Lovell as payback for her father's betrayal, four years after he died? What would be the point of that?'

'Revenge is not always rational, is it? I'm just saying, if you think the girl was killed as punishment, it could as easily be about the Lovell family as the Norths.'

Stolen ground, Anthony thinks. Plenty of Catholics thought that Queen Elizabeth's throne was stolen. John Lovell's supposed treachery against his brother would certainly count as a hidden sin. The problem with that doggerel verse was that it could be twisted to fit any meaning you wanted; everyone has sins they'd rather keep buried (Anthony has more than a few himself). There was still the matter of Sophia's cipher to narrow it down, though. Walsingham had used English Catholics as informers in the 1580s; at least half of them were double-crossing him. Could some Catholic spy have come across the cipher and used poor Agnes Lovell to show what happens to those who betray their faith?

'Where's this Vincent Lovell now?' he asks.

'He was in the Clink for about a year, but they didn't have enough to try him. After his brother died, he was released on bail. I don't know who paid it or where he went, but I can ask around.'

'Thanks, Nat. Anything you can find about the Norths or the Lovells, I'll make it worth your while.' At this rate, he will have spent the payment for the new play before it is even written. He knows that Sophia would gladly cover the costs of his enquiries, but he balks at asking her for money.

So Vincent Lovell was at liberty: a man with connections to a supposed plot against the queen. Did Vincent feel he should have been granted the wardship of his niece, or inherited his brother's estate? A Catholic with coastal land in Suffolk where priests could come ashore safely would be invaluable to the mission. A younger brother robbed of that asset might well consider it stolen ground.

Nat is looking at him with concern. 'I hope they're paying you well for this, Munday, whoever they are,' he murmurs, pushing his stool back. 'Someone who'd kill a young girl to send a message isn't going to think twice about shutting you up if you become a threat to him. I'm going out to take a piss and see if there's a link-boy to light us back.'

Anthony drains his cup and rests his elbows on the table, weighing up Nat's warning. He will need to decide whether helping Sophia with this business is really worth the risk, when he has a family to think of. After all, it's highly unlikely that she would suddenly return his feelings as a result, and what could he do about it, even if she did? He rests his head in his hands and thinks about his wife. It's not that he doesn't love Beth; he does of course, but his love for her is a thing of duty, and has been from the beginning. Not the *very* beginning, perhaps; there were those few heady weeks of youthful lust – but since the day she informed him, trembling, that she was pregnant, he had felt obliged to do what was right, even as the fervour rapidly cooled. They were married a month later, and a fortnight after that she lost the child. He was twenty-two years old. Though he doesn't look much more than that now, with his clean-shaven face and mop of tousled hair, there have been four more children since, and he would walk through fire for any one of them, including little Rosie who died at two years, but he has never been able to shake off the obscure sense that a fraud was perpetrated on him somehow. Not by Beth herself – at times he suspects she feels the same way, though this is a conversation they will never have. Still, he accepted the bed he had made for himself and poured his passion into his work instead; he took a quiet pride in providing for his family, and for nearly fifteen years he was able to sustain a kind of equilibrium – perhaps, though he knows this does not reflect well on him, precisely because he spent so much time travelling. And then Thomas Phelippes asked him to look for a boy in Canterbury.

Well, he has done what Sophia asked of him, he thinks, as he and Nat ride back to London, and faced down a pistol in the process. He can report what he has learned about the Norths and the Lovells, and if she is determined to pursue the matter, that's her business. He has no doubt that she will, and not just because of Tobie; he caught the spark in her eyes when she talked of her cipher and the life she thought she had left behind.

He tries to shake the lingering feeling of unease; his nerves are wound tight, and more than once he thinks he sees a movement at the edge of his vision. But every time he whips around, the road is empty, and it's only the wind playing tricks with the flickering torchlight.

TEN

On arriving back at Broad Street, Sophia's plan is to change her wet clothes, fillet Agnes Lovell's letters for anything that might be unhelpful to Tobie, then write to every person of influence she knows who could get him out of Newgate before he can be hurt. But as she unpins her cloak, Hilary sweeps into the entrance hall, her expression stonier than usual. She takes in Sophia's appearance and pointedly refrains from comment.

'You have a visitor, madam.'

For a moment Sophia allows herself a flicker of hope; could it be Thomas Phelippes again, come to reassure her that Master Secretary has heard about Tobie's wrongful arrest and intends to intervene? But a second glance at her steward's face dashes that hope on the instant. Sophia knows exactly who is here.

'I'm sorry,' Hilary says, spreading her hands wide and dropping her voice. 'He insisted. We could have used force, but I thought that might create more problems than it solved. I made him take off his sword though.'

Sophia sighs. 'No, you did the right thing. Where is he?'

'In the library. He asked for wine. Lina brought him a bottle – that was about ten minutes ago. He's probably finished it by now.'

Sophia takes off her boots and heads along the corridor, her shoulders braced.

'Wouldn't you prefer to change first, madam?' Hilary asks, following close behind. 'You don't want to take a chill.'

'I'd rather get this over with,' she says. 'Before he starts on the next bottle.'

'I'll be outside, just in case,' Hilary murmurs.

'Thank you. I'm sure I can handle him.' She takes a deep breath and pushes open the door.

The library fire is stoked high and she sees a pair of legs in riding boots, stretched out with heels resting on the hearth, dripping melted snow on the rug. Their owner is hidden behind the wing of a high-backed chair, but he leans around at the sound of her approach and greets her with a lazy grin.

'Mother dearest.'

'Don't start.' She picks up the bottle next to the chair and tips it to gauge how much he has drunk.

'Are you going to tell me off? I like it when you're stern with me, Mother.'

He rises unsteadily to his feet; she immediately steps back to avoid an embrace. Jasper de Wolfe: her stepson, though the designation is absurd; he is a mere six years her junior. Humphrey's only child favours the portrait she has seen of the boy's mother, the first Mistress de Wolfe, who died when he was ten; Jasper is slight, dark-haired, handsome enough in his lean-jawed way, though she finds something rodenty about his face, the way his eyes dart around the room and he seems to twitch as if scenting the air for his best advantage. He has none of her late husband's amiably patrician bearing, nor any of Humphrey's other good qualities, it appears. She stands next to the fire, leaning on the mantel and letting the heat spread painfully through her frozen limbs as his eyes rove over her from head to foot.

'Have you been out rolling in the snow?' he enquires, slumping back into his seat.

96

'Something like that. What do you want, Jasper? I have business to attend to.' She notes that his hair needs a wash and the sleeves of his doublet are frayed, and this bothers her. He is usually vain over his appearance, and if he is letting his standards slide it can only be because he is in some kind of trouble.

'Of course. I appreciate that you are a very busy woman.' He is over-enunciating, in the way drunks do, though he is remarkably coherent given that he has put away most of the bottle, and no doubt more before he arrived. 'I'll come to the point, Sophia – I find myself in a delicate situation.'

'I can't give you money,' she says brusquely, moving far enough away that he can't lunge at her – he has an unpredictable temper. But this time he only laughs.

'I knew you'd say that. I came to appeal to your tender womanly feelings.'

'That's unfortunate, I have none.'

'Well, I'd be inclined to agree, except I know for a fact that you give plenty of my family's money away to the poor scholars at Christ's Hospital. And the Chamberlain's Men, of course – they regularly arouse your charitable instincts.'

'Jasper, must we have this conversation every time you incur a gambling debt? Humphrey's decisions are not my responsibility.'

'Not your—' He lurches forward in his chair; spots of colour rise in his cheeks. 'Yes, we will have this conversation every day until one of us dies if we have to, or until you give me what I am owed. My father was worth fifty thousand pounds at his death. He was one of the most successful exporters in the entire history of the Merchant Adventurers Company.' He slaps his hand on the arm of the chair. 'And you live here like a duchess, in the home I grew up in, throwing my inheritance to fucking jongleurs and orphans, while I have to live in rented rooms, forced to beg scraps from your table.'

She exhales slowly, determined to keep her temper, though

she is hardly in the right frame of mind for any conversation with Jasper, let alone this old tune.

'You're not forced to do anything. Humphrey left you a manor and its lands in Northamptonshire.'

'Yes, but I'd have to live in bloody Northamptonshire, wouldn't I – what kind of life would I have there?'

One where you don't run up hundreds of pounds of debt, she thinks, though it's probably not true: Jasper would find trouble wherever he fetched up. He had been educated at Cambridge and the Inns of Court, but after one brawl too many had been expelled before he could qualify in the law – not that he had ever shown the slightest interest in practising that or any other profession. He had presumed on a well-paid sinecure in his father's business before eventually inheriting it, but Humphrey, whose commercial acumen had indeed made him one of the most prosperous merchants in London, had chosen to sell his company to a rival cloth exporter shortly before he died rather than leave it to collapse in Jasper's hands. Periodically, throughout the boy's twenties, he had settled Jasper's debts with threats that it would be the last time, but no one had expected to find that his will left his son so little.

'The income from that manor is two hundred pounds a year,' Sophia says evenly.

'And *you* dare tell me to live on that? When you have taken everything, you shameless—' He stops just short of an insult he can't retract. His eyes are shining with a manic light; he might just as easily punch his fist through a window or collapse sobbing on the floor. Both have happened before.

'I took nothing that wasn't given to me. I know you don't believe it, but Humphrey didn't consult me on the terms of his will. He did what he judged best.'

'I was out of favour with my father when he made that will, as you well know. If he hadn't been gathered to God so unexpectedly, we would have reconciled, and I would have been given what I'm owed as his only heir.'

He tilts his chin defiantly; they both know that is highly improbable, but Jasper has talked himself into believing it. The suddenness of Humphrey's death had been a shock – he was sixty-one, but outwardly hale and active, when his heart gave out one September morning in 1596. But the meticulous care with which he had put his effects in order in the six months before it happened has always made Sophia suspect that it was not a surprise to him. It still pains her to think he might have known he was sick and kept it from her.

'Anyway,' Jasper says, tracing the puddle of melted snow with the toe of his boot and pointedly not looking at her, 'it isn't a gambling debt this time. It's a girl.'

Of course; it had to be one or the other. Sophia bites down her anger; sometimes she does feel that she has been unwillingly cast in the role of mother to this man who is almost her age. She wants to cuff him around the head for his stupidity.

'Who is she?'

'A grocer's daughter.' He curls his lip. 'She says it's mine, but how would I know? She lifted her skirts for me willingly enough – she may do the same for others. Her father is demanding I do right by her. I was hoping I might pay him off instead.' He raises his eyes with a smile that he presumably imagines to be appropriately contrite and appealing.

'You should marry her. Take her to your manor house in Northamptonshire and raise a family. You're nearly thirty years old, Jasper – long past time to give up the roistering.'

The smile dries instantly on his lips. 'Don't be absurd. I've no intention of marrying into a family of grocers. Frankly, I would count it a blessing if the girl fell under the wheels of a cart. My mother was a knight's granddaughter, you know.'

Sophia does know; Maud de Wolfe had been the youngest of six daughters from one of those old families that long ago lost all their lands backing the wrong side in the wars that brought the Tudors to the throne. Humphrey always said they were only too glad to give her away to an ambitious young merchant who didn't ask much by way of dowry, but the lineage has given Jasper ideas about his own status.

'So ask your high-born family for money.'

He snorts; they both know that will never happen. 'I shouldn't have to ask anyone for money.' He rises from his chair and takes a breath, composing himself. 'Look, Sophia, must we always argue?' His tone has shifted and she feels herself tense as he moves closer; she prefers it when he's cursing at her. 'I think I can aim higher than a grocer's daughter, don't you?' He reaches out and traces a line down her arm with a tobacco-stained forefinger.

Sophia leaps back as if she has been burned. 'Should have thought of that before you tupped her.'

His wheedling expression curdles to a sneer. 'And who's tupping *you* these days? Because, let me tell you – no one in London believes you're living here chastely like an abbess. Is it that writer, Munday? I hear he's a frequent visitor. Or maybe it's one of the players – is that why you lavish my money on them? Buying yourself some pretty young boy to ride? Did you do that while my father was alive too?'

She has crossed the space between them and fetched him a slap before her mind has had time to process the decision; the sound echoes around the high ceiling. Jasper stares at her, a hand pressed to his cheek; she looks back at him, astonished at herself. In all their altercations over the past two years, though she has wanted to hit him many times, she has always managed to exercise restraint. A line has been crossed, and they both feel it.

'Get out,' she says, through her teeth. 'Get out of my house.'

He steps towards her; her hand moves to her hip pocket. He leans in until his face is six inches from hers and she can smell the tobacco and wine on his breath.

'Do you think I don't know what you are?' he hisses. 'How you came to be here? This is *my* house by birthright, and you have robbed me.'

She doesn't flinch, though her heart is hammering. 'Don't make me tell you again.'

'I'm leaving.' He turns abruptly and picks up his hat; as an afterthought, he drains the glass of wine on the table and hurls it into the fireplace, where it shatters into fragments. Sophia starts, but grips her hands together and tries not to betray any emotion; this, too, has happened before. At the noise, the door bursts open and Hilary stands in the doorway; at her back is Mick, the servant who does the heavy work in the gardens and is also a useful presence in situations such as this, being built like a standing stone.

'Master de Wolfe is on his way out,' Sophia says, with greater composure than she feels.

Jasper looks as if he is about to say something, but glances at Mick and thinks better of it. He gives her a last glare and settles his hat on his head. As the servant accompanies him down the corridor, Jasper's protests carry through the open door: 'I don't need you to show me the way, for Christ's sake – this is my family home.'

'Are you all right?' Hilary asks. 'Did he propose again?'

'Not this time.' Sophia crouches to pick shards of glass from the hearth. 'I hit him, Hilary. I was distressed about something else and I lost my temper.'

'He probably deserved it,' Hilary says with a sniff. 'I've wanted to myself many times over the years. Leave that, madam, Lina can do it.'

Sophia stands and leans on the mantel, brushing flecks of glass from her fingers. A wave of tiredness rolls over her. She is never in a good frame of mind after an encounter with Jasper, but this one has disturbed her more than usual.

'You should eat something,' Hilary says. 'Baked eggs? I can have it brought to you in your room.'

'Thank you, yes.' Her steward's brisk practicality rouses Sophia from her ruminations; she follows Hilary down the corridor. At the foot of the stairs, she pauses. 'Did Humphrey ever lend money to Sir Thomas North, that you know of?'

If the question surprises Hilary, she doesn't show it.

'I'd have to check the ledgers. Quite possibly. Half the nobility in England came to him at one time or another, as you know.'

Hilary's late husband, Dennis, had been Humphrey de Wolfe's household steward for more than thirty years. As his eyesight began to fail, he had relied increasingly on his wife to read the account books to him and record the calculations. In her role as housekeeper, Hilary had already proven that she had a remarkable head for figures; when Dennis died, she continued to manage Humphrey's private accounts as well as the household expenditure, and after Humphrey was buried a year later, Sophia's first act in organising her affairs was to appoint Hilary as her official steward. A female steward was unheard of; one more reason for the merchants' wives to gossip about Sophia at the dinners to which she is not invited (nor has any wish to be), but there is no one she trusts more.

She thinks of Sir Thomas North's barbed comment: 'I hear he disinherited his son for you.' Not true, but she has no doubt that this is what Jasper has been telling anyone who'll listen for the past two years. He believes this house is stolen ground, and Sophia certainly has sins she has taken great care to keep buried. The implication sends a wash of cold fear through her; she puts a hand out for the polished banister to steady herself. It's not possible that he could know anything, she thinks, but then she recalls Jasper's bloodshot eyes inches from hers, and his twisted smile as he insisted he knew what she was. She had assumed he was insinuating, as he has many times before, that she is no better than a common whore who attached herself to his father for the money, but there is an outside chance that Jasper is more subtle than that. He is well practised in listening at doors; if he had the slightest inkling of his father's work for Walsingham and Burghley, might he have extended that suspicion to Sophia? She reminds herself to breathe; the idea is absurd. Jasper lacks the self-control to hoard information as potent as that; if he knew anything about her past, he would have thrown it at her long ago. Besides, he may be many things, none of them admirable, but she doesn't think he's a killer of young girls.

'Baked eggs,' Hilary says firmly, noting Sophia's slight stumble, her tight grip on the banister, and ushers her up the stairs.

In her chamber, Sophia strips off her wet clothes and finds a dry shift, hose and wool dress. She wraps a linen cloth around her hair to soak up the damp and pulls a chair to the fire to warm herself, staring into the flames. In her mind's eye she revisits over and over the moment when the guards dragged Tobie away, his arms pinned behind his back, his fearful look as he protested that he would never harm Agnes. She should have stepped in then, threatened them with lawyers. What might be happening to him even now, in Newgate, after the searchers told North they had found nothing in Tobie's room? A hot wave of rage surges through her; how dare Sir Thomas North bring his own private army to arrest a fifteen-year-old boy on the strength of a few love notes? There could be no legal justification for such a needless show of force; it was designed purely to intimidate.

Eventually she rouses herself and retrieves her bag with the letters from Tobie's room; she is about to open it when there is a knock at the door.

'One moment,' she calls, stuffing the bag under her pillow, but it is only the maid, Lina, with a dish of baked eggs and bread.

'I'll take your wet things down to the laundry, madam,' Lina says, scooping up Sophia's discarded clothes. 'These are soaked through – what happened to you?'

Sophia gives her a sharp glance; it's unlike Lina to be so direct in speaking to her mistress.

'I was caught in the snow,' she says crisply; she does not want to encourage the idea that she is obliged to explain herself to the servants. 'Thank you, Lina, that will be all.'

The maid blushes and hurries from the room. Sophia forces herself to eat a few mouthfuls, but her anxiety about Tobie tightens her throat and she can barely taste the food. Her stomach knots with dread at the prospect of a whole night stretching ahead, in which her son might be facing interrogation with torture while she waits here, helpless. There must be something she can do. She sets the dish aside, half-eaten, and crosses to her writing table. She could send a message to her lawyer; he will be at home with his family at this time of the evening, but with the right incentive he might be persuaded to accompany her to Newgate and make some threats. But if North has given orders for Tobie to be roughly treated, the gaolers will have no fear of legal repercussions. North must believe himself above the law, with his brother on the Privy Council. If that is the case, there is only one person who can intervene for her, and she can't trust that request to a messenger.

'Madam. Where are you going now?' Hilary appears with her most forbidding expression in the entrance hall as Sophia retrieves a dry cloak and riding boots from the closet. Even in a house this size, it is impossible to escape her steward's notice.

'There's someone I need to see.'

'You can't ride alone after dark, in this weather. It's snowing again, and the wind is up. At least take Mick with you.'

'Don't fuss, Hilary.'

'Madam! Think what the master would say,' she calls, as Sophia pulls on a rabbit fur hat and hurries to the yard before Hilary can rally the servants to hinder her.

ELEVEN

At the junction of Eastcheap and New Fish Street, Anthony draws his horse to a halt. He could turn left towards home, or right to London Bridge. The snow is coming down harder, spinning in a gusting wind, and the bells have struck seven; he pictures a good fire stoked in his parlour, Beth sitting by it with her sewing in her lap and her expression of enforced stoicism, the smell of roast meat drifting from the kitchen and the children running in with their clamour and good-natured bickering. A sensible man wouldn't even hesitate. He sighs, and spurs the horse to the right. He will just do this one thing, he assures himself, and then he can tell Sophia he has followed every lead. After that, he will absolutely, definitely leave her to get on with it.

Gaolers in all the London prisons make the best part of their income from bribes, but the Clink in Southwark is notoriously liberal when it comes to its Catholic inmates. The warden reasons that, since the majority are educated men, locked up for crimes no worse than harbouring priests or defaulting on their recusancy fines, they are unlikely to become violent, and since the Catholic prisoners have ready funds sent by their wealthy friends and supporters, he is happy to turn a blind eye to most things short of escaping. At night, the cell doors are unlocked and the prisoners mingle freely; there is always a priest ready to say Mass for them, with consecrated bread and wine smuggled in. It's said that there is even a rudimentary printing press in one of the cells, rolling out Catholic pamphlets. Naturally, the place is also crawling with informers, which is why this lax regime is tolerated by the authorities. Periodically, the Privy Council grow anxious about plots germinating too abundantly in this fertile soil and make a show of clamping down, so Anthony is not surprised to find the warden initially wary of being questioned.

Once he has handed over enough money to suggest he is probably not a government agent come to carry out a covert inspection, Anthony is shown by a guard into a small room furnished with a table and two chairs, one of which is occupied by a red-faced man in his sixties, who introduces himself as Warden Martin and motions for him to take the other. A fire is built high in the grate, and Anthony leans gratefully towards the heat as he explains his enquiry.

'Certainly I remember Vincent Lovell,' the warden says, lighting a clay pipe and resting his boots on the hearth bricks. 'A real gent, and his family paid well for his comforts.'

'His family?' Anthony is taken aback; if Sir John Lovell had been instrumental in having his brother arrested, why would he then pay to keep him comfortable in prison? Guilt, perhaps – unless it was in Sir John's interests to prolong Vincent's time in the Clink.

'How long was he here?'

'Just over a year.'

'That's a long time without trial.'

Martin nods. 'They had nothing on him really, except his name on the lease of a house that was used to shelter priests coming in from France. Vincent maintained he knew nothing about what went on there, and they couldn't prove otherwise. He should have been let out months earlier, and he had plenty of wealthy friends who would've put up bail, so it obviously suited someone to keep him here. These things happen.'

'Did his family ever visit him? His brother, for instance?'

'Not that I recall. But there was a little girl used to come sometimes, with an older woman. They brought food in for him, and letters.'

Anthony raises an eyebrow.

'Nothing untoward, sir – we read everything first, to make sure. The girl often brought him childish drawings, all very innocent.'

Innocent drawings could conceal secret messages written in lemon or orange juice, Anthony thinks, but he doesn't mention this.

'Was the woman Vincent's mother?'

'No, a servant. Probably the girl's nurse. The child was a bonny creature though, lovely manners. Her name was Agnes, as I recall. Vincent was always more cheerful after her visits.'

'Was he generally melancholic, then?'

'Prone to brooding, sir. The men can get that way. I tell them to look on the bright side, they could be in Newgate. As long as they can pay their way in here, things could be a lot worse. But Vincent Lovell was angry, and desperate to get out. Even Father Gerard couldn't placate him, and that man could charm the birds out of the trees.' Martin smiles fondly and puffs on his pipe.

'Father John Gerard?' Anthony blinks against the smoke. John Gerard was the de facto leader of the Jesuit mission in England, coordinating the placement of priests who came in secret from the French seminaries for the purpose of converting people back to the Catholic faith: a treasonable offence. Gerard had been moved to the Tower for interrogation after his time in the Clink, and the previous autumn had staged a daring escape that involved sliding down a rope strung from a high window to the riverbank; the pamphleteers had revelled in the story for weeks. He has still not been caught. The incident had caused serious embarrassment to the government, and having the charismatic Gerard at large to inspire the Catholic resistance was currently one of their biggest headaches.

'They knew one another?'

'They had cells next door for a time,' the gaoler says. 'They overlapped in here by about three months, give or take. Vincent Lovell was released shortly after his brother died, make of that what you will.'

'When was that?'

Martin leans back and takes a long draw on his pipe. 'Must have been autumn of '94. Round October time, as I recall, because Gerard came to us in the July.'

Anthony shifts in his seat, his mind racing in his efforts to fit all this together. The warden's information seems to confirm the suggestion that Sir John Lovell had been responsible for his brother's prolonged incarceration. But if Vincent Lovell had been at liberty for more than four years, why would he wait until now to kill his niece as revenge for Sir John's betrayal? And why kill the girl in the first place – to what end? If it was to punish his brother, it was four years too late. Unless Vincent believed there was someone else involved in his incarceration, someone who was still around to understand the cryptic message left with Agnes's body. And what connection could Vincent have to Sophia and the cipher? He shakes his head briskly, as if the movement will cause his scattered thoughts to settle into a convincing pattern.

'Was he a violent man?' he asks.

'Vincent?' Martin laughs. 'He was a scholar.'

'The two things are not incompatible,' Anthony says, thinking of the fights that regularly break out among writers. Ben Jonson has only just been released from prison after he killed Gabriel Spenser in a duel this September past. Spenser was irritating, granted, but he hadn't warranted that. A pointless waste of both men's gifts.

The gaoler rubs his chin. 'True enough. In fact, now that you mention it, there was one incident. We had to drag him off another prisoner, a young priest. Vincent had the fella up against a wall with his arm across his throat, bellowing "Your sins will be found out", or some such, in his face.'

'Really?' Anthony straightens. 'Do you know what he meant?'

Martin sniffs. 'Thought the priest was an informer.'

'And was he?'

'I wouldn't know, sir,' he says primly. 'There's a lot of accusations get thrown around in here, men cooped up with too much time to think and their nerves frayed. Feelings run high.'

Anthony suspects the gaoler knows exactly who the prison informers are, and that their continued protection is part of the elaborate agreement he has with the Privy Council that allows everyone to profit.

'What's your interest, anyway?' Martin asks, narrowing his eyes as if it has only now occurred to him that Anthony might be a Catholic, here to winkle out traitors to the faith.

'That girl you mentioned – Agnes,' Anthony says, reasoning he may as well tell part of the truth. 'She was murdered last night. I'm looking into it.'

The gaoler looks genuinely astonished. 'God's blood, that's a terrible thing. And, what – you reckon Vincent Lovell had a hand in it?'

'I'm just making enquiries,' Anthony says evenly. 'She was his niece.'

'No.' Martin shakes his head emphatically. 'No, I can't believe that. Vincent doted on the girl, you could see it. Besides, he doesn't have it in him to kill a child.'

'How can you be sure? You've just said he had a temper.'

The keeper sits back in his chair and gives Anthony a long look. 'In this job, sir, you get to see pretty much everything men are capable of. You learn to recognise those who'll flare up and throw a punch in the heat of the moment, and the ones who have a cold kind of cruelty in them, those who'll do whatever is necessary for their purpose, and have the patience to bide their time. The first type can't govern their feelings, the second lack feeling altogether. And I'd stake my life on Vincent Lovell being of the first sort.'

In Anthony's experience, religious fervour can make people capable of all manner of actions they might not otherwise countenance, but he doesn't argue.

'Do you know where Vincent is living now?' he asks.

The gaoler laughs. 'They don't tend to leave a forwarding address. The family had land in Suffolk, I heard – maybe he went back there.'

'Would any of your prisoners know?'

'Oh, certainly there'll be men out there who know,' he says, jerking his head towards the door. 'But they won't talk to you.'

'I can't go in there anyway. Someone might recognise me.' Anthony pauses. 'I used to be a pursuivant.'

'Is that right?' The gaoler assesses him with new respect. 'So we're on the same side. You should have said.'

Anthony fetches up a faint smile. 'What about this informer? Would he know?'

'Maybe. It'll cost you.' His eyes flick to Anthony's purse.

He sighs and produces a shilling; the gaoler hauls himself up from his chair with some effort and cracks the door, exchanging a few whispered words with the guard outside. After a moment, he returns with an encouraging smile.

'This man here will take you to him.' He nods to the guard, who approaches holding something behind his back.

Anthony feels a prickling in his scalp. Too late, he realises it might have been a mistake to offer information so freely; there is no knowing who is in whose pay here.

'Just a precaution, sir – like you said, we don't want any of the prisoners recognising you. This young priest is very useful to us, we don't want his cover blown.'

Before he can object, Anthony finds his wrists grappled

behind his back and a rough sack pulled over his head. He breathes in dust from the material and coughs; it all happens so fast, the last thing he sees is the gaoler's self-satisfied smile.

'Take him to solitary,' Martin says, and he is bundled out of the door with his arms still pinned behind him.

'It's just for show, sir,' the guard whispers as Anthony is pushed along a passageway and made to stumble down a flight of steps. All he can smell is damp and mould from the sacking, but the air is colder here, and as they turn a corner he catches the sound of voices; he guesses they are passing a row of cells. His heart gallops as he curses his own stupidity in coming here alone without telling anyone. Eventually, he is pulled to a halt; there is a jangle of keys and Anthony is roughly shoved between the shoulder blades, his wrists released from the guard's grip. He rips the sack off and looks around to see a small circular cell with one narrow window above his head. Trails of green moss have formed where damp runs down the stone walls, the rivulets now frozen to ice. He breathes in the foul air, the stench of soiled straw on the floor, and gags, pressing a sleeve across his mouth.

The guard lights a candle from his own lantern and sets it in a wall sconce. 'Wait here,' he says, as if Anthony has a choice, and slams the door shut behind him. The key is turned and the bolt shot home with a terrible finality.

Anthony stands in the middle of the cell, arms wrapped tightly around his chest, not wanting to lean against the wall or sit on the floor. *You bloody fool*, he tells himself as his breath clouds around his face in the freezing air, thinking of his parlour with the fire, the supper cooking. He has walked into a trap and paid for the privilege, and all because he can't cure himself of Sophia de Wolfe.

TWELVE

A bitter wind rises from the river, driving the snow into flurries that sting Sophia's face and blur her vision as she rides west through empty streets, the horse's hooves skidding at every corner. There is a kind of insanity in what she is doing, she acknowledges: not only setting out alone in this weather, but to her intended destination. But what choice has she? There's no chance that she could sleep tonight in her warm, comfortable bed, thinking of Tobie in a Newgate cell; she must do *something*. Hilary's reprimand pricks at her, and as she rides, she wonders what Humphrey would say if he could see her now. He had always understood her desire for autonomy, her need to act for herself; it was one of the many things she had come to appreciate about him. Though she had never been clear on how much Francis Walsingham had told Humphrey about her past – they never discussed it – her husband knew that too much of her life had been shaped by other people's choices, and that she was not willing to tolerate that again. Of course, Humphrey's wealth had afforded him the freedom to disregard convention, up to a point, and to laugh off society's disapproval; in any case, people will forgive a great deal from a rich man. The same indulgence is not extended to women, however large their fortune. But she suspects that, in this instance, even Humphrey would have told her gently that you can't just ride up to the Palace of Whitehall and bang on the gate demanding to speak to the queen's Secretary of State.

She doesn't know where Master Secretary Cecil lives, but she has heard that since his wife died in childbirth two years ago, he spends all his time working, so it's a good bet that she'll find him at Whitehall. Along the Strand, the going is easier; snow has been cleared from the roadway, no doubt by prisoners with shovels, so the residents of the grand houses that back on to the river are not inconvenienced.

At the Charing Cross, she almost loses her nerve and turns back. But she thinks again of Tobie, pictures him being dragged out in chains to clear snow from the streets, and her resolve hardens. She approaches the Great Gate and dismounts.

Sophia has never set foot in the palace – though Humphrey's connections included courtiers and privy councillors, he was not invited to meet them here – and even the gatehouse is daunting. When she explains her business to the guards, they laugh at first, then confer rapidly among themselves when they realise she is serious. Sophia removes a glove and takes a gold ring from her little finger. It was a gift from her late husband and is engraved with the de Wolfe crest. The old families of England sneer at men like Humphrey who buy themselves a coat of arms, but, as Hilary reminded her, they were not above asking for a loan when it suited them. She wonders again if Sir Thomas North was among those who had borrowed from her husband. Tonight, when she returns, she will ask Hilary to help her look through Humphrey's accounts.

In her most imperious voice, she tells the soldiers on the gate that her business is urgent and cannot wait. Eventually one of them agrees to make enquiries and disappears across the courtyard. Taking pity on her, the other invites her to shelter under the gatehouse arch, close to his brazier, but to her relief he doesn't try to engage her in conversation. After a good twenty minutes have passed, she curses her own stupidity; most likely she won't see the man or her ring again, and there would be very little she could do about it. But at the point where she can no longer feel her hands and feet, the guard returns with the ring and the information that Master Secretary is not at the palace this evening. She gives him a coin for his trouble and his honesty, turning away to hide her frustration.

'I heard someone say he was dining with his brother tonight,' the guard murmurs. 'But you didn't get that from me.'

Sophia thanks him. She knows where Sir Robert's older brother, the new Lord Burghley, lives; she has just ridden past it. She mounts and returns in the direction of the Strand.

Burghley House is a large, red-brick residence on the north side of the street, three storeys high with four corner turrets, set behind a high wall. At the gate she repeats the business with the ring, though the armed men stationed here seem less surprised by someone demanding to see Sir Robert. After a shorter wait she is led through a side gate into a yard, where her horse is taken by a groom and she is shown across the courtyard into the servants' quarters at the back of the house. Heat and noise from the kitchens travel along the passageway as her silent attendant leads her to a room that is evidently used to store barrels of beer. The man tells her to wait and closes the door on her.

Sophia tucks her hands into her armpits and stamps her feet to keep warm, her anger rising with every minute that passes. She had not expected a congenial welcome, but she suspects that leaving her in here is a deliberate punishment on Cecil's part, and she is not in the mood for his strategic reminders of who holds the power. When the door eventually slams open, she is taut with impatience, poised on the balls of her feet with her fists clenched like an inn-yard fighter.

Even so, she falters at the sight of his face. Cecil is more intimidating than you would expect from a small man, and she can see immediately that he is incandescent. He glares at her for a long moment, his lips pressed into a white line, before he speaks.

'Have you lost your wits, woman?'

Sophia bristles; she is always riled by men who use *woman* in that tone, as if the word itself is an insult; it makes her think of her first husband, which is something she tries never to do.

'What were you thinking, coming here?' Cecil says, before she can speak. His voice remains cold and steady, but she can hear the fury vibrating in it. 'You may as well ride through town with a sign saying "Informer" pinned to your back. To say nothing of the disrespect to my family.'

'What about *my* family?' Sophia says, recovering herself. 'Tobie's been arrested.'

'Ah. You heard.'

'I was there! At the playhouse, I watched it happen. I saw him dragged away by Thomas North's armed men for the girl's murder. Of course, you knew. You couldn't have warned me?' She has raised her voice to him, compounding her offences against etiquette, but she is too far in to row back now.

Cecil weighs his answer. 'It was a fait accompli by the time I found out. The coroner is keeping me informed, but the discovery of those letters was unfortunate.'

'*Unfortunate?*'

'Please try to stay calm, Mistress de Wolfe,' he says, in a tone that seems designed to provoke her further. 'North is an angry man who wants to see someone punished, and finding that the boy had had some kind of liaison with young Agnes was a gift to him. I couldn't have stepped in without raising questions.'

'But you know Tobie can't have killed her.'

'Do I?'

She stares at him, at his enquiring brow, and is seized by an urge to pin him against the wall by his embroidered lapels. She is a good four inches taller than him; she could do it too. She breathes hard through her nose and masters herself.

'Because of the note. Tobie couldn't have written that – where would he get hold of my cipher?'

Cecil merely looks at her.

'Are you serious? I haven't thought about that cipher myself in ten years. You really think I would share it with him, when he doesn't even know who I am?' Her voice catches on these last words and she stops abruptly. 'Besides, he was working that whole night. All the players were – they were unloading the timbers at Peter Street's warehouse till the early hours.'

'Alas for Master Strange, that's not the case. He dropped the end of a beam on his foot early in the evening, and as he appeared to be in pain, Burbage sent him home. This was about nine o'clock. The two boys he shares rooms with stayed on at the warehouse, so there is no one to vouch for his movements that night.'

'But that's—'

Cecil holds up a hand. 'To answer your question, Mistress de Wolfe – no, of course I don't think the boy is responsible. But in the absence of evidence against any other party, those letters do not look good for him. He writes that he would do anything to make sure she doesn't marry Edmund North.'

Sophia is about to protest, when a thought occurs.

'Do the Norths know about the cipher note?'

'To the best of my knowledge, they do not. The coroner had it brought straight to me and I have impressed upon everyone who saw it the importance of keeping it quiet.'

'But if you tell North about the note, he would know it can't be Tobie.'

'The note mentions hidden sins. If that refers to something Thomas North or his son did in Ireland, I want to know. And if they suspect we are looking, they will take pains to cover it further. Whereas, for now, North appears to think the murder is the act of a hot-headed jealous youth in love. It will make my job easier if he goes on believing that while we investigate the real motive.'

'I see. You're willing to let Tobie suffer in prison so that Thomas North thinks he's safe?'

'Mistress de Wolfe.' He is losing patience; an edge has crept into his tone. 'It seems beyond doubt that the girl's death was intended to send some kind of message, and my guess is that it concerns the Irish campaign. I need to find out why now, why Agnes Lovell, what the ramifications may be. With Tobie in custody, the murderer will also believe himself safe. He may make a mistake. Let us not forget, this killer has a connection to you as well. Have you examined your husband's correspondence yet?'

'I haven't had a chance,' Sophia says.

'Then perhaps the boy's arrest will provide the incentive you need to give the matter your fullest attention.'

She wants to hit him; she feels the urge rush like firewater through her whole body, and wills herself not to move; she has already slapped one man today in a lapse of self-control, and that will have repercussions, but nothing like the consequences she would face for striking the queen's minister. She, who has always prided herself on her ability to lock her feelings away so that they are never written on her face.

'How old is your son, Master Secretary?' Her voice is so tight it hurts her throat. She sees a flicker behind his imperturbable demeanour.

'William will be eight this coming March,' he says evenly.

'Can you imagine him in Newgate? Go on, picture it.'

Cecil allows a long silence to unfold while they glare at one another, hackles raised, like dogs sizing each other up for a fight.

'Very well,' he says, relenting. 'I'll see what I can do to have the boy moved somewhere less . . . stringent.'

'Tonight? Before he can be mistreated?'

He nods. 'I'll dispatch the order now. I can't have him released,' he adds, holding up a warning finger before she can argue. 'Not with the evidence against him. But I can make sure it doesn't go too badly for him while he's in custody. That will be difficult enough, considering.'

'Considering what?'

'The coroner had a physician examine the girl's body. She was no longer *virgo intacta*. I have not shared that information with the Norths either.'

Sophia does not know how to respond to this. *Thirteen*, she thinks.

'Was Tobie bedding her, to your knowledge?'

'I don't have that kind of conversation with him. I didn't even know he'd met her until this afternoon.' She hopes to God he'd have more sense than to bed a thirteen-year-old girl who was pre-contracted to someone else, but she knows sense doesn't come into it when you're fifteen and thinking with your loins.

'Find out. You're familiar with his friends – a boy that age, he'd have bragged if he'd deflowered a knight's daughter.'

Tobie isn't like that, she wants to say, but the truth is, she doesn't know him well enough to make such a claim. If he slept with the girl, it's a great deal more serious than a few love-struck letters.

'But if it wasn't Tobie who— then that means there's someone else with a motive for keeping her quiet. She could have been raped.' She pauses, remembering Jasper de Wolfe and his pressing problem with the grocer's daughter: *it would be a blessing to me if the girl fell under the wheels of a cart.* Had it suited someone for Agnes Lovell to end up in a trench for the same reason? 'Was she pregnant?'

'No evidence to suggest it, though we haven't opened the body. But you're right, worth finding out if anyone else had been sniffing around the girl.'

'What about Edmund North? His father claims she was pre-contracted to him.'

Cecil shakes his head. 'Any pre-contract was unofficial and therefore worthless, because the queen had not yet given her permission for the marriage. But the Norths were counting on it, clearly – meaning Edmund needed only to wait five months until she turned fourteen, and he'd have become a wealthy man by marrying her. And it would hardly have been in his interests to deflower her ahead of time – he'd want any child to be indisputably legitimate. No, the Norths would have been fully invested in preserving both her maidenhead and her life. The family's future prospects depended on her.'

'Did the physician say how she died?' Sophia asks.

Cecil gives her a curious look. Perhaps he thinks women shouldn't concern themselves with such details.

'Blow to the back of the head,' he says matter-of-factly. 'He thinks it caused bleeding on the brain. There were bruises on her upper arms as if she'd been grasped tight, but no other sign of injury. He said the freezing temperatures made it difficult to know exactly when she died, but he thinks the body was moved after death. Oh, and he did say that the discoloration of the flesh suggests she could have been killed a day or even two before she was found.'

Sophia digests this. 'So you are not just looking at last night, then?'

If that is the case, Tobie's lack of an alibi for that night may matter less. A blow to the head did nothing to narrow it down; unlike poison, which required specialist knowledge, or strangulation, which assumed a degree of physical strength, anyone – man, woman or child – could hit a girl with a heavy object. They might not even have intended to kill her. 'But if it was a day or two earlier, how did no one notice her missing?'

'The coroner is interviewing the servants. North was visiting his married daughter near Hampton – he left early on the twenty-seventh and only returned this morning – a messenger intercepted him on the road with news of the murder. And now, I must return to my dinner.' Cecil takes a step towards her and points a finger in her face. 'Let me make this very clear, Mistress de Wolfe. You are no use to me or your son if people discover the truth about you. When I have something to impart, I will send for you. But if you *ever* dare to seek me out uninvited, or come anywhere near my home or my family, I will make sure Tobie Strange is thrown into the deepest oubliette in the kingdom. Do not presume that, because you are a woman, you can play by different rules. Your actions tonight could have compromised your work and mine, and put you in considerable danger. Do we understand one another?'

She looks down at him. It ought to be comical, this little man jabbing his finger in her face, but she can see his absolute ruthlessness in his eyes. She has no doubt that he would do everything he has threatened to her and Tobie, just to show that he is not to be trifled with.

'Yes,' is all she can manage.

'Good.' His tone grows more conciliatory. 'Now go home, it's almost nine. I'll have a servant escort you. Remember, you can always get a message to me through Phelippes.'

What if I can't trust Phelippes? she thinks as the door closes behind him, remembering Ben's story about the cryptographer's debts. She doesn't know what to do with the idea that Thomas might be slippery.

Outside, the weather has worsened. She considers telling the servant that she has no need of his company, but decides it would probably be wise not to defy Cecil any further this evening, and in truth she is glad of the man's solid, silent presence and his lantern as they ride up the Strand through the blizzard, though the street is empty. Whirling flurries of flakes in the circle of lamplight make it hard to see more than a few yards ahead, but as they approach the junction with Little Drury Lane, she catches a slight shift in the shadows to her right. She turns in her saddle, and at the same moment a figure darts out, straight into her path, emitting a hair-raising scream; her mount, normally placid, rears up, pawing the air, and Sophia is thrown backwards over its rump. She lands in a thick drift of snow banked up at the street's edge, winded but unharmed. 'Get after the horse!' she yells at Cecil's servant, who hesitates a moment before giving chase to Sophia's black mare, who has bolted in fright.

Shaken, Sophia stands and brushes herself down, whipping her head from left to right. There is no sign of the figure who ambushed them. The servant's lantern narrows to a pinprick of light in the distance; she is alone in the dark, the only sound the wind and her own shallow breathing. She reaches to her hip, alert to any new disturbance in the air, but her fingers are made clumsy by her fur gloves; as she fumbles under her cloak for the knife, the weight of a body collides with her from behind, knocking her forwards on to the ground. She feels the pressure of a knee in her back, her face pushed into the freezing drift so that snow fills her mouth and nose and she can't breathe. She struggles but the person holding her is too heavy to push off, and her right arm is trapped beneath her chest. She feels her cloak lifted and a quick, sharp pain at the top of her left arm. Just as her lungs begin to burn, the load on her back suddenly eases; she is free to lift her head and snatch a mouthful of cold air. As quietly as he arrived, her assailant has vanished into the night.

Sophia sits up, gasping for breath and brushing snow from her face. Tentatively, she reaches under her cloak to her left arm, afraid that she has been stabbed, but instead she touches paper. Pulling off her right glove, she extracts a note attached to her sleeve with a hat pin. She holds it under her cloak to keep it dry until she sees the lantern appear again from Little Drury Lane; Cecil's servant is leading her mare by the reins. When he stops, she asks him to hold his light up, and with a shaking hand she unfolds the paper. There is a verse written on it, in her cipher.

THIRTEEN

Anthony waits, counting the minutes and trying not to panic. There is no sound except the steady drip of water. He recalls the warden saying 'solitary' and guesses that this cell is some distance from the other prisoners, meaning that no one will hear him if he shouts. How long, he wonders, would it take Beth to notice that he hasn't come home? She has never been shrewish about his absences; she has always professed to understand that his work often takes him away, without ever pressing him too hard with questions, and she knows him well enough to trust that he doesn't go out whoring or seeking other women. It's not as if he leaves her on her own, either (he says, in his defence, to the imaginary prosecutor in his head); Beth's widowed cousin Mercy Slade had come to live with them ten years ago to help with the children, and never left. Anthony knows that the implacable Mercy (was ever a woman so mis-named?) disapproves of him, she makes this clear with every glance, but she won't say anything to his face, mindful of the fact that he puts a roof over her head and food on the table. He has no doubt that she expresses her feelings forcefully to Beth every time he's out of the house, though. If he fails to come home, Mercy will merely see this as further proof of his shortcomings as a husband; neither of them would immediately think to worry about him. Would Sophia notice his absence? He has no answer for that. It occurs to him that the only person who would have the slightest idea of where to find him is Nat, and it might be days before Nat seeks him out.

Be reasonable, he tells himself, as the candle in the sconce flutters worryingly in a draught; what cause would the warden have to detain him here? The obvious answer is that he didn't like the tenor of Anthony's enquiries into Vincent Lovell, but that would make no sense – unless the warden were secretly Catholic and in their pay? That, too, is absurd. He understands that, in a place like the Clink, there is a delicate system of nods and winks, information passing silently from hand to hand, and that an outsider barging in asking awkward questions could threaten to upset that. Perhaps the warden simply wants to check that Anthony is who he says he is before offering him anything that might compromise that system; even so, it could take hours before they can find someone to vouch for him.

The candle burns lower; somewhere in the distance, he hears a church bell strike the half hour, though he's no longer sure which half hour. Eight? He measures his breaths, fighting down the fear of being left here in the dark, and is on the point of giving in and hammering at the door with his fists when it opens to allow a thin slant of light. A small man slips through the gap, a candle in one hand.

The door shuts again behind him, and he looks at Anthony with wary eyes and a taut stillness, the way a fox will when you surprise it on the path at night. After a moment, he takes a step forward. He's no more than twenty-five, with a harried expression that Anthony recognises immediately as guilt. It's one he wears frequently himself.

'Do I know you?' the young man asks, holding up the light. It sounds like an accusation. His face wavers in and out of shadow.

'I don't think so.'

'They said you were a pursuivant.'

'Years ago.' Anthony understands what he is asking – was he responsible for putting this young man, or his friends, in here? In truth, he can't answer that; the midnight raids, the broken-down doors, the sobbing women and terrified men dragged from hiding places babbling desperate prayers – all the faces began to blur after a while. But he thinks this man is too young to have crossed his path. 'You're a priest?'

The young man bites his lip. He doesn't offer his name and nor does Anthony. 'They said you had questions about Vincent Lovell.'

'You know him?'

The man nods. 'I was taken at the house in Colchester that was leased in his name. That's how he ended up in here.'

'I heard the four priests were executed.'

'Three of them were.' He looks at the floor. 'My friends. They were better men than me. I thought I'd be ready to suffer for Christ, but I was wrong. They didn't even have to use the instruments before I crumbled.'

Anthony can hear the self-loathing in his voice. 'So you were spared in return for staying in here and informing?'

He nods. 'Officially, they said there wasn't enough evidence against me. But my friends knew the real reason I wasn't taken to Tyburn. Vincent Lovell knew it too, when they brought him here.'

'You're the man he attacked?'

The priest nods again. 'Let's be brief. What do you want to know?'

'Tell me about Vincent's relationship with his brother.'

He gives a dry laugh. 'No love lost there. Vincent was the younger son. The family had money and land, and Sir John wanted to hold on to it, so he renounced his faith, signed the Bond of Association declaring his loyalty to the queen, the whole lot. He argued that he had a responsibility to his

124

motherless daughter, and what would happen to her if he was thrown in prison and his lands forfeit? Vincent still couldn't forgive him. He accused John of being weak.'

'When he was arrested, Vincent Lovell thought it was his brother who betrayed him to the authorities. Is that true?'

'I don't know. Vincent was a key part of the mission, he was one of the people who organised safe houses for priests coming in from France. I heard Sir John's manor was searched a few times on account of his brother's activities. Vincent said John had offered him money to stop his involvement with the mission and make a show of conformity – he was afraid Vincent would bring the whole family into disrepute.' The priest shrugs uncomfortably. 'So when the four of us were arrested and Vincent was picked up too, everyone assumed it was Sir John who had decided to put a stop to it. Supposedly he was paying one of Vincent's servants for information.'

Anthony digests this. 'The warden said Vincent was in here for over a year.'

'That's right. He had any number of friends who would have paid his bail, but they weren't given the chance. Vincent thought his brother was behind that too.'

'Did he strike you as the kind of man who would seek revenge?'

At this, the young priest lifts his head, frowning. 'Who's there to be revenged on? Sir John died four years ago, before Vincent got out.'

'You mentioned he had a daughter.'

'Yes. Vincent thought his brother had betrayed him there too.'

'How do you mean?'

He stamps his feet against the cold. 'Well, Vincent had only been in here a couple of months when he had word that Sir John was sick. A canker, I believe – anyway, it was clear his brother was dying. Vincent was cock-a-hoop. I know – not very Christian,' he says, off Anthony's look. 'But like I said, they'd come to hate each other – Vincent blamed John outright for the priests' deaths. I heard Vincent telling Father Gerard that once John was dead, he – Vincent – would surely be released and made guardian of the little girl, and that would give him control over eight miles of Suffolk coastline to land boats. It would be invaluable to the mission. They took it as proof of God's favour to our cause – they were delighted with themselves. Of course, things didn't turn out that way.'

'Vincent didn't get the girl's wardship.'

'No, even though he was her next of kin, legally it should have gone to him. Instead it was bought by Sir Thomas North. Vincent thought his brother had made sure to keep him locked up until that was all signed and sealed. So if you want to talk of revenge, I suppose he may well carry a grudge against North.'

'Vincent has a temper, I heard. Do you think it's possible that he would seek extrajudicial revenge on North?'

The priest thinks for a moment. 'If he found out North had mistreated the girl, I'd say he'd be capable of violence.'

'But would he hurt the girl to hit back at North?'

'His niece?' The priest stares at him, shocked. 'Absolutely not. He adored her. That's another reason he was furious about the wardship – he said he didn't trust North, he was only in it for profit, and she deserved a guardian who cared about her welfare.'

'So it wasn't just about the land?'

'Well, that was a big part of it, obviously. But he clearly loved the little girl too. He might have gone after North through the courts, or even thrown a punch if he'd had the opportunity, but I can't believe he'd ever willingly harm the child.' His eyes widen. 'Why, has something happened?'

'I'm not at liberty to say.' The news will be all round the prison by tomorrow, Anthony has no doubt, but there is no need to help it on its way.

The young priest pauses, as if a new thought has struck

him. 'How old is the girl now?'

'Thirteen,' Anthony says.

He nods. 'So that wardship would be coming to an end soon. Vincent's niece will have control over her own lands at fourteen – I imagine he'll hope to sway her in how best to use them. I can't imagine North would give up an asset like that without a fight, and the government wouldn't want a known Catholic sympathiser getting his hands on an estate with that kind of coastal access. Plenty of potential for friction there, all right.'

Anthony watches him, trying to process the ramifications of all this. 'Vincent's still actively involved in the mission, then?'

The priest gives him a mirthless smile. 'Oh yes. But he's a lot more careful these days.'

'Do you know where I would find him?'

'I could make an educated guess.' The man gives him a level stare. 'What can you offer in return?'

Anthony tamps down a sigh as his hand moves to his purse.

'I don't need money,' the priest says, pre-empting him. 'I have all the material comforts I could wish for in here.' He gestures around the cell with a short, bitter laugh. 'If you were a pursuivant, you'll know people. Speak to them for me.'

'To say what?'

'I've paid my debt.' The man lowers his voice and clutches at Anthony's sleeve with an urgency that makes him step back in alarm. 'I can't go on like this indefinitely – too many of the prisoners here suspect me of double-dealing. The day will come when they decide to silence me, and the authorities won't care if I'm no longer of use to them.'

'Surely your fellow priests wouldn't—'

'Don't be an innocent. You've encountered zealous Catholics – they think murder is no sin if it's in the service of their holy war. Even regicide.' He shakes his head. 'I'm on borrowed time anyway – it was made clear to me that I should have died with my friends at Tyburn, and I'm only alive on sufferance. Speak to the authorities for me – please. Say I have done what was asked. Only let me go quietly abroad, I won't trouble England again.'

His fear rises off him, raw and animal; Anthony can almost smell it.

'I'll do what I can,' he says. 'What's your name?'

'Prior. Stephen Prior.' A pause. 'Father Stephen Prior.'

'All right, Prior. Where's Vincent Lovell?'

'He lives in the village of Upper Homerton, by Hackney Marshes, in the house of a widow named Crowley.'

Anthony thanks him, and Prior bangs on the cell door three times. They exchange a last look before the guard comes, and Anthony submits to the bag over his head again. He means to keep his word to the young priest, though privately he doesn't think much of the man's chances of being allowed to slip away over the sea and live out the rest of his days in a private agony of conscience.

At the prison gate, the guard leans in close as he removes the sack.

'Warden says he'd prefer not to see you here again,' he says, and Anthony hears the threat in it. He has never felt such relief to find himself outside in the snow, breathing in the filthy air of Southwark.

128

FOURTEEN

Sophia arrives home, shaken and frozen to the core. She did not show Cecil's servant the note thrust at her by her mysterious assailant, and asked him not to mention the incident to his master, though she doubts he will comply with this. Hilary looks Sophia up and down with pursed lips as she helps her off with her cloak, but knows by the set of her mistress's jaw better than to ask questions. She sends the maid Lina to stoke the fire in Sophia's room and warm another set of dry clothes.

Once Sophia has changed and given instructions that she is not to be disturbed, she wraps herself in a thick wool shawl, sips a cup of hot wine and pulls a chair close to the hearth, where she takes out the paper delivered by her attacker. It's her own cipher again, no question, and the realisation sends a spike of fear through her: this can only mean that for those brief moments she was held down in the snow, she was entirely at the mercy of the person who killed Agnes, or someone in his pay. And yet, beyond a little bruising from the fall, she had not been hurt, or robbed; the sole purpose of the encounter appears to have been to intimidate her. Well, she will not give them the satisfaction, she thinks, though her hands are still shaking – whether from shock or cold, she can't tell.

A wave of exhaustion rolls through her; she allows her eyes

to close briefly and feels sleep stealing over her, but she wrenches herself awake and forces her attention back to the note. She wishes she had asked Phelippes for a copy of the original verse found with Agnes; she could have worked backwards from there. There was a time when she had the key to this cipher by heart, and could translate a message in a matter of minutes in her head, though that was ten years ago. She had been taught memory techniques, but those too have grown rusty with lack of use. Her daily fencing bouts may keep her body agile, but she has allowed her mind to slacken; this is what comes of an easy life, of no longer living on her wits. If only she wasn't so tired, and anxious about Tobie. But she summons her remaining strength, crosses to her writing table and sets to work, beginning with those characters she can remember.

As she works – slowly at first – she finds the letters falling into place, the patterns returning to her like a familiar tool fitted to her hand. It takes her the best part of an hour, but eventually another doggerel couplet takes shape on the page, and a cold dread lodges like a stone in her gut.

> *Those who hide their past behind a lie*
> *Should hold their tongue, lest they be next to die*

She stands, agitated, and paces the room; it's a clear threat, from someone who appears to know or suspect something of her history. 'Next to die': a reference to Agnes, surely, and the warning to hold her tongue suggests that the writer knows she has been asking questions about the girl's murder. But how? Besides Anthony, only Robert Cecil and Thomas Phelippes know that she was charged with looking into it. Her pulse is beating in her throat, and she feels starkly how alone she is with this. She would like to talk to someone, but who is there to confide in? Cecil will have to be told, of course, but she does not expect much sympathy from that quarter. He may even consider it best to stand her down from the investigation, and she can't let that happen; now that Tobie's life depends on it, she needs to be sure that the real killer is caught. She could go to Anthony, but he would pointedly refrain from mentioning that he warned her about the dangers, and it would only reinforce his belief that she needs looking after. Even Leila would tell her to step away. The only two people whose advice she would welcome in this moment are Humphrey and Sir Francis Walsingham, and both are dead. She will have to find a way through this on her own.

She throws the paper with the translated verse into the fire and locks the original in a compartment of her writing table to show Cecil. Her eyes are heavy, her right shoulder aches from the fall; she lies down on her bed and is about to blow out the candle when she feels a lump under the pillow. Reaching in, she draws out the bag she had hidden earlier, containing Agnes's letters to Tobie. She sits up. It would be sensible to leave them until the morning, give herself a chance to rest, but she knows she won't be able to sleep for wondering if they contain anything that might exonerate Tobie or point to the murderer. She pulls her shawl tighter and brings the light close to give them her full attention.

Unfolding the first, she feels an uncomfortable sense of trespass; this is her son's private world, his first love, not meant to be raked over and sifted by adults. It makes her wonder again how their relationship would have turned out if she had been allowed to be his mother: would he, at this age, keep secrets from her, defy her? It's what she had done with her own parents. She likes to imagine that, had Tobie grown up in her care, they would share an unbreakable bond of complete frankness, that he would have felt able to confide in her about anything, but from what she knows, this is rarely the case in youth.

The letters are not dated, which makes it difficult at first to order them, but, skimming the contents, she begins to assemble the pages into a logical progression. The earliest are written with a breathless, girlish excitement that makes Sophia smile; Agnes was too young and too innocent to dissemble or feign indifference to pique a man's interest.

I could hardly believe that you wrote back to me! I have watched and waited at the window all this morning and all of yesterday in hope of a reply, the way my lady North's dog Pipkin waits for her to come home. I have repeated our conversation at the play-house over and over to myself since Thursday and had begun to fear that you must have thought me an ignorant, silly girl who knows nothing of the world but what she has read in books . . .

So it was Agnes who had made the first move, Sophia thinks, turning to the next sheet. She wonders how the young lovers had effected the exchange of letters; she suspects Jo's hand in it, but there must have been another intermediary. A couple of pages later, her guess is confirmed.

T, you cannot know how it lifted my spirits at the end of a dark week to see you this morning at St Gabriel's – I have never been so eager to go to church! And then to have the luxury of walking and talking together in the churchyard after the service, though poor Grace was glancing to left and right and fretting all the while that we would be seen by some acquaintance of the Norths and she would be blamed. It grieves me that we can only contrive to meet when Sir Thomas is away from home.

Grace, Sophia supposes, is a chaperone or governess who has colluded in this tryst under cover of a church service, in which case she is right to fret; Sir Thomas North would surely see it as a gross abuse of his trust, especially if Agnes was promised in marriage to his son. The only St Gabriel's Sophia can think of is the one on Fenchurch Street. She wonders what could have caused a thirteen-year-old girl in the flush of first love to have a dark week. Something at home, surely; Sophia concludes that she needs to push Leila harder for what she knows of the North household. If the wife, Judith, couldn't have children of her own, she might well have resented her husband's young ward. Or perhaps his adult daughter from his first marriage was jealous, if her father doted on Agnes – though, on balance, Sophia doesn't think this so likely. While it's true that some men show grief as anger – her own father was one – from what she had seen of North that afternoon, he did not seem a man bereft by the murder of a child he had regarded with paternal affection. No: unless there was overt cruelty or abuse to Agnes in the North house, the most obvious source of the girl's unhappiness was surely the knowledge that she was expected to marry a man more than twice her age in five months' time, and that she had no say in it. The tone of the later notes would seem to confirm this.

Touching the matter we spoke of last week – I wish I could be sure of her friendship, but there is some reserve in her that causes me to doubt her motive. When she shows me affection, I have the sense that she is doing as she has been instructed. Often she tries to pry into my secret thoughts, in the guise of concern for my future; she presses me to know if there is some other man who has caught my eye, that I would prefer for a husband, and she sings his virtues to me constantly, though I do not think she believes her own words. I pity her sometimes; I sense she dislikes the task imposed on her. Of course, I have said nothing about you; I guard the knowledge of you like a locket held tight in my fist, and glow with the power of

*having a secret that is all my own. But time is short,
and if I dwell on the future, I grow afraid.*

Poor child; her power didn't last long. Sophia feels her jaw
tighten; the girl's fear is too horribly familiar to her, and an
impotent anger rises in her chest at a world that treats young
women as no more than counters to be moved strategically
around a board for the advantage of their fathers or guardians.
She knows too well how it feels to be pressed into marriage
with an older man for use as a brood mare when your heart
belongs elsewhere, with no way to fight the inevitable – though
Sophia had been nineteen when it happened to her, not thirteen. No wonder the girl was afraid. Agnes was too sharp to
put names in writing, but it seems clear from the letter that
she is speaking of her anticipated marriage to Edmund North.
Presumably the 'she' whose friendship seems insincere is Lady
North, pressured by Sir Thomas into convincing Agnes of his
son's worth. It sounds as if Judith North is an obedient and
dutiful wife, doing her husband's bidding to persuade his
reluctant ward into accepting his will for her, as if a woman's
encouragement will make it palatable. Again, Sophia feels that
flare of anger as she remembers how her father had used her
aunt, his sister, to lay the prospect of marriage before her all
those years ago, chipping away at her refusal with the insistent
threat that her only alternative was to end up on the street.

The final letter sends a chill through her, despite the fire.

*You make promises of running away and marrying in
secret, like Romeo and Juliet, and I can't tell if you
mean it, or if you are only trying to comfort me. You
must know that my guardian would come after us and
would not rest until I was brought back and you in
gaol. I have told you over and over that I would
gladly forfeit my inheritance to live in one poor room
with you, but I am not wholly sure that you would so*

readily leave the life you love with the players for a future of obscurity with me. But there is planted in my mind the seed of an idea that may yet spare me this detested match, and offer us the freedom to plot our own course. I will not unfold it to you until it is clear in my head, but I mean to call on my uncle while Sir Thomas is out of London for the holidays, and I hope by Twelfth Night I may bring you news of my progress. Until then, my love, go with God, win the queen's favour with your angel voice (but do not let her ladies make eyes at you!) and I will wait impatiently until your arms are around me once more. No pre-contract could be as strong as my oath to you: my whole heart is yours, and you take it with you wherever you go. Always, Your lamb.

Sophia folds the paper with an overwhelming feeling of sadness. *Poor child*, she thinks, for the thousandth time; she had no idea she wouldn't live to see Twelfth Night. *Your lamb*: a play on her name and the Latin for lamb, *agnus*. There is no hint in the letter that Agnes believed herself to be in danger at the time of writing, but Sophia wonders if the girl's embryonic plan had led directly to her murder. Had someone discovered it? If Agnes thought she had found a way to get out of her marriage contract with Edmund, that would certainly provoke the Norths to anger, but – as Cecil had pointed out – they would gain nothing by the girl's death, at least, not until she was securely in possession of her inheritance and legally married. It seems from Agnes's words that the execution of this plan depended in some way on her uncle; the next step was to find out whether the visit actually happened. Sophia also wants to track down this Grace and see what she knows of Agnes's intentions; any loyalty Grace owed to the girl will do her no good now, and if she was fond of Agnes – as her willingness to risk her position for the girl's sake suggests – she would surely want to see the murderer brought to justice. Sophia makes a note to herself to speak to Leila the next morning. She will also visit Tobie, to make sure that Cecil has kept his promise to improve his conditions, and see if she can persuade the boy to tell her anything Agnes may have confided in him; she must also see about finding him the best possible lawyer.

As she locks the packet of Agnes's letters in the compartment with the threatening note, a thought strikes her, bringing a cold fear in its wake: if Tobie had written of his proposal to run away and marry in secret in his notes to Agnes, that would give the Norths ample evidence to claim he had motive to kill her. Foolish boy, she thinks, shaking her head, half in anger and half in sorrow. She, too, had been reckless in the giddy heights of her first love. Tobie's father had promised her that they would elope and marry in secret, but at the last moment she had been prevented from reaching him. Occasionally she wonders how her life would have turned out if she had not been impeded, if they had managed to escape. There were those who tried to tell her afterwards that he had never intended to marry her, but rather had planned to kill her; that his true and ardent passion was not for her but for his mission, for the Catholic faith, and that she had become an unwelcome obstacle he needed to remove (she thinks again of Jasper, willing his paramour to fall under a cart). Sophia has long ago given up trying the case in her head, rehearsing all the arguments for and against. Even if he had been speaking the truth when he made those promises to her, there was no guarantee that they could ever have built a life together. She had always known that his faith was her greatest rival, and that she was destined to lose. A tiny part of her still wants to believe that if he had ever had the chance to lay eyes on his son, that might have been enough to convince him, but she knows in her heart that this is self-delusion. And if she had misjudged him back then, if he had indeed meant her harm, then neither she nor Tobie would be here today. Her own death does not frighten her as much as it might – she has looked it in the eyes more than once – but the thought of a world without Tobie in it chills her to the marrow.

She is grateful for the knock that interrupts these thoughts; it opens to reveal Hilary, looking extremely put out.

'Master Munday is here, madam.' The steward folds her hands together. 'I told him it's far too late to be calling – it's gone ten – but he insists that it's urgent. He's also in a . . .' she hesitates '. . . a less than respectable state. But I thought I should ask what you wish to do?'

'How do you mean – drunk?'

'I don't think so.'

'Then what? Oh – has he been in a fight?' She feels a sudden pang of conscience, and hopes Anthony has not put himself in harm's way pursuing her enquiries.

'I wouldn't like to guess where he's been, madam. Rolling in a midden, by the smell of him.'

Sophia frowns. That doesn't sound like Anthony.

'Take him to the library, will you?' she says, dropping the shawl and putting on a heavy brocade gown. 'And ask Lina to bring us something to drink.'

There is a long pause; Hilary is still giving her that inscrutable look. 'If you're sure, madam,' she murmurs, and slips away.

FIFTEEN

The library bears no sign of the earlier skirmish. All traces of broken glass and spilled wine have been magicked away by Lina. She finds Anthony pacing by the fireplace, as if he is unwilling to sit down without her permission. He starts as she enters, and takes a step towards her, smiling, then dithers, uncertain of how to greet her. She indicates the chair that her stepson Jasper had occupied. She notes that he is indeed unusually dishevelled, and smells like the Fleet ditch. He must notice the wrinkle of her nose, because he glances down self-consciously and brushes his breeches before sitting.

'Forgive my appearance – I've come straight from prison.'

'Prison?' Sophia pulls up the chair opposite and stares at him. 'Did you see Tobie?'

'Tobie?' It is Anthony's turn to look bemused. 'What?'

'He's been arrested. You didn't know?'

'How would I know?'

'I thought news might have reached The Rose.'

Anthony shakes his head. 'I've been in Whitechapel and then to the Clink, on the trail of the Norths. Whyever has Tobie been arrested?'

Sophia explains about the letters, then listens as Anthony shares his afternoon's discoveries; between them, they piece together a clearer picture of the eddying currents surrounding Agnes Lovell.

'My guess is that she planned to ask her uncle to help her get out of the marriage contract, perhaps even to elope with Tobie,' Sophia says, when they have finished comparing notes.

Anthony frowns. 'I can't imagine he'd have encouraged her in that. The informer in the Clink said Vincent Lovell was careful these days, he must know the authorities are watching him. Drawing down the ire of the Norths by helping to rob them of their prize would attract exactly the kind of attention he'd want to avoid.'

'But it would be in Vincent's interest to prevent the marriage to Edmund North,' Sophia says, standing to poke the fire and wincing slightly as she does so. Her right shoulder is still sore and she doesn't want Anthony asking about it. 'Your priest said Vincent wanted access to the Lovell lands to benefit the Catholic mission. Perhaps he saw his chance. What if he bargained with Agnes – he'd help her run away with Tobie in return for access to her lands when she inherited?'

'Surely Vincent would know that the Norths would bring all their legal firepower to the matter if he tried that.' Anthony sighs. 'It all comes back to the same problem, though. Everyone needed Agnes to stay alive until her fourteenth birthday, until that estate was hers.'

'Unless . . .' Sophia turns to face him, tapping her teeth with her fingernail as she thinks. 'Who gets the estate if Agnes dies before she turns fourteen?'

'It would depend on the terms of Sir John Lovell's will, I suppose. Not the Norths, though – the wardship would only give them the right to manage her lands while she was still a minor. But unless John Lovell had specified otherwise, I'd imagine it would go to the nearest male relative.'

'Which would be Vincent, surely?'

They look at one another. Anthony's blue eyes appear opaque in the firelight.

'Both the warden and the young priest said Vincent loved his niece,' he says quietly.

'He might have loved his faith more.'

Anthony considers this. 'All right. Let's suppose Vincent stood to inherit if Agnes died before she came of age. Why has he waited until now? He's been out of prison for four years. If he's ruthless enough to take her out of the picture, he could have done it long before and had the benefit of the estate all this time.'

'Perhaps he didn't have the opportunity before. It sounds from these letters as if the Norths kept Agnes under close watch – see how she had to wait until Sir Thomas was out of town before she could visit her uncle.'

'True. Or it could have something to do with the prospect of Agnes's marriage,' Anthony says, leaning forward with his elbows on his knees and his fingers steepled. 'Vincent might have initially thought that he'd be able to persuade Agnes to let him have the run of her coastline, once she inherited. She was young, fond of him by all accounts – he was her only living relative. Perhaps he was confident that he could influence her, rather than get rid of her. A husband would change all that. A husband would have legal ownership of Agnes and her estate. The only way for Vincent to secure those lands would be if Agnes died before she could inherit or marry.'

'That all makes logical sense,' Sophia says, reaching for the decanter to pour them both another glass of wine. 'What doesn't add up at all is why Vincent Lovell would choose to make such a display of the girl's murder, if he was behind it. Surely if her death benefitted him, it would be in his interest to make it look like an accident. None of this business with the cryptic note and verse.'

'Unless that's a deliberate misdirection, intended to point the finger elsewhere,' Anthony says. 'The riddle about stolen ground could be a dig at the Norths for taking her from him in the first place. And if she'd told her uncle about Tobie, leaving her at The Theatre could have been designed to incriminate him.'

'Seems unnecessarily elaborate. And what about my cipher?'

'I confess, I don't have an answer. It's a mystery.' He pauses. 'Except . . .'

'What?'

'It's been worrying me, you know. How anyone could get hold of it – Walsingham kept his records so carefully. But after he died—' He stops, biting his lip. 'There's no knowing who might have had access to those papers. That's a lot of sensitive information to have floating around.'

Sophia frowns. 'Hardly *floating*, surely. It's not as if anyone could have walked into his house off the street. And in any case, only Phelippes would know how to make sense of anything relating to cryptography, so— What?' She stops at Anthony's look.

'Exactly.'

She stares at him. 'You think *Phelippes* betrayed me?'

'Not deliberately.' He sighs and runs a hand through his hair. 'But you know about his disastrous escapade with the Earl of Essex, after Walsingham died?'

She shakes her head. 'I was out of the service and married by then. I didn't keep in touch with Thomas – I didn't even know he'd carried on searching for Tobie until he wrote to say you'd found him.'

'After Walsingham died,' Anthony says, pressing his hands together between his knees, 'everything to do with intelligence was badly managed. All those carefully wrought networks of communication he had built up over decades – Burghley didn't want the expense of maintaining them, and they collapsed from lack of nurture. Essex saw his opportunity to advance himself with the queen. One high-profile intelligence coup – one credible plot against her life foiled by his ingenuity – and she'd be in his debt, so he thought. But he had no experience or skill in espionage.'

141

'So he used Thomas Phelippes?'

'He needed Thomas. And Thomas needed him – he had no master at this point. Burghley wasn't giving him a regular income. But the whole venture was a mess from the outset.' He stands and resumes his pacing, as if to gather his thoughts. 'Essex was never going to replace Walsingham. He hadn't the patience for the groundwork of intelligence-gathering – he wanted a big dramatic result and he thought you could get that in a matter of weeks. He recruited men with no experience in the field and sent them to France and the Low Countries to infiltrate networks of English Catholics in exile. Phelippes was left to handle them, but they were either unmasked immediately or panicked and ran home.' His face tightens. 'Innocent people were imprisoned and tortured as a result of their rushed accusations, Phelippes was left out of pocket, and Essex soon decided that leading military campaigns offered more glory than undercover work. But the point is—'

'—that Thomas might have shared secret information with Essex.' Sophia pauses to weigh this. 'But there's no reason to think Essex had anything to do with Agnes Lovell. He certainly has nothing to do with me.'

'Given the incompetence of the whole operation, there's no knowing who in the earl's circle might have got hold of that cipher. You're right, that means it might not even be about you,' he adds, more cheerfully.

Sophia rolls her bruised shoulder. She could tell Anthony about the attack and the new note, which seem to suggest beyond doubt that it is very much about her. She would value his view of this development, but she has to weigh that against the inevitable fussing.

A log falls in the hearth with a cascade of sparks, startling them both from their thoughts. She brushes a damp strand of hair from her face, impatient.

'All this is speculation. Let's concentrate on Vincent for now. We need to speak to him.'

'He's living in Upper Homerton. I thought I might go in the morning, if the road is passable.'

'Don't you have to be at The Rose?'

'Henslowe won't miss me.' He hesitates, then raises his eyes to her. 'I'll do whatever I can to help Tobie, you know that. You just have to ask.'

There is a terrible hope in his expression; Sophia thinks of Leila's words and feels a small twist of guilt. She is no fool; she sees how Anthony looks at her, but she also knows that he cares for his wife and children, and she has always believed that he would do nothing to jeopardise either their friendship or his family's happiness. She hopes she is not taking advantage of him.

'Thank you. I mean to visit him tomorrow, and I also want to find this Grace – it sounds as if she knew Agnes better than anyone. I'll do that while you talk to Vincent Lovell, and perhaps we can meet here again in the afternoon? If you're not needed elsewhere, of course,' she adds hastily.

'I'll be here at four,' he says. His gaze searches her face. 'Sophia – is everything all right?'

'Aside from my son being in prison for a murder he didn't commit, and the possibility that someone in the Catholic network has discovered my secret work for Walsingham, you mean? Absolutely fine.' She tries to keep her voice light, but she hears how it comes out strained.

'Only – you have a bruise, here—' He takes a step closer, lifting his hand to her; for a moment it seems he will touch his thumb to her cheek, but he stops, uncertain, his fingers hovering an inch from her skin. The firelight makes shadows and hollows of his fine-boned face. For the space of a heartbeat, they look at one another and a tiny filament of possibility stretches between them. She allows herself to imagine how it would feel to be held, the solace of a pair of strong arms around her. It's been a long time since she let anyone take care of her in that way. She takes a breath; fortunately, the smell rising off his clothes is enough to banish those thoughts on the instant. She turns abruptly away, pressing her palm to her cheek.

'I slipped on some icy steps,' she says. 'It's nothing.' She decides not to tell him about the attack or the note just yet. One of the great advantages of being a widow with her own money is that, for the first time in her life, she doesn't have to submit to any man telling her what she can and can't do (that's Hilary's role). She forces a smile to soften the blow and sees him step back, his hand dropping uselessly to his side. 'You should go home, Master Munday,' she says, in a too-bright voice that sounds odd to her own ears. 'Your family will be worrying that you're stranded in a snowdrift. Besides, you could do with a bath.'

He laughs, though she catches a note of melancholy in it; he knows he has been gently rebuffed. 'Yes, that will take some explaining,' he says. 'Until tomorrow, then.'

She accompanies him to the hall, where the maid fetches his cloak. After he has left, with promises to return at four the next day with news of Vincent Lovell, Sophia leans against the panelling and looks up at the portrait of Humphrey de Wolfe hanging above the stairs. In the painting, her late husband stands tall with his right hand resting proprietorially on a globe, his twinkling brown eyes watching her shrewdly, one corner of his mouth lifted in private amusement above his silver beard, as if he can see past her to some joke she is not party to. Not for the first time, she finds herself missing his wisdom and gentle guidance more than she had thought possible. But Humphrey is not here, and she must find her way out of this thicket alone.

SIXTEEN

30th December 1598

The next morning finds Anthony back on the road east out of London, bundled against the weather, as stray flakes drift loosely from a sullen sky and the horse's breath steams in air cold as a blade. His mount picks its way fastidiously through the snow, resentful at being taken from its warm stall. Anthony, by contrast, is glad to be out of the house, away from Mercy's stony looks. Beth had been in bed by the time he returned home the night before – 'she's bad tonight,' Mercy had informed him curtly – but Richie and Priscilla were still up, squabbling over a game of cards by the parlour fire. He had stopped to kiss them both on the tops of their heads, though Richie had squirmed away, protesting; at eleven, he finds any show of affection from his parents mortifying. Priscilla had risen to hug him and he had held her tightly, unable to keep his thoughts from straying to poor Agnes Lovell, violated and murdered at the age his elder daughter is now. Eventually even Priscilla, the most accommodating of children, had laughingly complained that he was crushing the breath from her, and he had left them to their game. He had cracked the door of Beth's room as silently as he could, and seen two fair heads close together on the pillow, breathing softly; little Annie, who at nine still liked to curl into the warmth of her mother at night, had a tendency to sneak in whenever he was out, though he had tried half-heartedly to tell Beth that her baby was getting too old for this habit.

'Does Beth good to have someone to hold at night,' Mercy had said, tight-lipped. Anthony had turned away to his own chamber, the weight of failure heavy on his shoulders.

The marshes around Homerton are blanketed thickly with snow; few people have dared to venture abroad, and the only sound is the occasional mournful cry of a curlew over the frozen marsh. One benefit of the cold is the way it has muted the ripe smells from the tanneries that usually hang over this area. Anthony passes a man digging drifts from the path outside a cottage and asks for the Widow Crowley's house; most of the landmarks the man gives him are buried under a white shroud, but eventually he finds his way to a street of red-brick dwellings behind the churchyard and ties his horse to a post.

The door is opened at his knock by a woman in her fifties with small, suspicious eyes, who asks what business he has with Vincent Lovell.

'My name is Munday. Tell him it's about his niece.'

The widow's gaze shrinks further. 'Wait there,' she says, before closing the door in his face.

Anthony stamps his feet and breathes on his fingers. Mistress Crowley must have connections to the Catholic community, he supposes, for her to have taken in Vincent Lovell as a lodger (or lover, he wonders, not that it's his business), so her wariness is probably justified. As he begins to think he might have done better to have invented a pretext, the door opens again and she beckons him inside, not troubling to hide her reluctance.

The house is bigger than it appears from the frontage, reaching back a fair way through a series of connected rooms.

She shows him into a parlour with high-backed settles arranged around a well-stoked hearth. A bearded man regards him impassively from red-rimmed eyes. The Widow Crowley closes the door behind her without offering to take Anthony's cloak or hat; clearly she does not expect him to stay long.

He puts Vincent Lovell in his early fifties, though it's hard to tell; he's long-limbed and solidly built, with few traces of grey in his hair and beard, but his face is haggard. He has evidently been crying – though if he had played any part in Agnes's death, you would expect him to put on a show of grief to deflect attention.

'Sit, then.' Vincent indicates the seat opposite. 'Mistress Crowley says you bring news about my niece, God rest her.'

'I'm sorry,' Anthony says, removing his hat. Where to begin? 'I'm looking into Agnes's death and I wanted to ask you about the last time you saw her.'

If Vincent is discomfited, he doesn't show it. 'I've been through all this,' he says evenly. There is a stillness about him that Anthony recognises; it's the comportment of a man who is used to being questioned, to having his every gesture and expression scrutinised, and is practised at giving nothing away. But Anthony knows those tricks too; he learned them in Walsingham's service. 'Are you from the coroner's office?'

'No. I'm here on behalf of the young man who has been arrested for her murder.'

At this, he catches a flicker of curiosity in Vincent's eyes. 'Tobie Strange. I see. So you're a lawyer?'

'A colleague. I'm a writer,' he adds, never sure if this will make things better or worse.

Vincent frowns. Anthony can almost hear his mind making connections. 'Munday,' he says eventually, tilting his head. When he speaks again, his voice is cold. 'I know you. You're Topcliffe's man.'

There is a long silence while Anthony considers how to respond. Richard Topcliffe, Elizabeth's self-styled queen's pursuivant: executioner and torturer, scourge of Catholics, a man with a reputation as a violent bully, who took pleasure in the pain he inflicted in the name of national security. While it's true that Anthony did report to Topcliffe during his early days as a pursuivant, it was partly Topcliffe's lust for persecution that drove Anthony away from the profession; in recent years, he has even written satirical verses about the executioner, who is retired now. He doesn't think this would carry much weight with Vincent Lovell. In fact, he is surprised that Vincent has not ejected him bodily from the house on the instant.

'Master Lovell, I realise it will be no consolation to you to learn that, when I began work as a pursuivant, I had no knowledge of what went on in Topcliffe's house,' Anthony says. Vincent lets out a short, eloquent snort. 'I've been party to things that give me no pride to look back on, I admit it.'

'Are you still in the pay of the queen's ministers?' Vincent asks.

'I write plays now.'

'That wasn't my question.' Vincent folds his hands together. 'It would be reasonable to assume that you are here on their behalf to entrap me in some way.'

'Except, if that were my intention, I would not have given you my real name, knowing you would likely kick me out the moment you put two and two together.'

Vincent almost smiles. 'If Mistress Crowley knew who you were, she'd kick you all the way back to London.' He looks at Anthony as if indulging a disobedient child. 'What on earth makes you think I would have anything to say to you, Munday, after all you have done to my brothers and sisters in Christ?'

It's a fair question, and Anthony knows it would be pure sophistry to protest that he never personally hurt anyone. He takes a deep breath, flexing his hands as the warmth returns to his fingers. 'I don't believe Tobie Strange killed Agnes.'

'Good. Neither do I.'

Anthony sits up straighter.

'That surprises you, I see,' Vincent says. 'You're no doubt thinking that, if *I* had killed her – which I presume is your hypothesis – it would be very much to my advantage to have this young player take the blame. But since I'm prepared to insist on his innocence, that should be proof enough that I did not murder my niece.' For the first time, he allows his face to betray his disgust at the idea.

'There are many people who will attest to your affection for her,' Anthony says carefully. He has no doubt that Vincent Lovell is clever enough to play a double bluff.

'I would go so far as to say I was the only person who genuinely cared about that poor child's welfare,' Vincent says, with some force. 'Aside from her old nurse, but certainly the only person in her family who saw beyond the use they could make of her. My brother never got over his disappointment that Agnes was not born a boy, and didn't trouble to hide the fact from her. I showed her more fatherly affection than John ever did, and in turn she confided in me. It's my belief that, as soon as he knew he was dying, he engineered a situation that would prevent me from becoming her legal guardian, purely to spite me.'

'Betraying your priests to the magistrate, you mean?'

Vincent looks at him with contempt. 'They were not *my* priests. You won't induce me to say anything on that subject, Munday. I was imprisoned with no evidence of wrongdoing against me, while Sir Thomas North and Lord Burghley cooked up a plan with my brother that would profit them all, no thought for Agnes or her wishes. She deserved better. I should have foreseen this outcome, and I add that guilt to the considerable burden I already bear.'

'You should have foreseen that she would be murdered?' Anthony leans forward.

Vincent takes a moment to choose his words. 'I feared for her, yes. The moment the Norths became involved. But I didn't think it would be so soon. I thought there would be time to intervene.' He passes a hand over his beard and Anthony can see him struggling to master his feelings.

'You thought they would get rid of her once she was legally married to Edmund and had taken possession of her lands.'

'Agnes was *nine* years old when her father took ill,' Vincent says, his level gaze fixed on Anthony. 'Edmund North was a married man of twenty-five. I saw through their plan immediately – it was so transparent, a child could have worked it out. My brother made sure I was out of the way, in a place where I could not obstruct or raise a legal challenge. The Norths bought Agnes's wardship – God alone knows how Sir Thomas afforded it, but I'm sure Lord Burghley, as head of the Court of Wards, would have been pleased to facilitate that, rather than let such a strategic estate go to someone of my reputation. I have no doubt that money changed hands to the advantage of all parties. Then all the Norths had to do was marry Agnes to Edmund when she came of age, and the transfer of wealth would be complete. After that, she would be superfluous.'

'I didn't realise Edmund North already had a wife,' Anthony says. The business seems to grow murkier with every step.

Vincent gives a dry laugh. 'He kept her out of the way, up in Cambridgeshire. He'd married in haste at nineteen, not a particularly advantageous match for the Norths, certainly nothing like the wealth Agnes would bring. And two years after Sir Thomas purchased my niece's wardship, wouldn't you know, Edmund's wife took a sudden illness up there in the fens and died, poor creature.' The thin line of his lips shows what he thinks of this story.

'My God. You think she was murdered too?'

'I don't suppose we'll ever know. But I think it was extremely convenient for Edmund North to find himself free to marry just as Agnes was about to come of age. So, yes, I had grave concerns about what might happen to my niece once she had served her purpose for them. I consulted a number of lawyers on how I might prevent the marriage, but they were not optimistic.'

And did you then look for another way to prevent it? Anthony wonders, watching Vincent's face. He is inclined to believe the man's sincerity, but he also knows how foolish that would be in the circumstances.

'Who inherits your brother's estate, now that Agnes is dead?'

'That would be me.' His neutral expression is back in place like a mask. 'I do see how that could arouse the suspicions of anyone who didn't know how much I loved my niece.'

Anthony says nothing. Plenty of people have killed in the misguided belief that they were protecting the person they loved.

'Listen, Munday,' Vincent says, more briskly. 'Though it sticks in my throat to collaborate with you in any way, I will help, if I can. Because I want to see those rogues brought to justice, and because I would not like to see another innocent young life lost to their scheming. But you'll understand I'm reluctant to have the shadow of suspicion lifted from Tobie Strange, only to have it fall on me. The government would love any excuse to be rid of me once and for all.'

'You're certain the Norths killed her, then?' Anthony frowns, unconvinced. 'With what motive? They needed her alive until she turned fourteen, or all their schemes and outlay were for nothing.'

'She was planning to defy them,' Vincent says heavily. 'She wanted to run away and marry this boy Tobie in secret.'

'Surely she must have known that could never work,' Anthony says. 'Unless she was especially—' He wants to say 'stupid', but feels that would be insensitive.

'She was no simpleton,' Vincent says. 'She'd given it a great deal of thought. Her plan was to transfer the estate legally to me. She reasoned that, without her lands and fortune, she would be of no interest to the Norths and they would leave her alone.'

'Was that even feasible?'

'I thought it absurd at first. But the more I considered it, the more I grew to think there might be a grain of possibility in the idea. Once the estate was hers, she could in theory dispose of it however she wished, provided she did not have a husband to countermand her. I promised Agnes I would consult a lawyer on the matter as soon as the holidays were over.' He rubs his face again. 'It would have depended on keeping Agnes away from the Norths until her fourteenth birthday. They were planning to marry her to Edmund the same day, so that there was no gap in which she was free of their control. But it would have had to be done in such a way that neither I nor Master Strange could be accused of abduction. Five months is a long time.'

'She would have given up her inheritance for the chance to marry Tobie Strange?' It sounds to Anthony like the sort of decision one might make at thirteen and live to regret. Except that Agnes had not had the chance to do that.

Vincent allows a sad smile. 'Oh, she had thought it all through. She proposed that, since I am not likely to have children, I should make any child of hers my heir once she had signed the estate over to me. So it would not be lost to her line, only skip a generation. For Agnes, those lands had come to represent nothing but misery.'

Anthony wants to ask why Agnes was so sure Vincent would have no heirs of his own. Is there a chance the man could be an ordained priest? Surely if anyone suspected that, he would have been interrogated, and Anthony has heard no mention of it. But he wonders now if Lord Burghley guessed at something of the kind. 'She told Tobie she was planning to visit you over Christmas,' he says. 'Did she?'

Vincent pauses for a long time before he nods. 'She arrived on the twenty-seventh. She had to wait until Thomas North had left the house. His wife was not a particularly diligent guardian – she preferred Agnes out of sight, which made it easier for her to disappear when Thomas's back was turned.'

'Surely she didn't travel alone, in this weather?' Anthony gestures to the window.

'I was as shocked as you when she turned up that morning, believe me. She told me with a great air of triumph that she'd slipped out of the house, leaving her nurse to tell Lady North that Agnes was unwell and confined to her chamber, if anyone asked. Then she'd hired a horse at a nearby inn, rather than take one from the North stables. Agnes is . . . *was*' – he falters, and recovers – 'an accomplished horsewoman, but she had a child's understanding of danger. She didn't stop to consider what could have befallen her on the way.'

Anthony feels his admiration for Agnes Lovell grows the more he learns of her.

'She sounds like a strong-willed girl,' he says.

'You don't know the half of it.' Vincent sets his jaw. When nothing further is forthcoming, Anthony shifts in his seat and tries another tack.

'So what happened during that visit on the twenty-seventh?'

'We talked. We exchanged new year's gifts. That was it. She was here from perhaps eight in the morning until around two. Mistress Crowley brought some food and Agnes told me of this plan she had formed. Tobie Strange, the estate.' He shakes his head. 'I had not seen her so animated in a long time – I think she barely felt the cold that day. She was flushed pink and her eyes shone – after seeing her so crushed by her life with the Norths, it gladdened my heart to glimpse a spark of her old spirit. I hadn't the heart to point out all the potential flaws in her proposal.'

'You encouraged her, then?'

'I tried to urge caution. As I mentioned, I told her I would speak to a lawyer after the holidays. But I advised her not to provoke the Norths in the meantime, and to make no hasty pledges to Master Strange. I didn't want her escaping one man's control for another's.'

I bet you didn't, Anthony thinks. 'So she returned to the North house the same day?'

Vincent leaves a pause, as if deciding how to answer. 'So I believed. Agnes began to fret about the time, she didn't want to ride back in the dark, and she worried that Lady North would notice her absence by supper. This would have been about two in the afternoon, as I say – the light was fading and we had already lit candles in this room. I insisted on accompanying her, though she made a great fuss – didn't want me coming in case we might be seen together and word somehow find its way to Sir Thomas. She needn't have worried – there was hardly anyone on the road. They all had more sense.'

'And you delivered her directly to the North house?' Anthony makes his tone as light as possible. Much depends on Vincent's answer, but he doesn't want to make the man defensive.

'Not to the door, if that's what you're asking,' Vincent says shortly, and it's clear from his expression that he understands the tenor of the question. 'She wouldn't let me. I rode with her as far as Aldersgate Street and she insisted on making the rest of the journey alone.'

'And she went straight back to the Norths' after you left her at Aldersgate Street?'

'I had no reason to think otherwise. She needed to return the horse to an inn on Smithfield. I said I would take it for her – I didn't like the idea of a thirteen-year-old girl alone at an inn yard, surrounded by stable boys and men drinking. So outside St Botolph's I bade her farewell and told her we would speak in the new year.' He pauses to draw a steadying breath. 'She set off on foot along Little Britain as the bells were striking half past three. And that was the last time I saw her.'

'I'm sorry,' Anthony says again, and allows a moment of silence while Vincent composes himself. Although returning the horse himself was convenient for Vincent, he thinks; that way, no one at the inn could confirm whether or not Agnes made it back from Homerton. 'So, you may have been the last person to see her alive?'

Vincent looks at him with naked contempt. 'Well, no, because she could only have gone home. Oh, I know what the Norths are saying.'

Anthony, who does not know, tilts his head with an encouraging expression.

'I went through all this with the coroner,' Vincent says, not troubling to keep the impatience from his voice. 'They're claiming she never returned, but of course they're bound to say that, they want suspicion to fall on me. Whatever was done to her, it happened between half past three on the twenty-seventh and whatever hour her body was left at The Theatre on the night of the twenty-eighth. And if I had had the slightest inkling that she was walking into that kind of danger, I would have kept her here with us and damn the consequences.' He rises and lifts a poker from the hearth; instinctively Anthony tenses, but Vincent leans in and stabs repeatedly at a log as if it's Thomas North's heart. The flames leap up and subside as the wood settles.

'You have no doubt that the Norths killed her?' Anthony asks. 'But Sir Thomas was absent.'

'I have never thought Sir Thomas killed her,' Vincent says, still staring at the fire. 'He is too level-headed to lash out like that.'

'Edmund, then?'

Vincent turns and fixes him with a weary eye. 'Edmund is not level-headed, far from it. If I had to guess what happened to my poor niece that day, I would suppose that Edmund caught her sneaking back in, an argument ensued, in the heat of the moment she must have blurted something about her intention to refuse him, or taunted him that she had a sweetheart, and—' He brings the poker down hard on the stone floor with a resounding clang, making Anthony jump.

'With a poker, you think?'

'Poker, candlestick, sword hilt – he could have thrown her against a wall, who knows. One way or another, he broke her head. She was only a slender little thing.' He rubs his left hand across his eyes. 'Then he left her at The Theatre to point to the Strange boy.'

Anthony watches him. Robert Cecil had told Sophia that Agnes died from a blow to the head, she had shared that with him last night, but it was surely not common knowledge? Yet Vincent seems clear on the manner of his niece's death. Possibly the coroner let it slip during questioning. Anthony recalls George Grinkin's story about Edmund North and the young whore in Ireland, the unbridled temper when he was thwarted.

'So the Norths are claiming she never returned?' he asks.

'I assumed you knew?' Vincent examines the end of the poker. 'They say no one in the house saw her after she left that morning. But the discovery that she had been to visit me works out nicely for them, so of course they'll say she didn't come back. They'll claim I was in league with Tobie Strange.'

'What about the nurse?'

Vincent grimaces. 'She suffers with severe headaches that affect her vision. I'm told she had a bad attack that afternoon and took to her bed.'

'Even so. What about later? She knew that her charge was out alone in the city, a thirteen-year-old girl, and she didn't check to make sure she'd returned safely?' Anthony hears the outrage in his tone; he is picturing Priscilla running about London on her own with a hired horse.

Vincent spreads his hands in a gesture of helplessness. 'Apparently there is a tincture she takes for her headaches, she slept right through. She woke all in a fluster the next morning to find the house in uproar because Agnes was missing. But of course that could have been staged. So you see, it's my word against the Norths'. And who do you think the Privy Council are more likely to favour? But I swear to

156

you' – he grips the handle of the poker – 'I would never have hurt that girl, not for all the money and land in England. So if you want to put right the harm you have done, Munday, in your Topcliffe days, start with this. Bring Edmund North to justice.'

They stare at one another for a long moment. Vincent Lovell is convincing, Anthony thinks, but he has been around the English Catholics enough to know that they are extremely good at dissembling – the ones that survive, anyway. A thought strikes him.

'What if you are both telling the truth?'

'What?'

'Well – you say you didn't see Agnes to the door. Might she have gone somewhere else after leaving you?'

'Where would she have gone, three hundred yards from home, with dusk falling, in this weather?' Vincent looks incredulous.

'I don't know. I'm simply saying it's a possibility that someone else met Agnes that afternoon. If she was reluctant for you to accompany her all the way home, she may have had other plans.'

'And some mysterious stranger killed her along the way?' Vincent pinches his mouth. 'I can see why you wouldn't want to go up against the Norths, Munday, but you're clutching at straws here.' He sets the poker into its stand and stretches out his back. 'Still, if anyone would have an idea, it's Grace Parry. Agnes's nurse. You should talk to her.'

Anthony nods and stands, gathering his coat. 'What was the gift? Your new year's gift to Agnes?'

'A locket,' Vincent says warily. 'It belonged to my mother – her grandmother. Agnes was named for her, I wanted her to have it. I don't suppose I shall ever see it again now. It would not occur to anyone that I might want Agnes's things to remember her.'

Anthony wonders what might have been inside the locket,

and whether it was found with Agnes's body. If so, that would argue against Vincent as the killer; why leave something of value that would point back to him? Anthony pulls on his hat; he suddenly feels very tired, and the warmth of the room is making him sleepy. The ride from Homerton to The Rose will slap him awake. But there is one more question he needs to ask.

'I'm sorry to bring this up, Lovell, but did your niece speak to you frankly about her relationship with Master Strange?'

Vincent's eyes narrow. 'How do you mean?'

'Did she confide . . . ?' How does one ask a man about his thirteen-year-old niece's maidenhead? He could not imagine having this conversation with any of his nieces, let alone his daughters, but Vincent was all Agnes had by way of confidant, apart from the nurse. 'Do you know if they were intimate?'

The colour drains from Vincent's face and he grips the bench for support. 'Oh dear God. Tell me she wasn't with child?'

'No, no. I only wondered if she had said anything to make you think they had consummated . . . ?'

Vincent shakes his head. 'She would not have broached that subject with me.'

'Did she ever say anything to make you think Edmund North had behaved improperly towards her?'

'Not in that regard. But you must have a reason for asking. Was she violated?' His right hand curls into a fist; he clasps it in the palm of his left. 'Because, by God, if he touched her, I'll kill him myself and gladly hang for it.'

'Edmund North, or Tobie Strange?'

'Either.'

'I don't know,' Anthony says, trying to soften the blow, 'but the Norths may try to claim Tobie had relations with her, as part of their case against him. I only wondered if you knew—'

'You'd better ask him about that,' Vincent says, his expression grim, his fist still bunched. 'He'd better pray I don't get to him first.' Anthony remembers Warden Martin's story of Vincent threatening the young priest, his sudden temper. Here was a glimpse of it.

'Anyone else Agnes might have confided in about such matters?'

'Only Grace Parry. Or—' He stops, frowning. 'I worried about her having no female friends, no feminine influence besides her nurse. Judith North clearly had no interest in her. But the last time I saw Agnes – before the other day, I mean, this was at the start of summer, six months past – she hinted to me that she had found a new friend. A fine lady who was going to help her stand up to the Norths.'

'No name? Could you take a guess?'

'She said she would tell me when the time was right. She enjoyed playing games like that, and I indulged her because she had so little control in her life. If I'm honest, I suspected she was inventing it – a fantasy version of the mother she never knew. Do you have children, Munday?'

'Three.' *Four*, says a voice in his head, accompanied by an image of a small coffin, and he pushes it quickly away.

'Well, then. Find out who killed Agnes, because I swear on all that is holy, it wasn't me.'

He holds his hand out and Anthony shakes it. In the street, icy air hits him like a punch to the throat. He rides away with the uncomfortable feeling that he has only added to the man's grief, and has to remind himself sternly that Vincent Lovell may yet prove to be a murderer.

SEVENTEEN

'Hilary, can you find Humphrey's ledgers for me?' Sophia asks, pausing in the doorway of the dining room. 'The ones detailing private loans.'

Hilary's eyes narrow. Those ledgers are kept locked away; plenty of people with status and influence at court would prefer there to be no record of the fact that they needed Humphrey's money to prop them up. Sophia has often wondered how many of those loans her husband recovered before his death, or whether he made them in the first place with little expectation of repayment, it being worth more to him to have certain courtiers in his debt. The thought always makes her uneasy – that there are powerful people out there who might have concerns about whether she will suddenly decide to chase up the money owed. They need not worry; Humphrey recorded his transactions in a code that only he could interpret, and Sophia has no idea who the abbreviations might signify. But Hilary knows.

'Which year?' the steward asks.

'Let's start with the most recent – '94 to '96. Can you bring them to my room when I've eaten?'

Hilary gives her a look that implies objections, but after a pause she dips her head and retreats.

The dining room is chilly; it is too early for the fire to have taken the edge off the air. Sophia would much prefer to break her fast in the kitchen with the cook and her servants, where it's warm and full of brisk motion and easy chatter, but she understands that she must preserve her authority, so she eats alone at a long polished table, where the maids deliver her food with a curtsy and say nothing beyond 'God give you good day, madam.' She misses Humphrey's good-natured outrage at the scurrilous penny pamphlets that used to be bought up and brought to him by the servants.

But she feels rested this morning, and ravenous. As she works her way through warm bread with honey, slices of dried apple and smoked ham, she rolls her bruised shoulder and thinks back over the assault of the night before, with its childish threat. She is resolved not to be intimidated, though she is still troubled by the question of who could have known that she was involved in the pursuit of Agnes's killer.

While she eats, the servants bring a flurry of messages: one from Richard Burbage to say that Tobie Strange was moved during the night to the Clink, where he is being kept in better conditions in a room with a bed; Burbage clearly believes this is Sophia's doing and thanks her extravagantly, with a reminder of her promise to provide the boy with a lawyer. Sophia feels a profound relief; if Cecil had a hand in the move, it is to be hoped that he also gave instructions that Tobie is not be to harmed (she can't admit the word 'tortured', even in her head). She will to go to the Clink herself later and see if she can buy a private audience with Tobie. A note also arrives from Leila, asking her to come as soon as she can, because someone wants to speak to her. It must be that boy, Badger, Sophia thinks, her pulse quickening; with luck, the child will still have the brooch and she may be able to discover the insignia.

After breakfast, she returns to her chamber and writes a note to Humphrey's attorney, asking him to meet her at the

Clink at noon. She is sanding the paper when Hilary appears, her arms grudgingly full of leather-bound account books.

'Lay them on the table, if you would,' Sophia says, trying to conceal her impatience.

Hilary sets the ledgers down and swipes at the uppermost with her palm, brushing away a layer of dust. 'What is it you hope to find, madam?'

'I want to see if Humphrey ever lent money to Sir Thomas North or his son, Edmund.'

'When would this be?'

'That's the problem – I don't know.' Sophia catches Hilary's look. 'Sorry. Did they have any dealings, to your knowledge?'

To her surprise, Hilary nods. 'The master and Sir Thomas were thrown together because of the boys. This would be ten years ago, mind you.'

'The boys?'

'Master Jasper and the North boy were law students together. Not that there was much studying involved – they seemed to spend their days dicing and whoring and racking up debts. Even managed to get themselves arrested a couple of times.'

'What for?'

'Drunken brawling. And on one occasion, a girl in a tavern accused them of lewd behaviour, but of course she was a servant, so that never went anywhere. I expect she was paid off. Once they were thrown in the cells for causing damage to an alehouse. I recall Sir Thomas asking the master to put up the money for bail, as he didn't have the ready funds, and Humphrey refusing. He said it would do the lads good to have a couple of nights in gaol and reflect on their actions.' This pulls a rare smile out of Hilary.

'So when Thomas North was short of money he came to Humphrey? Did that happen often?'

'He was certainly a regular visitor to the house ten years or so ago, usually on the pretext of some concern about the boys' latest disgrace. Dennis took care of the accounts back then, so I didn't involve myself too closely. Once the boys were no longer at Gray's Inn, we saw less of Sir Thomas.' Hilary pauses, tracing a finger over the cover of the top ledger. 'This would have been just before you married the master.'

'That must be why I never met him. Odd that Humphrey never invited him for dinner over the years, if they were friends.'

'I wouldn't say they were *friends*, exactly. And Sir Thomas never came for a meal, even back then – only ever to see the master in his study. I heard the second Lady North dislikes social occasions and makes any excuse she can to avoid them.'

'Can't say I blame her,' Sophia mutters, with feeling. Though Humphrey had respected her independence, she had not been able to shirk the duties of a successful merchant's wife entirely, and playing the charming hostess at his supper parties had been her least favourite role; the performance always left her depleted. 'So you don't know if Humphrey had anything to do with Thomas North in the years since their sons left Gray's Inn?'

'I don't recall him coming to this house since you married the master, no. I suppose they could have met at his offices in Threadneedle Street. Although—' She breaks off, frowning. 'There was that peculiar incident a few years ago, with the painting.'

'Which painting?'

'Sir Thomas sent it as a gift. Ugly great thing. The master asked me to have it valued. It wasn't a vast amount, Sir Thomas was too cheap for that, but enough to make it worth selling on when enough time had passed. It's in the back guest room. The master thought it was hideous – he used to call it the Idiot Sheep.'

'*That* one?' Sophia stares at her. She knows the exact picture: a depiction of a sheep standing on an altar, radiance emanating from its head, blood spurting from a wound in its breast into a chalice, a remarkably stupid expression on its face. A copy of a work by a minor Flemish artist of the last century, Humphrey had told her, a gift from a grateful client. He'd joked that he'd hate to see what the man sent when he was ungrateful. He had not mentioned North's name. *Agnus Dei* was the picture's official title.

Not a sheep, but a lamb. Agnes.

'When exactly did Thomas North give it to Humphrey?' she asks.

Hilary purses her lips. 'It would have been four years ago, if I'm not mistaken.'

'Let's look in the ledgers for '94, then. See what North might have been thanking him for.'

Sophia brings more candles to the table for Hilary, but there is little she can do to help except hover while her steward traces a forefinger down endless columns of figures and tiny letters for page after page. Sophia watches with impotent fascination; one day, she thinks, she will ask Hilary to teach her how to read these signs, as foreign to her now as cuneiform. Although it might well be a waste of time; Sophia knows her own strengths, and mathematics has never been foremost among them, to the despair of her childhood tutor (though she was still quicker than her brother, she recalls, with a flash of pride). Hilary closes one ledger and opens the next, while Sophia privately concludes that this is a fruitless search. Suddenly her steward stops, taps an entry decisively and says, 'There.'

Sophia peers at the page and sees the clearly marked sum of three thousand pounds.

'Seventeenth October, 1594,' she reads. 'And you're sure this is Thomas North?'

'Quite sure,' Hilary says. 'And the painting arrived about a month later. I remember because we were beginning to get the house ready for Christmas guests and we didn't know where to put it.'

'I remember that too.' Sophia can't take her eyes off the ledger and that enormous sum. 'That's a lot of money. Did Thomas North ever pay it back?'

'No,' Hilary says shortly. 'I warned the master at the time that he was unlikely to see it again. He just laughed and said it was an investment.'

'Did he explain what he meant by that?'

'Humphrey de Wolfe rarely explained himself,' Hilary says. 'And I didn't ask.'

Sophia nods. It was true that Humphrey never felt the need to justify his decisions or share his reasoning; there was a presumption that his staff (and his wife) would simply trust in his sound good sense. But there it was, in fading black ink: a direct connection between Thomas North, Agnes Lovell and Sophia's own family. She would need to check the date of Sir John Lovell's death, but the obvious conclusion was that Humphrey had lent North the money to buy Agnes's wardship; the gift of the *Agnus Dei* painting must be a sly reference to the purpose of the loan. And four years ago, in 1594, the Court of Wards – the legal body that bought and sold the wardship of minors – was headed by Lord Burghley, Robert Cecil's father. In blunt terms, Agnes had been sold to the Norths by Burghley, presumably for profit, using Humphrey's money. None of this explained how anyone involved in the girl's murder had gained access to Sophia's cipher, nor the meaning of the cryptic verses, but the nearness of the connection makes her deeply uneasy. She can no longer claim that Agnes Lovell was nothing to do with her. She wonders how much of this Cecil knows or guesses. He was right to upbraid her for the utter recklessness of riding to Whitehall and Burghley House last night. Her assailant did not come upon her by chance; she was obviously followed, meaning that someone must have watched her leave Broad Street. She darts a quick glance at the window.

Why, though? This is the question she can't fathom. Why

anyone would want Agnes dead, and why they would want to implicate Sophia.

'Were these loans made privately?' she asks Hilary, tapping a finger on the open ledger. 'I mean, did I inherit them, or the business?' If the loans were made through Humphrey's company, they would now belong to its new owner.

'You did, madam,' Hilary says warily. 'The business accounts were separate, the master was very particular about that.'

Sophia frowns down at the page, considering. 'So, in theory, I could call in this sum from North?'

The steward inhales sharply through her nose. 'In theory. I wouldn't advise it.'

'Why not?'

'Sir Thomas is a difficult man, and well connected. And if word spreads that you are in the business of calling in old debts, you will turn a lot of powerful people against you.'

Sophia waves a hand, makes a pffft noise of dismissal, but Hilary folds her arms and stares her down.

'Madam. You profess to care nothing for the good opinion of society, and you can afford to take that stance, up to a point, because you are the widow of a respected man, and wealthy. But . . .' She hesitates, weighing whether she is permitted to speak so frankly to her mistress.

'Go on,' Sophia says, an edge to her voice.

'You are one woman alone. You do not have connections you can call upon. You have enemies. It would not be in your interest to make more.'

'You think I care a fig what Thomas North might say about me?' Sophia speaks hotly, because she knows Hilary is right.

The steward tilts her chin towards the ledger. 'There are people weightier than Thomas North listed in there. If they think you are coming for them, they have an arsenal of weapons at their disposal to deploy against you. Or anyone connected with you.' She levels a meaningful look at her mistress, and Sophia pictures Tobie, chained up in a dark cell.

'I have connections,' she says, but hears her own lack of conviction. Robert Cecil is not her friend; he would not support her if she were in trouble, the way Walsingham would have done. There is only one person of influence in London that Sophia could call on *in extremis*, but it is a long time since they have seen one another; she is no longer sure how she would be received.

'Ask yourself, madam, if gaining three thousand pounds you knew nothing about until this evening would be worth the ill feeling you would stir up as a result. People looking to discredit you. Making enquiries about you. Or do you harm in other ways. And after what occurred last night—' She breaks off and drops her gaze.

'Last night? How do you mean?'

'You have a bruise on your face.' Hilary indicates on her cheek. 'There were spots of blood on the sleeve of your gown.' She holds up a hand before Sophia can articulate an excuse. 'I do not presume to tell you your business, Mistress de Wolfe. I merely point out that if you knowingly put yourself in harm's way, you provide opportunity to those who would find it convenient for you to meet with an accident.'

Lest they be next to die.

Sophia glances at the ledgers. Hilary is right; it would indeed cause ripples through London and the royal court if word spread that Sophia was calling in Humphrey's loans, and if there are people more powerful than Thomas North listed in those columns of figures, they may be inclined to try and stop her by any means. Sophia is well aware that the man who ambushed her in the Strand – she assumes it was a man – could easily have stuck a knife in her if he had wished to, and made it look like a robbery; next time she may not escape so lightly.

'Is there anything else you need here?' Hilary indicates the books.

'Not for now.' Sophia pulls her belt tight at the waist. 'Better lock them away.'

'I always do, madam,' Hilary says, gathering the ledgers. 'There are people who would like nothing more than to see these destroyed.'

Before Sophia heads south to meet Leila and the boy, she decides it's time to pay a visit to the North house. Her principal aim is to see if she can find a way to talk to this Grace mentioned in Agnes's letters, who was clearly party to her relationship with Tobie and might be able to tell her something useful. Her pretext, she decides, will be interceding with Sir Thomas North for Tobie. She intends to remind him of his erstwhile friendship with Humphrey, and in doing so allude to the fact that she knows about his unpaid debt. If Sir Thomas is an intelligent man with a view to his own interests, he will understand the deal she is proposing, and there will be no need for anything as crude as a legal threat. She knows what Hilary would have to say about this course of action, so she makes sure to tell her steward that she is going to see Leila.

She considers sending the stable lad to find Ben at the Saracen's Head, but she doesn't want to delay, and she is conscious of having kept him from the tavern for most of the previous day. Ordinarily she might have set out for Southwark alone, but the bruise on her cheek and the ache in her shoulder are present reminders of last night's encounter, so she asks Lina to fetch Mick. He comes straight from chopping wood, brushing sawdust from his heavy leather gauntlets, and if he is surprised by the request to accompany his mistress with a stout stick at his side, he makes no complaint, and she is relieved to see he rides competently enough. Her black mare, Nyx, usually so even-tempered, seems skittish today, dancing sideways and tossing her head at any movement in the corner of her eye; evidently it is not only Sophia who is feeling unsettled by the events of the previous night.

As they ride along Moorgate, Sophia glances sidelong at Mick and wonders if she ought to make more effort at conversation; not for the first time, she wishes she had Humphrey's gift for chatting easily with all members of the household staff without ever sounding condescending. She knows very little about Mick, she realises; he is one of the few household servants who has not been around since Humphrey's time, though he came recommended: some relative of the cook's, she thinks. Hilary had seemed satisfied. She asks him where he's from and he says Hertfordshire, and since she has nothing to offer on that county, they lapse into silence again. She is secretly grateful; it gives her a chance to order her thoughts.

She leaves him with the horses at the Starre Tavern on Smithfield without telling him her destination, only that she will be back shortly. The North residence is well guarded by armed men; she supposes it would be, if resentful veterans of the Irish wars are likely to hang around the gates throwing buckets of pig's blood and threatening retribution. She states her name and her business; after a cold wait, she is informed by a servant that Sir Thomas is away from home this morning, but that Lady North will see her. This surprises her; she wonders what interest Judith North would have in her, but she is not about to turn down the opportunity: the lady of the house is more likely than her husband to have an idea of Agnes's comings and goings, and to point her in the direction of the nurse.

As she is led through the entrance hall and along a panelled corridor, she notes details of the North residence the way she learned to in Walsingham's service: the quality of the carpets and furnishings, their provenance and state of repair, and what that tells her about the family's circumstances. It appears to her that, though the Norths like to fill their home with fine things, many of them could do with mending or replacing. Where is Sir Thomas's forty pounds a year pension going, then? Paying off his debts, perhaps, although not the one to Humphrey, which he presumably thinks forgotten. No wonder they were so eager to annexe Agnes Lovell's estate.

She is shown into a small receiving room furnished with wall hangings (fraying at the edges) and immediately sees where a portion of Thomas North's money has gone: his wife is wearing it. Although she is clothed in mourning dress, her bodice, skirt, sleeves and hood are exquisitely tailored in black velvet and taffeta, and sewn over with tiny seed pearls. Lady North is tall and reed-thin; her face remains hidden behind her veil, and the only part that is visible are her hands, which are surprisingly coarse for a noble lady. Evidently she has a condition that leaves her skin dry, red and flaky, like a washerwoman's, and as she gestures Sophia to a seat, she scratches absently at the inflamed patches. Sophia tries not to look; it sets her teeth on edge.

'This is most irregular, Mistress de Wolfe, for you to call uninvited. Particularly as we are a house in mourning.'

Her voice is cultured but affectless; it's hard to read anything from it.

'Forgive me, my lady. I wanted to offer you my condolences in person. I met your husband yesterday and there is a matter I wished to discuss with him.'

'He's not here. You can talk to me. Would you like wine?'

'It's a little early.'

'As you wish. I've been curious to make your acquaintance, as it happens. I've heard a lot about you.'

None of it good, Sophia is sure. 'I believe we have a friend in common,' she says. 'Leila Humeya.'

Lady North makes a small noise that conveys shock or outrage. Sophia immediately regrets her words; Leila would be furious to think she had betrayed a confidence. But Lady North pushes back her veil and stares at Sophia, her expression softening as she realises.

'Ah,' she says, nodding slowly. 'So you had the same trouble.'

Sophia looks at her with polite puzzlement and Lady North leans in confidentially.

'Children,' she whispers.

'Oh – yes. Exactly.' Sophia sees the sympathy in the woman's eyes, her need to confide in someone she hopes will understand. Judith North is a few years older than herself, she guesses, not yet forty but not far off; the hourglass is running out for her. She is not an unattractive woman, but her skin condition creeps up the side of her neck under her ruff, red and angry, and her face is drawn with grief, her eyes puffy and shadowed.

'Tell me,' Lady North says, in the same low whisper, 'you had no success with Leila's tinctures?'

'Sadly, no. But then my husband died, so who is to say what might have happened?'

'How long did you try?'

'We were married six years.'

Lady North nods again. 'It's a hard burden, is it not? To be barren. I have been married near twelve years now. And as my husband likes to point out, it cannot be his fault, since he has two grown children from his first wife.' Her mouth twists. 'I try to have faith in Leila's methods, because what else have I? Sir Thomas hoped for a bigger family. That's why he was so willing to take Agnes in after she was left orphaned.'

Sophia would like to point out that Thomas North did not take Agnes in as an act of charity, rather he bought her in order to profit from her lands, but she bites her tongue. She wonders if Lady North has genuinely persuaded herself that her husband acted out of altruism and a fondness for children.

'Her death must be a hard blow for you all,' she says. 'I can't imagine.'

'No, you can't. My husband and I – we had hoped she would be our daughter-in-law before too long. And now some lowlife player has cruelly robbed us of that future. I can't bear to think of what she must have suffered.' Her fingers creep up to her neck and rake at the exposed skin.

'Actually, that was the matter I wanted to discuss with your husband,' Sophia says, her sympathy for the woman rapidly diminishing. She sees Lady North's gaze sharpen. 'I have some involvement with the Chamberlain's Men as a patroness of sorts, and I wanted to speak to him on the boy's behalf. He swears he never harmed Agnes, and I thought—'

'Well, of course he says that.' Lady North looks at her as if she is simple. 'But I've seen the letters, Mistress de Wolfe. Agnes was young and very innocent, and that boy was intending to elope with her. Which would be a crime even if he hadn't killed her, since she was pre-contracted to my stepson.'

'Was she? Officially?'

Lady North stiffens. 'It wanted only the queen's blessing, and Her Majesty likes to withhold her favours. But it was generally understood that Agnes would marry Edmund once she came of age. We surmise that she lost her nerve about running away, and when she told the boy, he killed her in a fit of rage. If he couldn't have her, no one would. He as good as says so in his letters.'

'But – how was Agnes able to arrange a tryst with this player boy?' Sophia asks, sensing that Lady North is keen to end the conversation. 'Does she not have a chaperone?'

'She had a nurse.' Lady North makes a conscious effort to clasp her hands in her lap. 'Grace Parry – we've dismissed her. The woman had been Agnes's nurse since she was an infant and out of charity my husband took her into our household when Agnes became his ward. The girl was only nine and he thought it would make her less homesick. But Grace Parry indulged her in everything. I blame that woman as much as I blame the boy for allowing things to reach this pass.' Her face closes up. 'So if you've come to beg clemency for him, I'm afraid you are wasting your breath, and you are fortunate my husband is not here – he would give you very short shrift. Sir Thomas is determined to see Agnes's murderer face the full force of the law. But I will tell him you called by.'

Sophia nods; she knows when to make a tactical retreat.

'Please do. Say that I am sorry for the way I spoke to him at the theatre yesterday and I would like to make amends. And please let him know . . .' She pauses, weighing her words. 'Tell him I keep the *Agnus Dei* painting in pride of place at home. Every time I look at it, I think of the friendship he had with my husband, and how valuable that was to them both. Not that one can put a price on friendship, of course.' She gives her a benign smile.

Lady North regards her closely. 'I'll be sure to pass that on.'

Sophia stands, smoothing her skirts. 'I'm sorry to have intruded on your grief, my lady. And I wish you all the luck with—' She places her palm flat on her belly with a knowing smile.

'I hardly need say that is between us, Mistress de Wolfe.' Anxiety flits across her face.

'Naturally. Women in our situation must look out for one another.'

'Thank you. It's done me good to talk to someone in the same boat.'

Lady North gives her a grateful smile as she rings a bell for the maid to show Sophia out. Sophia is not sure what to make of her; she is hard to read. Judith North is a woman in pain, that much is evident, but she is not convinced it's on account of Agnes. If Lady North is sorrowing for anyone, it would appear to be herself. *In any case*, Sophia thinks, *we are not in the same boat. I have a son, and I will not let your husband punish him for a crime he didn't commit.*

EIGHTEEN

The snow is no longer falling as Anthony rides back to the city along the route Vincent Lovell took with his niece only days before. Overhead the sky remains a belligerent grey. The visit has left Anthony unsettled, and his horse appears to pick up on his mood, growing jittery and irritable, starting at shadows, resisting the bit. It's not just his instinctive feeling that Vincent is telling the truth; it's the way his encounter with the girl's uncle has exhumed memories he would rather have left buried. Richard Topcliffe was a name he had hoped to leave in the past; increasingly, now, the years he spent working for that man haunt him with a sick sense of complicity, a hot-cold rush of guilt. It had seemed so simple to him when he was young: Catholics were the enemies of England. The death of one priest on the scaffold was infinitely preferable to the mass slaughter of innocents in the streets that would follow a Spanish invasion, he always told himself. These days, that kind of certainty feels out of reach. Fervour on either side only makes him tired. But there is no denying that both he and Sophia, and all those who worked for Walsingham, have indirectly contributed to the suffering of others, many of whom were guilty of no greater crime than idealism.

Thomas Phelippes, though. He is not a man of unshakeable

faith, unless it is in the systems of the state. In all the years he has known Thomas, Anthony has never had the sense that he is driven by anything other than a commitment to the work for its own sake, a fascination with spycraft and all its complex machinery, the same way a certain type of boy is obsessed with chess stratagems. He has no idea what Thomas actually believes. He was loyal to Walsingham, but Walsingham has been gone almost a decade; did he transfer that loyalty to the Earl of Essex? It would be reassuring to think that a man as intellectually gifted as Thomas Phelippes would have reservations about someone as nakedly self-serving as Essex, but Thomas was always a better reader of ciphers than people, and even a man of genius needs money.

The Saracen's Head is surprisingly busy given it's not yet eleven; or perhaps not so surprising, Anthony thinks, looking around the tap-room at the men pressing close to the wide hearth with its blazing fire: cheaper for many to buy a pot of beer and keep warm here all day than pay for wood to heat their own houses, costs being what they are. Nonetheless, there is still a holiday atmosphere among the regulars; people making the most of the season's cheer before the Epiphany plunges them back to the workaday bleakness of January. The tavern keeper, Dan Hammett, crossing from the serving hatch with a mug in each hand, gives him a nod but doesn't greet him by name; in the Saracen's, you never know what name a man might be using that day. Walsingham had trusted Dan; the Saracen's was a meeting place, a clearing-house, the dove-cote in the yard (which had never had doves) a place to leave and collect letters.

'You after Ben?' Dan murmurs as he passes. His hair is greying now and Anthony notices that he moves more stiffly these days, legacy of a life spent hefting barrels and sacks, but he still has the natural authority that can quiet would-be troublemakers with a look.

He lowers his voice to match. 'Has Thomas Phelippes been in?'

Dan nods to a corner table by the yard door, the coldest spot in the room, where a hunched figure sits with his back to them. Anthony asks for a jug of hot wine and weaves through the bodies to slide into the bench opposite.

Thomas raises his head and lets his eyes flicker over him. 'Munday,' he says, after a moment. 'I thought you'd turn up sooner or later.' There is nothing in his tone to suggest how he feels about this. He turns an empty mug between his hands. 'Strictly, she should not have told you anything.'

'You're going to complain of what others should or shouldn't divulge? You *lied*.' Anthony jabs a forefinger on the table for emphasis. He has known Thomas long enough to know there is no point going at things sideways; he doesn't pick up on hints and allusions.

Thomas lets out a short, cheerless laugh. 'That's what we do, isn't it? That's the job.'

'Not to our comrades.'

Thomas gives him a pitying glance and Anthony remembers his own first mission to Rome, all those years ago: looking around the English College and wondering how many of the other young men were sending back reports on their fellows for Walsingham. He supposes he'll never know.

He tries again. 'Sophia's cipher. You said it was never reused. But it was, wasn't it?'

Thomas studies the backs of his hands for a long moment before briefly glancing up. His gaze swerves away as soon as it meets Anthony's, as it always does.

'There was a lot of pressure,' he says eventually. 'He wanted everything done immediately, it wasn't like Walsingham's way. He had no concept of how these things must be built, a little and a little – he only wanted to get ahead of the Cecils. He had men at the ready and gave me no time to develop new communications.'

'You're talking about the Earl of Essex?'

Thomas nods. 'I have always thought it essential to create new ciphers for each operative – reduces the chances of them becoming familiar to the enemy. I tried to tell the earl this. I kept my own records of those that had proven impenetrable and those that were weaker. I used them to refine my methods. It was my intention one day to create a code that would be impossible to break. But Essex was in a hurry, so I was forced to fall back on existing ciphers.'

'Why Sophia's?'

'It was robust. And she was married by then and no longer active.'

'Her husband was.' Anthony thinks of Humphrey de Wolfe's ships crossing the English Sea, steering their course to all points of the compass carrying couriers posing as merchants, with Burghley's secret correspondence sewn into their clothes.

Thomas frowns. 'That has no bearing. No one among the men Essex used could possibly have known that cipher was previously attached to her.'

As understanding dawns, a wash of relief floods through Anthony so suddenly that he has to sit back and lean against the wall.

'Then – potentially, all this' – he makes a sweeping gesture – 'the dead girl, that note – it has nothing to do with Sophia?' He rubs his jaw as the implications settle. 'But you didn't tell Cecil that. You let him involve her in a murder that could easily put her in danger, when in fact that cipher is not unique to her at all. Why didn't you say something at the outset?'

Thomas motions to him to lower his voice. He keeps his eyes on the table.

'I didn't want to remind Cecil of that blunder with the Earl of Essex,' he says quietly. 'I need this work, Munday. I need to be back in the game – it's the only thing I'm suited for. I didn't want Sir Robert thinking I can't keep track of confidential information. My reputation took a knock after the

Essex business – the queen herself lost faith in my skills. Of course, if I'd been allowed to vet the men Essex was using, or if I'd been able to recruit them myself, it would never have ended in such a botched job, but he wanted all the credit. Then, when it ended badly, he left me to take the blame.'

'The privilege of being an earl, I suppose.' Anthony shifts on the bench. 'Who were they, Essex's men?'

'Double agents. Catholics. At least, men supposedly known and trusted by the English Catholic networks in France and Flanders. I would not, with hindsight, have used them myself.'

'How did he find them?'

'I believe they approached him to offer their services.'

They look at one another. Anthony says nothing; he doesn't need to.

'People used to do the same with Walsingham,' Thomas says, defensive.

'But Walsingham would have tested them thoroughly before entrusting them with information. Where are they now?'

'No idea. It was five years ago. And a lot has happened since.' His face closes for an instant and Anthony remembers his two stints in debtors' prison. Briefly he pities the man, until he remembers that for the sake of his own reputation Thomas has plunged Sophia into an investigation that could make her a target. He thinks of the bruise on her face and wonders if she has already suffered repercussions.

'Holy God, Thomas,' he says softly. 'They were probably Catholic spies all along, congratulating themselves on how readily Essex was duped. And he would have been too sure of himself to doubt his own judgement or have it questioned. So Sophia's cipher could have ended up in the hands of Catholics abroad . . .'

He tails off; it's as if the whole picture has spun away from him and reassembled in an entirely new pattern. If the cipher was not Sophia's alone, then none of this was their problem (it was never your problem in the first place, says the purse-lipped voice in his head). The cipher had been let loose in the world, it could have been circulating among the Catholics of the English Mission for the last five years. The reference to stolen ground was nothing to do with The Theatre or Ireland, but a message to those who had taken the kingdom of England away from its rightful duty to Rome, to a queen who had stolen the throne from her Catholic cousin. And if that were the case, it could only point the finger back in the direction he has just come from – to Vincent Lovell. Vincent, with his close ties to the mission, who stood to inherit an estate with miles of useful coastline, who in all likelihood had never heard of Sophia de Wolfe and her work for Walsingham, but had appropriated a cipher he knew to have been used by those working against the Catholic cause, as a way of thumbing his nose at his enemies. Considered from this angle, it all made far more sense than someone making an oblique reference to Sophia.

He outlines this theory to Thomas, pushing aside the nagging feeling that the only thing wrong with the argument is his conviction, hard to shift, that Vincent Lovell could not have hurt his niece.

Thomas studies the table, a slight crease above his nose, as he calculates the probability.

'The man I gave that cipher to was named Cloudesley. As far as I know, he stayed out in Paris. Cecil has had Vincent Lovell watched since he came out of prison – I can check to see if they've corresponded or have associates in common. But you're right – it seems a likely lead.'

'You need to tell Cecil right away.' Anthony leans in as Thomas instinctively rears back. 'Swallow your pride and get Sophia out of this business. I've just been to see Vincent Lovell – by his own account, he saw Agnes the day she disappeared, and no one appears to have seen her after her visit to Homerton. They'd have more than enough reason to take him in for questioning.' He pictures the red-eyed man by the fire and tries not to think about what that questioning might involve.

'Sophia won't step away until Tobie is released,' Thomas says.

'Then you can kill two birds with one stone. As soon as Cecil knows about this Cloudesley and the cipher, that will tip the weight of evidence towards Vincent Lovell. They can't keep Tobie in gaol for writing a few letters.'

Thomas looks as if he is about to raise a further objection, but thinks better of it and nods. He hasn't touched his wine. 'What do you think, Munday? Do you believe the uncle killed her? I never met the man, but I know he is zealous for the Catholic cause.'

Anthony hesitates. 'He had the motive and the opportunity,' he says carefully. 'I've heard reports that he is a man of quick temper. You and I have both seen over the years how a man's dedication to his faith may eclipse all other bonds and affections. And if he was acquainted with that cipher through the Catholics in Paris – well, then. It all argues against him.' He is aware that he sounds as though he is trying to convince himself.

'The only part that jars,' Thomas says, pulling at his lower lip, 'is why he would make a public display of the killing. If he stands to inherit, he must have known that suspicion would fall first on him. If I were in his position, I would seek to pass the girl's death off as an accident.'

Anthony watches him; there is something chilling in the way Thomas can consider a child's murder as if it were a practical problem to be solved.

'Perhaps he'll explain it under questioning,' he says quietly. 'There's one other thing,' he adds, as Thomas reaches for his hat. 'Vincent told me he gave Agnes a locket as a new year's gift when she visited him on the twenty-seventh. Was there one found with her body?'

Thomas settles the shapeless lump of wool on his head.

'Cecil will know,' he says. 'I believe he had an inventory taken of the girl's effects. Though there's no telling who might have robbed the body before it was reported.'

'Ask him,' Anthony says. The fact of the locket pricks at his conscience. Would Vincent Lovell have given his niece a precious family heirloom mere hours before he beat her to death? If so, would he not have recovered it before leaving her body, lest it point obviously to him – in which case, why did he ask Anthony to enquire after it? He shakes his head, quashing his unease, conscious that, in his eagerness to steer the investigation away from Sophia, he may be plotting an equally misguided course.

'I'll go directly,' Thomas says, sounding reluctant. 'In the meantime, you had better tell Sophia that she should continue her enquiries until she hears otherwise from Master Secretary. If I know her, she won't want to let the business drop now she's started.'

Anthony grimaces. This is what he's afraid of.

NINETEEN

Outside the North house Sophia notices a boy of about Tobie's age leading a grey horse through the rear gate and calls out to him.

'Hey. You work here?'

He nods, surprised.

'Do you know Grace Parry, the nurse?'

He glances around, instantly guarded. 'She's been dismissed.'

'Where would I find her?' She holds up a twopenny piece.

'She said she had a friend in Southwark,' the boy says. His ears protrude from his cap, red with cold, and he pulls it down to cover them. 'I don't know the name.'

Sophia can hazard a guess. She collects Mick from the Starre and sets out towards the bridge.

At Leila's, she asks Moll to make Mick comfortable by the fire – she can't keep leaving him in taverns – while she heads out to the workshop. Here she finds Leila in the company not of the badger-haired child, but a plump woman in her fifties weeping copiously into a well-used handkerchief. The woman looks up as Sophia enters and halts, mid-sob, pressing the cloth to her mouth in an effort to contain her feelings.

'Grace Parry?' Sophia asks.

The woman nods miserably. Leila gives Sophia a brisk

embrace and nods to the visitor.

'Grace was Agnes Lovell's nurse. I suppose you know that. Sir Thomas wants her arrested but as yet they have no evidence. I thought you should hear what she has to say.'

Sophia pulls up a stool opposite the weeping woman and leans forward to her. 'I'm so sorry about Agnes,' she says gently. 'God rest her.'

Grace Parry raises her swollen eyes and nods her thanks. 'Forgive me, mistress – I didn't know where else to come after they threw me out, and when I told Leila my story she said you would want to know. Truthfully, I can't believe any of this is real – only a few days ago it was Christmas, and she seemed so happy – glowing, she was.' The memory prompts a fresh cascade of tears.

Sophia rests a hand on the woman's wrist. 'You can call me Sophia,' she says. 'Begin at the beginning.'

Grace Parry takes a ragged breath, and through another sob, a rush of incoherent words tumbles out. Leila gives Sophia a minute shake of her head, and presses into Grace's hand a beaker with a pleasant herbal steam rising from it. When the nurse has managed a few sips, she wraps her hand around the cup and, staring into the fire, tries again.

'I didn't know Agnes planned to go to her uncle Vincent that day, not until she was already gone. I used to sleep in her chamber, you see, but Sir Thomas put an end to that last year, he said she was too old to have a nurse in with her, as she was almost of age, and she must learn to do without me in preparation for her marriage. Well, that's come home to roost for him, hasn't it, because if I'd been there I could have stopped her leaving.' She bunches the handkerchief in her fist.

'So how did you find out where she'd gone?' Sophia asks.

'I woke and there was a paper under my door,' Grace says. 'This was about the hour of seven, I suppose. Folded inside it was the key to Agnes's room. The note said I was not to worry, she had gone to her uncle in Homerton and would be back before dark. If my lady North should ask after her, I was to say she had taken to her bed with a fever.'

'You knew she was riding around London alone in the snow and you didn't do anything?'

'What could I do?' Grace flares up, roused from her grief. 'I couldn't send anyone after her, they'd all report back to Lady North, and there would have been hell to pay if anyone discovered Agnes had slipped out – the only thing I could do was to stay home and cover for her, and trust she came back safe. I knew Master Vincent would see her home, and she knew the way to his house well enough.'

'But she didn't come back?'

Grace shakes her head and spreads her hands in a gesture of helplessness. 'The Norths say she did not, and I can't argue otherwise, because I didn't see. At noon, one of the kitchen girls brought a tray of food for Agnes. I said I'd take it in to her. So I went into the empty room, ate the meal, and after a quarter hour I locked the door again and stacked the empty dishes outside on the landing. No one in the household cared enough to look in on her, as she knew they would not. But in the afternoon I had one of my headaches. Often worry brings them on, see. I tried to carry on, but it got so bad I thought I might faint, so I went to my bed and I took – God forgive me, I have a tincture from the apothecary that dulls the pain, and it must have been a strong dose, because it knocked me out so I slept right through.'

'Until the next morning?'

'Yes, God forgive me. I woke to a great hammering on my door – the maid had tried to take Agnes some breakfast and, finding no reply and her chamber locked, had gone to my lady North, who kept a spare key. Which, until that moment, I did not know she had,' she adds bitterly. 'So then they thought she had run away, with my help. At first I claimed I knew nothing, but my lady said she would have me whipped until I told them all, so eventually I said if I had to guess she might have gone to her uncle, it being Christmas. I'd burned her note, you see. But in truth I was worried sick – I couldn't think what might have happened to her. At least Master Vincent would be able to say whether she arrived at his or no. I never for a moment believed he might have harmed her. He loved that child better than her own father ever did, for all he was a papist.'

'So that was the morning of the twenty-eighth. Did Lady North inform the constables that Agnes had run away?' Sophia asks. 'Send the hue and cry after her?'

'Not to my knowledge. She said she'd sent household servants out looking. I think she wanted to avoid any scandal – she was waiting for Sir Thomas to return and make the decisions. At that point, they only thought she'd run off, probably with Master Vincent's help.'

'And what did you think, Grace, when you first learned she was missing?'

'I thought . . .' The nurse dips her head and speaks into her substantial bosom. 'Well, I thought she had gone to—'

'To Master Strange?'

'Yes. This was before she was found, you understand. And, God forgive me, I did a terrible thing.'

'What?' Sophia feels herself tense. 'You told them?'

'No – the letters. In all the fluster, I slipped into Agnes's chamber and took her letters from Tobie. I knew where she hid them. And I know I should have destroyed them there and then, but I thought' – she shakes her head – 'they were precious to her, you see, and I thought at some point in the future she would want them to look back on. All those poems. I meant to save them for her. But the next day, after she was found and Sir Thomas returned, he didn't believe that I knew nothing, and he had the servants turn out my chamber. And the letters were discovered, and now Master Strange is taken up for her murder, and I am dismissed, and Sir Thomas says I must have known all along and he will see me arrested as accessory to abduction and murder, so I ran with only the

185

clothes on my back. And I came here because Leila has always been so kind when she came to the North house, and Jo—' she breaks off, glancing up guiltily at Leila.

'Jo carried Agnes's letters to Tobie,' Sophia says flatly.

'The Norths don't know about that,' Leila interjects. 'And Thomas North doesn't know that I attended his wife, and I think it unlikely she would mention it, so for the moment there is nothing to link us.'

Sophia leans forward, elbows on her knees, and steeples her fingers. Grace is right: if she had destroyed those letters before Thomas North found them, Tobie would not now be in prison, but she can't allow herself to dwell on that.

'They think Agnes was left at The Theatre sometime during the night of the twenty-eighth. If she left before seven on the morning of the twenty-seventh, that means there is a space of thirty-six hours or more between her leaving the North house and her body being placed in the trench.'

Grace affirms this with a hiccuping sob.

Sophia taps her nails against her teeth. 'The Norths says she never returned on the twenty-seventh. What does her uncle say?'

'Vincent Lovell told the coroner he brought her back almost to the door that afternoon. If only I hadn't taken that draught, I would have been there to see, may God—'

'Could she have gone anywhere else?' Sophia cuts in, before Grace can ask God's forgiveness for the thousandth time (her own capacity for forgiveness is reaching its limit). 'After her uncle left her, if she thought she wouldn't be missed till evening, might she have taken advantage of the fact to go on somewhere?'

'I suppose she could have gone to Master Tobie,' Grace says, looking miserably into the flames. 'If she did, I dare say they'll have that out of him in prison, one way or another.'

Sophia digs her nails into her palms, even though she had expected this answer.

'Or else I suppose she could have gone to Essex House,' Grace adds.

'What?' Sophia glances up, exchanges a look with Leila, who shakes her head and makes a blank face. 'You think she would have gone to the Earl of Essex? How? *Why?*'

Grace turns slowly with a sad half-smile. 'Not the earl. The countess.'

Sophia can't order her thoughts fast enough to settle on the right question.

'They were friends,' Grace explains, taking pity on her confusion. 'That is to say, my lady Essex had made a pet of Agnes as a friend to her daughter Lizzie. They were of an age.'

'So – Agnes had been spending time at Essex House? Did the Norths know?'

'Oh yes.' Grace twists her mouth. 'They encouraged it. Couldn't believe their luck, especially Lady North – that woman is obsessed with rank, and her father only a minor gentleman with no fortune from somewhere upcountry. She was delighted that a countess should deign to take notice of their ward. Sir Thomas, too – you know his elder brother had all the money from their father, Thomas was left with near to nothing and has to go cap in hand to Lord North all the time. He thought if he could get close to the Earl of Essex through Agnes, he'd be a short step away from the queen herself.'

'But why?' Sophia asks. 'Why did the countess take an interest in Agnes in the first place?'

'You'd have to ask her,' Grace says, her round shoulders slumping again.

'I will,' Sophia says, half to herself.

'Careful,' Leila murmurs. Their eyes meet. Frances, Countess of Essex, is known to both of them. She was born plain Frances Walsingham, daughter to the queen's master intelligencer; at seventeen she married Sir Philip Sidney, England's brightest young poet – she had her eldest daughter, Lizzie, by him, though he died before he could see the child, of an infected wound taken while fighting in the Low Countries. That was when Sophia first met her. She had liked Frances then; one of the few women she knew with an education to match her own, and a remarkably shrewd grasp of statecraft and intelligencing from observing her father at work. But in 1590, in the same month her father died, she had married Robert Devereux, the young Earl of Essex, a marriage made without the queen's permission and briefly incurring Her Majesty's wrath. Sophia too had married and, after Walsingham's death, her circle no longer overlapped with that of the new countess, though Sophia has a strong suspicion that Robert Devereux's name would appear in Humphrey's ledgers if she asked Hilary to look. Frances was the one person close enough to the queen that Sophia might have petitioned her on Tobie's behalf, if it came to it. To find that the countess is already entangled with Agnes Lovell, however tangentially, comes as a shock. Especially after what Anthony has told her about Thomas Phelippes's abortive attempt at running agents for the earl. Here is the connection Sophia had claimed did not exist.

She understands, too, why Leila is urging caution: Essex is the queen's darling, about to embark on a glorious campaign to put down the Irish rebels for good and for all. The suggestion that he might have anything to do with a murdered girl is unlikely to end favourably for the person doing the suggesting. And yet, Sophia thinks – what if someone at Essex House could confirm Agnes's movements for the twenty-seventh, if their word could prove definitively that she could not have been with Tobie? The testimony of a Devereux, or a member of their household, would trump the accusations of a North. But if the girl had been to Essex House that day, would they be willing to draw attention to the fact?

'I believe it was the earl who suggested it,' Grace says suddenly, and it takes Sophia a moment to realise she is answering the previous question. 'Lady Essex's interest in Agnes, I mean. Sir Thomas had mentioned to the earl that

Agnes lacked company her own age, and the next thing we knew, my lady North received a letter inviting Agnes to Essex House, with a view that she might become a suitable companion for the countess's daughter.'

'Did you go with her?'

'No.' Grace almost laughs. 'They didn't want her old nurse tagging along. I think Lady North was hoping for an invitation herself, but they didn't ask her either.'

So no independent chaperone, Sophia thinks.

'How long were you Agnes's nurse?'

'Since the day she was born. Oh, she was a bonny baby, you should have seen her smile—' Grace subsides again, blowing her nose copiously into her sodden cloth. Leila moves in discreetly to press a clean one into her hand.

'I'm surprised Thomas North didn't provide Agnes with a nurse from his own household when she came to him,' Sophia says, remembering what Lady North had said about her husband's charity in retaining Grace.

'Oh, he tried, believe me.' Grace snaps her head up, indignant. 'Sir John, Agnes's father, stipulated in his will that I was to stay with her until she came of age – a rare gesture of kindness on his part, although I think even then he guessed the Norths would not be a loving family to her and she would need someone to be a comfort. Sir Thomas disliked this idea, you may imagine, and as soon as he took the wardship he gave me half a year's wages and told me I was no longer needed. Oh, it was awful. I thought of going to law, though what chance did I have against the Norths? But Agnes took matters into her own hands. She refused to eat or speak until I was restored to her.'

'That was brave, for a girl of – what was she, nine?'

'Nine years old,' Grace confirms proudly. 'They thought at first it was a child's piece of foolishness. But they reckoned without Agnes's determination. She made herself so ill, Sir Thomas feared losing his prize altogether, so I was recalled. They made clear I was there on sufferance, though. I always felt they were watching me for the slightest misstep, so they could throw me out.'

'And yet, despite that, you encouraged Agnes in her correspondence with Tobie Strange?'

'Did I not just tell you about Agnes's strength of will?' Grace rounds on her. 'She'd set her heart on that boy, and she'd have found a way to pursue it with my help or without. I reasoned if she felt able to confide in me, I'd at least be party to her plans and could stop things going too far. But I failed in that.'

'You knew she meant to run away with Tobie?'

'I knew they talked of it. I thought he'd have more sense, he seemed a level-headed lad. Besides, they had no money. Sir Thomas kept every penny of the income from Agnes's lands, that he was supposedly managing for her. She had to beg Lady North if she wanted so much as new stockings without holes.'

'Was that why she went to her uncle?' Sophia asks. 'To ask for money to elope?'

'She didn't say. She'd have known Vincent Lovell had no spare money – what he did have, though, was contacts. Ways to arrange passage across the sea.'

Sophia feels her eyes widen; the prospect of Tobie taking off to France with no way to keep track of him stops her breath in her throat, so that it takes a moment to remember this is not going to happen; Tobie is locked up, and Agnes is dead.

'The Countess of Essex has money, though,' Grace adds with a sniff.

'You think Agnes would have asked the countess to help her elope?' Sophia remembers Frances as wilful, fixed of purpose when she had set her sights on a course, but not foolhardy. Especially after her own illicit marriage had brought a temporary loss of the queen's favour – would she risk that again for a young girl and a player?

'I agree it sounds unlikely,' the nurse says, as if following her thoughts. 'I only mention it because Agnes told me the Countess of Essex was not in favour of the forced marriage with Edmund North. Agnes claimed the countess had promised to help her find a way out.'

Grace lapses into a silence punctuated by small hiccups; Sophia clasps her hands together, questions chasing through her mind. She wonders what motive could have prompted Frances Sidney – Lady Essex, as she must now call her – to offer her assistance in the business of Agnes Lovell's marriage. It would not have been to benefit Tobie, that much is certain. The only way to find out is to ask her.

Sophia stands and brushes down her skirts. She has learned from her experience with Cecil the night before that you do not simply turn up on the doorstep of a noble house and expect to be welcomed. On the other hand, if she writes to Frances, as decorum demands, that will give the countess time to prepare an excuse. She doesn't really have a choice.

She rests a hand on Grace Parry's shoulder; small comfort, she knows, but the nurse reaches up and presses her own hand over Sophia's with a watery smile. Sophia tries to think of something helpful to say, but the moment is broken by a commotion outside; the workshop door is flung open and a girl of about ten with a smudged face and windblown hair appears, her eyes wide.

'Mistress Leila! You have to come right away.'

Leila wipes her hands on her apron; Sophia admires the speed and sureness with which her friend reaches for the leather bag containing the tools of her trade. She is well used to the sudden emergencies that can befall the women of the Southwark stews: usually a miscarriage or a client too handy with his fists.

'Which house?' Leila asks.

The child shakes her head, hopping from foot to foot. 'It's Badger. We found him.'

TWENTY

'I had the street children out looking for Badger since last evening,' Leila calls over her shoulder as she runs sure-footed across icy ground towards the quays, the little girl pulling her by the hand. 'Since Jo gave me your message. When they said he was not to be found in his usual haunts, I began to have misgivings, but I told myself that boy comes and goes according to his own rules, he knows how to look out for himself . . .' Her voice trails off as she quickens her pace. From the river Sophia can hear the muted thud and splash of men with mattocks breaking up ice around the jetties.

The small body is laid face down on a piece of sacking on the cobbled quayside outside the row of brothels facing the river. The moisture on his clothes has begun to refreeze, glazing him with a cracked pattern. He is wearing one boot, too big for him, the other lost to the water, and his skin has a blue tinge. Leila pauses and breathes in sharply; Sophia sees her eyes glisten, before she crouches by the body and presses the back of two fingers to the boy's neck. A boatman stands over him, leaning on his oar, and a little way off, the girl who fetched them has been joined by a smaller girl. They hold on to one another, staring and sniffing.

'Well, he didn't drown,' Leila says briskly.

The boatman looks unimpressed. 'Anyone who knows the river could have told you that. It was only chance I found him, poor little bastard – the ice had trapped him up against the landing stage by the Elephant. Otherwise he'd have been taken downriver with the tide, never seen again.'

Which presumably was the intention of whoever threw him in, Sophia thinks. Leila turns the body over; even frozen, the child looks insubstantial, like a fledgling fallen from its nest. There is frost on his eyelashes.

'There you go,' she says, indicating. Sophia nods; she has already noted it. On the front of the boy's ragged jacket, a neat round bloodstain below his left ribs. A short-bladed knife, she guesses, such as every man in Southwark might carry. She lowers her eyes and turns away.

'Did you know him?' she calls to the shivering children. They nod mutely, clutching one another's hands. 'When did you see him last?'

She takes two pennies from her purse and lays them in her palm as inducements.

'Yesterday,' says the older of the girls, reaching out with frostbitten fingers. 'We went to the kitchens at the Unicorn, the cook sometimes gives us leftovers after the supper rush. Badger was there. He was showing off – said he was going to make a great fortune from some gentlemen with a jewel he'd got from a murderer.'

'He said that? Those exact words?'

The child nods again. 'He showed it to us, he kept it wrapped in a cloth inside his belt.'

'But he wouldn't let us touch it,' pipes up the smaller girl. 'He said it would bring us bad luck, as he found it in the grave of a dead girl and it was dropped by her killer.'

It certainly brought Badger bad luck, Sophia thinks, and no wonder, if he was shouting that story around the inns of Bankside. She has an urge to wrap her fur-lined cloak around the girls, bareheaded in this weather. 'Did he say where the grave was?'

'Over north,' the bigger girl says, jerking her chin towards the river.

Sophia senses that this is the best she is going to get. 'What about these men who wanted to buy the jewel?' she asks. 'Do you know where he met them?'

The little one points behind her, to the Unicorn. 'He was showing it around in there, and one of the girls told him she knew a man who'd pay good money for it. She said to come back at night when she'd had a chance to send him a message.'

'Badger said she wanted to take the jewel for safekeeping but he wouldn't let her,' says the elder. 'He boasted that he was too clever to be tricked like that.'

'He promised when he had the money he'd take us for a fine supper,' adds the small girl. Her tone is blank and empty; neither child is crying. Sophia supposes that death – violent or otherwise – is so familiar to a street child in Southwark that it loses its power to shock.

'You didn't get a look at the men he was meeting, I suppose?' she asks, though this would be too much to hope for.

The older girl shakes her head. 'We took our bread and went to the stables. The head ostler lets us sleep in the stalls when it snows. Don't say I told you that – he might get in trouble.'

'You have my word.' Sophia gives the girls another penny each and turns to Leila, lowering her voice. 'I need to speak to this woman at the Unicorn.'

Leila nods. 'I can arrange that.' To the boatman, who is still loitering, half-dismayed, half-curious, she says: 'Help me carry him, will you? We'll take him to the inn, I'll clean him up. They can send one of their kitchen boys to fetch the constable, get it reported.'

The boatman lifts the slight, stiff body and carries it through the snow towards the yard of the Unicorn, Leila and Sophia following behind. As an afterthought, she turns back; taking off her fine woollen scarf, she crouches to wrap it gently around the necks of the two staring children. They are so small it encircles both of them with fabric to spare. 'Don't mention the jewel or the murderer to anyone else, will you?' she murmurs, trying to put a smile into her words so as not to frighten them, in case the sight of their friend's corpse hasn't already taught them the value of silence.

She waits by the fire in the tap-room of the Unicorn, feeling increasingly self-conscious. Though this is one of the more up-market establishments on Bankside, with all its goods priced to match, it is nevertheless indisputably a brothel; as such an unaccompanied gentlewoman is a rare sight, and one that attracts a good deal of attention from the male clientele, who have either arrived early in preparation for a day of debauchery or staggered downstairs to refuel after a night of it. Mick, her handyman, having belatedly caught up with them at the inn, sits at a neighbouring table and stares around him in slack-jawed amazement; this is proving quite a change from his usual working day, but he seems to be taking it in his stride.

The Unicorn's formidable madam keeps Leila on a retainer to tend to her girls, has done for years, and there is a specially appointed room in the basement for her to treat her patients. This is where they have taken the boy's body to await the constables, though Leila has already expressed scepticism about how much concern the authorities will show for the murder of a homeless child. Sophia pulls her cloak tighter despite the warmth and thinks of those two little girls sleeping in the stable with the horses. No doubt they'll sell her scarf to buy food. There must be more that could be done for those children and others like them, she thinks, before they end up like the girls upstairs, and she remembers the three thousand pounds that Sir Thomas North took from Humphrey to buy Agnes Lovell. You could build a whole school to feed and clothe them with that money, which rightly is owed to her.

She is pondering on this when one of the maidservants pops her head around the door to call her upstairs.

Sophia is led to a lavishly furnished and overheated bedroom that, in defiance of the heavy perfumes that hang in the air, smells thickly of sex; she has an urge to fling the casement open and let in a sweep of clean, icy air. She resists, for the sake of the slight young woman who sits on the edge of the bed wearing no more than an undershift, her bare arms wrapped around her knees. Leila stands beside her, a hand on the girl's shoulder.

'This is Jen,' she says, with a curt nod. 'Jen, this is Mistress de Wolfe. Tell her what you told me.'

The girl raises plaintive eyes, ringed with purple shadows. She has a delicate beauty, not yet worn down by her trade; clear skin so white you can see the tracery of blue veins at her temple. She can't be out of her teens.

'I never knew they'd kill him,' she says. Her voice sounds hollow; like the children on the quayside, she looks too jaded to cry, but she is clearly distressed. 'I just thought to make some money. I meant for it to help Badger too. He was a good boy, we were all fond of him, cheeky little fucker.' She stares at her narrow naked feet, pressing one on top of the other.

'Start from the beginning,' Sophia says gently. 'You saw Badger with a brooch, is that right?'

Jen nods miserably. 'In the afternoon, it must have been. He hangs about the tap-room sometimes, does tricks with cards or juggles cups, the men give him a coin if they're feeling generous. Yesterday he was flashing this thing about, boasting that he'd found it, inviting the men to bid for it. I told him to watch himself or he'd be hanged for a thief.' She bites her lip. 'His answer was that he didn't rob it, he found it in the grave of a dead girl. I thought he was making up one of his stories. So I asked him for a closer look. He gave a great bow and presented it to me like I was a princess and he my suitor.'

196

She gives a tight little laugh and her voice trembles.

'And you recognised the design?' Sophia prompts.

'It was a crest. Red band across with three red circles above. Picked out in red and white stones. I knew I'd seen it before. Not the brooch, but the device.'

'Where?'

There is a long pause. The girl flicks a glance at Leila, who gives a firm nod.

'On the Essex arms,' Jen says to the floor.

Sophia feels a shot of cold run through her like ice water. 'To be clear,' she says, hoping the girl has made a mistake, 'you mean the Earl of Essex's coat of arms? How would you know?'

She hadn't intended to sound condescending, but Jen must have taken it that way, because she looks up at Sophia with a flash of hauteur. 'Because he's been here,' she says, as if the question is self-evidently foolish. 'With his two friends. They come in disguise, that's part of the game, but he can't help telling you who he is, he wants to be admired, even by whores. And his servants all have that badge sewn on their jackets, under their cloaks.'

Sophia digests this. The shock is not that the Earl of Essex uses brothels, nor that he is indiscreet about it, but hearing his name in this context, right after Grace Parry's revelation that Agnes Lovell had been visiting the earl's wife. Never trust coincidences, Walsingham used to say.

'You said you saw a chance to make some money?' she prompts.

Jen drops her gaze again. 'I never thought there would be harm in it. I told Badger to put the brooch away, I knew a man who would pay double what any of those curs downstairs would offer, if he'd hold off and let me negotiate. He was interested – he likes a good deal, Badger, likes to haggle. *Liked*,' she adds, clenching her jaw. 'So I sent one of the stable boys to Essex House with a message.'

'You wrote to him?' Sophia can't keep the surprise from her voice.

Jen draws herself up, ruffled. 'What? I know my letters – my pa taught me when I was small, so I could help him in the shop. Before he died.'

'I'm sorry, I didn't mean – what did the note say?' Sophia doesn't bother to ask how a girl from a Southwark stew can get a message direct to the Earl of Essex; she supposes there are channels.

'I told his lordship he'd left something of value that might reflect badly on him if it came to light, but for a finder's fee he could have it back tonight. I said ten o'clock on the fore-shore by the Barge House stairs.'

'You put all that in the note?' Sophia tries to hide her impatience, but really. She has always thought of the Southwark girls as canny, but this one appears to have given no thought to the risks of blackmailing a powerful man.

'I meant to go with Badger. I knew the earl would be well disposed to me.' She preens a little. 'He has been with me more than once. He has a special name for me.'

And one for all the girls at every other house he visits, Sophia thinks. 'You imagined the earl would come himself?'

Jen looks indignant. 'Well, yes. Because I signed it with my special pet name. I thought he would be grateful that I had recognised the brooch before anyone else spotted it and started wondering how it came to be in a dead girl's grave.' She wraps her arms tighter around herself. 'But in the event I couldn't go, I had to work. There was a new client particularly wanted me, and Madam Rosa wouldn't let me pass him to one of the others. So Badger went alone.'

'And in the event, whoever met him there considered it a deal cheaper to stick a knife in him and throw him in the river so he couldn't tell any more tales about girls and graves,' Leila says.

At the reproach in her voice, Jen's lip quivers and a shaky sob escapes.

'I never thought—'

'No,' says Leila, 'you didn't.'

'You should thank Madam Rosa,' Sophia says. 'You'd probably be in the river with him if not for your client.' She sees Jen's face turn even whiter and wonders if Essex will send someone back to dispatch her, and how that might be prevented. She softens her tone. 'Thank you for telling me this, Jen. Perhaps you could go out of London for a while, until it all blows over.'

'But how would I live? I'll lose my place here.' The girl's eyes grow wide with fright.

Sophia exchanges a glance with Leila. 'I'm sure something can be arranged.'

She leans back against the door, trying to order her thoughts. This is more than she bargained for: the Earl of Essex, implicated in the murder of both Badger and Agnes Lovell. It's definitely time she visited the woman she still thinks of as Frances Sidney.

'Sophia?' Leila is looking at her with concern.

She blinks herself back to the present, forces a smile, and reaches for her purse. 'For your pains,' she says to Jen, passing her a silver tester. 'Do not speak to anyone else of this brooch, much less mention the earl, do you understand? Leila will make sure you are safe.'

Downstairs, at the tap-room door, Leila lays a hand on Sophia's arm. 'I know a woman out Dulwich way who would take her in, if she'll agree. I can't force her to go, though. Madam Rosa will put another girl in her room before the door's closed behind her, and Jen knows that.'

'Do what you can. Let me know what it costs. And for Badger's burial, too.'

'Sophia.' Leila's face is grave. 'Have you thought about what you're doing here? The Earl of Essex – you know as well as I do that if he is behind this, there's no prospect of justice. They won't touch him for the murder of a street boy.'

'Not for Badger, maybe,' Sophia says, 'but if he had the boy killed, it's because he was involved in the death of Agnes Lovell, and the authorities might stir themselves for her. Her guardian's brother is on the Privy Council.'

Leila twists her mouth, unconvinced. 'Even so – do you really want to get involved? Men like Essex will always wriggle past the law, and all you will achieve is to make a powerful enemy, which you cannot afford to do. Humphrey's money will only protect you so far.'

'Leila, my son is in prison accused of this girl's murder.' Without meaning to, she has raised her voice; she casts a glance around the tap-room but no one appears to be listening. Mick is still sitting at his table, staring blankly ahead, seemingly baffled into passivity by the unexpected turn his day has taken. She drops to a whisper. 'I will do whatever it takes to prove he could not have done it. You'd do the same for Jo. Speaking of which – what is the time? I need to get to the Clink.'

'The bells just struck the half hour – you'll be fine. I'll stay and lay out Badger's body – the least he deserves is a kind touch at the last.' She gives Sophia a brisk embrace. 'Think on what I said. You will be no use to Tobie if you end up in the river with a blade in your heart.'

Next to die, Sophia thinks, and shivers. Briefly she considers confiding in Leila about the previous night's attack, but she knows what the response will be. 'If Grace Parry remembers anything else, send word to me. Mick – fetch the horses,' she calls, and sees her servant jolt his attention back to her with surprise, as if he had forgotten why he was there.

'*Vaya con Dios*,' Leila says in a low voice, squeezing her hand as she leaves, and Sophia shoots her a sharp glance. If Leila is invoking God, it's a sign she is seriously worried.

TWENTY-ONE

Anthony stays at the Saracen's long enough to see Thomas Phelippes mount and ride away; he doesn't entirely trust the cryptographer to prioritise admitting his mistakes to Robert Cecil, but the sooner he shares the information about Sophia's cipher, the sooner she can be relieved of the responsibility Cecil has wrongly thrust upon her, with all its attendant dangers. Once Thomas has left, Anthony rides to Broad Street; he is already hopelessly late for rehearsals, and his news is too pressing to wait until his appointed hour with Sophia this afternoon.

At the de Wolfe house, her steward tells him tersely that her mistress left early for Southwark; he might find her at the house of Leila Humeya or at the Clink prison, where she is meeting a lawyer at noon. She gives this information grudgingly; Anthony knows Hilary doesn't approve of him, though he thinks this is less to do with his personal qualities than the fact that his friendship with Sophia attracts rumours that do nothing to help her standing among the city wives. This being so, he is always careful to treat the steward with the utmost courtesy; he makes a small bow before setting out again, though the look she gives him in response suggests she thinks he is being facetious.

If he hurries across the river, he can catch her at the Clink. He tries not to think about the wisdom of returning to the prison after last night's warning, but if he is in time, he will not have to step inside.

In the Clink gatehouse, he sees a well-dressed man in his fifties wearing a lawyer's coif under his fur hat, stamping his feet against the cold and casting his gaze around impatiently.

'Are you waiting for Mistress de Wolfe?' Anthony asks.

The lawyer regards him with understandable wariness from beneath black brows that contrast startlingly with his neat silver beard. 'And you are?'

'Munday. I'm an associate of hers. I write for the Admiral's Men,' he adds, as if this would improve his standing with the man.

The lawyer appears unmoved. 'I don't get to the theatre as often as I'd like. Brother Timothy Whyte,' he says, offering a hand. The brows knit together a fraction. 'I was under the impression this boy was a member of the Chamberlain's Men?'

'Yes, but he used to be one of ours,' Anthony says, improvising. 'We wanted to offer our support.'

'The young man is fortunate to have so many friends.' Whyte slaps his hands together as he peers into the courtyard, breath clouding around his face. 'I must say, this is not my usual milieu. I'm more accustomed to dealing with export disputes and shipping rights than murder, but Mistress de Wolfe was insistent that I come. It is very good of her to take so much trouble over a minor player.' He watches Anthony as he says this.

He's fishing, Anthony thinks, but he keeps his face a perfect blank. Humphrey's lawyer, then, clearly; he wonders how much the man charges by the hour. 'She is a great supporter of the playing companies,' he says, 'and she believes in the boy's innocence.'

'Let's hope she is not deceived,' Whyte says pointedly, as two horses pull up at the gate, hooves sliding on the icy cobbles. Sophia dismounts lightly, handing the reins to her thick-necked companion.

Anthony feels the same charge in his belly that he always feels on seeing her, however much he tries to suppress it. He has time to notice that she looks shaken, before her gaze lights on him and she stops, surprised.

'Anthony? I didn't expect – has something happened?'

'I wanted to speak to you, that's all.'

'Will it keep? Only I have brought Brother Whyte to see Master Strange and our business is urgent.' Her eyes search his face, and he sees the flicker of fear in them; she is wondering what has caused him to seek her out now rather than waiting until the afternoon.

'Of course. Nothing to worry about.'

She nods, but he can see she is not persuaded. He watches her cross to the inner gate and exchange a few words with the guard; between their hands there is a brief glint of silver and the gate opens smoothly. Sophia turns back to him.

'Come with us. Tobie will like to see a friendly face.'

He demurs; he thinks Tobie will have little interest in anything other than securing his release, and Anthony has not forgotten the warning after his visit the previous day. But she is waiting for him, and if the lawyer's view of the situation is not encouraging, she may need a shoulder to lean on. He is embarrassed for himself even as he pulls his hat low on his brow and follows her through the gate.

They are led up a flight of stairs and along a gallery over-looking the prison's inner courtyard, empty now except for a lone figure sweeping snow from the cobbles in slow, monot-onous strokes. Anthony watches as the man pauses to lean on his broom and wipe sweat from his face, and realises it's the young priest he met yesterday, Father Prior. An idea strikes him; he excuses himself and before anyone can object, he slips away from the others to the nearest staircase and descends to the yard.

The priest has resumed his sweeping; the snow muffles Anthony's steps so that the prisoner doesn't look round as he approaches.

'Prior,' he says softly, when he is a few feet away.

The priest snaps his head up, and Anthony sees a livid bruise swelling over his left eye. As soon as Prior recognises his visitor, his eyes widen in panic and his gaze veers wildly from one side of the yard to the other, to the windows on the upper levels, like a bird trapped in a hall.

'Do you want to get me killed?' the priest hisses, looking past Anthony. 'I told you all I know, for God's sake let me be.' Then his expression changes to a terrible fledgeling hope. 'Or do you bring good news?'

'Not yet,' Anthony says. 'Is this because you talked to me?' He gestures to the man's blackened eye.

'They don't know it was you, only that I was taken to speak to someone in secret,' Prior says, touching a finger gingerly to his brow. 'But they soon will, now that you've come charging in to accost me openly and confirm all their suspicions.'

'I'm sorry,' Anthony says, pulling his hat down further as if that might undo the damage. 'There is one more question I need to ask. Do you know a man named Cloudesley?'

Prior leans heavily on his broom and drops his voice to a whisper. 'I know of him. He's based in Calais, I believe.'

'And does Vincent Lovell know him?'

'Oh yes. Tom Cloudesley organises the transport and passports for priests coming into England from the French ports.'

'So they would have corresponded?'

'I've never seen their letters, but I presume so.'

And there it is, Anthony thinks: the connection with Sophia's cipher. Or rather, not Sophia's, but a cipher repurposed by Phelippes for a double agent in the pay of the Earl of Essex, an agent who went on to use it in correspondence with Vincent Lovell, who later employed it in a note attached to the body of his murdered niece. If Anthony remains less than convinced by Vincent's motives for doing so, he has at least found conclusive proof that the cipher need not point to Sophia, and indeed has a readier explanation. He can't help a small flush of triumph; when Phelippes takes all this to Master Secretary, Cecil will have no choice but to stand Sophia down from the investigation. Presumably, once Vincent Lovell's guilt comes to light, Sir Thomas North can be persuaded to drop any charges against Tobie, and Sophia can resume her comfortable life as a patroness of the theatre. He does not expect her to be grateful to him for protecting her in this way; his reward will be only to know that she is safe.

'Thank you,' he whispers to Prior, turning to leave.

'Wait,' the priest says. 'You haven't forgotten your promise? To speak to someone about removing me from this situation?' His eyes flicker nervously around the galleries again.

'I will,' Anthony says, though he hardly knows where to start. Perhaps Sophia could speak to Cecil, once she knows her debt to Prior. He can feel the priest's eyes on his back as he crosses the courtyard to the door, and unseen other eyes from the windows all around, noting the exchange.

He has no knowledge of where Sophia and the lawyer were taken, so he returns to the gatehouse and skulks with his chin sunk into his collar, hoping not to be recognised. The best part of an hour passes, during which he stamps his feet to keep warm and exchanges banal observations about the weather with the guard while he thinks of all the work he should be doing. He vows to go straight to The Rose once he has informed her that she need not concern herself any longer with the murder.

But on her return, her face is grimmer than when she went in. The lawyer Whyte clasps her hands and murmurs something placatory; she nods and bids him farewell. When they are left alone outside the gate, she turns to Anthony and he sees the strain in her face. There are blue shadows under her eyes; she looks as if she hasn't slept.

'Bad news?' he asks. 'Do you need a drink?'

She shakes her head. 'Let's walk. I need clean air after that place.'

They walk west away from the bridge, on to the quay in front of the Bankside inns. A bitter wind knifes off the river into their faces; when he glances at Sophia, he can't tell if it's distress or cold bringing tears to her eyes.

'Has Tobie been mistreated?' he asks, dreading the answer.

'He says not.' She wipes the drops from her cheeks with gloved forefingers. 'He has a room of his own, a bed, blankets and hot food. I gave the warden a generous gift to ensure he is kept comfortable. But Whyte says he must be arraigned at the next assizes, and there is no prospect of release unless conclusive evidence is found against another party for the murder of Agnes. And God only knows how we are to bring that about.'

He sees the muscles working in her jaw as she grits her teeth, determined not to show weakness, and feels a rush of tenderness for her.

'I have some good news on that score,' he says. He tells her of his visits to Vincent Lovell and Thomas Phelippes, of Essex and Cloudesley and the cipher, and when he has finished, she turns and looks at him with a desolate expression, which is not at all the effect he'd hoped for.

'Essex,' she says flatly.

'Well, but he is not germane to the business – the point is that we have found a direct connection between your cipher and Vincent Lovell,' he says, trying to encourage her to the desired response. 'Phelippes is on his way to Cecil now to explain it. All the available evidence points to Vincent as the killer.' Except the evidence of his obvious love for his niece, says the voice of his conscience, which he does his best to stifle. 'Don't you see,' he adds, when her face does not change, 'this means the murder, the note – they're nothing to do with you?'

'I'm afraid that's not true,' Sophia says, after a pause, looking down as she kicks drifts of dirty snow out of her path. As they walk, she tells him about a brooch with a crest, a boy with a streak in his hair and a knife wound in his chest, a whore with a connection to the Earl of Essex, and an attacker who lurched out of the shadows the night before, leaving Sophia with an unambiguous threat.

'Shit,' Anthony says feelingly, when she has finished.

'Exactly.'

'For God's sake, Sophia – why didn't you tell me about this man last night? You could have been killed. You have to tell Cecil immediately, and abandon this business right now.'

'I didn't mention it because I knew you'd react like this,' she says, pulling her cloak tighter as if to keep him out.

Anthony decides there is nothing to be gained by pursuing it. 'Vincent Lovell said Agnes had hinted at a special friend she confided in,' he says. 'You think she meant the countess?'

'According to her nurse, Agnes was a regular visitor to Essex House. And if Phelippes reused my cipher during that fiasco when Essex tried to run his intelligence operation, the earl could easily have got hold of it. Think about it,' she says, with a hint of impatience, when she sees Anthony's frown. 'Suppose Essex sees Agnes on one of these visits. He takes a liking to her. He seduces or rapes her, perhaps she threatens to expose him. So he decides she has to be silenced. He leaves her body at the site of The Theatre with a note written in a cipher he has from years earlier, but later he realises he's dropped a brooch. Well – probably not the earl himself, but one of his trusted servants in his livery. Then he gets a message from this girl Jen at the Unicorn, saying his brooch is being touted around the taverns by a boy who can testify to where he found it. So Essex – or, again, one of his men – dispatches Badger.'

'Then where do you come in? What reason would he have to threaten you?'

She considers this. 'You know Essex and Robert Cecil are always in competition for the queen's favour. They both keep spies in their rival's household – somehow Essex must have found out that Cecil asked me to make enquiries about the girl's death. He could have set someone to watch me, and seen me go to Burghley House. That assault last night was a warning to leave the matter alone. I have even wondered' – she hesitates, half-turning to him – 'if Thomas Phelippes can be entirely trusted. If he took money from Essex once, he could do so again.'

'Not now he's working for Cecil, surely?' Anthony looks at her. 'In any case, I don't think Essex ever paid him what he was promised – that's partly how Thomas ended up with debt problems in the first place. He financed that mission for Essex out of his own pocket, and all it achieved was to ruin his professional reputation with the queen. I can't see Thomas going out of his way to do the earl any favours, especially not if it would put you in danger. I think Thomas is fond of you.'

He sees the surprise register on her face. 'Well, someone must have told Essex about my involvement,' she says, her chin jutting stubbornly. 'But if he thinks I will back down and let my son pay the price for his crimes, he is a bigger fool than I suspected.'

'Why would Essex make such a display of the girl's body, though?' Anthony says. He can see where her thoughts are tending, and hopes he might divert her. 'The first part of your theory I can credit, but the cipher, the riddle about stolen ground? If he killed her, would he not just have her buried somewhere she wouldn't be found?'

'To divert attention,' Sophia says immediately. She has clearly thought this through. 'To imply that the murder was payback to the Norths for Ireland, or – as you suggest – to cast suspicion on the Catholics. It was vague enough to point in several directions. If he or his servant hadn't lost that brooch, we might never have connected the girl with him.'

208

They walk on in silence while Anthony tries to process this unexpected turn of events. On balance, he still prefers his Vincent Lovell theory; it too has flaws, but on the whole it appears neater, if he could only persuade himself that Vincent's affection for his niece was a skilled pretence. Certainly it will be a good deal less problematic to accuse a known Catholic sympathiser who has already flirted with treason and served time in prison than to make a case against a peer of the realm, beloved of the queen. The young earl is undoubtedly reckless; Anthony can picture him forcing himself on a girl and even fetching her a blow to the head on an impulse, but pausing to compose a verse – even a bad one – to misdirect attention seems unlikely. And how would he have known about Tobie Strange, to make the connection with The Theatre? He can see that he will have a job convincing Sophia; for her, the brooch is conclusive.

'So what will you do now?' he asks, apprehensive. 'Take these suspicions to Cecil?'

Sophia shakes her head. 'Cecil will not move against the earl without clear proof – their rivalry being as it is, he wouldn't risk the repercussions if he made an accusation he couldn't stand up.'

'Then I don't see—'

'So I will have to bring him proof.' She doesn't look at Anthony as she says this; her face is set determinedly into the headwind.

He has the sensation of missing a stair; only moments ago, he had expected to come away from this conversation having lifted the burden of the investigation from her shoulders; instead, somehow, it has ended with her on the verge of accusing one of the most powerful men in the kingdom of rape and double murder.

Anthony feels suddenly very cold and very tired. Not for the first time, it occurs to him that trying to save Sophia from herself is a thankless task. He should be elsewhere. He stops dead; she continues for a few paces before she realises he is no longer in step with her, and turns to face him.

'What will you do?' he asks. 'Accuse Essex to his face?'

She catches the disbelief in his tone.

'I was planning to talk to Frances,' she says.

He lets out a dry laugh. 'You think if Frances knows anything, she will confess it to you? Against her own husband? Perhaps you know her better than I, but she is not her father's daughter for nothing – Frances Walsingham is a pragmatist to her core.'

'She is the mother of a thirteen-year-old girl,' Sophia says, looking mutinous.

'A girl whose future depends on her stepfather,' Anthony points out. Why must she be so unreasonable? 'God's blood, Sophia – that man could have killed you last night! He has as good as promised to try again if you persist. Will you not put this into Cecil's hands and let him deal with it?'

'And leave Tobie to rot in prison while Cecil havers and delays so as not to put a foot wrong around Essex? Thank you for your help, but you need not involve yourself any longer if you don't like it. Go home to your wife.' She lobs the final word at him with particular force; turning on her heel, she strides off, cloak pulled tight around her narrow shoulders, back in the direction they came from.

He sighs and hurries to catch up. 'I am only trying to save you from your own impulsiveness, damn it! How does it help Tobie if you get yourself knifed in an alley before you've even told him who you are?'

She whips around to face him, tawny eyes flashing. 'It's not your job to save me, Anthony. What would you do if it was Richie in gaol?'

He bows his head. 'I would do exactly what you are doing, I suppose. Though . . .'

'Though, because you are a man, you would be less vulnerable?' She glares at him; her body is held so taut that for a moment he thinks she might swing her arm back and aim a punch at him, but the breath goes out of her with a small laugh, as if in surrender, and again she wipes away the water that spills from her eyes.

'I was not going to say that,' he says, though it was more or less exactly what he had been thinking. 'In truth, I don't know what I'd be doing if it was Richie, beyond tearing my hair out. I would not face it with your fortitude, that's for sure.'

She smiles sadly. 'Women have long apprenticeships in fortitude.' She lays a hand on his arm. 'Forgive me, Anthony – I hope you know I am grateful for your help. I had thought we might be able to secure his release today, with enough inducements, and it was a bitter disappointment to leave him there. But we must go forward. Are you coming?'

He looks at her, alarmed. 'Where to?'

'Essex House.' She catches his hesitation. 'No, of course – I've kept you from your work long enough.'

'You're going now? You think Frances will receive you, just like that?'

'I think she will want to hear what I have to say.'

Her jaw is tight; he sees he will not dissuade her. 'She won't speak frankly to you in her husband's presence.'

'The earl is always at court. You don't have to come in, but I would be grateful if you would ride with me – then I could send Mick home to chop wood. I'm not sure I want him knowing about Essex House.'

He has to think for a moment to remember who she means, then recalls the bull-necked man who led her horse away. 'You don't trust your servants?'

'I'm not sure I trust anyone at the moment,' she says grimly.

TWENTY-TWO

Essex House occupies a substantial acreage at the eastern end of the Strand, adjacent to the Middle Temple, its gardens sloping down to the Thames and its grand frontage overlooking the church of St Clement Danes on the north side. Though Essex has supposedly given up trying to run his own private intelligence service from his residence, he still maintains a busy network of informers, spying for him on any other courtiers he regards as current or potential enemies, on his mistresses, on his creditors. The place is full of side and rear entrances where visitors may come and go in the shadows, unobserved. Sophia considers this approach and decides that her best option is to present herself openly, as someone who has nothing to hide. Her visit will find its way back to the earl one way or another, so she may as well minimise any cause for suspicion. Naturally, it is against all rules of etiquette for a woman of her status to request an audience with a countess uninvited, but she is gambling on the idea that Frances will be too intrigued to turn her away.

Around the imposing gatehouse on the Strand side, a crowd of poor men and women cluster, with pinched faces and blank eyes, stretching out red raw hands for alms to any visitor who looks as if they might have coin to spare. Sophia sees them size up her horse and her cloak before they press in on her; she sees frostbitten noses and fingers, desperate eyes, blackened gums. She feels Nyx jib and sidestep, and in an instant a sharp memory of the previous night threatens to engulf her: the weight of her attacker on her back, the snow in her mouth and nose; she finds herself gulping for breath, swaying in her saddle, gripping the reins too tight as her panic transmits to the animal, its nostrils flaring. For a moment she thinks she might fall, but there is a shout of 'Get back!' and the beggars skitter away; Anthony has drawn his horse alongside her with a hand on his dagger. She steadies herself, glancing sidelong at him; she ought to be grateful, she supposes, but in fact she feels irritated. She had not intended to tell him about last night's attack, but he was so determined to persuade her that the cipher had nothing to do with her that she felt perversely compelled to prove that it did. Either way, after seeing Tobie in that cell, she has no choice but to be involved. He didn't appear to have been harmed, but he was so obviously terrified and on the edge of desperation that she fears he could easily make his situation worse by lashing out, or being bullied into a confession; she needs to find a way to free him as soon as she can.

She announces herself at the gate as a friend of the countess, adding that she has no appointment, but her business is a matter of urgency. The guards look dubious, but she sees them size up the quality of her horse, her furs, her bearing; they confer among themselves, and a messenger is dispatched to the house.

'Where did you disappear to, in the Clink?' she asks Anthony while they wait.

'I saw the young priest I spoke to yesterday – I wanted to ask him about this Cloudesley. He's been beaten since I last saw him.'

'For talking to you?'

He nods. 'That place is a seething pit of conspiracies, and

the warden allows them to flourish in the hope of skimming off information, but I have the sense that he is not in control as much he likes to think. This priest says the Catholics in there know he's a spy and will kill him eventually. I said I'd try to help. Could you speak to Cecil about him?'

She twists her mouth. 'I have not exactly endeared myself to Cecil lately, I doubt I'm in a position to ask him for favours. You shouldn't have promised.'

'What else could I do? I needed him to tell me about Vincent Lovell, and now he's been made to suffer for it.'

She sighs. 'Cecil has made it clear that I am not to contact him unless he sends for me. But I suppose I could write via Phelippes. Truthfully, Anthony – did Vincent Lovell really strike you as a guilty man?'

'Honestly? I thought his grief was genuine, although I suppose the two things could coexist. But all the evidence seemed to fit so well. Until I knew about the brooch and the boy. I could almost wish you had not discovered that,' he adds, nodding towards Essex House.

Sophia rounds on him. 'Oh yes – simpler to send an innocent man to the gallows than hold the earl to account for anything he does,' she says tightly. 'I am so heartily sick of men like him, who believe their title and standing allow them to go through life doing whatever suits them, without once paying a price for their actions. Cecil may be afraid to stand up to him, but I'm not.'

Anthony begins to say something – she can guess at the gist of it – when the messenger returns and confers urgently with the men on the gates.

'The lady can go in,' one of them tells her, 'but your man will have to wait in the servant's quarters.'

Sophia bites down a smile as she glances at Anthony. She half-expects him to turn and leave for the sake of his dignity, but he is watching her as if awaiting instructions.

'Maybe you could find out if any of the servants admit to

214

being at the Unicorn last night,' she murmurs as she dismounts.

He gives her a long look, and eventually flashes a grin. 'Very good, madam,' he says, taking Nyx's reins as he bobs her a bow. She tries to arrange her face as she follows the guard under the gate.

Through a vaulted marble entrance hall hung with pine boughs and holly wreaths for the season; past antique busts and tall portraits of venerable Devereux forbears, along stone corridors muffled by tapestries and Turkey carpets, she is escorted via a seemingly endless series of heavy doors that open silently before them, to a comfortable receiving room with a blazing fire, where the servant wordlessly takes her hat and cloak and withdraws with a bow. In a window embrasure, a thin girl of about thirteen hunches over a table, laboriously picking out a tune with two fingers on the virginals. The room smells of good beeswax and resin. By the hearth, one hand resting on the mantel in a carefully artless pose, Frances Walsingham, now the Countess of Essex, allows a silence to elapse before she deigns to turn and acknowledge her visitor.

Sophia dips into a curtsy; when she raises her head, she sees that Frances is appraising her in the way that women do when they haven't seen one another for a long time, to see how well the other has aged. She is conscious of doing the same thing. Frances has her father's long face and watchful dark eyes; she has kept her figure in spite of childbirth, and her skin is good, though Sophia notes lines of strain around her eyes. She wears a dress of plum-coloured velvet, the bodice sewn all over with gold thread and seed pearls, and her brown hair is caught up in a simple silk net. There is a wariness about her, as if she has already guessed that this will not be a pleasant social call.

'Mistress de Wolfe,' she says, with easy charm. 'What a surprise. It must be more than ten years since we met.'

Sophia inclines her head. 'So much has happened in that

215

time, my lady. I have not had the chance to offer my condolences on the death of your father, God rest him. England misses him every day.'

She has judged this opening gambit correctly, it seems; Frances visibly softens a fraction.

'As do I,' she says. 'And I am sorry for the loss of your husband. My father held Humphrey de Wolfe in high esteem.'

'Thank you. He was a good man.'

'He was a kind husband to you?'

'The best. I will always be grateful to Sir Francis for introducing us.'

Frances's eye rests on her for a moment with a wistful expression, as if a kind husband is something she has vaguely heard about in stories. Sophia thinks of the young whore at the Unicorn boasting of the earl's special name for her, and wonders if Frances knows what Essex does when he is away from home. No doubt of it, she thinks; Frances is not Walsingham's daughter for nothing. The girl continues to wrest the same repetitive phrase from her instrument; the high, melancholy notes echo around the painted ceiling.

'I am glad of it,' says the countess briskly. 'But I don't suppose you came here to exchange condolences several years overdue.' She raises an eyebrow expectantly; Sophia nods a warning towards the girl in the window.

'Lizzie, you can stop torturing those poor keys now. Come and meet my friend Mistress de Wolfe.'

The girl pushes back her stool, tucking a lock of hair behind her ear. This, then, is Philip Sidney's daughter. She is almost as tall as Sophia, though she hunches awkwardly as though her height were an uncomfortable garment she had been made to wear against her will. She curtsies, looking nervously from beneath long lashes. She has evidently been crying.

'Mistress de Wolfe and your father had a dear friend in common, many years ago, when you were a baby in the cradle,' Frances says, a hand on her daughter's shoulder to encourage her upright. 'And her late husband was a friend of your grandfather.'

'I wonder that we have not met before, Mistress de Wolfe,' the girl says politely.

Sophia exchanges a glance with Frances. 'Well, your lady mother is very busy. But I am glad to have met you now, Mistress Sidney,' she says, then immediately worries that she has misspoken; does the girl use her stepfather's name these days?

'Lizzie, you are excused your music practice – go and find something useful to do,' Frances says, with a touch of impatience. She watches her daughter to the door and waits until it has closed behind her. She lowers her voice. 'She is so like her father that sometimes it pains me to look on her.'

'That must be very difficult,' Sophia murmurs.

'It is. As I'm sure you can imagine.'

There is a silence. Frances holds her gaze as Sophia wonders what she is supposed to read into that. Could Frances know about Tobie? If so, she could only have found out from Thomas Phelippes.

'Come and sit,' she says. 'Do you want something to eat?'

'Thank you, no.' Sophia takes one of the high-backed chairs by the fire. 'My lady Essex, I need to ask you about Agnes Lovell.'

'Honestly, Sophia, call me Frances, we've known each other long enough. That poor child.' The countess leans towards the flames and warms her hands. 'She was my daughter's friend – Lizzie has taken it very hard, and no wonder. Did you know her?'

'No.' There is an art to judging how much of your hand to reveal. Sophia meets her eye. 'I have some involvement with the Lord Chamberlain's Men. One of their company, a boy of fifteen, has been arrested for the girl's murder. None of us believe he did it.'

Frances looks interested. 'Why not?'

'Because he loved her.'

'Love does not preclude violence. Ask Master Shakespeare.' She rearranges her skirts. 'So why are you here?'

'I heard that Agnes visited you, I thought you might have some idea of her associates. Could she have confided in Lizzie, for instance, if there was someone who wished her ill?'

'If Lizzie knew anything, she would have told us right away,' Frances says immediately. 'She's heartbroken over what happened to Agnes, she wants the killer caught.'

This little speech sounds rehearsed. 'How did they come to be friends?' Sophia asks. 'Agnes's family are not your equals in status.'

Frances picks at a loose pearl on her sleeve. 'She was a knight's daughter, Lizzie is a knight's daughter, in that regard there was no discrepancy. But yes, you're right that we did her a favour to notice her.'

'How did they meet?'

'My husband had business with Thomas North, six months back. He visited their house, I believe Sir Thomas mentioned that his ward lacked company her own age. Knowing that Lizzie often felt the same, Robert suggested Agnes should visit us.'

'So it was the earl who first took notice of her?' Sophia tries to keep her tone as neutral as possible, but she sees Frances stiffen.

'He was trying to do a kindness for Lizzie,' she says crisply. 'It's not an easy situation – well, you're a stepmother, perhaps you'll know. Lizzie has never warmed to Robert – it's as if she's convinced herself that it would be an act of disloyalty to her father to show him any affection, never mind that Philip never even laid eyes on her. And she's not an easy girl – it's hardly surprising that Robert is more invested in his own children, but he's been good to her, not that you would know it from her demeanour towards him. Finding a companion for her was one more example of his thoughtfulness.'

Sophia wonders how far Frances believes this. It occurs to her that Lizzie is not the only one who lacks companionship; the countess's willingness to unburden herself to a virtual stranger surprises her, so much so that she suspects it is not as candid as it might appear.

'So Agnes came here?' she asks.

'Yes. And we all adored her – she was a charming girl, lively, beautiful too. Face of a Botticelli nymph. She and Lizzie took to one another immediately, which was very pleasing to me and to Robert – we felt she brought Lizzie out of herself. With the Norths' blessing she became a regular visitor.'

'When did you see her last?'

Frances laughs, but her eyes are narrowed. 'I begin to feel that I am under interrogation, Sophia. It was some time before Christmas, I forget.'

'Perhaps Lizzie would remember?'

'I can ask her. But she's much too fragile at the moment to be questioned by someone who was trained by my father.' She smiles to soften the refusal.

'Of course,' Sophia says hastily, not wanting the audience to end prematurely. Anthony was right; if there is any connection to the earl, Frances will close ranks to conceal it. She feels obscurely disappointed, as if she had expected better from Walsingham's daughter. 'Did you ever hear Agnes suggest she was afraid of anyone?'

Frances leaves a long pause while she stares into the fire, her fingers steepled together at her lips as if she is weighing up how much to confide. 'I'll tell you this,' she says eventually. 'There was no love lost between her and the Norths. She said repeatedly in my hearing that she wished she could be free of them.'

'Really? Was she mistreated, did she say?'

'I don't think they were beating her, if that's what you mean. But Lady North resented her, and Sir Thomas and his son regarded her purely as a source of income. She was lonely and unhappy. Hardly surprising if she looked for a kind word elsewhere.'

What does she mean by that? Is she pre-emptively excusing her husband for seducing the girl?

'Edmund North intended to marry her, I believe,' Sophia says.

'So she told me. But there was no formal pre-contract – the Norths wouldn't dare. The queen hadn't approved the match, and men have been put in the Tower for marrying without her consent.' She gives a little shudder, perhaps thinking of how narrowly her own marriage might have incurred the same penalty. 'Edmund North obviously thought he had staked a claim, though. Agnes asked me to help her get out of it.'

'And?'

'And I told her the best way to avoid an unwanted marriage was to pledge herself to someone else. That, or divest herself of her estate.'

'Did you have someone in mind?'

An affect passes across Frances's face, too fleeting to be scrutinised, but there nonetheless. Guilt, perhaps?

'I was not being entirely serious in either case. I had no idea about the player boy at the time, you understand, but it seems she took me at my word. Thomas North is putting it about that they intended to elope together, and the boy turned violent when Agnes changed her mind.'

'That's not what happened.'

'Were you there? Wanting to believe something doesn't make it true,' Frances says.

There is such a brittleness about her; Sophia is sure she is not telling all she knows, but she can't impel a countess to talk.

'I am hoping to find out who else might have seen Agnes on the day she disappeared,' she says, trying a different tack. 'The twenty-seventh. You're sure she didn't come here?'

'No.' The answer is instant and final. 'She hadn't visited

since before Christmas, as I say. She was obliged to spend the festive season with the Norths.'

'Did she mention any plan to visit her uncle over the holidays?'

'The one who's a recusant?' Frances looks surprised. 'Not in my hearing. But then I don't suppose she would have advertised it if she was in touch with him. The Norths didn't approve.'

Sophia feels she is running out of road. She can sense Frances preparing to bring the meeting to an end, and wonders if she should have asked for food after all, if only to have a reason to linger. There is more to discover here, she is sure of it, but it seems clear that Frances will not waver in her wifely loyalty for the sake of a mere player. She glances up and, for the first time, registers properly the portrait above the mantel: a young man in black-and-gold ornamental armour and neat starched ruff, his left hand resting on a plumed helmet, his black eyes looking sidelong out of the frame. In the upper left corner of the picture a complex heraldic shield is emblazoned. Sophia rises for a closer look.

'That's my lord husband's father, the first Earl of Essex,' Frances says.

'These are his arms?' Sophia points.

'The Essex crest, yes. Don't ask me what they all mean. Different illustrious forebears, but I forget all their names.'

Sophia peers at the device. The shield is counter-quartered in sixteen, each square showing a different emblem.

'And all your household servants wear this crest?' she asks, trying not to sound overly interested.

'Yes, on their tunics and caps. You can imagine the headache it gives the embroiderers. Why, are you interested in heraldry? Didn't your husband buy himself a coat of arms?'

Sophia ignores the snide tone. 'He thought it was expected.' She points to the shield. 'That square, the top left – it looks familiar.'

This one square is the only part of the shield that corresponds to Jen's description of the brooch: a white background with a red horizontal band, above it three red circles.

'Canton,' Frances corrects her, proud to display her knowledge. 'Dexter chief. That is the Devereux emblem. Robert's family design.'

Devereux. Sophia stares at the canton. White background, red band, three red circles – there is no mistaking the description. Jen made no mention of all these other squares and patterns that make up the Essex arms. So was the man who dropped the brooch some Devereux kinsman of the earl, not a member of his household?

'Do any of your servants wear that emblem alone as their badge?' The question is too direct; she regrets it as soon as it is asked. The countess's expression hardens.

'Sophia – what is it exactly you are trying to say? If you think you know something about Agnes, I had rather you spoke frankly than go at it sideways.'

She turns to face Frances, but before she can think how to frame it, there is a commotion outside the room and the door is flung open; in strides Robert Devereux, Earl of Essex, snow still clinging to his riding boots and flecking the sleeves of his leather jacket. Behind him, two young men of a similar type: expensive clothes and fashionable beards, all swagger and bluster. One stocky and dark, the other fair and nervy, both a good ten years junior to the earl, who at thirty-three would like to believe himself still in the first flush of youth. Essex is not, in Sophia's opinion, a handsome man, but he is tall and athletic and rich, which many – men and women alike – mistake for attractiveness.

Frances rises immediately and drops into a deep curtsy; a moment behind her, Sophia does the same.

'Imagine my surprise,' Essex says, in a voice too loud for the chamber, 'when they told me at the gate that a city widow had presumed to call upon my countess, without invitation, against all custom of propriety, and – more astonishing still – my wife had consented to receive her.'

'My lord—' Frances begins, but the earl holds up a hand. 'Quiet. I'm talking to your visitor.'

Sophia straightens and looks Essex in the eye. This is the first time she has encountered him in person, though she has seen him from a distance in public parades, but she has met his sort before. Her first husband was such a man. She is older now, and knows enough not to be cowed.

'My lord of Essex. I humbly beg pardon for presuming on your hospitality. My name is Sophia de Wolfe.'

'I know who you are. Why are you here?' The earl is shamelessly sizing her up, allowing his eyes to travel over her body as if she were horseflesh and he a prospective buyer. Any moment now she expects him to walk around her in a circle. She knows she is too old to be of any real interest to him (his flirtation with the queen notwithstanding), but he is a man who can't help but look at women as if seeing them naked. He wants to unnerve her, and she doesn't shrink from his gaze as she considers her answer. To claim any mutual acquaintance or prior friendship with Frances would betray her own connection to Walsingham, although she has the sense that it is her husband's name that has provoked the earl's hostility. She thinks of those ledgers, the neat coded entries, and wonders what she would find in there under Devereux.

'My lord, I am looking to raise funds to found a school for the street children of Southwark, and since you and my lady Essex are known as great patrons of learning, I hoped I might prevail upon you for a donation?'

Essex looks briefly confused, as if he doesn't recognise this version of himself but realises it is not in his interest to deny it.

'What need have you to go begging, mistress? I heard your husband was worth fifty thousand when he died.' One of the men behind him lets out a low whistle. 'You could fund five schools out of your own coffers and not even notice,' the earl adds.

'My husband was not as wealthy as people think, if you take into account the sums owing to him at his death,' Sophia says easily. 'But I thought, my lord, that your name and patronage would lend the venture greater prestige.'

His eyes narrow. 'Southwark, you say? What's your interest? Spend a lot of time there, do you?'

The young men snigger; Frances clicks her tongue as if embarrassed by and for him.

'There is great need in that liberty, my lord. Children going about unshod in the snow, forced to thievery just to buy bread. Young boys murdered and thrown in the river for no more than selling trinkets,' she adds, looking him square in the face. Her eye drifts downwards, to the half-cape he wears over his left shoulder, pinned with an enamel brooch. It shows the coat of arms on his father's painting, the crest of sixteen squares, not the simple Devereux design.

'If they're thieving, they should be hanged, not taught grammar,' says the dark-haired hanger-on, and his companion gives a sycophantic laugh.

'You'll have to excuse my friends, Mistress de Wolfe – they have little interest in the light of learning, as you would see if you read their poetry.'

'Hey,' says the fair youth in mock indignation.

'May I present the Honourable Augustine Moynes and Roger Manners, Earl of Rutland.'

Sophia offers them a perfunctory curtsy; she has barely registered which was which. The young men regard her with indifference, but Essex is watching her closely, not with appetite now, but with calculation.

'Well, Mistress de Wolfe – it sounds like an admirable project, and your charitable impulse does you credit. It may be that we can contribute – I'll have my household steward contact you. In future, though, please address any such requests in writing. I know your husband had no reservations about dealing with his betters as if he were their equal, but you are a woman.'

'I'm grateful for the reminder, my lord.'

'It is not a fitting association for my wife, and I fear that by coming here in person, you seek to take advantage of her generous nature. The servants will show you out. Now, my lady – where's your daughter?' He turns to Frances as if Sophia were already out of his sight. 'Lizzie should have been here to greet her bridegroom. Roger is impatient to see her.'

In one sharp glance, Sophia catches the way Frances suppresses a shudder of revulsion at these words, at the same time as the dark-haired youth makes a lascivious face at his friend.

'I expect she is making herself ready, my lord husband,' Frances says, and Sophia recognises instantly the placatory tone, the one women use to pre-empt a man's anger or criticism. In that one exchange, she feels she has the measure of the Essex marriage. 'I'll go and fetch her.'

'Let a servant do that, I want to speak to you,' the earl says, clicking his fingers as a man in the Essex livery steps forward holding Sophia's cloak to usher her into the corridor. This time Frances stands her ground.

'She is naturally shy with my lord of Rutland, as you would expect from a chaste little maid,' she says firmly. 'This requires a mother's encouragement.'

'Then be quick,' Essex calls after her, as she follows Sophia out.

'I will see Mistress de Wolfe to the door,' Frances tells the servant, as they progress back through the tapestried rooms. When the man hesitates – these were not the earl's instructions – she adds, impatient, 'Make haste and see that her horse is ready.'

'And my, uh – manservant was taken below stairs,' Sophia

says. 'Please tell him we're leaving.'

Reluctantly, the man departs. When they are alone, Frances turns to Sophia.

'Quick thinking, about the school. Your wits are still sharp, I see.'

'Will you tell your husband why I was really here?'

Frances hesitates. 'No. But I will have to answer for receiving you.'

'Frances – he won't hurt you, will he?'

Frances gives her a tight smile. 'Oh, not with his fists, don't worry. That's not his way. But you must promise you won't come again. There is nothing I can tell you about Agnes Lovell that will help the player boy, I'm sorry.' She looks frightened.

'But if you think of anything – or if Lizzie remembers a conversation with her friend, however insignificant it may seem – you would let me know? I am at Broad Street – or you could send a message by Leila. Please, Frances – you wouldn't let an innocent boy hang for murder, if you could stop it?'

'As I told you, Lizzie knows nothing useful, or she would have said so.' Frances looks straight ahead as she speaks. They pass along a dim corridor without wall hangings; it seems she is leading Sophia to one of the side entrances, for visitors who should remain invisible. For a few moments, the only sound is the swishing of the countess's skirts.

'Lizzie is betrothed already, then?' Sophia asks, as they approach a door.

'It's a good match for her,' Frances says, so swiftly that it is clear she is on the defensive. 'Roger Manners is Earl of Rutland. The dark-haired man with my husband just now. He's very loyal to Robert.'

'But she's so young,' Sophia says. 'He must be a good ten years her senior. How does she like the idea?'

'Lizzie is headstrong, like all girls. She'll come to realise the value of the marriage in time, and see that her stepfather has chosen well for her.' Her eyes dart away; Sophia takes this to mean Lizzie hates the prospect. No wonder the girl formed a bond with Agnes Lovell; they could commiserate over being sold off to older men. 'My father was the son of a vintner,' Frances adds, with unexpected vehemence. 'You know this, Sophia. He worked himself to death for the queen and in recompense, both his daughter and his granddaughter will be countesses of England. That is cause for pride, is it not?'

'As long as you are both happy,' she says mildly.

'Oh, *happy*.' Frances spits the word as if it were a blasphemy. 'I count any woman a fool who looks for happiness in her marriage. I'm glad if it worked out that way for you,' she adds, mollifying, 'but most of us have to shift for ourselves and make the best of it. The sooner Lizzie learns to let go of romantic dreams and accommodate herself to reality, the better for her in the long run. Look at Agnes Lovell. Did she really imagine that she, an heiress, could marry a penniless player for love? It was a child's fantasy.'

'But they *are* children,' Sophia points out. 'Agnes was thirteen. Same as Lizzie.'

Behind Frances's anger is something less easily defined; the countess holds her arms wrapped around her narrow chest and her jaw tight, as if she is barely keeping her feelings in check. On impulse, Sophia reaches out and embraces her (how is that for a breach of propriety, my lord of Essex?); for an instant she feels the tension in Frances's shoulders subside as she leans in, before she pulls away abruptly.

'I must fetch my daughter, or my lords will be displeased,' she says, brisk and formal once more. 'I am glad to have seen you, Sophia, but don't come back.' With a fleeting kiss that barely touches Sophia's cheek, the countess turns and walks away, her silks whispering down the corridor.

Sophia opens the door on to a covered walkway that leads to the stable yard. Not even mid-afternoon and the light is already fading, blue shadows creeping over the piles of snow banked against the walls. She pulls her cloak tighter; the cold air tastes of woodsmoke, a welcome relief after the thick scented heat of those rooms. She has some sympathy with Frances – Sophia has not forgotten what it was to be married to a man who rides roughshod over you – but to allow your thirteen-year-old daughter to be bargained away for your husband's advantage without a fight: this she can't compute. Or perhaps it is Frances who is in the right; God knows, following her heart has brought Sophia nothing but trouble. She is brooding on this, hoping Anthony will not be too long, when she senses the familiar prickling at her nape, a flicker of movement behind her; her hand goes instantly to her knife, her blood surges, she whips around on the point of drawing when a small voice says, 'Mistress de Wolfe?'

Lizzie Sidney, her slight form materialising from the shadows. Sophia lets her hand drop and hopes the girl won't see her shaking.

'Mistress Sidney. You startled me.' She forces a smile.

'Sorry. I wondered – did you know my father? My real father, I mean – Sir Philip.'

'Oh. No, I knew a friend of his, years ago – about the time you were born. Though I did see your father once.' She had almost said 'in Oxford', but stopped herself in time.

The girl's face lights up. 'Was he very handsome?'

'Handsome and elegant – he was everything a young knight should be. And you are the image of him – I would know you for his daughter anywhere.'

This was the correct response; Lizzie flushes pink with pleasure, before her face falls again. 'My mother says I must think of Essex as my lord father now, but I cannot. She was lying to you back there,' she adds.

'Which part? How do you know?'

'Behind the tapestry of the Muses there's a connecting door to the next room. I listened outside. Because I knew you were talking about Agnes. Let's step out of the cold.'

She gestures Sophia to an outbuilding on their left that appears to store animal feed. Lizzie pulls the door closed behind them and they look at one another in the grainy light through narrow windows. There is a strong smell of horse.

'Agnes did come to us that day before she died,' Lizzie says. 'Though my mother told you she didn't. I suppose she doesn't want anyone connecting her with us, now that she is murdered.'

Sophia stares at her. 'The twenty-seventh of December? You're certain?'

'It was late in the afternoon. Around four, I think, because I had not long finished my dancing lesson. She came on foot through the snow, and presented herself at the kitchen door so her arrival would not be announced. She wanted to see me in secret, without the earl's knowledge. One of the cooks – I won't say her name, to spare her trouble – she is fond of me and sent for me to say Agnes was here.'

'What did Agnes want?'

'Money.' Lizzie makes a face. 'She planned to run away. With the player boy, Tobie Strange. Perhaps you know that?'

'I had heard. Did she say why she had suddenly decided on that course?'

The girl sighs. 'Before Christmas, my stepfather Essex had promised Agnes he would go directly to the queen to argue against the match with Edmund North. He said he was high in favour with Her Majesty at the moment because of Ireland, so he was certain she would grant him his request. If the queen forbade the marriage, there would be nothing the Norths could do about it.'

'And I presume your stepfather was not spending his credit with the queen out of the goodness of his heart? He had his own reasons for preventing the North marriage?'

'Naturally. But Agnes chose not to think about that part.' Lizzie's face is still hidden; she looks as if she is fighting back tears. 'In any case, he had not yet done it, and Agnes was afraid of the Norths. She thought if they found out about Tobie, they would straightaway rush through her marriage to Edmund, even without the queen's permission, and then she would never be free of them. She had to put herself beyond their reach.'

'So what happened that day when Agnes came here unannounced?'

Lizzie swipes a hand across her eyes and sniffs. 'The cook sent a maid to fetch me and I went with Agnes into a pantry off the kitchen, where I thought we could be private. She begged me to give her money, any coin I could lay my hands on. She said she had to escape the Norths, and remain hidden for the next few months, until she turned fourteen and her wardship was ended, for she would marry no one but Tobie, she said.'

'Did she mention her uncle?'

'Vincent? Yes. She told me she had just come from seeing him, and she had a plan to make over her inheritance to him, in name only – she thought that would be enough to make any other suitors lose interest in her. I told her she was playing with fire, that she would be caught and punished.' The girl's head drops again. 'She was impatient with me. She said, "I am not meek like you, Lizzie – in five months I will have my own money, and I will not be pressed into an empty marriage, not now that I know what true love is." That was cruel of her, because I do not agree to Rutland out of meekness, but because I have no choice.'

'You don't like the Earl of Rutland for a husband?'

Lizzie's eyes flash. 'Would you? He's a roistering braggart who boasts of his whoring and talks about women as if they were animals. But he is a protégé of my stepfather, and what the earl wants, he will have. Gus Moynes is the same. All the men who follow Essex are cut from the same debauched cloth.'

Sophia lays a hand on the girl's shoulder. She would like to tell her that she understands what it is to be sold off by a father, but she will never speak of her past. All she can do is offer sympathy.

'So did you give Agnes money?'

The girl lets out a dry laugh; she sounds older than her years. 'What money? I have none of my own, I told you. My father, God rest him, left nothing but debts, and my grandfather Sir Francis settled a sum on me at his death, but that was for my dowry, so I could make a good marriage. He would be turning in his grave if he saw Rutland. I don't know what Agnes expected me to do – break open my stepfather's strongbox? I said as much to her, but she was crying and begging – she said she meant to leave that night, and if I ever loved her I should find some means to help her, because she had no friend in the world except me.'

'She did not count your mother a friend?'

'Not in this matter,' Lizzie says bluntly. 'But she was exaggerating, as she always did. She had plenty of friends. Grace, her nurse. Leila's daughter, who carried her letters. The Norths' stable boy, Fred, who made her a key to the servants' gate. She always got people to do what she wanted, even when it would get them in trouble. But I was firm with her this time.'

'So what happened when you told her you couldn't help? Did she leave?'

Lizzie presses the knuckle of her thumb against her mouth and shakes her head. 'That was when my mother walked in. The maid who was sent to fetch me wanted to curry favour with her, because she ran straight to my mother and told her Agnes was here to see me in secret. The countess found us in the pantry, sent me to my room and took Agnes off with her to her chambers.'

'And I presume you disregarded the instruction and found a way to listen at the door?'

Lizzie draws herself up with a hint of pride. 'I know every back staircase and hidden door in this house. I am not a royal spymaster's granddaughter for nothing.'

Sophia smiles. 'And?'

'Agnes was crying again, asking my mother to lend her money, saying she needed to escape the Norths before they forced her into marriage. My mother said she could stay here for the night while she talked to the earl about how best to resolve the situation. Well, Agnes didn't want that – she said she already had a solution, she just needed money so she could leave while Sir Thomas was away from home and the Norths couldn't trace her. And my mother grew impatient then and told her she was being foolish, did she really expect the Countess of Essex to fund her elopement with a player? She said if Agnes wanted their help, she had a choice and the player boy was not one of the options.'

The girl is starting to shiver; she is wearing only velvet indoor slippers and a thin woollen wrap around her shoulders. She must have come running out the moment she saw Sophia leaving.

'How did Agnes respond?'

'She lost her temper. She called my mother a false friend, and said she was as bad as Sir Thomas North, and that she – Agnes – would not be forced into any man's bed unless he was someone she loved. My mother told her to calm down, and then I knew no more because my stepfather walked into the room where I was crouched and grabbed me hard by the arm saying "eavesdroppers hear no good of themselves" or some such, and called for the servants to take me to my own chamber and lock me in until I learned to behave like a lady.' This last part comes out in a great rush of breath as she winds her thin arms around her chest in a gesture that exactly mirrors her mother.

Sophia has the lurching sensation of missing a stair. 'So you don't know when Agnes left?' Or if she left alive, is the part she doesn't need to say aloud.

Lizzie shakes her head miserably. 'All I know is she was not there when they let me out the next morning. My mother said she went home. The following day I heard that she'd been found dead at The Theatre.'

Her gaze drops again and her shoulders slump forward; Sophia steps in and wraps her arms around her. It's like holding a bird between your hands: fragile bones, wildly skittering heartbeat.

'Mistress de Wolfe!' The call carries across the courtyard; it's Anthony's voice.

Lizzie pulls away. 'I should go,' she says, looking up at Sophia with fearful eyes. 'My mother will be looking for me.'

'Have you told anyone else about Agnes coming here that day?'

'No. My mother made me swear I would deny it, after she was found. She said it would cause bad blood with the Norths, when she and the earl were only trying to help Agnes.'

'But the servants saw her.'

'Only a couple, and I expect they have been paid to keep quiet, or threatened. Listen—' She clutches at Sophia's sleeve. 'Agnes loved Tobie Strange. He should not have to die for her murder. If you find enough evidence to prove he didn't do it, Mistress de Wolfe, I would testify to what I have told you today.'

'If your own mother denies seeing Agnes, you would testify publicly that she's lying?'

'Yes. But only if the outcome were absolutely certain. Do you understand?'

Sophia nods. She understands all too well; if there is no prospect of the earl being convicted – and she finds it hard to imagine – then Lizzie gains nothing by telling the truth except to make her own life unbearable.

'Lizzie – did you ever see your stepfather or one of his associates with a jewelled brooch in the pattern of the Devereux arms? Not the quartered Essex crest, just the white with the red band and red circles?'

'Not that I can recall, but I don't know every piece of

jewellery he owns.' She pauses to consult her memory. 'Though if I think, I have never seen him wear any heraldic device that was not the Essex arms. He likes to remind people of his title. Why – should I look out for such a brooch?'

'You could keep your eyes open, if it doesn't put you at risk.'

'Oh, I do that anyway. But I will double my efforts.'

'If you find anything, you can always get word to me at my house in Broad Street, or through Leila Humeya in Southwark, if you have a messenger you trust.'

Lizzie nods. 'I know Leila. My mother sent for her when I first had my woman's curse, she made me a brew that helped with the pains. My stepfather doesn't know she visits.' She presses a finger to her lips and grins.

Sophia opens her mouth to thank her, but the girl has already slipped from her grasp, darting around the door like quicksilver and gone.

She walks out into the courtyard, where thin flakes drift down over a lightless afternoon. Anthony is making conversation with a boy who holds the reins of their horses; when he sees her, he makes an ironic bow and says 'Madam', though his humour fades when he sees her expression. She mounts Nyx easily, ignoring his offer of help, and when they are past the guards on the gate she turns to him and speaks through gritted teeth.

'It's Essex. I'm certain. God only knows how we are to prove it.'

TWENTY-THREE

They ride back along Fleet Street towards the Ludgate sunk in a bleak silence. It's not yet three and already dusk is falling.

'But *why* would Essex kill Agnes?' Anthony says eventually.

'I told you. I think he wanted to bed her. That's why he offered to get her out of the North marriage. That was the choice Frances spoke of.'

'So Frances *knew*?' He shakes his head; he can't bring himself to believe it.

'You'd be surprised, Anthony, what some women will accommodate or look away from to keep a man happy.' Sophia sounds infinitely weary. 'However it played out, I don't think Agnes left that house alive on the twenty-seventh.'

For a few minutes he can't speak.

'So what do we do?'

'Take it to Cecil.' Sophia rides upright, looking straight ahead, but he can see the tension in her back and shoulders. 'Whatever his objections, I have to see him face to face. And if he won't act, then I will have to go direct to the queen herself.'

He wants to laugh, but the set of her jaw makes clear that she means it.

'How? Bang on the gates of Whitehall and demand an audience?'

She considers this. 'You said the Admiral's Men are playing before her on Twelfth Night?'

'Yes, but – oh, no, Sophia, that's—'

'Take me with you.' She turns imploring eyes to him. 'I can come in the guise of a seamstress – just so I can get into the palace.'

'And then what? Stop the play halfway through to denounce Essex in the queen's presence? Don't be insane – they'd clap you in chains before you could get a word out. And Ned would never let you near the company, anyway.' *Not while you're supporting the Chamberlain's Men*, he adds silently. 'You'll have to trust it to Cecil.'

'I don't trust Cecil an inch with this. Don't you see how it will go, Anthony?' she bursts out, her voice tight with tears barely held in check. 'They'll pin it on Tobie. All the evidence points to the Earl of Essex, but the repercussions for moving against him will be too severe for Cecil, not while Essex is in the queen's good graces and about to lead a glorious force in Ireland. Agnes Lovell is not significant enough to topple him, even if everyone suspects he killed her – not when they have a convenient and expendable scapegoat ready in the form of her young admirer.' She breathes in hard through her nose, mastering herself. 'Even if he knows Tobie is innocent and Essex guilty, Cecil won't spend his political capital pursuing justice in this matter at a potential cost to himself. Hanging Tobie would keep the Norths quiet and avoid the need to confront Essex at a time when the queen would likely take the earl's part.'

'But Tobie was in custody when the Southwark boy was murdered, so they won't be able to blame him for that.'

'No one will care about Badger,' she snaps back. 'There's nothing to link the two deaths except his idle boast about a brooch, and he can't repeat that now. The authorities will say he was a street thief, he crossed a gang over a stolen trinket, happens every night in Southwark. They won't waste a moment of their time making a connection with the murder of Agnes.'

'What about this girl from the Unicorn – her testimony links Badger's death to Essex?'

'The word of a Winchester goose against the queen's favourite?' She gives a bitter laugh. 'I think she's scared enough to know that she'll be in the river next if she ever mentions that brooch again. She might be anyway, if she doesn't take my advice to leave town.'

'And whose advice will you take, Sophia?' He turns to her as they cross Holborn Bridge, but she won't meet his eye. 'Essex knows you're looking directly at him now – if it was he who sent that man after you, he'd have good reason to believe you haven't heeded the warning. He might think you need it spelled out more clearly.'

She doesn't reply. Ahead, at the junction of Snow Hill and Cow Lane, the painted sign of the Saracen's Head comes into view, its lighted windows beckoning.

'Do you want to stop by and see if they know where to find Phelippes?' he offers. She nods, and they ride through the arch into the yard.

In the tap-room they find Ben, hauling in a basket of firewood.

'Thomas?' he says. 'Haven't seen him, but a boy came with a message for him, about a half hour back. Said if he turned up, I should tell him he was to go to Homerton urgently. You might catch up with him there, if the lad found him elsewhere.'

'Homerton?' Anthony exchanges a glance with Sophia. 'Did this boy say why?'

Ben leans in and lowers his voice. 'Suspicious death. He seemed to think Thomas would know what that meant. I wouldn't normally have told you, but I know you're working on something with him, so . . .' He drops his basket by the hearth and feeds a couple of logs into the flames. A girl emerges from the kitchen carrying a tray of hot meat pies and the scent of fresh pastry twists Anthony's stomach; he realises he has not eaten since breaking his fast that morning.

'Can we take a couple of those for the road?'

Ben grins. 'Course. Pay me later.'

He nods to the girl, who obligingly wraps two pies in a cloth while Sophia stamps impatiently.

'Don't you want yours?' he asks, cramming half of one into his mouth as they wait in the yard for the boy to bring their horses.

'Not hungry,' she says, swinging herself up and wheeling Nyx around while he is still trying to stop the cooking juices running down his sleeve. 'Hurry up, or I'll go without you.'

'It's Vincent Lovell,' she says as they ride north through Smithfield, the market deserted in the snow. 'It must be. Do you think Essex has had him killed as well?'

'I don't know what to think.' Anthony thumps his chest. He has never eaten two pies so fast – criminal to let one go to waste – and now they are stuck in a solid lump behind his breastbone, and he has burned the skin off the inside of his mouth. He sticks his tongue out to the freezing air, as if that might help.

'I mean, now we know Vincent was telling the truth about bringing her safely back to London.' Sophia is not to be deterred. 'She must have waited until he was out of sight, then slipped away to Essex House instead of going home. So we know he wasn't the last to see her. What if he didn't tell you the whole truth this morning? If Essex had made advances to Agnes on previous visits, assaulted her even, she could have confided in her uncle. The earl might have been afraid that Vincent would report it – to the Norths, to the queen – and decided he needed to be silenced as well.'

'Let's hope he dropped a ring with his full name inscribed on it this time.'

'Is this a joke to you, Anthony?' She swivels in her saddle

so abruptly her horse throws its head back and whinnies. 'Vincent Lovell could have testified against Essex. It would have made one more voice in Tobie's defence.'

'You're getting ahead of yourself,' Anthony says, chastened. 'We don't even know that Vincent is dead.'

'Who else would Phelippes have eyes on in Homerton?'

'Phelippes moves in mysterious ways.' He gives an involuntary hiccup and tastes seasoning again. 'Of course it's not a joke, Sophia. I'm afraid for you, and for Tobie. I feel with every step we're tangling ourselves deeper in something that can't end well.'

She pulls her horse up short, so abruptly that its hooves skid on the frozen ground. He brings his own mount around to face her.

'You can turn back now. I'm serious,' she says, seeing his expression. 'You would have never have been mixed up in this if I hadn't charged in accusing you of telling Cecil about Tobie, and I'm grateful for your help, but with the turn this has taken . . .' She lets the sentence fall away and shakes her head. 'We could not have known it would bring us to Essex. I don't know how this will end, but you should not risk making an enemy of the earl. You have your family to think about. Whereas I' – she looks away and spurs Nyx on again, past him – 'I will have no family left unless I can find a way to prove Tobie innocent. I have no choice but to keep entangling myself.'

'I know.' They ride on in silence. Anthony well understands the increased danger to Tobie; even if they turned up a dozen willing witnesses who all saw the Earl of Essex rape and murder Agnes Lovell, the queen would still find some excuse to look the other way, if she could. Elizabeth Tudor likes to spar and bicker with young Devereux, it's part of the odd relationship between them, and she allows him impertinences and liberties no other courtier would dare; Anthony sometimes wonders what offence Essex would have to commit for the queen to say, *enough*. Sophia is right, too, about the danger to himself; she doesn't have to think about money, but he thinks of nothing else. He is a writer, and writers need patronage; he can't afford to make an enemy of Essex, who could easily poison the queen against him and, by extension, the Admiral's Men. He should turn around. But another part of him is pleased by the possibility that Vincent Lovell is not guilty of his niece's murder, if only because it vindicates his own judgement of character. He had looked into the man's eyes and been convinced by his grief; it was the one aspect he could not square even when the evidence seemed to point to Vincent.

'I'm not going to let you ride all that way alone,' he says. She makes a face, but he suspects she's secretly relieved.

The journey out to Homerton feels longer than it did that morning. The hedgerows are stiff with ice, cobwebs fixed like glass. Lone crows flap up from white fields with desolate cries.

'Are you going to ask me what I found out at Essex House, while I kicked my heels masquerading as your manservant?' he says, as they traverse the snow-bound fields of Shoreditch, largely to shake her out of her gloomy thoughts.

She turns to him, more animated. 'Something useful? The brooch?'

'Nothing as helpful as that, I'm afraid. I was put to wait in a room off the kitchen with a cup of hot cider, only turnspits and skivvies coming in and out, not the earl's men. So I took myself off for a wander backstairs with the excuse of looking for the privy.'

'And?' Her eyes gleam; she enjoys any tale of subterfuge.

'Down one passageway I chanced on a couple of kitchen girls talking. One said she was taking a tray of food to Mistress Lizzie. So I pressed myself into a niche to listen. "Waste of good broth," said the other. "She won't touch a bite since her friend was killed", and then she made some comment about how Lizzie had no spare flesh to lose to begin with.'

'Anything to the point?'

'I'm coming to it. So then the first girl said, "I suppose we can say goodbye to a double wedding in the spring now", and her friend was grumbling about how Cook had promised there would be extra wages if the wedding feast was held here. The first girl said boldly that she'd step in if there was a spare bridegroom going, and the other giggled and said, "Not that one, you wouldn't, he's a whoremonger and they say he already has the French pox." Then they passed out of my hearing.'

'A double wedding?' Sophia frowns into the wind. 'Meaning Lizzie with the Earl of Rutland, and Agnes with – who? That makes no sense. I can comprehend Essex wanting her for a mistress, but he's hardly in a position to marry her. And I can just about credit that Frances would encourage her visits if she thought it would keep her husband happy, but not if she imagined he was lining up a new wife.'

'Perhaps they had Agnes in mind for some other man, then.'

'You're right.' Her face twists in disgust. 'God, it was bad enough thinking Essex wanted Agnes as an amusement on the side – this sounds like he was planning to give her away like a prize to one of his friends.'

'Some Devereux kinsman, perhaps – that might explain the badge.'

'That's no help, though – that family has more branches than a vine. There was another boy there hanging on the earl's elbow – Gus Moynes. Do you know anything about him?'

He shakes his head. 'Never heard of him.'

'Lizzie implied that he was debauched as well. I wish I could speak to her again, but Essex made clear I won't get a welcome next time. I've half a mind to go back there with the paperwork for his outstanding debts to Humphrey.'

'That might be unwise,' Anthony says, alarmed. She would do it, too. 'What astonishes me is how Essex could imagine himself in a position to bestow Agnes on anyone? He is nothing to do with her. The Norths thought she was theirs.'

'Lizzie said he intended to ask the queen to intervene. She could forbid the match with Edmund North, if she chose, and she might do it for Essex. And that could explain the argument Lizzie heard between Agnes and her mother, that last day – Frances told Agnes she had a choice, and Agnes said she would not be forced into any man's bed. Perhaps she didn't mean Essex himself, but whoever he was proposing as an alternative husband.'

'But if that's the case,' he says, 'it brings us back to the same question we had with Edmund North – why kill her? If Essex wanted her estate for some cousin, they needed her alive until she turned fourteen.'

'I don't know,' Sophia says. Her spirits appear to have sunk again. 'Something must have happened that day. We know she didn't die a virgin. Suppose she was raped at Essex House – perhaps by this prospective husband wanting to stake his claim – and she resisted. A blow to the head – that could have come during a struggle. Or else she threatened to report it and they decided to cut their losses and silence her. Either way, I am certain she did not leave Essex House alive that day. And Frances knew about Tobie, which would explain their decision to leave the body at The Theatre.'

'There are a lot of maybes in this theory,' Anthony says, knowing he needs to tread carefully. 'If Essex was going to the trouble of petitioning the queen to intervene in Agnes's marriage, why would this relative or friend of his risk such long-term gain by violating her?'

'Because men always want to prove their power,' she says, under her breath.

'Well – not all of us.' He waits for her to concede that he is not like that, but she doesn't. 'Although,' he goes on, 'this whole business is making me increasingly ashamed to be a man, when I see what young women must put up with. I keep thinking of Priscilla.'

'These great families don't see their daughters as people with feelings of their own,' Sophia says. 'They're just bargaining tokens, or brood mares. Not only great families either.'

Once again, he finds himself wondering about the parts of Sophia's life that remain a closed book to him. They ride on in silence for a while longer, until a cluster of small houses appears flanking the road ahead, smoke trailing from chimneys into the bitter air.

'Hackney,' he says, gesturing. 'Perhaps we'll find some answers here.'

TWENTY-FOUR

The last of the scant daylight is fading at the edge of banked clouds when they pull up outside the Widow Crowley's house in Upper Homerton. A small knot of curious neighbours stands at a distance, bundled in layers of wool that make it impossible to determine their age or sex. They turn to look at Anthony and Sophia and, as one, take a respectful step back; evidently their clothes or their horses suggest officialdom, he supposes. A tall man is stationed on the front doorstep; he is not obviously brandishing a weapon, but he looks as if he could produce one quicker than you could move out of its way if the need arose.

The neighbours exchange muffled whispers as Anthony and Sophia dismount.

'Can anyone watch these horses for fourpence?' she asks with an air of authority, casting her gaze around the huddled figures. A man steps forward.

'You can leave them with me, mistress – I live two doors down.'

'Did any of you see or hear anything?'

Anthony can't help but admire her; the way she framed that so as not to reveal that they have no idea what's happened.

A woman's voice emerges from the general murmur:

'She said he's dead, but we know no more than that.'

'We know they weren't legally wed,' says another, with a sniff.

'God's blood, woman – as if that matters now,' a man chimes in.

'Matters to Our Lord,' she says piously, and someone else swears at her.

One goodwife in a thick cap with ear flaps tugs at his sleeve. 'Here, sir, I've been neighbours with Joan Crowley for more than twenty years, and yon fellow says I can't even go into her house to see if she needs anything. What's that all about?'

Anthony pats her hand and approaches the guard at the door. 'Are you Thomas Phelippes's man?' he asks, in a low voice. 'Is he here?'

The man jerks his head at the house. 'Inside. He said to keep people out.'

'Tell him Sophia de Wolfe is here,' Sophia says, at his shoulder. 'And Anthony Munday,' she adds, as if she has just remembered. He tries not to mind.

The man disappears into the house and returns almost immediately, nodding them through. It feels to Anthony like days since he was last here in this parlour, though it is only a matter of hours. Thomas Phelippes is kneeling on the floor in front of Mistress Crowley, who sits rigidly upright on a settle; he looks impatient. The fire in the hearth has burned low; no one has thought to stoke it and the room is cold. The widow stares blankly at a point beyond Phelippes's head; she is visibly shivering.

Phelippes appears relieved rather than surprised to see them.

'I can't get any sense out of her,' he says, jabbing his thumb in the woman's direction as if she is incapable of hearing. By the look on her face, she might well be.

Sophia steps forward. 'For God's sake, she's had a shock. Did anyone think to get her a drink? Anthony, put some logs on that fire, I'll find some liquor.' She takes off her cloak and wraps it around the woman's shoulders; for the first time, the Widow Crowley stirs and focuses on Sophia with gratitude for a crumb of comfort.

Anthony coaxes the fire back to life while Phelippes crouches beside him.

'What happened?' he asks, in a low voice.

'I've had a man watching the place,' Phelippes whispers back. 'The fellow you saw on the door. About two hours ago, the woman came rushing out to her neighbour and asked her to send her kitchen boy to friends in the city with a message to say Vincent Lovell was dead. My man intercepted the boy and paid him to bring the message to me instead. I arrived about half an hour ago but she's not very coherent. She keeps repeating that she went out and came back to find him dead, and that she can't believe it.'

'What happened to him?'

Phelippes nods at the ceiling. 'See for yourself.'

With some trepidation, he follows Phelippes out to the passageway that gives on to the back room and the stairs, just as Sophia returns with a cup of something that smells as if it would take whitewash off a wall.

'They're not well provided with strong drink in this house,' she whispers as she passes. 'I think this is some kind of fortified wine, it'll have to do.'

'It's probably been consecrated. See if you can get her to talk,' he says, as Phelippes disappears up the bend of the stairway.

On the first floor there are two bedrooms; whatever the woman in the street believed, Anthony thinks, Vincent Lovell and the Widow Crowley at least kept up the appearance of propriety. Phelippes pushes open the door to the room overlooking the back yard and Anthony instinctively flinches.

He has seen hanged men before, of course; when he was a pursuivant, he was expected to attend executions as part of the job. The bulging eyes, the lolling tongues, the grotesquely swollen faces; the stains on their breeches where they lost control of their functions as they fought for life. He has seen enough to distinguish between the appearance of those whose necks were mercifully broken and those who strangled slowly; to judge by appearances, Vincent Lovell was the latter. His body sways gently from the central beam, not more than three feet off the floor, a low stool under him. Anthony feels the meat pies roil in his stomach.

'What do you think?' Phelippes says quietly.

Anthony understands the question. He lets his gaze travel around the room, taking in peripheral details, until – reluctantly – it comes to rest on the unavoidable fact of the dead man's face.

'That stool,' he says, nodding to it. 'You'd expect him to have kicked it over. And there's a cut on his lip. He didn't have that when I saw him this morning.'

'Exactly. And this.' Phelippes crosses the room to a space between the bed and the window and crouches, pressing his forefinger to a damp patch on the boards. He proceeds to sniff it and hold it aloft. 'Urine. So tell me how he pissed himself over here and not under the place he's hanging.'

'So. Not self-slaughter.'

Phelippes wipes his finger on his breeches. 'The woman downstairs is adamant he never would have. He considered it a great sin. But someone's gone to some trouble to make it look that way.'

'You're sure she didn't right the stool?'

'I asked her that. She doesn't recall, but I think her mind is not at its sharpest at the moment.' He pinches his lips together as if he considers this inefficient on her part.

'Surely your man watching would have seen if someone entered?'

'He was only watching the front door, from a house across the street. I didn't have the funds to set two watchmen. I regret that now.'

Anthony turns away to the door; he can't look at that face any more. 'I was only talking with him a few hours ago.' He shakes his head.

'How did he seem?'

'As I told you – distressed. His grief for his niece seemed genuine. But not like a man in fear of his life.'

Phelippes rubs at the stubble on his chin. 'I feel we are missing something. Why kill Lovell and dress it up as suicide?'

'To stop people looking for another perpetrator.' Anthony drops his voice further. 'Sophia thinks Essex is behind the murder. It fits, now we know about the cipher. She has a theory that the earl planned to marry Agnes off to one of his friends.'

Phelippes closes his eyes. 'This is a bad business, Munday. No accusations against the earl will stick.'

'You tell that to Sophia, then, for she won't listen to me. I'm sorry, I can't be in here any longer.'

He rushes down the stairs to find Sophia seated with her arms around the Widow Crowley, rocking her gently. The woman still has the same blank expression but she has allowed the tension to go out of her body; she looks like a cloth doll in Sophia's embrace. Sophia disentangles one arm and reaches towards him; he sees that she is holding a paper.

'Joan says this was in Vincent's chamber when she found him. She was going to burn it so no one could see the slanders it contains, but I persuaded her that it might help us find whoever did this.' She gives him a meaningful look over Joan's head.

He opens the paper and reads.

I, Vincent Lawrence Lovell, being now 55 years and sound in mind and body, do hereby make my last confession: that, having stained my soul with the sin of murder, I add to the list of my offences the sin of self-murder. I freely confess that on the twenty-seventh

*day of December in this year of grace 1598, I did kill
my niece Agnes Lovell, only surviving child of my late
brother John and his wife Catherine, thereby to benefit
from the inheritance of my brother's estate, the better
to give safe harbour to the queen's enemies, and in
retribution for the lives of my fellow Catholics lost as
a result of my brother John's betrayal. But the weight
of my sin so crushes my soul that I cannot go on, nor
will I see another innocent life lost on my account. I
repent my vile deeds and may God have mercy on my
soul.*

The note ends with a looping signature. Anthony folds the
paper and looks up. Sophia has done well; he doubts Joan
would have handed this over to him or Phelippes.

'Every word is a lie,' Joan Crowley says, focusing on him
for the first time.

'It's not his hand?'

She hesitates. 'It's *like* his hand, I grant. Whoever wrote it
took care over that. But the words are not his manner of
speaking. Besides, he would never have laid a finger on that
girl, nor so offended God as to die in such a way' – she
gestures to the ceiling – 'without hope of absolution.'

He meets Sophia's eye. He can see that she believes the
woman too. Her look says, *we have a problem.*

'Have you told anyone else?' Anthony asks.

Joan shakes her head. 'I sent a message to a friend who
would know what to do. But he has not come yet.'

Because your message was intercepted by Phelippes's man,
Anthony thinks. 'The coroner will need to examine him to
determine what happened,' he says gently. 'Is there someone
you could go to while they work?'

She nods. 'But they will not take him away without telling
me? We – his friends – will want to see that he is given
Christian burial. Once they rule that he did not die by his

own hand.' She juts her chin and he sees a streak of determination. 'I'd have cut him down, but I couldn't reach. And I thought – better to leave him, so the constables would see he had not done it himself. I thought they'd be able to tell.'

'You did the right thing,' Sophia says, rubbing the woman's arm.

Phelippes appears from the stairway. 'We'd better get the coroner in. What's that?' he says, seeing the paper in Anthony's hand.

Anthony passes it to him and watches his face as he scans it; fruitless, as Phelippes gives nothing away.

'Second thoughts, let's hold off on the coroner. Can we get her somewhere else?' he says, indicating Joan. But before any of them can react, the door opens and three men in heavy coats appear. Two pass straight through towards the stairs; the third beckons Phelippes into the hall.

'What will they do with him?' Joan, galvanised, leaps up from the settle and starts towards the stairs; Sophia catches her arms and holds her back.

'They will need to examine him to determine how he died,' she says. 'I will make sure they return his body to you and his friends after.'

'They won't cut him up?'

Anthony wants to step in, to stop Sophia making promises that are beyond her power to keep. The door opens again and Phelippes reappears, his face grim.

'We need to go with this man,' he says. 'Now.'

From the room above comes a clatter, like the sound of a stool being kicked over.

TWENTY-FIVE

Sophia watches as Phelippes rides ahead conferring with the man in black. Link-boys follow them before and after with lanterns; dusk has settled in, though it is only half past four. She and Anthony ride side by side, keeping enough of a distance from the others that their voices won't carry.

'Go on, say it,' Anthony prompts, after a while.

'It's too sophisticated. The forged confession, the attempt to mimic his writing. That's not what Essex's people do. They knife a child in an alley and throw him in the river. They don't take this degree of care.'

'So we're thinking the same thing?'

She glances over at him. It hardly needs stating; they both know one person with skilled forgers at his beck and call, and the kind of men who could enter a house, kill someone and leave without being seen.

'I suppose we're about to find out.'

A different nondescript house this time, off St Martins Le Grand. Their escort shows them to a door and melts away into the interior. Phelippes knocks and enters.

Cecil is seated behind a desk again on a high-backed chair. Sophia suspects he is elevated on cushions.

'Close the door.'

Phelippes obeys, and the three of them range themselves in front of him like children awaiting punishment. Cecil takes Vincent Lovell's confession and reads it with a solemn expression; he makes a good show of affecting never to have seen it before, she thinks. Finally he sets it down and regards them like a father who regrets having to exercise discipline for their own good.

'Well,' he says. 'It seems I owe you an apology, Mistress de Wolfe. Thomas assured me initially that the cipher used in the note was particular to you.' He glances at Phelippes, who is hanging his head. 'If I had known it had been in other hands, I would never have brought you into this sordid business. Anthony Munday – I have no idea what you're doing here, except that Mistress de Wolfe must have breached my strict instructions about confidentiality. But I think we can all be grateful that we have our answer' – he taps the confession in front of him – 'and we can consider the matter closed. I will see you recompensed for any inconvenience, of course.'

This is the point, she knows, where she is supposed to nod and walk away. She notes that he has not asked them to sit down. How simple life would be if she were the sort of person who could quash her conscience so easily. She can feel Anthony willing her not to make trouble.

'Vincent Lovell didn't kill Agnes,' she says, looking Cecil in the eye. 'He didn't kill himself either. As I think you well know.'

Cecil crooks an eyebrow. 'I have his written confession in front of me in his own hand. You've read it.'

'I've seen an account that contradicts everything about the man and his character.'

'You knew him, did you?'

She feels herself flush. 'No, but – Anthony spoke to him. I talked to the woman he lived with. Everyone says he loved his niece.'

'He loved Rome more,' Cecil says. 'He never forgave his brother for the deaths of those priests, and he wanted that estate with its sea coast, the better to aid England's enemies.'

'Who gets the estate now?' she asks. 'Who inherits that land now there are no Lovells left?'

'I believe it reverts to the crown,' he says, looking away and shifting a stack of papers from one side of the desk to the other.

'That's convenient.'

'I beg your pardon?' Cecil's eyes are on her again; he has gone very still. She can feel Anthony bristling with the desire to clamp a hand over her mouth.

'Master Secretary, may I speak plainly?'

Cecil sighs. 'Do you ever do otherwise, Mistress de Wolfe? Go on, then – let's have it out in the open.'

Her hands are clenched at her sides. 'You asked me to look into the murder when you thought the cipher implicated me. So I looked. Anthony assisted me, asking questions in places I could not go. And as soon as the evidence pointed to Essex House, you came to the same conclusion we did.'

'Which is?' He sounds as if he is indulging her.

'That Essex killed Agnes Lovell. Perhaps not with his own hands, but he is responsible. He saw her the day she died. I believe she was raped and murdered at Essex House. I think you suspect it too, and you knew you had no hope of bringing a conviction against the earl, so you took the opportunity to dispatch a Catholic conspirator who had been a thorn in your side and wrap the whole business up neatly so it wouldn't jeopardise the Irish campaign. And you get a nice fat estate out of it into the bargain, for the queen to hand out as she pleases.'

This is met with a cold silence.

'You presume to know me inside out, Mistress de Wolfe,' Cecil says eventually. 'It's true that I learned only this morning that Agnes Lovell had been seen at Essex House the day she died. That, together with what Thomas told me about the cipher, pointed in a direction we could pursue no further. You'll know that I am no admirer of the Earl of Essex. But often in politics one is forced into temporary alliances for a greater cause. You are quite right to think that Her Majesty will not risk the Irish campaign – the rebels must be put down, or Spain will use Ireland as a back door to invade us. The queen believes that at this stage, only Essex has the charisma to win public support for another effort there.' He pauses to shift his papers back again. 'As for Vincent Lovell – you have no idea what he was capable of. We've been watching him for some time – we have copies of his correspondence with traitors in France and the Low Countries who believe it is no sin to shed blood in the cause of bringing England back to Rome.'

'That's how you had his handwriting,' she says.

Cecil ignores this and continues:

'We know he has arranged passage for priests who entered this realm with the express purpose of harming the queen's person – thanks be to God, they were apprehended in time. He may have been a doting uncle, but he was a zealot for the Catholic faith. We recently intercepted letters from him to one of his contacts in the Clink urging the murder of a young priest he believes to be an informer. In truth, I have enough letters between him and traitors in the pay of Spain to have arrested him for treason months ago – we left him at large in the expectation that he would lead us to others. I assure you, that man would have found himself on the end of a rope sooner or later – at least this way he didn't have his guts pulled out for an audience. And if you can't understand the importance of putting the defence of prime Suffolk coastline into the hands of someone whose loyalty to England is beyond question, then I can only assume such matters are outside the scope of a housewife.'

Sophia summons all her self-control to keep her jaw clamped

shut and her hands by her sides. She would like to pick up his obsidian paperweight and throw it at his head.

'In any case, I would have thought you'd be relieved,' Cecil continues, with the smile of a man playing his ace. 'Vincent Lovell's confession means there is no reason for Tobie Strange to remain in custody. I've just drafted a letter to the warden of the Clink ordering his release.'

Sophia lets her breath escape slowly, not quite trusting herself to speak. 'Thank you, Sir Robert.'

'Who will get the Lovell estate?' Anthony asks. 'Not Sir Thomas North?'

'I wouldn't have thought so. It will be for Her Majesty to grant as she sees fit.'

So you'll get it, Sophia thinks. *Of course you will.* She can see it in his almost insouciant manner, shuffling his papers again as if to dismiss her. She takes a deep breath.

'There was a boy, in Southwark. He found a brooch with the Devereux crest in the trench with Agnes's body. He tried to sell it. Last night he was thrown in the river with a knife wound in his chest. Was that your doing?'

Cecil wrinkles his nose fastidiously. 'I consider that question offensive. But no. Not my methods. The boy was a notorious pickpocket, as I understand it.'

That part must have been Essex, then. She glances at Anthony. The brooch, the cipher note – anything that can't be explained away by Vincent Lovell's forged confession will simply be erased from the record.

'So the earl will get away with murder.' It's not a question. The words stick in her throat.

Cecil's eyes narrow. She expects him to rebuke her for her tone, but for a brief moment he lets the haughtiness drop.

'Justice is imperfect. You would know that better than anyone.' He leaves a pause here and looks at her, long enough for her to understand he is talking about what happened in Canterbury. 'Do you not think I would like to see Essex held to account, for once in his life? But the first lesson my father taught me was, read the queen's moods as a sailor reads the weather, and steer your course accordingly. At present, since he volunteered for Ireland, Essex is high in her favour and any man who speaks against him will find the barb rebounds and wounds only himself. I could make these accusations to the queen, the earl would deny them and it would be the worse for me. But take heart, Mistress de Wolfe – Essex will undo himself before long, you may be assured of it. In the meantime, someone must carry the blame for the murder of Agnes Lovell – better a traitor who would have died anyway than your boy, don't you agree? And if you're thinking' – he leans across the desk and points a finger at her – 'that the sainted Francis Walsingham would never have allowed such a travesty of justice, well, then, I have two words for you. Mary Stuart. Isn't that so, Thomas?'

Phelippes lowers his head. Sophia says nothing, because she knows he is right.

Cecil's eyes flick from her to Anthony. 'You have both been loyal servants of Her Majesty in the past. I need hardly impress upon either of you the need not to breathe a word of what you know or suspect. And you, Munday – you would do better to direct your efforts towards your writing if you want to please the queen.'

Cecil stacks his papers and taps the edges on the desk to square them off; the interview is evidently at an end.

'One last question,' Sophia says. 'How did Essex know? That I was investigating the murder of Agnes, I mean?'

Cecil looks faintly incredulous. 'Possibly because you marched into his house and started interrogating his wife?'

'No. Before that. Last night I was attacked. After I—' She has the grace to look abashed. 'After I called on you. On my way home, a man knocked me off my horse and held me down. He pinned a paper to my sleeve with another ciphered verse threatening that I would be next to die if I didn't keep silent. Essex must have sent him to warn me off. So I'm wondering – how did he know?'

Cecil's expression reminds her of the way Anthony looked earlier when he had indigestion. Anthony's attention is fixed studiously on his boots. They are all trying not to look at Phelippes.

'I have informers among Essex's servants, naturally, so I suppose it's not impossible that he could have them among mine,' Cecil concedes. 'Although no one except Thomas knew that I had a meeting with you about the cipher note. Or did they, Thomas?'

The cryptographer's face remains as expressionless as ever. 'Not from me, if that's what you're implying.'

'You've had dealings with Essex before.'

'And after the way that fell out, Master Secretary, do you think it likely that I would entangle myself with him again?'

'Not willingly. But he is a man to make threats. Do you still owe him money?'

At this, Phelippes recoils. 'I owe the Earl of Essex nothing,' he says quietly.

'That's reassuring, I suppose. And yet Essex did not learn of Mistress de Wolfe's involvement by divine revelation. What about you, Munday? An unguarded comment in the hearing of one of your colleagues in the Admiral's Men, someone with a connection to the earl?'

She sees Anthony pull his shoulders back, his professional pride stung.

'Master Secretary, I have served in intelligence work on and off since I was eighteen. I do not make unguarded comments.'

Cecil sizes him up and nods. 'Well, there is clearly a breach somewhere. I will look into it. Once the news of Vincent Lovell's suicide is made public, you should have no further trouble from Essex, Mistress de Wolfe, if he is content that you are not a danger to him.'

She hears the warning in his tone: *Don't even think of*

pursuing proof against the earl, or I take no responsibility for the consequences. 'I wasn't hurt, you'll be pleased to hear,' she says, irked.

Cecil blinks. Apparently it hadn't occurred to him to ask. 'That's a mercy. I expect he just wanted to frighten you. And as I told you at the time, your reckless visit to my brother's house will have given him all the confirmation he needed that you were working for me. Even before you harassed his wife. I must say, Mistress de Wolfe – I had been led to believe you operated with a little more subtlety.' He gives her a disappointed look. 'Still, I don't suppose our paths will need to cross again. You'd better see yourselves out – I want to speak to Thomas.'

Before she can argue, she feels Anthony's hand grip her elbow and steer her to the door. He makes a reverence to Master Secretary on the way out; she does not. Thomas Phelippes watches them go with the face of a man who is about to be whipped.

TWENTY-SIX

Anthony doesn't let go of Sophia's arm until he can be sure she is not about to give offence to the queen's minister. They stand outside in the dark street, the air so cold it seems to sparkle.

'That's that, then,' he says. But she is looking into the middle distance, brooding; he knows the mutinous set of her jaw. 'Sophia. There is nothing to be done about Essex now. You have to let it go.'

She turns to him, eyes flashing, but then he sees the fight go out of her.

'He's right, you know,' she says. 'I used to be good at this. But I have been clumsy, careless – I've blundered around like a cow escaped in the market.'

He smiles at the image. 'It's been ten years since you were called on to do this work, and you were thrown in with no time to prepare – hardly surprising if you're out of practice. It's not as if you need to make your living as an espial now.'

She looks wistful. 'No, but – I had hoped to make a better impression on him.' She jerks her head back towards the house. 'It's Phelippes, isn't it? Spying for Essex. It must be.'

'I think Phelippes hates the Earl of Essex.'

'That wouldn't make the first thing untrue. Essex could be

compelling him to betray Cecil. I don't see how else he would have known about me.'

'Come on, let's find a link-boy and I'll see you home,' he says. 'Essex may not have heard about Vincent Lovell yet and called off his thugs, you had better not be out alone.'

She doesn't protest. They don't speak much on the ride back to Broad Street; each tangled in their own thoughts. Once or twice he thinks he hears something, a disturbance at their back; each time he twists in the saddle to look, but the shadows offer nothing, and his jumpiness is only making his horse jittery. But he notices Sophia is the same, riding upright and alert, her eyes twitching to left and right, though the snow muffles all sounds.

'I liked Vincent Lovell,' he says sadly, as they turn towards her house. 'In spite of everything. I must be out of practice too. I thought myself a better judge of character.'

At this, she laughs. 'A man may be several things at once, Anthony. Just because he was a Catholic conspirator doesn't mean he couldn't be likeable. One of the most dazzling men I ever knew turned out to be—' She breaks off, and he feels disappointed; for a moment it had seemed that she was going to confide in him. 'In any case, never forget that Vincent Lovell didn't kill Agnes. I wonder if there is something I can do for Joan, that woman he lived with.'

'Be careful. Whatever Vincent was involved in, Joan's up to her neck in it too. You don't want your enemies saying you channel money to Catholic plotters.'

'My enemies.' She repeats the word as if it is unfamiliar. 'Yes, I suppose I have those now. The Earl of Essex as well as my stepson. Essex won't like the fact that I know the truth about Agnes. Do you think he may try to threaten me in spite of the official version?'

'I think,' Anthony says, weighing his words carefully, 'that unless Essex finds out about your conversation with Lizzie Sidney, he doesn't know that you know Agnes visited that day. And I can't imagine Lizzie would tell him – from what you say, she seems well able to keep her confidences. But if I were you, I wouldn't go riding around London alone until the earl has had a chance to forget about you.'

They draw up outside her house, and the guards on the gate nod to her in greeting.

'Thank you for everything, Anthony,' she says in a low voice, as a boy comes to lead Nyx away. 'I could not have made progress in this business so well without your help. I'm sorry I've been so short-tempered – just, with Tobie . . .'

'Don't worry. We make a good partnership,' he says, and instantly regrets it, though she seems not to be listening.

'I can't help but wonder what we did achieve, in the end. Three people dead, and no justice for any of them. It makes me sick to my stomach that men like Essex believe they never have to pay for the damage they do.'

'Forget Essex. Think instead that Tobie is free,' he reminds her. 'Without your persistence, he might have been left to take the blame. I'd bet right now the Chamberlain's Men are plying him with terrible beer in some Southwark drinking hole and he's embellishing his tales from prison to regale them.'

He meant to cheer her, but her face closes. 'I doubt he's regaling anyone – his first love was brutally murdered. He'll need to grieve her. I wish he had someone to talk to, but boys don't, do they? They don't unburden their hearts to anyone. Perhaps Jo could try.'

'And what about you?' He waits until she looks at him. 'Do you have anyone you can unburden your heart to, Sophia?' He hesitates. 'Because I hope you know that you can always—'

'Leila,' she says firmly. She steps forward and gives him a brisk embrace. 'You should get home to your family, they'll have missed you these past couple of days.'

He forces a smile. 'Not as much as the Admiral's Men.'

'It will do Henslowe good to miss you. He ought to value you more.'

'That'll be the day. He wishes I was Will Shakespeare.'

She squeezes his arm. 'Then he's a fool. Give my best to Beth. I mean it – you must both come for dinner soon.'

He watches her disappear into the house and remains there after the door has closed behind her, until his horse snorts, impatient to move, and reluctantly he mounts and sets out for home.

Beth is sitting by the fire in the parlour when he arrives; she sets down her book and stands to kiss his cheek.

'You're freezing,' she says, taking his hands between hers. 'Come and warm yourself. Have you eaten?' She doesn't ask where he has been, only observes that he looks tired.

'I had a pie earlier. It's been a long day,' he says, easing his boots off in front of the hearth.

'Henslowe works you too hard. I've a good mind to come down to The Rose and tell him so.'

'Well, he might listen to you,' he says, smiling, while simultaneously praying that she is only joking. There might be a difficult conversation if Henslowe were to tell her he has barely seen his principal writer for two days in the week leading up to a performance at court. 'You're looking brighter today.'

It's true, there is more colour in her cheeks. 'I have felt much better,' she agrees. 'I know I've been poor company this festive season, Anthony – I hope I can make it up to you. I said to Mercy that we should have a dinner here for the new year, invite some friends, give the children a chance to celebrate. You've been so busy and I've been so unwell, it hasn't been much of a Christmas for them. We could hire musicians. You could ask Mistress de Wolfe to come.'

He stares intently at the fire until he is sure his face is steady. 'Why would – I mean, what made you think of her?'

'Well, she's on her own, isn't she? She's a widow, she has no children nor wider family in London – I didn't like to think of her spending the festive season alone in that big house.'

'I'm sure she has plenty of friends,' he says, feeling a little desperate. Why is he so resistant to the idea? Beth is only being kind, he knows, and yet he wonders if some sixth sense has prompted her to mention Sophia's name; the same intuition that he has long feared would make his thoughts transparent to his wife if she were to witness him in Sophia's company for any longer than ten minutes. But the disappointment on her face is enough to make him relent. *She lacks company*, he thinks, with a pang of guilt; *stuck here all day with only Mercy and the children, and me always elsewhere, even when I'm home*. 'If it will make you happy, then of course we'll have a dinner,' he says, and is briefly heartened by her flush of pleasure. But before they can discuss it further, the door slams open and the children come bowling in, all talking at once: Richie with some device he is carving from a piece of wood, Priscilla with her drawing book and Annie hurling herself on to his lap like a puppy, and he sees that Sophia was right: his family have missed him, and he them.

A man may be several things at once, Anthony, he thinks. But can he be a loving and devoted husband and father, while also longing, with a force that at times threatens to stop his breath, for a woman he can never have? Can he be content with a prestigious position writing royal entertainments and crowd-pleasers for The Rose, while also hankering for that life he used to know in Walsingham's service, where you are permanently on edge, always living on your wits?

The restlessness he feels, even now as he tickles Annie until she squeals while admiring Priscilla's sketch of the cat, is a dissatisfaction with the outcome of the day. It's not precisely the same as Sophia's anger at Essex's ability to dodge justice; it's more a sense that the story lacks a proper resolution. (And he should know – didn't Francis Meres, only this year, describe him as 'our best plotter' in his book *Palladis Tamia*? Take that, William of Stratford.) The short while he was working with Sophia in pursuit of the killer he had felt that sense you have sometimes when galloping a horse, when your body and the animal's find the same rhythm and all parts of your combined minds and bodies move as they should, through pure instinct, in perfect harmony. When Cecil told them the investigation was over, that feeling of rightness dropped away abruptly. It feels like denying the audience a fifth act, he thinks. Too much still unanswered. But only a fool would go against Master Secretary, and Sophia is right: he has too much at stake.

He kisses the top of his little daughter's head and tells himself sternly to count his blessings. But he knows he will see Vincent Lovell's face tonight when he tries to sleep.

TWENTY-SEVEN

'Hilary, I need to see those account books again,' Sophia says, before she has taken off her cloak and hat. 'I want to know how much Humphrey lent the Earl of Essex.' If Essex can't be made to pay for murder, she thinks, he can be made to pay in other ways. When she finds his name in those ledgers, she will have a weapon to use against him.

Her steward puts a warning finger to her lips and nods towards the parlour. 'Visitor, madam.'

Sophia doesn't wait for an explanation; she anticipates a messenger from the Chamberlain's Men assuring her that Tobie is safe and free. She rounds the corner into the formal room she never uses, and her heart drops at the sight of Jasper de Wolfe. He still looks unkempt, but at least he doesn't smell of spirits this time, and he has not asked Hilary for drink.

'Mother,' he says, with a sarcastic bow. She gives him a stony look. 'Sorry. Sophia. I must speak with you on a personal matter.'

'The answer's still no,' she says. She is too angry about the Earl of Essex to entertain another spoilt boy who thinks the world should bend to his whims.

'I'm not here about that,' he says. 'And you might show me a little more courtesy, considering I was just assaulted on your account.'

'What?' She looks him over; he doesn't seem damaged in any way. 'On *my* account – how?'

He sits heavily in a tapestried chair and crosses his legs at the ankle. 'I was at the Half-Eagle and Key in the Barbican earlier with some friends – spare me your disapproving look – and I left to walk home alone. I was looking for a link-boy when a fellow came up behind me and pushed me into a doorway with his arm across my throat. He moved fast, otherwise I'd have had my knife out,' he adds.

'No doubt,' she says drily. 'The father or brother of the girl you've ruined, most likely.'

'I feared so, at first. But he said he wanted to ask me about you. If I answered his questions truthfully, I could leave with all my limbs intact.'

Sophia feels a wash of cold run through her. 'How did he know me?'

'He said, your stepmother's been running around London asking questions that are none of her business. He wanted to know why.'

'What did you tell him?'

'I said I was not in your confidence.' He says this with a hint of petulance; as if he thinks he should be. 'He said you've been all over Southwark talking to street children and whores about the girl found dead up at The Theatre. He thought you were looking for something. And apparently you've been visiting the Clink.' His small green eyes fix on her, waiting to see what she will give away. 'I told him my stepmother is a respectable widow, she wouldn't go near Southwark whores, and if she visited a gaol it was to do Christian charity. But he didn't believe me. And I have since spoken to your servant, who confirms that it is true – you were in the Southwark stews today, and the prison. And apparently you visited that Moorish witch.'

Bloody Mick. She makes a mental note never to take him with her again.

'You're right – I was doing charitable work with the girls of Southwark, and at the prison. And Leila Humeya is a midwife. Not a witch.'

'Huh. Perhaps you'd be more inclined to give me my father's money if I were a criminal or a whore?' When she doesn't answer, he presses on: 'This man who threatened me seemed very sure that you were looking into the murder of Agnes Lovell.'

It takes considerable effort to keep her expression neutral. Surely this must be the man who has been following her, the one who held her down in the snow and left her with that warning note. Essex's hired muscle, no doubt. Enterprising of him to seek out Jasper, she thinks, though a sign that he has no understanding of their relationship.

'Well, he's mistaken. If he wants information about Agnes Lovell, perhaps you should direct him to your friend Edmund North. Wasn't he betrothed to her?'

Jasper flushes, as if he has been caught out. 'She was his father's ward. The family are grieving sorely.'

'I'm sure they are. That's a big estate to lose.'

'Not everyone marries for financial gain, Sophia. Don't judge by your own standards.' He pushes himself to his feet and wanders to the mantelpiece, where he picks up a small blue ornament of Venetian glass. 'This man says he knows where I live, and he will break my legs next time if I can't give him answers about how much you know. I realise that you have no family feeling for me, not even for my father's sake, so you probably don't care, but if there is anything you can tell me, I would prefer on the whole not to be crippled. He knows where you live as well, by the way,' he adds.

'I know no more than the general news in the street,' she says. 'And you're wrong, Jasper – I have no desire to see your legs broken. If you will take some motherly advice' – she gives it the same ironic tone – 'don't go walking about London alone and stay sober enough to defend yourself.'

'Appreciated.' He gives a dry smile, turning the ornament

between his hands. 'So you weren't hunting for something in Southwark, then?'

A small, high note of alarm sounds in the back of her mind, like a knife striking a glass.

'What did he look like, this man?'

'I didn't really see him. It was dark and he was wrapped up in a scarf and hat.'

'But you must have had a sense of him, nonetheless, if he had you pinned against a door. Tall, short, heavy, thin?'

Jasper falters. 'Tallish. Strong enough to hold me. I don't know, it all happened so fast and I was afraid.'

She nods. Briefly, she had wondered if Jasper had invented this man as a pretext for asking his own questions – on behalf of Edmund North, perhaps. If she hadn't encountered a man of similar description the night before, she might have entertained this suspicion for longer. But it can only be Essex's man.

'I hope you won't have any more trouble from this person,' she says, trying to sound soothing. 'But if he approaches you again, tell him he is mistaken. My business in Southwark is only the relief of the poor. I have no interest in the girl's death beyond a sorrow that anyone could commit such an evil deed in London.'

He doesn't seem mollified. He glares at her a moment longer, then casts his eyes around the walls.

'Where is my parents' wedding portrait?' he asks. 'It used to hang here, above the mantel.'

The space he indicates is now filled by a painted copy of Ortelius's *Theatrum Orbis Terrarum*. The globe and its possibilities: a more enduring passion of Humphrey's than Jasper's mother. There is a wedding portrait of Sophia with her husband, but it lives in an upstairs chamber; she had disliked the idea of being exposed to the scrutiny of guests.

'I don't know. Humphrey moved it years back.' She tries frantically to recall where it ended up; in one of the bedchambers, or was it packed away for storage?

'I want to see it.'

'I'll have Hilary look it out for the next time you come.'

'It's grossly disrespectful to my mother for you to hide it away in some cupboard, as if there were never any wife but you. Considering her lineage, and yours. If you don't want it, I'll take it. It should be mine anyway.'

He probably wants to sell it, she thinks.

'I've said, we'll find it for you.'

'I can look for it now.'

She sighs. 'Jasper, it's supper time. I'm sorry you've had a fright from this man, and thank you for warning me. We'll find your mother's picture for you. But I need to rest now. I can ask one of my guards to see you home, if you're afraid?'

Jasper makes no sign of taking the hint. A heavy tiredness pulses behind her eyes; she realises she has eaten nothing all day. Is he expecting her to traipse through every room in the house in search of this picture while he waits?

A knock at the door: Hilary's head appears.

'Madam – someone else to see you. From the Chamberlain's Men.'

Her face clears; you can always rely on a player to script a timely interruption. No doubt an emissary bringing the good news of Tobie's release and Burbage's profuse gratitude for her help.

'Thank you, Hilary. Master de Wolfe was just leaving – would you ask one of the men to accompany him home and make sure no ill fortune befalls him on the way? Not Mick, though, he's had enough riding around today.' She will have to have a talk with Mick about the meaning of discretion, she thinks, and the fact that Jasper is not a part of this house-hold, whatever he may believe.

At the door she turns back. 'Oh – Jasper. I think that little blue dish has accidentally fallen into your sleeve – Hilary can help you find it before you leave, I'm sure.' Passing her steward, she whispers, 'Have him escorted off the grounds right away. He wants his mother's wedding portrait – don't let him go wandering around the house on the pretext of looking for it.'

She feels a prickling of unease as she walks down the corridor to the entrance hall. Whatever Jasper thinks, she is not so heartless that she would countenance him being hurt on her behalf, but she is more troubled by the idea that this man – whoever he works for – knew how to find people associated with her.

Her thoughts are interrupted by the sight of Richard Burbage pacing the hall; he turns as she approaches and his face does not speak of relief or gratitude.

'What?' she says, fear clutching at her again.

'It's Tobie.' He rushes to her and seizes her hands.

'Is he free?'

'No. That's the thing. He should be. I had a message to say they've dropped the murder charge – apparently the girl's uncle killed her and then couldn't live with the guilt and hanged himself. You couldn't make it up.'

Oh, you could, she thinks. 'Then why is Tobie not released?'

'There are new charges. I don't know the details – only that he's been accused of heresy.'

'*What?*' She stares at him.

Burbage spreads his hands, helpless. 'I know. It makes no sense. I thought, since you had spoken to a lawyer, perhaps we might prevail on your generosity again . . .'

'Of course – I'll do whatever I can. Have you seen him?'

'Not yet. I was going to ride down now – I suppose it's too late for you? I have a couple of the boys with me, so we should be safe on the streets.'

She glances at the wall-clock; it's not yet six. 'Give me ten minutes,' she says. 'Your boys can wait here in the warm if you like.'

Her appearance in the kitchen startles the cook into a flurry of consternation. 'I had no instructions, madam,' he says, wiping floury hands on his apron. 'Hilary didn't know if you'd be home for supper. I have a capon to roast, if you—'

'Don't worry,' she tells him. 'Anything cold will do, I don't have long.'

She settles on a piece of baked egg and cheese flan from the cold store, which she gulps down standing at the worktop while the cook looks on with disapproval and mutters about the importance of a hot meal in this weather. She accepts a packet of sweet pastries wrapped in a cloth to take with her, and promises to eat properly when she comes home.

'*Heresy?*' she says to Burbage, as they wait in the yard for a new horse to be saddled (Nyx has had enough excitement for one day). 'I didn't know Tobie was even interested in matters of religion.'

'He's not,' Burbage says, through a mouthful of pastry. 'He's fifteen – he's interested in girls and music. That's why I can't understand it. I wondered if it was a confected charge by Thomas North, to score a point against us, now that the accusation of murder no longer stands. The Lovell girl, you see – if she was swayed in her beliefs by the Catholic uncle, there might be some matter in the letters between her and Tobie—'

'What, points of doctrine? Did you write love letters debating the eucharist when you were fifteen?'

In the flickering torchlight, she sees him grin, his beard flecked with crumbs. 'I might have, if I was trying to impress a girl.' His face turns sombre again. 'We must demand to see the evidence – that's why your presence would aid our cause, Mistress de Wolfe. They are more likely to listen to a woman of your standing, who can use your persuasive charms—'

'Offer a hefty bribe, you mean?' She smiles wearily, hoisting herself again into the saddle and wondering if this day will ever end.

TWENTY-EIGHT

'A Catholic relic,' says the warden of the Clink, after Sophia has paid out enough for herself and Burbage to be admitted to his presence. 'Concealed in his belongings. It pains me to say this, because he seems a good boy. I received word that he was no longer under suspicion of murder, and we were set to release him, but it's our practice to search those on their way out to make sure they're not carrying letters from fellow prisoners. We found no messages, but we did discover this relic, as I say. So it's my belief that he has Catholic affiliations. He may have been sent to make contact with some of our inmates.'

'I've never heard such horseshit,' Burbage says, slapping his palm on the warden's table.

Sophia gives him a warning nudge. 'What affiliations? Which inmates? Tobie doesn't know any Catholics.'

'Begging your pardon, madam, but he had connections with the Lovell family, and Vincent Lovell was at the centre of a network that includes the fugitive John Gerard. We don't know exactly what the boy's role is, but we aim to have that out of him sooner rather than later.'

Sophia almost leaps out of her seat; this time Burbage has to lay a restraining hand on her.

'I'm sure there's been a misunderstanding,' he says, with the dazzling smile that works so well on female groundlings but less so on this grizzled gaoler, who merely stares him down. 'Can we see the offending object? This so-called relic? There might be a perfectly innocent explanation.'

Reluctantly, the warden reaches into a box on his desk and withdraws a pendant on a silver chain. The locket is about the size of a starling's egg, with filigree patterns on the outside.

'Looks innocent, I'll grant you,' the warden says, as he springs the catch. 'But mark this.'

One half of the inside is decorated with a miniature painting of a young girl holding a lamb, a halo shining behind her. The other side offers a recess lined in crimson silk, inside it a fragment of something grey and brittle.

'What is that?' Burbage asks, frowning.

But Sophia has already understood. She can feel the blood draining from her face, as if her body has processed the implications before her mind has fully caught up.

'It's a reliquary,' she says faintly.

'That's right. It's a relic of St Agnes, to be precise. That's a fragment of her skull.' The warden indicates with his finger-nail.

'Really?' Burbage peers closer.

'Well, no, obviously not – it's probably a cat. But the fact that he had it concealed suggests that he practises the veneration of saints in secret.'

That's not all it suggests. Sophia pushes her chair back abruptly and stands.

'I need to speak to him. Immediately. Alone.'

'I'm afraid I can't allow that.' The warden turns the locket in his hands. 'For all I know, you might be smuggling messages yourself.'

'Now look here,' Burbage says, drawing himself up, 'Mistress de Wolfe is a highly respected patroness of—'

'How much?'

The warden blinks at her.

'How much to let me have ten minutes of conversation alone with him? Will this do?' She takes a gold angel from her glove and holds it out to him.

He regards it for the space of a heartbeat before snatching it up in his fist as if she might change her mind. 'Ten minutes only,' he says, looking at her with a mixture of disgust and reproach, the way men often look at women, as if they blame them for their weakness.

She is relieved to see that Tobie is still in the chamber where she saw him that morning; they have not taken the opportunity of this new charge to move him somewhere worse. If it were not in the Clink, you would say it was a pleasant enough room; certainly she has stayed in inns that lacked this level of furnishing and comfort. The guard knocks on the door and steps back to let her in. 'Ten minutes,' he says again, as the door is locked behind her.

Tobie raises his head and she can see that he has been crying. Then, most unexpectedly, he hurls himself across the room and into her arms. Instinctively, she enfolds him; she cups the back of his head with her hand and draws his face into her shoulder, murmuring soothing words as you might to a little child who has woken in the night, and every fibre of her being is shot through with a rush of pure love almost frightening in its ferocity; she understands those stories of mothers possessed by superhuman strength who can lift carts to save their children. She feels she could punch through the stone walls of the Clink to free him. His hair is dirty, but the smell of his scalp triggers something deep and animal within her; she knows his scent, it is part of her. It occurs to her that this is the first time she has held him to her since he was an hour old; if she were not so well practised at hiding her feelings, she could weep with the enormity of it.

Abruptly, he pulls away as if shocked by his own outburst. He swipes his tears away with his knuckles and retreats to sit on the bed, mumbling an apology.

'Forgive me, Mistress de Wolfe,' he says, when he has recovered himself. 'It's a lie. They told me I could go free, they knew I didn't kill Agnes, and then they found – and they accused me—' He lets out a juddering breath. 'I'm no heretic. I go to church as the queen commands. I never pray to saints, my parents were good Christians, they never hankered after the old ways like many did in Canterbury.' His eyes flicker to her, imploring. 'It was a gift. The locket, I mean.'

'I know. A gift from Agnes.'

He stares at her, horrified. 'How did you know?'

'Agnes's uncle gave her that locket when she visited him. It was a new year gift. The day she disappeared. Tobie, we don't have much time.' She glances at the door. 'I need you to tell me when exactly you last saw her.'

He presses his hands between his knees, his gaze on his feet. 'It was that day. The twenty-seventh. The day before we took The Theatre down.' He gives another hiccupping breath.

'When, though?' Her mind is racing through the possibilities. Before or after she went to Essex House? 'What time of day *exactly*?'

He looks surprised at the sharpness of her tone. 'It was the evening, after six. She came to my lodgings. I remember because my room mates had gone out to a tavern when the bells rang six. I said I'd join them in an hour – I had some lines to learn first. To think – if I'd gone with them, I'd have missed her.' His face is burning with embarrassment, his entire body twisted away from her with the excruciating awkwardness of having to discuss this with a woman he barely knows, and thinks of as a benefactor. 'It wasn't my idea, Mistress de Wolfe,' he bursts out. 'I wanted to wait, but Agnes – you didn't know her. She could be very determined.'

'So – explain it to me – she came to your lodgings sometime after six.' Sophia forces herself to speak slowly and clearly, to tamp down the rising panic. 'You're certain?' If Agnes was with Tobie at six, then she didn't die at Essex House.

'Certain,' he says quietly.

'And you – forgive me, Tobie, but I must ask – you went to bed?'

You would think the boy couldn't turn a deeper scarlet, but he does. When he answers, his voice is barely more than a whisper. 'Agnes wanted to. She said it was no sin as we were pledged to one another. She had this idea that we could run away and marry in secret, like Romeo and Juliet. I kept reminding her how that tale ends.' He smiles sadly. 'She was upset when she arrived. She said time was running out. In five months she would be forced to marry Edmund North, or if not him, the Earl of Essex would press her to marry a friend of his who she disliked equally. She said two things made her a prize as a bride – her maidenhead and her father's estate.'

'So she set out to rid herself of both,' Sophia says, half to herself. Agnes was nothing if not enterprising. She wishes they could have met.

'She said she had talked to her uncle Vincent about signing her inheritance over to him, he was going to help. She had tried to borrow money so that we could elope that night, but she failed. So then she' – he can't look at her – 'she said that if we were married in the sight of God, it would mean that I had a prior claim on her, and the other suitors would not want her. She practically dragged me to the bed.'

It would have meant nothing of the sort, Sophia thinks; a couple of hours between the sheets is not legally binding, and a ruined maidenhead would not weigh much against the value of Sir John Lovell's estate, but perhaps Agnes was innocent enough to believe that a pledge made with her body was sacred.

'So you took her to bed. And – again, I'm sorry, but this is important – are you sure it was her first time?'

Tobie tucks his chin into his collar. He can't look at her.

'Well, I'm no expert in such things, Mistress de Wolfe, because, uh – it was my first time too. Agnes said she had not been with a man before, and why would she lie?'

'Was there – forgive me – did she bleed?'

'Oh. Yes. A little. I thought I'd done something wrong. I fear I was not very skilled.' Tobie has pressed his back against the cell wall as if trying to disappear through it. This is not a conversation he had imagined he'd be having. 'We joked that we would have time to practise once we were married.' He covers his face with his hands.

'And afterwards – what happened? I need you to tell me the absolute truth, Tobie, or I won't be able to help you.' She can feel her pulse beating in her throat.

He speaks through his fingers. 'Afterwards, we talked for a while, and when the bells struck nine she said she had to leave before Lady North noticed her missing. And she gave me her locket as a gift, as we didn't have a ring to mark our vows. She said it belonged to her grandmother and she wanted me to keep it until we next saw each other.' His face crumples again. 'I had no idea it contained papist relics, I swear. I didn't even open it – my mind was too full.'

'I believe you,' Sophia says. 'But I need you to tell me how Agnes got home. You didn't let her walk alone?'

'Of course not. I brought another lantern and went with her as far as Aldersgate. She didn't want me to come any further, she was afraid we would be seen together.'

'Did you have any sense, on that walk, that you were being followed?'

'Followed?' He lowers his hands and frowns. 'Not that I noticed. But then, we were only looking at each other.'

'And you didn't see her after she left you at Aldersgate?'

'I followed her. It was only a short distance but I wasn't going to let her walk alone in the dark, whatever she said. I kept to the sides of the street so she wouldn't see me.'

'Did you see her enter the North house?'

He shakes his head. 'She turned down Little Britain and I kept her light in view, but then she cut through the grounds of the old St Barts priory, behind the hospital. There's a path that leads to Long Lane, and she knew her way, where I was stumbling around in the snow – there's so many fallen stones where they pulled down the chapels. I fell and my light went out. By the time I had picked myself up and got my tinder-box to work, I'd lost sight of her. I went around the back of the church to the gate, but there was no sign of her light in the street. The North house is only a couple of doors down, so I reasoned she was home already. I thought I'd better leave before anyone caught me hanging about.'

Sophia takes a deep breath. 'So, to be clear – the last you saw of her was crossing the priory churchyard, sometime after, what – half past nine?'

He nods. 'About quarter to ten, I would guess.'

'How long, between losing sight of her and finding the street empty?'

'Minutes, only. Five, at most.'

'And did you hear anything to suggest she had been – intercepted?'

'No. But then the snow would muffle any footsteps, I suppose.'

'The Norths say she never arrived home that day.'

'They could be lying,' he says. 'They've lied about everything else.'

'Listen to me, Tobie.' She crosses to sit beside him and grasps his arm. 'You must never tell anyone that Agnes came to your lodging that night. Did your room mates see her?'

He shakes his head.

'And you didn't tell them?'

'What do you think I am? The sort of braggart who would dishonour a lady by talking up his conquests?'

'No. I don't think that at all.' She is touched by his indignation. 'But it seems you could have been the last person to see her alive, apart from her killer. Since you've been cleared of her murder, you don't want to give anyone reason for asking more questions.'

'They're saying her uncle killed her. I don't believe it, Mistress de Wolfe. He can't have done.'

'No. But he can't defend himself now, and if he is declared guilty, no one can point the finger at you. So you don't want anyone knowing that you saw her much later than he did.'

'Then the man who really killed her will just get away with it?' His eyes are round at the injustice of it.

Not if I can help it, she thinks. 'You mustn't worry about that now. Say the locket was sent to you as a Christmas gift by an anonymous admirer from the playhouse and you had no idea what it contained.'

He looks sceptical. 'You think they'll believe that? One of the guards said I would burn for a papist, and I can't even imagine – I have never seen a burning.' He seems to shrink into himself.

'He's just trying to frighten you. We'll get this charge dropped, don't worry. Tomorrow you'll be free and back at the Blackfriars.'

He gives her a brave smile and clasps his hand over hers. 'Mistress de Wolfe, you've been so good to me. I don't know how I'll thank you.'

'I know how much the Chamberlain's Men value you,' she says tightly. There is a fuzz of golden hair along his jaw and his upper lip, but from a certain angle, he still looks like a child in need of mothering.

'Lord Hunsdon has not lifted a finger to help, though he is supposed to be our patron. You know, Master Shakespeare says—' He breaks off, suddenly bashful. 'He says we're very alike.'

'You're a better actor than he is.'

Tobie laughs. 'Not me and him. Me and you.'

She holds herself very still. Master Shakespeare and his

famous perception. 'Well – I think we're both determined people. Perhaps he meant that.'

'He says we both have eyes like a lynx.'

His golden eyes are fixed keenly on hers; there is a moment of held breath, broken by the sound of a key in a lock.

'Time's up.' The guard holds the door for her, to ensure she doesn't linger. She gives Tobie's hand one last squeeze before she leaves, fighting with every sinew to keep herself steady. She had almost told him.

TWENTY-NINE

'You were magnificent back there, Mistress de Wolfe,' Burbage says, as they ride back over the bridge. 'That warden looked as if he were about to soil himself by the end. I thought I might, and you weren't even shouting at me.'

She gives him a wan smile. 'I wasn't *shouting*, I was speaking forcefully.' She had declared that she was going straight to the Privy Council and if one hair of the boy's head was touched in the meantime, the warden would wish he'd never been born. 'I will do whatever I can for Tobie. You should also send to Lord Hunsdon right away, ask him to stir himself. I know you'd rather he didn't find out that one of your actors was in prison, but he'll hear eventually – better if he learns it from you with a true explanation.'

'*Is* it a true explanation?' Burbage asks. 'The locket being an anonymous gift, I mean?'

'It's the only one you're going to get.'

'You don't think the boy *is* a papist, do you?' He looks anxious. 'He came from Canterbury, you know – a lot of people cling to the old ways there, in secret. We don't know much about his people.'

'I'm fairly sure that, as you said yourself, he's never spent even a moment pondering transubstantiation.'

They continue in silence for a while. At the corner of Leadenhall Street, she turns to him.

'Will Shakespeare,' she says. 'Is he a man of discretion?'

'In what sense? Ohhh.' Burbage grins, a glint in his eye. 'Well, his wife's all the way back in Stratford, so I'm sure what she doesn't know won't hurt her.'

'Christ, Burbage, not that. I mean, only – if he suspected – no, never mind. You can leave me here, I need to call on someone.'

He doesn't ask questions, though she is sure he is supplying the answers in his imagination, given that it is almost nine o'clock. Well, let him. One of the things she likes about actors is that they are rarely scandalised by anyone's personal arrangements. She waits until he and his companions have turned the corner before she rides through the archway to the yard behind Thomas Phelippes's lodgings. The place is deserted; only one torch flickers in a wall bracket by the back door. She ties her horse to a post and knocks.

When a second knock brings no reply, she thumps her fist against the door and curses in frustration. If Phelippes is out, she needs to find another way to contact Cecil, and her best hope is the Saracen's Head; Dan or Ben might know how to send a message quickly to Master Secretary. She is exhausted; the sensible course would be to wait until the morning and try Phelippes then, and if it weren't for the thought of Tobie spending another night in prison, she would go straight home.

She turns to leave when an idea strikes her. She glances up; there are no lights in any windows overlooking the yard, and this is an opportunity that might not come again. Peeling off her gloves, she crouches and slides her knife out from its hidden pocket, then removes a silver pin from her hair. She could do with someone to hold the light closer, but she will have to manage by balancing it on the doorstep. The lock is sturdy, as you'd expect from Phelippes, and she is out of practice; add to that the fact that she doesn't have the right tools and she can barely feel her hands, but she tries to remember how Ben had done it at Tobie's lodgings, and allow the old familiar movements to return to her. It takes time; more than once the knife slips and nicks her, and she fears that Phelippes or one of his neighbours will appear at any moment, but the lock is well-oiled and with patience she begins to feel the mechanism engage. When the bolt finally springs back, she has to suppress a small exclamation of triumph.

Behind the door she finds a ledge with a stump of candle. She lights it from the torch outside and pulls the door shut, looking around. The passage runs from the back to the front of the house; a flight of stairs leads up to Phelippes's lodgings on the first floor, and beneath them, facing her, a door with two solid bolts, both secured with padlocks. Cursing softly, she goes to work again with her makeshift instruments, pausing to wipe bloodied fingers on her skirts, but eventually she has them open, and before her is a set of steps leading down into a void.

Feeling her way, the weak light small comfort in that dense dark, she finds at the bottom a spacious cellar, divided at intervals with tall stacks like a library, but in place of books, the shelves hold wooden chests. Her heart sinks: even if she knew what she was looking for, where would she begin? And what *is* she looking for? Some evidence that Phelippes is in the pay of Essex, and betrayed her? And then what? Not much she can do now, but Cecil should be warned.

Except she now knows that Agnes didn't die at Essex House that day. Nor was she violated by the earl or his friends; she lost her virginity willingly to Tobie. Foolish boy, she thinks, the severity of it only now striking her; what if the girl had become pregnant – what would the Norths have done to him then? Christ, and she would have been a grandmother. The thought stops her cold. Though, of course, Agnes will never be pregnant. She leans her head against the shelves and thinks that she could easily fall asleep here, though she can picture the result if the candle fell among so much paper and wood; she needs to concentrate.

The chests are labelled alphabetically. Passing along the stacks, curiosity gets the better of her; she wants to know what information Phelippes holds on her. But which of her names would it be filed under? He had code names for all Walsingham's agents, back when she was recruited, taken from mythological figures. Hers was Lyssa, goddess of rage and madness, which had seemed fitting: she has been raging all her life, for as long as she can remember, at one thing or another (usually the actions of men). But she begins with W, for Wolfe.

The first box contains page after page of cipher alphabets, all written in Phelippes's tiny, meticulous hand. There are bundles of letters, also in cipher, neatly tied with ribbons, nothing she recognises. Some of the dates go back to the 1580s, to the time when the Catholic rebels wanted Mary, Queen of Scots on the English throne. Sitting on the floor, she pauses to look down the length of the shelves as they disappear into blackness beyond the reach of her candle, and tries to imagine how many hundreds of thousands of papers are contained in all these chests, the cumulative record of a decade in Walsingham's service. And the majority of their contents, she has no doubt, held also in the extraordinary memory of Thomas Phelippes.

But it was folly to think she could find anything here that would shed light on the present business. She is about to give up when she lifts a paper and feels a jolt at the sight of a familiar hand. The letter is dated July, 1596 and is written in plain English, unciphered.

My dear Thomas
    I was shocked to receive your letter and can only
wonder how you did not come to me before things

reached this pass. It grieves me greatly to learn of your
travails; I have heard the Marshalsea is not the worst
of London's gaols but that will be cold comfort to
you, I'm sure. In recognition of your unique gifts and
the long years of service we have undertaken together,
I would willingly help. Send me a list of your creditors
and I will see what may be done to secure your
liberty.

   Your loving friend
   Humphrey de Wolfe

Seeing his signature causes an ache behind her sternum. So it was not the Earl of Essex but her own husband who had bailed Phelippes out the first time. Does this mean, then, that Phelippes is not playing double, that he has no loyalty to Essex?

'You could have just asked me if you wanted to know,' says a flat voice behind her. 'You're filed under G, by the way, for Gifford.'

She whips around, almost dropping the light.

'Careful,' he says. 'We don't want the whole place going up.'

'Mother of God, Thomas – you nearly killed me with fright. I didn't hear you.' He must have come down those stairs in the dark, she thinks, by touch alone.

'No. I'm well practised at discretion. Unlike you – there's a bloody great horse in my yard. Still – you did a good job with the lock, it's not an easy one. A lot of people wouldn't have managed. Good to see the skills I taught you haven't gone to waste.'

'I only wanted to talk to you, but—'

'But you didn't know if I could be trusted.' He sounds regretful.

'Someone knew I was looking into the murder of Agnes. They threatened to kill me. I thought it must be Essex.'

'And you thought I was the one leaking to him.'

'You did work for him.'

'True.' He slides down the stack to sit on the floor beside her. 'I needed employment. Unfortunately, Walsingham didn't provide me with a rich spouse, as he did for you. But I told Master Secretary, I have no loyalty to Essex. I consider him in part the author of my misfortunes these past years.'

'I thought perhaps he was extorting you. If you owed him.'

'Ah. You thought he had cleared my debts.' He gives a dry laugh. 'No. Essex would not lift a finger for me, nor did I ask.'

'I realise that now.' She taps the paper. 'It was Humphrey who got you out of prison.'

'Yes. The first time.' His head is lowered, but she couldn't see his expression in this light in any case. 'I think, Sophia, if you want to know who is watching your every move, you should look closer to home.'

'You think there's a spy in my household?' Her shoulders stiffen. 'But that's—' She was going to say 'impossible', but of course it's not. You never know what people will do for money.

'I think it would be the obvious place to start.'

'But when I was attacked, the note said that I would be the next to die. It was a clear reference to the murder, and no one in my house could have known I was investigating. I never mentioned Agnes to anyone.'

'Unless they were in the pay of the person who killed her.'

'Essex?'

'You're still sure it's Essex?'

Sophia slumps back against the stacks. 'I don't know, Thomas. That's why I wanted to talk to you.' She tells him, with minimal detail, of her conversation with Tobie – the heresy charge, the locket, his tryst with Agnes. It feels like a monstrous betrayal of trust. 'So my theory – that she was raped by Essex or his friend and killed to keep her silent –

falls apart. We know now she didn't die at Essex House that afternoon. But that doesn't mean the earl wasn't behind it.'

'With what motive? Now we know she wasn't raped.'

'Perhaps she refused his friend and he was angry. He could have had someone follow her from Tobie's and attack her in the priory churchyard behind St Bart's.'

He frowns. 'They would have had to come well prepared. Where did they leave the body for a day, until they could take her to Shoreditch? If this hypothetical killer was waiting for an opportune moment between Tobie leaving Agnes and her reaching the safety of home, he couldn't have known Tobie wouldn't walk her right to the door.'

'He could have hidden the body and come back with a cart.'

'Mm. Or there's a simpler explanation. Which is that she did reach home, and did not find safety.'

She stares at him. 'You think the Norths killed her after all?'

'What I think, Sophia, is that since it's been given out that Vincent Lovell killed her, it would be a good idea for you to stop asking questions.'

She thinks of Tobie's face when he asked if the man who killed Agnes would just get away with it. She wants to show him a world where justice is better than that, but such a world does not exist. Not in London, anyway.

'But then' – her mind is turning rapidly – 'if it was not Essex or Vincent Lovell, that means the cipher note had nothing to do with this Cloudesley in France or your work for Essex. It *was* aimed at me all along.'

Phelippes looks down at his hands. The candle is burning low; he is almost erased into shadow. 'When I was first imprisoned in the Marshalsea in '96, after I wrote to Humphrey, he came here. I didn't have this strongroom then – everything was piled in boxes upstairs in my lodgings. I'd had to grab as much as I could when Walsingham was dying, before Essex or Burghley got hold of it. Humphrey was concerned that there might be compromising material there that could fall into the wrong hands if I was known to be *hors de combat*.' He bites at the skin around his thumbnail and avoids her eye. 'Your husband went through all the papers and took away anything that might be damaging to his interests, or yours. Ciphers, letters, reports. After, when I was free, he paid for me to have this cellar converted and better security installed.' He gestures to the door. 'Not secure against his own wife, as it turns out.'

She gives him a wry smile and holds up her fingers to show the lacerations. 'It wasn't easy, I'll give him that. What did he do with all the material?'

'He said he wanted to put it beyond reach. I assumed he'd destroyed it, but he may not have meant that. You'd probably have a better idea of what papers he left than I would.'

Sophia shakes her head. 'It took months to go through everything belonging to the business with the lawyers and accountants. All his properties and investments. By the time that was done, I couldn't face starting on his personal letters, and once I'd closed the door on them, somehow I never made time to open it again. There are boxes of his papers I've never even looked at.' But Hilary has, she realises, and it is as if the ground is falling away beneath her; she presses her hands to the floor to steady herself. 'You think there's a spy in my household who could have found my cipher among Humphrey's letters and passed it on to whoever killed Agnes – Essex or the Norths? But why?'

'Money, I presume. It usually is.'

'No, I mean – why would anyone want my cipher in the first place?'

'As I understand it, Humphrey had made loans to just about everyone at court. My guess is that someone thought it would be useful to have evidence of your history to hold over you in case you decided to call them in.'

'Christ.' She puts her head in her hands as the implications rush at her. 'What other information did you keep on me, Thomas? Anything about Tobie, or his father? Or the events in Canterbury in '84?'

'Walsingham held files on all of it at one time, yes. Whether that matter was part of the papers Humphrey took away with him, I don't know. I don't keep a record of every document in my head.'

'Cecil knew about Tobie when he first sent for me. If you didn't tell him, then—' She lifts her gaze and looks at him in horror. 'Surely it can't be *Cecil* keeping a spy in my house?'

Phelippes shifts position and wraps his arms around his knees.

'Those last weeks when Walsingham was dying, it was chaos. He called me in to see him in his sickbed in Seething Lane, alone, and told me to take the most sensitive papers – all my ciphers, identities and codenames of agents, certain letters. The Earl of Essex had already moved in on Frances – he married her just before her father died, and he was manoeuvring himself into position to replace Walsingham as spymaster. Sir Francis told me what I needed to take from his house to keep it safe from Essex. But I couldn't access his offices at Whitehall – Lord Burghley's staff stripped all the files there. So I imagine anything Sir Robert knows about you, he learned from his father's papers.'

Sophia fears she might faint or vomit. The thought that every detail of her life – Tobie, his father, her brutal marriage in Canterbury and the suspicion of her husband's murder, her subsequent flight to France, all her work for Walsingham – was documented and out there somewhere for other people to consume as if it were a lurid drama, it gives her terrifying sense of dizziness, as if the world around her is no longer solid and might give way at any moment, leaving her to plummet to oblivion. Why, in God's name, did Humphrey not destroy the papers he took from Phelippes's house, if he had wanted to protect their content? Sentiment, perhaps; did he want to look back fondly in his retirement on everything he had done for queen and country? Then why had he needed to keep papers about Sophia's previous life? Insurance, she supposes, and the realisation saddens her. Had he never quite trusted her? Or maybe it was only that, once you have been in Walsingham's service, you learn to watch your own back in a way that has nothing to do with how you feel about the people around you; it's a purely professional instinct. Either way, it's probable that someone – besides Cecil – knows details of her past that could destroy the life she has now, and Tobie's future along with it. And that one of her own servants provided them with that information.

'You know all my secrets, don't you, Thomas?' She tilts her head and regards him.

He blinks. 'I know a lot of people's secrets.' It's a simple statement of fact. 'I think that was why Humphrey was so quick to get me out of prison when I wrote to him. He was afraid I'd be tortured for what I knew.'

She wonders that this possibility had never occurred to her. 'My God. Were you?'

'No. I was in the Marshalsea for debt, not politics. I don't think the keepers even knew who I was really.'

She wants to ask him how a man of his exceptional abilities could have found himself in that situation not once, but twice, but feels she would be overstepping. It's a weakness that leaves him vulnerable, though. That he wasn't tortured then doesn't mean it wouldn't occur to someone in the future. She should take better care of him, she thinks, given all he knows.

'You wondered why I didn't contact you when Humphrey died,' he says, not looking at her. 'The truth is, I was ashamed. I didn't know if you knew what I owed him. In every sense.'

'You worried I might ask you to repay the debt?'

'I didn't know. But I thought – out of sight, out of mind.'

'Listen, Thomas. If you ever have troubles of that nature, you come to me in future, understand? Preferably before you end up in gaol.'

His eyes meet hers and slide away.

'All right. And if you want to look at my papers, you ask before you break into my house.'

'Deal.' It's hard to tell, with Phelippes, whether he's making a joke, but she smiles anyway. The light has almost burned down, and she shivers. 'It's late, I should go. But I need a favour – I need you to go to Cecil urgently and tell him about Tobie's situation, this ridiculous heresy charge. If Cecil sends an urgent order for his release, they'll have to obey.'

Phelippes pushes himself stiffly to his feet. 'I'll see you home first.'

'There's no need.'

'There is. Someone out there is threatening to kill you.'

She concedes this point, and agrees to be accompanied. But who, she thinks? And who among her household could be complicit?

THIRTY

Sophia goes to her bedchamber, but she doesn't sleep. She sits at the writing desk surrounded by candles, picking at a bowl of nuts and running through lists of names in her mind, the histories of all her household servants: family backgrounds, religious allegiance, political views. Humphrey was rigorous about checking the stories of everyone he employed, with good reason – he feared commercial as well as political espionage – but since his death she has delegated that responsibility to Hilary, preferring to spend her own time and energy with the Chamberlain's Men, or among her books. She has not been as attentive as she should have been; if someone in the house has divided loyalties, she has only herself to blame. She has been terse with the servants tonight, and they can sense something is amiss. When Hilary asks if she wants the account books brought up to her room, she snaps that it can wait until tomorrow. Lina comes to put a warming pan in her bed, and Sophia chides her for letting a hot ember fall on the carpet. She sees Hilary's sharp eyes on her, assessing: is her mistress overwrought, sickening for something, expecting her woman's trouble? The idea that she might have to think twice before confiding in Hilary leaves her wholly unmoored. The only other time she had experienced such a feeling was when her father sent her away to Kent to spare the family the shame of her pregnancy, and she realised her mother was not going to fight for her. The destabilising realisation that the one person you believed was your ally was, in fact, not on your side at all.

She rests her elbows on the desk and presses the heels of her hands into her eyes. With the exception of Mick and one of the kitchen boys, all the servants have been part of the household since before Humphrey died, meaning they would all have been through his thorough checks. Mick has already shown himself willing to divulge her business to Jasper, but the one fact she can't get around is that the chests containing Humphrey's papers are in a locked room. She has one key and Hilary has the other. Even if someone had managed to steal or copy a key somehow, they would have to have known what they were looking for, and she doubts Mick – or any of the other servants – have the capacity for that. It all comes back to Hilary, and that is too enormous to process.

What motive could possibly inspire her steward to betray her? Not money, surely – Sophia pays her a generous wage, commensurate with her experience and discretion, and she could not hope for a better position elsewhere; any other household would demote her to mere housekeeper. Not faith – Humphrey would never have let her near the house if he thought there was even a whiff of Rome about her family. She has no children for whom she would risk her livelihood; who, then, could induce her to divulge Sophia's secrets?

She has no answer. She doesn't entirely rule out the Earl of Essex as Agnes's killer – there is the matter of the brooch to be explained – but Phelippes's theory that the girl made it home to the North house is also plausible. The difficulty is that she can't imagine either Essex or Sir Thomas North getting anything other than short shrift from Hilary; one glance from her would skewer the pretensions of both.

Gradually the house falls silent around her as the night's

tasks are wrapped up and the servants make their way to bed. When the clock in the hall strikes eleven, Sophia pulls her gown around her, takes a bunch of keys from her cabinet and, holding a fresh candle, pads down the stairs as softly as she can, to the room at the back where Humphrey's books and papers have lain in storage for the past two years. As she passes his portrait on the stairs, she lifts the light to catch his eye. *Well then*, she says to him, in her mind: *you created this mess, keeping those papers instead of burning them – what do you suggest I do about it?* And – though she is not superstitious and has never credited reports of visions or phantoms, indeed she hardly knows if she believes in the afterlife any more – she hears his voice in her head, clear as day, as he'd told her many times: *Trust yourself, Sophia. Trust your instincts.*

All very well for you to say, she thinks, *but my instincts have often brought me nothing but trouble.*

When she opens the door of the store room, it is obvious that the chests have been touched recently: handprints in the drifts of dust on top of each one give the intruder away. The prints are smudged and smeared where the boxes have been moved; impossible to say even what size the hands were. It is freezing in here; her breath clouds around her, but she shuts herself in, blows on her fingers to warm them and opens the nearest box.

She thinks of Sir Francis Walsingham, calling Thomas Phelippes to him as he lay dying; even as his body failed, his mind was working to secure the secret history of Elizabeth's reign. She remembers Humphrey in the last months of his life, meticulously transferring his business interests, remaking his will, putting his affairs in order. He must have known he didn't have long; even so, he can't have been expecting the end to come as abruptly as it did. If he had lived longer, would he have tackled the paperwork now looming over her in a dozen dusty chests? Might he have thought to destroy things that could compromise both of them?

As the candle burns down and she works her way through two boxes, she discovers that her late husband appears to have kept copies of every letter he ever wrote: there are missives from his travels, full of seemingly mundane detail which she guesses are coded references to secret matters; a significant amount of correspondence with the authorities at Cambridge and later at Gray's Inn, apologising for damage caused or rules flouted by his son, with generous offers of compensation to soothe aggrieved tutors or fellow students. She finds a touching letter to his former sister-in-law, with details of his first wife's illness, urging the sister to hurry up from Sussex if she wants to see Maud, and offering to cover the cost of travel.

Sophia sighs, wipes dusty fingers on her gown. She can hardly feel her feet, despite the fur slippers. This is the job of months, not one night. One more box, she tells herself. And there, in the third chest, it leaps out at her: a paper covered in Walsingham's elegant hand, and dated December of 1589.

Well, old friend – it seems this stubborn workhorse, my body, is failing me. The physicians tell me I must prepare to meet my Maker, and I would submit to His will were it not that so much remains yet to do to secure the realm and the succession against the threat of Rome. I beg Him every day: grant me just a little more time, Lord, and I will not waste it, though I fear He is not open to negotiations. But there is one matter I would resolve while I still have my wits about me; it concerns a young woman who has done good service to Her Majesty and to England, and I would like to see her provided for before I take my leave of this world. She goes currently by the name of Mary Gifford, but her true name is Sophia Underhill. Her father was John Underhill, Rector of Lincoln College in Oxford, though she was banished from the family

home at 19 years when she had a child by a Jesuit
conspirator, later executed at Tyburn (though I assure
you she has no affinity to the Catholic faith; quite the
reverse). The boy was taken from her at birth; Thomas
has been searching for him, as yet to no avail. There is
more I should tell you, but I had rather do it face to
face. You will like her, Humph – she is spirited and
intelligent, highly educated and – though I am past
noticing such things – extremely beautiful. Come and
see me. Do this last charity for an old comrade.
  Your loving friend,
  FW

Sophia folds the letter with trembling hands. She feels as
if the chill has spread from the floor to penetrate her very
bones. Half her life set down here, for anyone to read. What
was the charity, she wonders – visiting Walsingham on his
deathbed, or marrying her? So Humphrey had known every
detail about her past before they even met, and it had not
deterred him. She remembers their first meeting. A bare winter
garden, frost crackling on the ground. She was working as
governess for a family in Northamptonshire with suspected
Catholic connections (suspicions that proved correct, as she
had found out). They had been obliged to sell off some of
their land to pay their recusancy fines; Humphrey had come
out with a view to buy it. After his business was concluded,
he had asked her to walk in the grounds with him. They
talked for an hour or more – of books, plays, history – and
at the end he had produced from his coat a letter with
Walsingham's unbroken seal. It was brief, and the writing
heartbreakingly shaky:

My dear Lyssa,
  Humphrey de Wolfe is the best man I know. He
would take care of you when I can no longer do so. I

know you will balk at the thought of being traded like a commodity, but this is the only way I can offer you protection. Life has dealt you many hard blows, my dear; I pray you, take this chance to have the rough edges smoothed away. You have earned it.

Your loving friend,
FW

Humphrey had returned the following week and they had walked again. Shortly afterwards, the father of the family was imprisoned for correspondence with known traitors in France and Spain (letters Sophia had intercepted and copied) and his estate forfeit. Humphrey had bought the whole manor; it was the one he left to Jasper. When the house was sold and her position no longer existed, he had proposed to her and she had accepted. Walsingham died in April; she and Humphrey had married in May. She is surprised to find tears falling. Humphrey had been a gift she had not looked for; not because of his money, but because he had valued her for herself. Their marriage did not have the heat of her first obsession with Tobie's father, nor the combative tension of her relationship with Giordano Bruno, the Italian philosopher who had been her lover, on and off, more than ten years ago, the man who had first brought her to Walsingham. In place of passion, her marriage to Humphrey had given her, for the first time in her life (as Walsingham had foreseen), a sense of safety. Now all of that feels as if it is teetering on a knife edge.

She hadn't heard the door open, but she sees the spill of light creep along the floor; in a heartbeat, she slips the Walsingham letter inside her gown.

'Are you looking for something in particular, madam?' Hilary stands outlined in the doorway, her face in shadow. 'Can I help?'

'I couldn't sleep. I thought I might as well make a start on sorting these.'

If Hilary finds this implausible, she says nothing. 'Is this still about the Earl of Essex, madam?'

'What? No. I just wanted to see . . .' She can't think what to say. This new distance between her and her steward, it's unbearable. 'Hilary, has someone been through these boxes recently?'

'Not to my knowledge. How would they? The room is kept locked, you and I have the only keys.'

'True.' She still can't see Hilary's expression properly, but her tone gives nothing away. 'I think it would be best if I keep the keys from now on.' She pulls herself to her feet, wincing as the feeling returns to her legs, and holds out a hand to her steward.

'As you wish, madam.' Hilary unclips the ring of keys from her belt and removes one, passing it over without argument. 'Do you want me to question the servants about whether anyone could have gained access?'

'No. Let's leave it for now. You can go back to bed, Hilary.'

'Very good.' She hesitates at the door. 'If I may say, madam – you have been unusually agitated these past couple of days, ever since that man with the pocked face called on you. If there's anything—'

'Call him by his name, Hilary.' Sophia steps forward, her shoulders rigid. 'Don't pretend you didn't recognise him. You know everything that went on in this house.'

'And that is why the master valued me, madam,' Hilary says, with quiet dignity. 'I had thought you shared his trust.' She turns and stalks away with her head high.

Sophia leans against the doorframe and lets out a shuddering breath. If she has alienated Hilary, who does she have left?

THIRTY-ONE

31st December 1598

Sophia did not think she would sleep, but she must have, because she surfaces in her own bed, with Lina timidly shaking her awake and snow-light stealing through the drapes.

'Pardon me, madam, but you have a visitor waiting down-stairs. It's gone ten.'

Sophia struggles upright, cursing; as she moves, she feels the crackle of Walsingham's letter under her pillow. She must have fallen asleep reading it.

'Who is it, Lina?' Burbage or Phelippes, she hopes, confirming Tobie's release.

The maid bends forward and lowers her voice, as if whispering a blasphemy. 'The dark woman.'

'Do you mean my friend Leila?' She throws back the blankets, flinching at the shock of cold air, and frowns at the girl's sullen expression. 'What is it? I'd rather you said what you are thinking.'

Lina pouts. 'Master Jasper says she does not worship the Christian God, and she uses Saracen poisons to rid the Southwark whores of unwanted babies, in the womb and out.

He says it's unseemly for his father's widow to keep company with such a woman.'

'For God's sake, Lina – Leila is a skilled midwife. She goes to church as the queen commands.' Sophia is not strictly sure this part is true. 'And Master Jasper should not be discussing such matters with you, in any case.'

'Forgive me, madam.' The girl dips her head. 'Sometimes he comes here when he is in his cups, and then he speaks very freely.'

'I know. Make sure you don't encourage it. Go down and ask Cook for some mint tea and honey cakes, and bring it to us in the front parlour.'

She wonders as she dresses – pulling on her fencing breeches under her skirt, just in case – what Jasper might have said about *her* in his cups. She can guess. Could it be Lina spying on her? Would her maid be foolish enough to have had her head turned by flattery from Jasper? Her stepson would certainly have an interest in finding out anything he could use against her, but she doubts Lina would have the patience to sift through Humphrey's papers. Still, she can't rule it out. 'Suspect everyone,' she remembers Walsingham telling her once. At this rate, she will have turned her whole household against her.

Leila is waiting for her in the parlour, warming her hands by the fire, her back to the door. Sophia feels an overwhelming reluctance to step inside; she fears more bad news. These past couple of days, she feels she is permanently braced for the worst. But when Leila turns at the sound of footsteps, Sophia sees that her friend's cheeks are pinked by the cold, her eyes bright; she looks full of intrigue.

'Guess where I've been,' Leila says, kissing her cheek.

'Please – I don't have the energy for games.'

Leila steps back and examines her at arm's length. 'No, you look terrible,' she agrees. 'Well, then – if you will spoil my fun, I'll tell you. I've just come from Essex House.'

Sophia drops heavily on to a chair and stares at her. 'What? Why?'

'Poor little Lizzie Sidney was suffering dreadful monthly pains first thing this morning,' Leila says, taking the chair opposite with a glint in her eye and a barely suppressed grin. 'She wouldn't rest until her mother sent for me to take a look at her. I had to see her in the garden summerhouse to make sure the earl's people didn't spot me. It wasn't very summery, I can tell you.'

'*And?*' Sophia leans forward so far she almost falls off her chair. They are interrupted by a knock; Lina arriving with the tea and cakes. The girl takes her time arranging plates and cups on a small table; neither woman speaks until she has left and closed the door behind her.

'Well, she felt a lot better for seeing me. Turns out it wasn't even her time of the month. A woman's body is a mystery, eh.' Leila winks. 'She gave me this and said you would want it urgently.' She reaches inside her jacket and draws out a small cloth package, which she unwraps and lays flat on her palm. Inside is a brooch in the shape of a shield, about the length of a thumb, a pattern picked out in red and white jewels. Three red circles above a broad red band on a white background.

'Is it the same one Badger showed you?'

Leila nods.

'Can you be certain?'

'There's a garnet missing on the centre circle, see? I pointed it out to Badger.' Her good cheer dips at the boy's name.

'How did Lizzie get it?'

'She charged me with telling you the whole story, so listen. There's a man Essex refers to as his "agent", though Lizzie doesn't know what exactly he does and her mother doesn't like to hear mention of him – Lizzie assumes it's the earl's dirty work. She was watching from the window late last night when she saw this man arrive and head to the earl's private study in a great hurry, so she ran down and listened from the next room. There's a loose panel or a hidden door or some such.'

'Come to the point.'

'All right.' Leila ruffles herself gently; she is telling this in her own time. 'The earl was angry. He said, "Why am I hearing reports about a boy's body washed up in Southwark? I expect better from you." The man said something about ice in the river, and Essex snapped back that he should have thought of that. Then, as the man was leaving, Lizzie heard her step-father say, "And after all that, it wasn't even my fucking brooch. Never seen it before. Better safe than sorry, I suppose – we don't want a whiff of a rumour that I was connected with the business."'

'He's bound to say that, though.'

'To his own agent? Who's just killed a child to protect his master?' Leila shakes her head. 'Lizzie thinks the man must have offered to get rid of it, because then Essex said, "No, I'll hold on to it for now, it's safer here until we know whose it is. And tidy up after yourself better in future." Much later, when Lizzie heard the earl go to her mother's chamber, she slipped down again to his study and found it in a drawer of his desk. And this morning she sent for me. She said you'd asked her to look out for it.'

'Clever girl.' Sophia takes the brooch and turns it over in her hand. 'It looks old. Could be an heirloom. But if Essex is telling the truth it would have to be some other branch of the Devereux family, and they go back centuries, God knows who they might have intermarried with. Maybe the Norths have some connection, back in their family tree. Could Edmund's mother be a Devereux?'

'No good asking me – I've never understood these old English dynasties,' Leila says, shrugging. 'God didn't create earls and dukes, I know that much.'

'Careful expressing that kind of thought aloud.'

Leila laughs. 'You forget – I've seen under the skirts of half the noblewomen in London. We're all the same down there, believe me. The things I could tell you.'

'Please don't.'

Humphrey would have had all those dynastic details at his fingertips, Sophia thinks. He took a keen interest in the marriages of the noble families, largely because he liked to keep an eye on where their assets were at any one time, in case anyone should need to sell or borrow.

Leila stands. 'I'd better get back to work. I'll leave that thing with you,' she says, nodding to the brooch. 'Essex will notice it missing sooner or later, and I don't want to be accused of keeping stolen goods – that wouldn't help my reputation. And it would only remind me of Badger, poor little scrap.'

Sophia can picture all too easily how the scene played out: Badger, meeting his potential buyer in an alley by the wharf, swaggering as he named his price; Essex's agent affecting to examine it, a hand moving to his belt; instead of a purse, he draws out a dagger and puts it through the boy in one smooth move, easy as a hot knife through butter, then discards him. If not for the ice in the river, Badger would have simply disappeared, and only the little girls from the wharf and Jen at the Unicorn would have been able to guess at his fate.

'Is Jen all right?' Sophia asks, suddenly anxious.

'She's taken your advice, thank God, and got herself out of town. Not without a lot of persuasion,' Leila adds. 'I had to tell her you'd cover her loss of earnings while she's away.'

She nods wearily. 'As long as she's safe.'

'And what about you?' Leila says, laying a hand on her shoulder. 'Are you safe? You've run yourself ragged over this business – you look as if you haven't slept or eaten in the past two days. Is it finished yet?'

'I don't know.'

She thinks of Phelippes's advice the night before, to let the matter go. There is no hope of justice for Badger, that much she concedes, and if the world believes that Vincent Lovell killed Agnes, then Tobie will be clear of all suspicion, which is really all that matters. The Earl of Essex will lead his glorious campaign to Ireland as a hero, while the queen will smoothly convey the Lovell estate into Sir Robert Cecil's name, the better to protect England from priests and would-be assassins. There is nothing to be gained by pursuing the truth. Except that someone suborned a member of her household to steal her cipher, and then used it to attach a cryptic note to a dead girl's body: that was not a coincidence. Whoever killed Agnes wanted her, Sophia, to take notice, and to hint that they knew her history. And then it hits her like a punch to the chest. *Stolen ground.* She looks down at her feet, the carpet she is standing on, the boards beneath. This house. How did she not see it before? There is only one person who would choose her cipher to make a point about what she has stolen, and a threat to reveal her past sins.

'Jasper,' she says aloud. 'My God.'

'What about him?'

'I think . . . I think he killed Agnes?' But even as she says it aloud, it doesn't sound convincing.

Leila wrinkles her nose. 'Why would he?'

'His friend . . .' No. Agnes was Edmund North's passport to wealth and property; Jasper wouldn't want to deprive him of that, it doesn't make sense. But it would have taken two men to transport the body. If Edmund had killed her, perhaps in a fit of rage because he found out about Tobie – she recalls Anthony's story about Edmund beating the young prostitute in Ireland – then Jasper could have helped him dispose of her. And taken the opportunity to frighten his stepmother at the same time. But if it was Jasper who had taken her cipher, that ruled out Hilary as the conduit: she had nothing but contempt for the boy.

Before she can try her theory on Leila, there is a feathery knock at the door and Lina's head appears once more in the gap.

'Pardon me, madam, but there is a young man here to see you from Master Burbage. He says it's urgent.'

'Go,' Leila says, shooing her towards the door.

'Forget what I just said,' Sophia murmurs. 'We'll talk later.'

In the entrance hall she finds the young man with red hair she had seen sword-fighting with Tobie that day at the Blackfriars. He is flushed and sweating and looks as if he has run across London and back; there is a panic in his eyes that makes Sophia's stomach lurch.

'What is it?' she asks.

'Burbage sent me, Mistress de Wolfe – it's Tobie.'

All the worst scenarios play out in her mind's eye in the space of a heartbeat: they tortured him despite Cecil's instructions, and it went too far. For a moment she feels she can't draw breath.

'What's happened? He was supposed to be released.'

'No – I mean, yes, he was.' The boy places his hands on his knees; he, too, is struggling to breathe and speak at the same time. 'I share rooms with him, see. First thing this morning he walked in – I couldn't believe it. He said an official order had come overnight to drop the heresy charge. They let him out at first light. But then he started packing a bag.'

'What? Why?'

'He said he had to get out of London before they came for him again, because even Mistress de Wolfe couldn't protect him next time.'

'But – protect him from what?'

'Sir Thomas North.' The boy wipes his brow with the back of his hand. 'The prison warden told him they'd likely be seeing him again soon because Sir Thomas was preparing charges of attempted abduction and illegal marriage, and they had letters to prove it. I tried to stop him – I said let's go to Master Burbage, he'll know what to do, but he said there was no time. He just left. That was about eight.' He holds his palms out, helpless. 'I ran straight to the Blackfriars and Burbage sent me to come and tell you.'

'Thank you, ah—' She realises she doesn't know his name.

'Doug,' he prompts. 'My father's Scottish.'

She can see Lina by the stairs, beady-eyed and hovering, absorbing the conversation. She tries to keep her voice steady. 'Lina here will take you to the kitchen and get you a hot drink and something to eat.'

'Mistress de Wolfe?' The boy looks at her with fearful eyes. 'Burbage says Sir Thomas is doing this out of spite, because he hates the Chamberlain's Men. Now they can't get Tobie for murder, they'll go after him for something else, and make a great noise about it to discredit us.'

'You're his friend, Doug – can you think of anywhere he might go, if he was in trouble? Did he ever mention friends or family out of town?'

Doug grimaces. 'His parents are dead, I know that much. He always said the players were his family. I know he was fond of Master Munday from the Admiral's Men, who brought him to London. Beyond that, no idea – he's quite private. Will I tell Burbage you'll come and see him?'

She pats the boy on the shoulder. 'Have some breakfast before you go. I'll see Burbage soon – there's something I need to do first.' She turns to her gawping maid. 'Lina, where is Hilary?'

'She went out, madam, early – said she had some business in town. Oh, and she asked me to tell you – that picture you were looking for, it's upstairs in the Green Chamber with the *Agnus Dei*.'

It's only after Lina has begrudgingly left, trailing Doug in her wake, that Sophia realises Leila is still behind her.

'What can I do?' she says softly, laying a hand on Sophia's shoulder.

'Find Anthony,' she says. 'He should be at The Rose. Ask him to tell Phelippes and Ben. We need everyone out looking for Tobie, he can't have gone far if he only left a couple of hours ago. I doubt he's hitched a lift on a cart with the roads as they are, and he won't have money for a horse.'

'But we don't know which direction,' Leila points out.

Sophia takes a deep breath. 'Then we try every road out of London until we find him. I won't lose him again, Leila.'

'And where are you going?'

Sophia looks at her friend and clenches her jaw. 'I'm going to make Sir Thomas North wish he'd never been born.'

THIRTY-TWO

Leila had tried to deter her, of course, but Sophia would not wait to hear her arguments; she is raging inside and her jaw aches from keeping her fear and grief tamped down these past couple of days. Her anger at Thomas North is only the purest concentration of a more general fury at all the powerful men who think they can treat the powerless as disposable, a means to an end. She thinks of her namesake, Lyssa, goddess of rage and madness, and tries to imagine herself into that persona. *No wonder rage is embodied as a woman*, she thinks; *we have so much to be angry about, and spend so much of our lives having to hide it.*

Crossing the yard, she sees Mick bringing in a basket of logs. She calls out to him and he almost drops them; he looks anxious.

'Do you need me to ride out with you today, madam?' he asks. 'Only, I've the rest of the wood to finish.'

'No, I don't need you today. But I understand you've been talking to Master Jasper about our visits yesterday.' He starts to protest; she holds up a stern hand to stop him. 'What you have to understand, Mick, is that, whatever he tells you, Jasper is not a part of this household, and therefore nothing that I do is any of his business. So if he questions you in future, you tell him so, no matter how much money he offers you. If you want to keep your position.'

Mick shakes his head, stricken. 'No, madam, I never said a word to Master Jasper. It was Lina asking me about where we'd been yesterday. I told her because I didn't see harm in it, I thought she was just being curious. She doesn't get out much.'

Lina. There was the answer to that question. Sophia glances back towards the house; she will have to deal with that later.

'I apologise, Mick. I misunderstood.'

'That's all right. I wouldn't take money from that little prick.' He says it so vehemently that Sophia laughs. Not everyone's loyalty is suspect after all.

As she rides out towards Smithfield, she scans the streets for any sign of a youth alone, though she knows the chances of seeing Tobie are almost non-existent. Every time she passes a beggar or cripple huddled in a porch she imagines her boy doing the same tonight as the light falls. Will he have to beg or steal food? Even if she can bargain successfully with North to drop the charges – and she is confident that she can, given the size of his debt – if they can't find Tobie in time, it could all be for nothing. She wishes she had some idea of where he might go, who he would trust enough to ask for help. The thought of him believing he has no one outside the playing company cuts her to the heart.

At the North house, she hands Nyx over to the stable boy with the large ears and presents herself at the front door. She had considered bringing the ledger with her, but it was too unwieldy, and she only has Hilary's word that the coded letters next to the sum of three thousand pounds denote Thomas North. That could create difficulties if there were to be a legal case, she realises, but she is hoping that she can frighten North enough that it doesn't progress that far. All she wants is to make him drop his accusations against Tobie; in return, she will offer to forgive his debt. It seems a straightforward proposition – there can be no financial advantage to him if Tobie is found guilty of attempted abduction, Burbage is right that it's purely vindictive, but she suspects that North is not the kind of man who will respond well to being pressured by a woman. Whether she would ever be able to find sufficient evidence to prove that Edmund North killed Agnes, aided by Jasper, is another matter, and one she must put aside until she is sure that Tobie is safe.

The servant who opens the door tells her Sir Thomas is away from home. When she asks to see Lady North instead, the man disappears; he returns a few minutes later and ushers her inside.

Judith North looks as if she hasn't moved from her chair by the fire since Sophia's last visit. Her sewing hangs limply in her lap and when she raises her veil to acknowledge her visitor, her gaze seems unfocused. If Sophia appears underslept and underfed, Lady North looks worse; her face pinched and sallow, deep shadows under dull eyes. But she draws herself up with obvious effort and gestures for Sophia to take the seat opposite.

'Sir Thomas is out on business matters this morning. My steward is sending a message to advise him that you're here. I can guess what it's about, but perhaps you prefer to wait for my husband. Do you want something to drink in the meantime?'

Sophia has learned that if you accept someone's hospitality, however reluctantly offered, it puts them more at ease with you; she thanks Lady North, who rings a silver bell for the maid. When hot cordial has been ordered and the door closed behind the girl, they sit and regard one another warily. Lady North holds herself still but her fingers scratch ceaselessly at those red, inflamed patches on her wrists. Sophia notes flecks of blood on her lace cuffs where she has broken the skin.

'Does that pain you, my lady?' she asks, leaning forward

with a sympathetic expression. 'You should ask Leila to make you a balm to soothe it, she's good with skin complaints.'

'It's nothing.' Lady North pulls her cuffs down, embarrassed. 'I've suffered with it since I was a girl – it flares up when I am distressed or anxious.'

'You've had much to be distressed about these past days,' Sophia says, her head on one side.

'Quite. We feel our loss every waking moment.'

'I'm sure. Your stepson most of all, I imagine.'

Lady North's eyes narrow as if she is looking for a question behind the question. 'We had hoped for a summer wedding.'

'It would have been an advantageous match for Edmund too,' Sophia muses, as if the thought has only now occurred to her. 'Not just the land, I mean, but the lineage. Agnes was of good stock, I understand. The Lovells were an old family.'

Lady North bristles at this, as Sophia had guessed she would.

'My stepson is also of good stock,' she says, setting her embroidery down beside her so that she can point more emphatically. 'My husband's father was a baron, you know. And on his mother's side Edmund can trace his forebears back generations. His maternal grandfather was a descendant of the Bourchiers. Edmund was in no wise an inferior match for Agnes, whatever the Earl of Essex might have tried to imply. I suppose you know he hoped to turn the queen against the match in favour of one of his own friends.'

Sophia refrains from pointing out that, although Sir Thomas North's father may have been elevated to the peerage, his grandfather was a haberdasher. She tries again. 'Wasn't Edmund's mother also descended from the Devereux line, like Essex?'

Lady North frowns. 'No – you're thinking of the Daubneys.' She gives a tight little smile. 'Believe me, if my predecessor had been related to the Earl of Essex, we would never hear the end of it.'

Interesting, Sophia thinks. Standing in the dead wife's shadow, and resents it. That may be a crack she can force further. She is thrown by the denial of a Devereux connection, but covers it with another sympathetic smile.

'I understand,' she says. 'I have a stepson, as you know – it can be a tricky relationship. One is always made to feel like a usurper. Particularly when' – she hangs her head, as if it pains her to speak of it – 'one has no child of one's own to provide counterweight.'

I should be on the stage, she thinks. She raises her gaze cautiously and sees Lady North watching her, lips trembling. Sophia knows she must tread carefully; it's like picking a delicate lock.

'Sometimes,' she continues, 'I think my stepson hates me.'

Lady North takes a deep breath. She seems about to speak, when somewhere in the house a door slams; she starts, and the moment is broken.

'Well, he would,' she says tartly, blinking away the tears. 'You took his inheritance. It's common knowledge.'

'He and Edmund can console one another,' Sophia says. 'They are both grieving an inheritance lost.'

'Edmund is grieving the girl he loved,' Lady North says. It sounds like a rehearsed line; one that even she does not believe. Her fingers stray absently to her wrist again.

The woman's fretting at her own skin is setting Sophia's teeth on edge. How much does she know or suspect, she wonders. She pictures Agnes returning home on the last night of her life across the snowy churchyard of St Bartholomew's. Did Judith North see her that night? Did she witness what happened with Edmund, or did she deliberately look away? And how can Sophia persuade her to talk before Sir Thomas returns?

'Well, perhaps now that her murderer is dead and his vile crime made public, you can at least give her Christian burial and find peace,' she says, in a more placatory tone.

Something chases across Lady North's face, too quick to grasp. Fear? Guilt?

'We will never have peace in this house.' She spits the words. 'I mean to say – that papist, her uncle, may have killed her, but it was your boy who started all this. He is to blame. She would not have stolen away to her uncle that day if she hadn't been planning to elope. All this happened because a common player set his sights on a girl who was out of bounds to him.'

Sophia goes cold. '*My* boy?'

'Yes, that boy from the Chamberlain's Men you are so keen to defend. That's why you're here now, isn't it? Because Sir Thomas is bringing charges against him for conspiring to marry the girl illegally? Don't think you will persuade him out of it. We may have been cheated of justice for her murder, but we will have justice for this.' Her face is contorted with anger, as if all her rage at her situation has been concentrated into one fierce beam directed at Tobie.

'I sincerely believe the boy is innocent of any wrongdoing here,' Sophia says, fighting to keep her composure. 'His mistake, as you say, was to fall in love with a girl he could not have, but that is not a crime. If they talked of eloping, it was only the foolish dreaming of youth.'

'Innocent, you say? Tell me this, then, Mistress de Wolfe – is rape a crime?'

Sophia looks at her, confused. 'What?'

'That boy dishonoured her. He took her virginity, if you want me to speak plainly. And since she was promised to Edmund, that is *theft*.'

'How do you know this?' Sophia asks. She keeps her voice low, her body still, no sudden moves, as if approaching a cornered fox. Cecil had explicitly said he would not mention this detail to the Norths. 'Did a physician examine her? Could it not have been Edmund who did the deflowering?'

'It was not Edmund. He was careful to observe all propriety until they were married – he would not risk the queen's blessing. You ask me how I know – the girl herself told me. She boasted of it – how she would not marry Edmund because she was married to the player boy in the sight of God, and they were one flesh.' Lady North is shaking; there are flecks of spittle at the corners of her lips.

Sophia clasps her hands in her lap to quell any tell-tale sign of emotion. Judith North has just told her that she spoke with Agnes after she had been with Tobie. It's the clearest admission yet that Agnes did return to this house that night, despite the Norths' denials.

Lady North appears to realise this, because she adds, hastily, 'This was before Christmas.'

She doesn't realise, of course, that Sophia already knows Agnes could not have made this boast before the evening of the twenty-seventh.

'Before Christmas?' She frowns at Lady North. 'But I understood that Sir Thomas only discovered Agnes's relationship with Tobie Strange after her death, when his letters were found?'

'No. Yes, I mean – Sir Thomas didn't know. I – I didn't tell him.' The scratching has grown more frenetic; Judith North is entangling herself deeper in her own lies.

Sophia affects amazement. 'You didn't tell your husband that his ward was having a carnal relationship with a player? Did you tell Edmund?'

'I told no one. I knew they would be furious. I hoped I could talk Agnes into seeing sense before any greater harm was done. It's what we women do, isn't it – smooth things over, keep the peace?'

'Oh, yes – I'd have done the same,' Sophia says. 'Especially knowing Edmund has a violent temper.'

'Who told you that?' Lady North flares again; she is half out of her chair with agitation.

At that moment, the door opens and the maid enters with a silver tray and a jug of hot cordial.

Sophia spots her chance. 'I wonder, my lady, if I might trouble you to use your, ah, close-stool?'

Lady North is tussling inwardly; it's clear that she would like to throw Sophia out, but she is also afraid that she has said too much. 'There is a room at the back next to the scullery. The maid will show you. My husband will be here any moment,' she adds, as Sophia reaches the door. She makes it sound like a threat.

Sophia hurries down the corridor indicated by the maid, who mercifully does not insist on waiting outside for her. She has bought herself a few minutes, but for what? She needs to think. She should not have made that comment about Edmund's temper, she thinks; that was badly judged and she has made Lady North defensive. But she could see the woman was clearly rattled, and hoped she might provoke her into saying something more, now that she has as good as admitted that Agnes was last seen in this house on the night of the twenty-seventh.

She tries to picture what might have happened. Agnes snuck back into the house, aglow from her tryst with Tobie. Edmund North must have caught her; perhaps he confronted her, threatened to tell his father, told her she would not behave like that when they were married. Somehow, he provoked her into blurting out her secret: that she loved someone else, that she intended to marry him, that she had just come from his bed. Edmund North, the man who threw a young prostitute across the room in rage because he could not perform. Did he do the same to Agnes? Did Judith see it? And how can she, Sophia, possibly hope to prove it? Unless she can find a bloody murder weapon hidden in the close-stool, all she has achieved is to make herself even more of a threat to the Norths.

Except – it occurs to her – there may be a witness, besides Lady North. She recalls what Lizzie Sidney told her – Agnes had a friend in this house, the boy who looks after the horses, who had given her a key to the servants' gate. Sophia heads towards the back of the house until she finds a door to the yard.

By the stables she sees the boy who had taken her horse, forking soiled straw into a pile. His large ears stick out from under his cap; he is humming tunelessly as he works.

'I'm looking for Fred,' she says. 'Is that you?'

He jumps, glancing around in case they should be observed.

'Yes, mistress. Are you leaving? Shall I fetch your black mare? She's a pretty beast – you can always tell when a horse has a sweet temper—'

'Listen, Fred – I don't have much time.' She lowers her voice. 'I'm a friend of Jo Goodchild. Who brought letters for Agnes.'

His face colours so immediately that the flush reaches the tips of his ears. 'I can't talk to you,' he says, barely audible.

'You're not in trouble,' she says, catching his arm before he can turn away. 'No one knows – about the letters or the key. I just need to ask – did you see Agnes come back here on the twenty-seventh December? Four nights ago?'

When he doesn't answer, she gives him a little shake. 'Agnes trusted you, Fred. I'm trying to find out the truth. Doesn't she deserve that?'

'How will it do any good?' he blurts, pulling his arm away.

'Please. Whatever you tell me will be in confidence, I swear.'

He takes a deep breath. 'She slipped in the servants' gate,' he whispers, not looking at Sophia. 'I knew she was out because I'd seen her leave first thing. She gave me a wink and put a finger to her lips as she left. So I'd kept an eye out all day. I was relieved to see her back safe, it was getting late.' He stops abruptly and looks at the ground, leaning heavily on his fork.

'What time was this?'

'Shortly before ten. She went up to her chamber. I saw a light in her window.'

'And – do you know what happened after that? Did Edmund catch her coming in? Did you see them argue?'

He hesitates, frowning as if he doesn't understand the question. Thinking he needs persuading, she reaches for her purse, but he waves it away.

'Master Edmund wasn't home, mistress.'

'What?' She stares at him.

'He was out at the Hand and Shears.'

'Are you sure?'

'Quite sure – I had to go and fetch him.'

'Wait—' she shakes her head, as if that might dislodge the confusion. 'Fetch him? Who sent you?'

'Lady North. She came hurrying out into the yard with only her indoor slippers on and no coat, and told me to bring Master Edmund back as quickly as possible, it was urgent.'

Sophia takes this in, hardly daring to breathe. 'How did she seem?'

Fred considers the question. 'She looked – like she was somewhere else.'

'In what sense?'

'Like – her mouth was saying normal stuff like, "Fred, I need you to fetch Master Edmund and tell him he must come home right away, it's an urgent family matter", but her eyes were kind of skidding all over, do you know what I mean? Like her thoughts were in a different place altogether.'

'She wasn't crying or raging? Or frightened?'

'Nothing like that. She seemed calm on the surface. But – brittle, you know? Like she was made of glass. Like if you'd pushed her, she would shatter.'

Shock, Sophia thinks. 'And Edmund came back with you?'

'With a bit of grumbling, yes.'

'Did you see either of them again afterwards?'

'Not that night. But the next morning, Master Edmund told me to take the day off. He said I hadn't had a proper break for the festive season and I should go and visit my family overnight. I asked who would look after the horses, since the head groom was already away till the new year, and Edmund said he'd see to them, they'd be fine for one night. But I didn't go.' He glances up guiltily at the house. 'I don't especially like my family. I'd rather be with the horses. So I stayed up in my room.' He points to a loft above the stables where a small dormer window overlooks the courtyard.

'And . . . you saw something?' She realises she is holding her breath.

A furtive nod. 'That night, Master Edmund's friend came round, late. And about midnight, I heard noises in the yard so I looked out. I couldn't see clearly, but the two of them were out there with a barrow. It was heavy – they had to fight to drag it through the snow between them.'

'What was in the barrow, Fred?'

He shakes his head, but his mouth is pressed into a grim line. 'There was a cloth over it. But a couple of hours later, Master Edmund came back alone and the barrow was empty. The next morning, we heard the news that Agnes had been found—' He stops, biting his lower lip.

'Does Edmund know you saw him?'

'I pray not. After I'd seen that, well – I showed myself at midday and pretended I had been to my family overnight. And when I heard they'd arrested Agnes's sweetheart, I know I should have spoken up, but I was afraid. I'm only telling you, mistress, because – well, I had to tell someone.' He lets out a ragged breath. 'Now they're saying Agnes's uncle confessed to killing her. I only know Lady North and Edmund say she ran away and never came back to this house, but on my life, she did.'

'Which one is her chamber?'

'The tower room. At the top.' He points to the hexagonal turret in the lower left corner of the courtyard. 'I only know because some mornings I would see her at the window and she would wave.' He blushes violently again.

'Master Edmund's friend – did you recognise him?' Sophia barely needs to ask, but she wants to hear it.

The boy nods. 'He's been here before. They go drinking together. Ratty little face, speaks to the servants like we're all shit on his boots. Edmund calls him Wolf, something like that.'

A weight like a cold stone settles inside her. 'Listen, Fred – don't tell another soul what you saw that night. Don't let anyone in this house know you saw Agnes come back the day before either. It's for your own safety.' Seeing his alarm, she presses a sixpence into his hand. 'If you're afraid at any time, come and find me. My house is in Broad Street.'

'I don't know your name, mistress.'

'It's Wolfe. Sophia de Wolfe.'

'Oh shit. You're not—' Stricken, he takes a step back, afraid he's been tricked.

'We're not related,' she says tersely, turning back to the house. 'Have my horse ready – I may need to leave in a hurry.'

She stands at the foot of the tower stairs, peering up. She has already been absent too long, her excuse growing less plausible by the minute. This might be her only chance to understand what happened to Agnes; she doesn't imagine she'll be invited back to this house after today. The corridor is empty. She hurries up the stairs to the top floor, half-expecting Agnes's room to be locked, but the door opens and she stands on the threshold, taking it in.

The chamber is bitterly cold; no fire has been lit here since the day Agnes died. The girl's possessions are in a state of disarray, presumably from Sir Thomas North's search of the room for incriminating letters, but other than that, it seems as if she has only just left: combs and a silk hairnet are scattered on a dresser; a nightgown is crumpled on the pillow.

Sophia has her answer, in part, but Fred is right: what good will it do now? There is only Fred's testimony, and he couldn't swear that he saw a body, only a barrow. Even if he claimed he saw Agnes return to the house that same day, who would believe the word of a stable boy over that of Sir Thomas North and his whole family? Sophia closes the door silently behind her. She has promised she would not expose Fred to that risk, but if she could find anything that would prove Agnes died here, perhaps his word would not be needed.

Sophia casts around the room; she can see nothing that would make a potential weapon. The candle-holders on the dresser are squat and wooden; you couldn't deliver a killing blow with one. It's possible, of course, that the item Lady North used to hit the girl has been removed; she notices there isn't even a poker in the hearth. Cecil said Agnes was hit on the back of the head. She tries to picture the scene: if there was an argument, and Lady North was enraged enough to strike out, why would Agnes have turned her back? How did she not see the older woman pick up a poker or candlestick or whatever it was, and defend herself? Or was she trying to walk away?

A thought occurs; she crouches to look closely at the fire-place. It consists of a brick hearth with a carved marble surround set into wooden panelling. The light from the small casements is poor, but she leans in to examine the sharp edges of the mantelpiece and then she sees it, on the white stone: a fine, rust-coloured spatter. An attempt has been made to wash the worst of it away, but traces are still visible. She traces a finger down the line of the stain, under the ledge.

'Did you find what you were looking for, Mistress de Wolfe?'

Sophia turns; Lady North stands in the doorway. Her voice is glacial and her whole body is held so tight she looks as if she might snap.

'My lady. Forgive me, I—' She brushes down her skirt and lowers her gaze with appropriate humility. 'I confess I have trespassed on your hospitality. I worried that there might be more letters between Agnes and Master Strange that would make things go worse for him, so I wanted to see if I could find any.'

Lady North continues to stare at her as if she can't find the correct response. 'I could have you arrested for theft,' she manages eventually.

Sophia holds up empty hands. 'But I have taken nothing. Please accept my apologies – I won't trouble you any longer. I can speak to Sir Thomas another time—' She is suddenly overwhelmed by the need to get out of this room, this house, away from this woman who – she is now certain – killed Agnes. But there is nothing to be gained by confronting her; the best thing Sophia can do for herself and Tobie now is to speak to Cecil, however little he might wish to see her again.

'No.' Lady North moves to block the door, her voice oddly high and strangled. She darts a fearful glance over her shoulder and back to Sophia, her gaze fluttering like a moth, unable to settle, the way the stable boy Fred had described her that night she sent him to find Edmund. 'My husband will be here any moment. You mustn't leave.'

Sophia feels very strongly that she must. She has seen too much; Judith North knows it, and if Sir Thomas returns home now, they will contrive some way between them to ensure Sophia does not share what she has learned. Her heart is beating faster. She could physically push Lady North out of her way, she has no doubt that she would be the stronger, but she would have to make it down the tower stairs and through the house to the stables without encountering any servants who might hinder her; Lady North would need only call out to them to stop her.

Even so, she decides, it's worth a try. She launches herself at Lady North, who, caught off-guard, stumbles back against the door; Sophia dodges her grasp and rushes at the stairs, holding up her skirt, at the same time as she hears footsteps from below. She is barely a couple of steps down when a man appears around the curve of the stairwell, staring up at her.

'Edmund, stop her!' Lady North cries.

A strong fist clamps around Sophia's upper arm and she is forced back up to the landing and into Agnes's room, where he unhands her with a little shove. She recovers her balance and rubs her arm, glaring.

'The famous Mistress de Wolfe,' says Edmund North, looking her up and down as he kicks the door shut behind him. 'How nice to meet, finally. I've heard an awful lot about you.'

THIRTY-THREE

The Admiral's Men fall silent one by one and stare openly as Leila Humeya strides across the pit to the foot of the stage; partly because she's a striking woman, and partly because actors are superstitious, and some of the company are not entirely sure that the rumours about her powers are invented.

'I need Anthony Munday,' she announces, without apology, looking around for him.

'Oh, you have got to be joking,' Henslowe says, fists on his hips. 'This is the first we've seen of him in two days – we're performing at court on Twelfth Night, you know, and—'

Leila silences him with a look. Anthony climbs over the barrier from the seated tiers and meets her eye with a questioning frown.

'Outside,' she says, *sotto voce.*

'When will you have him back?' Henslowe sounds peevish.

'When I'm finished with him,' she says, turning on her heel. A ripple of ribald laughter follows; she shuts that down with a hard stare too.

'Tobie's run away,' she says, once they are outside. She explains the situation with Thomas North and the new charges. 'He was afraid they'd make him go back to prison. Sophia asked me to tell you, in case you could think of anywhere he might go. Did he ever mention a friend or relative, or a place he felt safe?'

Anthony shakes his head. 'I don't think he had any relatives left. Where is Sophia?'

Leila rolls her eyes. 'She said she was going to make Sir Thomas North wish he'd never been born. No,' she adds, laying a firm hand on his wrist as he tenses, poised to hare off in pursuit. 'You can't run to save her every time, Anthony. She's a grown woman and you're not her husband – let her fight her own battles. Thomas North's not going to harm her.'

'No, but his son might.'

Leila clicks her tongue. 'Sophia can look after herself. I've got to see patients this morning, but I'll be at the Unicorn at noon. Can I leave the Tobie business with you until then? Burbage has the Chamberlain's Men out looking, but Sophia thought you might remember something, as you befriended him in Canterbury.'

Crossing the bridge, stuck in traffic – the ice in the river is shifting, but not enough to allow free passage of boats – Anthony casts his mind back to the summer of '96, when plague closed the London theatres and the Admiral's Men set off on the road through Kent, playing in inn yards and guild-halls, and he with Thomas Phelippes's instructions in his pocket – the story of a boy, twelve years old, adopted and raised in the environs of Canterbury. In every town where they stopped through the north of the county, Anthony had made the time to ask questions of local people; coins passed between palms to jog memories.

In Canterbury he and Ned, with a few of the others, had gone to Evensong at the cathedral, less for the devotional aspect than to hear the celebrated music. He remembers it now as if it were yesterday: late sun slanting through the windows, casting jewel patterns across the worn stones, and a boy from the choir standing in a shaft of light, his fair hair backlit, singing a solo with a voice of such purity that you could feel your soul ascending.

'Look at him,' Ned had whispered, 'look at that face. People would pay well to see him play a maid, before his beard comes through. I'm going to speak to the choirmaster.'

So it had begun. The enquiries, the payment of more sweeteners; the discovery that the boy's parents had recently died and he was now a ward of the city, resident at the choir school, but that this was an arrangement that would not last past his voice breaking. Anthony had pressed further, tracking down servants of the Strange family, finally striking gold with a woman who had wet-nursed the boy and could confirm that Hannah Strange had not birthed him, that the baby – bastard of a disgraced girl of good family, so she'd heard – had been purchased as a newborn in a secret trade. These arrangements were not uncommon, the wet nurse said, with a sniff. When he learned the name of the woman who had brokered the deal, he discreetly punched the air: he had succeeded in his quest. The choirmaster had been understandably reluctant to part with the boy; more money had changed hands over the matter of his wardship, but when they left Canterbury, Tobie Strange was riding in the cart, the newest addition to the Admiral's Men.

How trustingly Tobie had come along with them: less than two months orphaned and leaving behind everything he had ever known, but he had done so without complaint, and with an eagerness to see new places that had touched Anthony, because it reminded him of himself at the same age. He remembers Tobie telling him about growing up in Whitstable, on the coast; how as a small child he would watch the fishing boats set out each evening and imagine them sailing over the horizon, beyond the edge of the world, and long to go with them.

'Shit,' Anthony says aloud. Turning downriver, he glimpses, in the gaps between buildings, the tall masts of seafaring ships moored along the wharves, ice-bound like stranded whales, waiting for a thaw to release them back to the ocean. Where would Tobie go, if he thought he was running for his life? Sophia imagines he would head for a familiar place, where he feels safe to hide, but as he recalls that conversation on the road, it seems to Anthony more likely that he would strike out for the unknown. There's always work for strong young men on board ships. Fortunately, he thinks, spurring his horse on to overtake a cart as the driver curses at him, the new horizons are currently frozen. If he moves fast, he might catch up with Tobie before he is able to set sail. He found the boy once; he can do it again.

On the north bank, he heads for the quays east of the bridge. Since he was a child, he has always loved the names here, the way they evoked a world beyond the mouth of the Thames: Fish Wharf, Fresh Wharf, Lyon Key, Somer's Key, Billingsgate, all the way down to the Customs House. Despite the weather, the wharves are busy: goods being loaded on to tall ships, barrels and crates stacked ready for winching aboard, men shouting and swearing and running up and down gangplanks or standing around braziers waiting for deliveries and complaining about the weather.

He tries the dockside taverns, asking if anyone has seen a young man of Tobie's description looking for passage on a ship. He's met with indifference at first – there are always boys hanging around the docks hustling for labouring work – or other kinds of work, some suggest, with a leer; no one cares to remember what they looked like. Anthony discovers, as always, that people are inclined to be more helpful if you are generous in buying drinks; suddenly men are appearing from dingy corners to tell him about blond boys they've seen, in return for a pot of ale. Most of it is garbled nonsense, but eventually, in the Mitre, an old fellow says he remembers a boy answering to Tobie's description coming in early that same morning, before nine. The man must be nearing seventy, Anthony thinks; fair play to him if he's been drinking since nine.

'I come here for my breakfast, and I stay to keep warm,' the old sailor says, as if reading his mind. 'And I remember this boy because when he come in, he was singing to himself, one of the old ballads, and we all stopped to listen – it was the sweetest sound. Like a window had opened to heaven,' he adds, pleased with his own lyricism. 'When he saw us gawping at him he shut up right away, poor lad. Turned red as a strawberry.'

'That sounds like him,' Anthony says. 'Where did he go?'

'Heard him asking if anyone knew of a place on a ship.' The man takes an appreciative draught of his beer. 'Most of 'em laughed at him – they pointed out no ships were going anywhere, he'd be quicker walking to France. But a couple of the lads from the *Goshawk* said there might be something, and he left with them.'

'The *Goshawk*. Is that a ship or a tavern?'

The old man gives him a pitying look. 'Three-masted carrack, moored up at Smart's Key. Bound for Antwerp, if she can ever get out.'

Anthony thanks him, and leaves him enough for another pot of beer.

On the quay, the snow has lost its fresh promise, trodden to brown sludge under boot heels. He picks his way through it until the *Goshawk* looms above him, its lines clanking in the sharp wind. Great lumps of ice creak and groan around its hull, not solid but moving with the swelling tide. Two men are rolling barrels of fresh water up the gangplank, swearing as their feet struggle to find purchase. At the top, a man in a sheepskin coat stands issuing directions with his hands tucked in his sleeves. Anthony approaches him and explains his business.

The man regards him suspiciously. 'What do you want with him, this boy? He calls himself Johnny, by the way.'

'He's a fugitive. He's wanted by the law.'

'And you're the law, are you? Where's your chain of office, then?'

'I'm a pursuivant,' Anthony says. 'We don't carry them. Just tell him I need to speak to him, will you?'

'What's he wanted for?'

'Witchcraft.'

'God save us.' The man looks horrified. 'Give me a minute.' Grumbling, he disappears below the deck.

Anthony feels a little guilty for this fabrication, but he knows sailors: they might not care about the law – half the men at sea are running from something – but they are more superstitious than a gaggle of grandmothers. No sensible captain would knowingly take a passenger or crewman suspected of dabbling in magic; his men would turn on him at the first rumble of thunder or rough water.

A moment later, he hears Tobie's voice raised in protest.

'He's lying, I swear to you, sir – this man only means me harm—' The boy appears above the side of the ship, his jacket in the grip of the sheepskin man. His expression turns to perplexity. 'Anthony? What are you doing here? I thought it would be—'

'I know who you expected,' he says. 'Come down here so I don't have to shout.'

'And you can stay off,' says the man, giving Tobie a little shove in the back as he steps on to the gangplank and throwing his bag after him. It lands with a soft thump at their feet.

Tobie picks it up and clutches it to his chest; he turns on Anthony, indignant and furious. 'What did you do that for? Tell them I'm wanted for witchcraft? Do you think I don't have enough trouble right now? I thought you were my friend, Anthony.' He kicks a pile of snow in impotent anger.

'I am your friend. That's why I'm here to stop you doing anything stupid, like running away to sea.'

'What choice have I?' He speaks urgently, but in a low voice; his colour rises with indignation. 'Sir Thomas North wants me arrested again for plotting to elope with Agnes, and

I can't deny it this time, they have the letters. They'll put me back in prison, and I'll be lucky if that's the worst they do. The Chamberlain's Men will wash their hands of me – they won't want the damage to their good name – and anyway, the girl I loved is dead and there is no justice for her killer.' He fights down a tremor in his voice. 'I have nothing and no one in London any more, Anthony – no future except a stinking gaol cell if I stay here. My only hope was to leave with that ship as soon as the tide allows and try to find my fortune in a new country where no one knows me. But you have destroyed even that for me, God strike you.' He pushes Anthony in the chest. 'Go back to that man and tell him it's a lie. I want to be gone.' His chin juts, his lip quivers; he looks in that moment like the boy who set out from Canterbury two and half years ago, not the young man he is becoming.

Anthony feels suddenly wearied by his intensity. *Was I so dramatic at this age?* he wonders. Granted, the boy has been through a lot in the past few days, but even so.

'It's not true that you have no one,' he says firmly. 'The Chamberlain's Men are all out searching for you – they want you back with them. I'm here, aren't I? And even now, Mistress de Wolfe has gone to confront Thomas North about these charges. She will do everything in her power to have them dropped, or to prove your innocence, as she has done tirelessly these past few days – at great cost to herself, I might add – so never say you have no one to look out for you—'

'I didn't ask her to,' Tobie cuts in, raising his voice to match Anthony's. 'She has been generous, I know, but she can't always step in with her purse and fix everything. Thomas North is determined to punish me, and he won't let Mistress de Wolfe stand in his way. The only place I will be safe is over the sea – I've made up my mind to go, and I won't be made to feel indebted just because some rich woman has decided to make a pet of me.'

Before he knows what he is doing, Anthony has flung out a hand and cuffed him around the head; not hard, but enough to knock the boy's hat off and leaving him staring in shock.

'She's not *some rich woman*, you ungrateful little shit, she's your—' He stops himself, clamps his lips together, breathing hard.

'My what?' Tobie stares at him, almost afraid.

He swallows. 'Your benefactor. She thinks you have promise, and she wants to help you. Most people in your position would be glad to have someone like her on their side.' Anthony stoops to pick up the hat and clasps it tight, so Tobie won't see his hands shaking.

The boy looks close to tears. 'I'm not ungrateful. It's just – the way she looks at me sometimes, Anthony, it makes me uncomfortable. I see her watching me closely, and I don't know what she means by it.'

Anthony hands him his hat. Does he think Sophia has some improper interest in him? Christ, this should not be his problem to unravel. She needs to clear matters up with the boy as soon as possible.

'That's just her manner,' he says easily. 'Look, Tobie – this isn't the answer.' He nods to the ship. 'There are more people in London who care about you than in Antwerp. What little money you have will be robbed the moment you step ashore, and there will plenty of men interested in making money from your pretty face.'

Tobie snaps his head away with a noise of disgust, but he chews anxiously at his lip. 'I'm afraid to go back to my lodgings, or the Blackfriars. I'll be constantly watching the door in a sweat, waiting for the soldiers to come for me.'

'Then come back to my house. You can stay there until the business is resolved, we'll be glad to have you. And it will be resolved, I promise. If anyone can deal with the Norths, it's Sophia. Mistress de Wolfe,' he adds hastily.

Tobie settles his cap back on his head with a knowing smile. 'You admire her,' he says.

'Everyone admires her,' Anthony says, trying to keep his composure.

'Most especially you.' Tobie reaches out and knocks Anthony's hat off, by way of payback. 'Little shit.'

The man in the sheepskin is still watching them from the deck of the ship. Tobie turns and waves. 'Go with God, masters,' he calls out. 'I will conjure a fair wind for your voyage.' The sailor crosses himself and spits, and tells them to fuck off for good measure. Anthony catches Tobie's eye, and they burst out laughing, but there is a slightly manic edge to it. The danger is not yet past.

THIRTY-FOUR

Edmund North is around thirty, tall and broad with his father's high forehead and sweep of hair. He wears his reddish beard close-cropped and his moustache curled.

'A pleasure to meet you – I'm afraid I was just on my way out,' she says, smiling sweetly, keeping her voice light and unthreatening, and despising herself for it. *This is what we do*, she thinks, *faced with a man who might turn violent: we fawn and simper and hope not to provoke.* Her arm throbs where he gripped it; she remembers again Anthony's story about Edmund throwing the girl across the room in Ireland.

'Oh, I think there's time for a chat, now you're here,' he says, rubbing a forefinger absently along his lower lip. 'My stepmother says you keep making a nuisance of yourself while our family is trying to grieve.'

'Your family—' She checks herself; moderates her voice before she can flare up, which is what he wants. 'There's been a misunderstanding about Agnes and the player boy, but easily resolved, I'm sure – I was hoping to discuss it with your father when he arrives—'

She sees it, quick as a blink: the glance that passes between Edmund and his stepmother, and in that moment she understands: Sir Thomas North is not coming. It was Edmund that

Lady North sent for as soon as Sophia arrived, to take care of the problem. Just as he did before.

'Ah.' She nods, looking from one to the other with a half-smile. 'I see. Sir Thomas doesn't know. No wonder you're in such a state, my lady. Your wrists, your neck.' She hears herself laugh abruptly; it's tinged with panic.

'Know what?' Edmund's brows lift in a question; his eyes glitter.

'Leave it,' Lady North says, moving closer, but he holds up a hand to stall her.

'No – I want to hear what Mistress de Wolfe thinks she knows. What she's planning to run and tell Sir Robert Cecil.'

Leave it, Sophia tells herself. Sensible advice. The only way to get out of this is to pretend she knows nothing. Placate him. Keep lying. Let them get away with it, the way people like them always get away with it. Perhaps it's that, together with Edmund's taunting face, that causes her to disregard the sensible course.

She turns to Lady North. 'Was it an accident?'

'I have no idea what you're talking about,' Judith North says, in that same strangled tone, but her right hand scrabbles at her left wrist as if she is trying to flay herself alive.

'You discovered, somehow, that Agnes had gone out that day, the twenty-seventh, when your husband was away visiting his daughter.' Sophia looks her in the eye. 'You were furious with her. You waited in this room so you could catch her out. A long wait – you must have been raging by the time she came home. And then what? You argued, obviously. My guess is that she told you her plan, just to spite you – that she had pledged herself to Tobie Strange, she meant to sign away her inheritance to her uncle and she would never marry Edmund. And you lost control. Somehow, in whatever tussle ensued, I think she hit her head on the corner of that mantel – there are blood stains. Did you push her? The coroner said the blow must have struck with some force to kill her. But perhaps

333

you didn't mean her to die – you just lashed out without thinking.'

Lady North continues to stare at Sophia, her jaw clenched; she is so pent with emotion that she is almost vibrating. Still she doesn't speak.

'Well, that's an interesting theory,' Edmund says briskly. 'But of course we all know that Vincent Lovell killed Agnes. He confessed to it and the matter is closed. What an imagination you do have, Mistress de Wolfe. By the way, we had the woodwork retouched recently – I expect what you see there are splashes of woodstain, the workmen can be careless. But the question is – are you intending to repeat this nonsense to anyone, because—'

'Why are you covering for her?' Sophia says, tilting her head to look at him. 'I'm genuinely curious – one outburst of temper and this woman robbed you of your future prospects. I don't suppose you were planning to keep Agnes around for long, once you'd secured the estate and title, but your stepmother made sure you didn't even get that. I don't understand why you would want to protect her?'

'She was a whore!' The words explode out of Lady North as if she can no longer contain the pressure of holding them in; her entire body is shaking. 'That girl – she opened her legs for a common player' – she fairly spits the word – 'and then bragged of it to me, as if she thought she had outsmarted us. After all we did for her. We took her in when she was orphaned—'

'You didn't *take her in*,' Sophia says coldly. 'Your husband bought her wardship, with money lent to him by my husband – three thousand pounds, which is yet to be repaid, by the way – in order to profit from her lands until your stepson could claim them entirely by marrying her. Don't pretend that any of it was done out of kindness to her. So she told you she had lost her maidenhead to the boy she loved – then what?'

334

'My lady, don't say any more,' Edmund says, but Lady North is like a river in spate; now that she has begun, there is no holding her.

'I told her Sir Thomas would lock her up when he found out, and she would have no liberty until she turned fourteen and could be married to Edmund and she should be glad he would overlook her disgrace. She said she was already married in God's eyes, and then she said to me' – she pauses to take a ragged breath – '"What if I should be with child from this night? How will you explain that away, if you have kept me prisoner for months?" So I told her she should pray hard that was not the case, for if it was, I would send for Mistress Humeya from Southwark to get the bastard out of her before it was formed, and I would personally hold her down while the job was done.'

'Jesus' sake, woman, will you dig yourself in deeper?' Edmund runs a hand through his hair, but he appears helpless to stop her. Sophia wonders if this is the first time he is hearing these details.

'She flew at me then, like a little wildcat, screaming that she would scratch my eyes out. I caught her by the wrists. And then she said—' Judith North looks right at Sophia, and for the first time her focus grows sharp. 'She said I was jealous, because I was a withered dried-up crone of forty who would never give my man a child and soon he would find himself a new wife who was fitter to be a mother, and that was when—' Her gaze darts to the mantelpiece. 'I shoved her, hard, and she fell back. I heard the sound her head made when it hit the stone. It was sickening. I shook her, but she didn't wake.'

'Fuck.' Edmund clasps his head in both hands and stares up at the ceiling, as if some solution might be written there.

'So you sent for Edmund?' Sophia prompts. She feels she needs every last detail now, to complete the picture. She is trying not to think about what will happen when Lady North has finished her story; it seems increasingly unlikely that they will bid her a good night and allow her to leave.

'I sent the boy to fetch him from the tavern. I didn't know if she was dead or not at that point.'

'It didn't occur to you to send for a doctor?'

'I wasn't thinking clearly.' Her voice is quieter now. 'I – I thought Edmund would know what to do.'

'It wouldn't have done any good, Mistress de Wolfe, if that's what you're wondering,' Edmund says. His fingers are still tangled in his hair, as if he is holding his thoughts together. 'I could see the girl was dead when I got here.'

'So you helped your stepmother hide the body for a day, until you could dispose of it? Weren't you angry with her?'

'I was fucking furious, obviously. But there was a practical situation to deal with. I was an army officer, you know – I have experience at thinking clearly under pressure.'

'Yes, your military heroics in Ireland are legendary,' she says drily. 'Why did you decide not to tell your father what really happened to Agnes?'

He lets out a long sigh. 'My father is terrible at cards, Mistress de Wolfe. Famously so – it's a family joke. Because he can't hide his feelings on any matter, you see – it's all written there on his face, plain as day. It's why his career as a diplomat was so short-lived. And I felt that the player boy should be made to suffer, since in many ways this mess was all his fault. He took my property.'

Sophia opens her mouth to protest, but he speaks over her.

'Hence leaving her to be found at The Theatre. But if the world was to believe that the boy killed Agnes in a lover's quarrel, then my father must believe it too, or he would inevitably let something slip. You say you can't understand why I would choose to protect my lady stepmother, when her recklessness had hurt my prospects. Well, I wouldn't expect you to understand it, since you don't know what it is to have a family name. Not in the way that we do. My uncle is on the Privy Council.' His condescension is almost comical.

'Whatever my feelings towards Lady North, the most important thing was to protect the family. If it was known that the girl died in this house, even by misadventure, it would do us a great deal of damage. Especially after—' He leaves the thought unspoken.

'After your first wife also died prematurely?' She gives him a tight smile. 'Yes, that might start to look like a pattern. It could hamper your efforts to find a replacement heiress, if it were known.'

He looks for a moment as if he would like to hit her, but he masters himself. 'Besides,' he says, with a nod at Lady North, 'my stepmother has never been the greatest admirer of mine – have you, my lady? Even before she married my father, she decided he was too indulgent with me. Many's the time she has whispered in his ear against me, talked him out of supporting me financially. She wanted to be the only influence over him. But now that we are bound by this matter' – he gestures to the mantelpiece – 'she has become a lot more *tractable*, shall we say.'

Lady North is leaning against the panelling as if all her bones have turned to jelly and only the wall is keeping her upright. Disburdening herself of the secret she has kept for the past few days has had the effect of a violent purge; she looks as if she might collapse at any moment.

'The question now, Mistress de Wolfe, is what to do about you, since you have insinuated yourself into our family affairs.'

'Excuse me?' Sophia stares at him, incensed. 'You insinuated me. You and Jasper – leaving that note with the body. What was the purpose of that, if not to involve me?'

Edmund's face darkens. 'That was none of my doing. I didn't know Jasper had left that letter until the next day. He said it would help to sow confusion in any investigation by making it look as if her killing was part of a greater conspiracy, but really he wanted to use the situation to take a shot at you. I was livid with him – I thought it would complicate things unnecessarily, and I was right, because here you are, like some kind of truffle-hound, determined to sniff out the truth and dig it up. He didn't bank on you trailing Robert Cecil in your wake.'

'I'm flattered by the comparison.' She sounds more insouciant than she feels.

'Well, you have the truth now, and somehow I can't picture you going quietly about your business and keeping all this to yourself.' He lets out a little impatient huff, as if he is irritated that she has been so selfish as to inconvenience him in this way. He glances at his stepmother. 'And I hope you feel better for your incontinent confession, my lady, because now you have saddled me with a problem.'

Lady North says nothing; she has retreated into her own private world. Sophia feels a chill snake its way down her spine.

'What would it profit me to repeat what I have heard here to anyone?' she says, working to keep her voice steady. 'As you say – the world thinks Vincent Lovell killed his niece. No one is looking for another killer. If your father will drop these charges against Tobie Strange, we can all go quietly about our business. In time, we may even come to believe the official version.' It sticks in her throat to bargain with him in this way, but she fears the alternative if she can't persuade him that she is not a threat.

'They may not be officially looking for another killer, but knowledge is power. What you've heard in this room would be worth a great deal to Sir Robert as leverage – I imagine he'd reward you well for it.'

'I don't need his rewards. And you chose to tell me,' she points out. 'I will give you my oath that I will never repeat any of this, if you can persuade your father not to pursue Tobie Strange.'

Edmund looks at her, considering, tapping his teeth with

his thumbnail. His swagger has ebbed away; now he seems rattled.

'I told several of my friends that I was coming here to confront Sir Thomas,' she persists. 'If I don't return, they'll know exactly where to look. You can't load me in a barrow and dump me at The Theatre with the same ease.' She should not have said that, she realises; she has given Fred away.

'Stop talking, woman, I'm trying to think.' He snaps the words at her; she remembers again the stories of his temper, and backs off. She can't afford to provoke him now.

Before he can speak again, there is a clatter of hooves on the cobbles outside. Edmund strides to the window and peers out to the courtyard.

'Damn, there is my father returned early.' He turns back to her. 'We can come to an accommodation on this matter, I am sure. I will speak to him about the boy. But I need you to wait here, and not make things worse by screaming or drawing attention to yourself. Understand?'

Sophia sees no option but to nod her agreement.

Edmund holds his hand out to his stepmother. 'Key.'

Roused from her thoughts, Lady North passes him a key from her purse. Sophia's heart sinks; he means to lock her in.

At the door, Lady North turns back to her. She appears to have aged ten years in the past hour.

'I never meant for her to die, Mistress de Wolfe,' she says, her voice dull again. 'I don't know what took hold of me – when she said those dreadful things, it was like a red mist in my head. I only meant to – I could not know she was so fragile.'

'She was a child,' Sophia says, as the door closes behind them and she hears the key turn in the lock.

THIRTY-FIVE

She watches from the window as Edmund North hurries across the courtyard to intercept his father. How much does Sir Thomas guess at, she wonders – or is he content to believe that Vincent Lovell killed Agnes? Easier for him, she supposes, than to acknowledge the currents of guilt and coercion playing out under his own roof.

The two men disappear into the house and Sophia turns her attention to the opposite window. She doesn't trust Edmund North an inch, and he has badly underestimated her if he thinks she will sit here patiently, locked in a tower like a lady in a courtly tale, waiting for him to decide her fate. On the west side of the room, the casement opens on to a gulley between the chimney and the pitched roof of the neighbouring wing. From here, as long as the tiles are not too icy, she could edge her way along the roof a few feet to the point where it meets a jutting section of wall, and from here drop down to the courtyard wall. It would be dangerous, even in the best weather conditions, but then so is staying put. She removes her knife from its hidden pocket, then unfastens her skirt from her bodice and lets it drop to the floor, where she steps out of it and tucks the knife into the waist of her fencing breeches. The sight of the crumpled material makes her smile;

when Edmund returns, it will look as if she has simply dissolved into the air.

The first part is easy, though out on the roof the cold air bites, and without her cloak she is soon shivering, her fingers numb and clumsy. She remembers hiding with Ben on the roof above Tobie's lodgings while Thomas North's men searched his room; it feels like months ago now, though it was barely two days. The danger comes when she emerges from behind the chimney stack; the exposed section of roof she must traverse is less than twenty feet, but there is nothing to hold on to except icy tiles, and a narrow gutter on which to balance. Below her is a fifty-foot drop to the courtyard; she will not survive that intact if she slips.

Taking a deep breath, feeling for purchase with her fingertips, she lies flat against the roof, face down, with the toes of her boots pressed into the gutter. Inch by inch, she works her way along, feeling the lead of the gutter bending under her weight. The snow soaks through her clothes, chilling her to the bone, so that she feels as if her hands belong to someone else; she must place them as if blind and hope they obey. Once her left foot slips and the sudden shift in weight almost tips her off the edge, but she jams her fingers into a gap in the tiles and clings on, righting herself, pulse hammering in her throat. Eventually she reaches the point where she can lower herself on to the abutting wall; she crouches there, shaking, while she recovers her breath. From here, it's a mere ten-foot drop to the rear wall of the courtyard, and below this is a pile of shovelled snow, into which she lets herself fall with a muffled thud, jarred but not hurt.

As she stands, brushing herself down, Fred rushes out from the stable leading Nyx by the reins. He stares at her in disbelief.

'What's the matter, Fred – never seen a woman escape from a tower before?'

'Mistress, you'd better hurry. I heard Master Edmund say

something to Sir Thomas about you being an unwelcome visitor.'

'Anything else?'

'Yes. Sir Thomas said he was not to deal with you here, and Edmund said, easy enough to have an accident on the road in this weather. He asked me to saddle his horse. I believe they mean you harm, mistress.'

'I believe so too. Listen, Fred – you may not be safe either. Get to the Saracen's Head on Snow Hill as fast as you can, ask for Ben Hammett. Tell him I sent you, and that I need his help – he should come to my house urgently. Mistress de Wolfe on Broad Street, remember?'

'I remember.' Fred hands her the reins. 'Mistress, you're shivering. You'll catch your death before you get home – take my jacket. I have another. Quick.'

He shrugs off the shapeless item and Sophia puts it on over her wet clothes: rough homespun, smelling of horses and male sweat. It's a gallant gesture, and oddly comforting. She mounts and wheels her horse towards the gate.

'Saracen's Head, Ben Hammett,' she says, as she spurs the animal on.

'Are you sure you'll be all right, mistress?'

'I can look after myself,' she calls back, and prays that it's true.

An accident on the road. She thinks of the man who ambushed her on the way back from Burghley House, delivering his threatening note with a dramatic flourish. That had been a performance, but Anthony was right: the next time it could be a knife in the gut, just as easily as Essex's man had done to the boy Badger. She is known to be a rich woman; it would be wholly plausible that she had found herself a target for robbers, out riding alone. Was it Edmund or Jasper who attacked her, she wonders. It doesn't seem, from Edmund's story, that they had involved anyone else in disposing of

Agnes – no servants or friends who might subsequently need paying off. It sounds as if they had managed it all themselves – even Jasper's story of the man accosting him at the Barbican sounds like a ruse to pry information out of her. In which case, every time she has sensed that she is being followed over the past few days, it must have been one or other of them. She suspects Jasper of the note: he had been at Broad Street that same evening, and could have hung about and followed her to Burghley House.

She rides with her knife in her hand and takes a circuitous route home, under the Aldersgate, down St Martin's Le Grand to Cheapside and back up to Lothbury, keeping to wider streets where there is less chance of someone surprising her from a doorway. Despite Fred's jacket, she is so comprehensively frozen that she can barely make her limbs obey her, but she forces herself to stay alert for any disturbance at the edge of her vision, any passer-by who looks at her a heartbeat too long, footsteps or hoofbeats at her back. At the Cheapside Cross, a crippled man lurches towards her, mumbling about alms for a soldier; she screams at him to get back, and afterwards feels guilty at the shock in his eyes. All the while she rides, she thinks of Jasper, laboriously penning that doggerel verse and translating it into a cipher he found in his father's papers, to send her the message that he could ruin her, then delivering it via the body of a dead girl. She had always guessed that Jasper was dangerous, especially after they learned the terms of Humphrey's will, but until now she had not understood how dangerous. *Stolen ground. Sins.* He read Walsingham's letter to Humphrey, she is certain. Which means he knows she had a son. At the time of that letter, Walsingham didn't know Tobie's identity. But, while Jasper may have many faults, he is not stupid. It would not take him long to work it out, if he hasn't already. And what will he do with that information, once he does? She needs to tell Tobie before Jasper has the chance.

She is so braced for combat that it is almost disappointing to arrive at her own house without incident. She tucks her knife away and tells the armed guards on her gate not to admit anyone unknown to the household, but to expect Ben Hammett shortly. In the yard she dismounts and calls out for her stable boy; after a moment, Mick appears, leading a fine chestnut gelding by the reins.

'What are you doing, Mick?' She frowns. 'That's not your job.'

'Stable lad's taken sick. Bad chest. I'm helping out.' He doesn't remark on her unusual outfit. 'You're shivering badly, mistress. You should get warm right away, or you'll get a bad chest and all.'

'I know this horse,' she says, as the gelding snorts impatiently and stamps a hoof.

'Yeah.' Mick jerks his thumb at the house. 'That little prick's here again.'

'For God's sake. Why did Hilary let him in?'

'Hilary's not back yet, mistress. Lina let him in.'

Of course she did. Sophia keeps a hand on the knife as she enters the house. In the back of her mind is a nagging thought: what if Hilary never comes back? What if she has walked out for good because she was so insulted by Sophia's distrust? It's a worry that will have to wait, eclipsed as it is by the question of what Jasper wants from her this time. He doesn't yet know what she has learned about his part in Agnes's death; she hopes that will give her some advantage.

She has barely set foot in the hall when Lina comes bowling up, twisting her hands together.

'Master Jasper is here, mistress.'

'So I see. Where is he?'

'He went upstairs to the Green Chamber, still in his cloak and boots with his sword at his belt. I couldn't stop him.' The girl is on the verge of tears. 'Mistress, I have done wrong,' she blurts. 'I beg your forgiveness. I let him deceive me.'

Sophia turns at the foot of the stairs.

'Oh God, you're not pregnant as well, are you?'

Lina looks horrified. 'No, mistress, I never – not that – but he gave me presents and sweet words, he said he would take me out to the bear-baiting, and I let him—'

'I really don't need the details, Lina.'

'—I let him look through the master's papers one time when you were out.' She bursts into messy sobs. 'He told me there were letters from his dear mother and you were keeping them from him out of spite. And I knew where you kept the key, you see, in your cabinet – I'm sorry, truly. Please don't dismiss me.'

'Why are you telling me this now?' Sophia sets off up the stairs. She is furious with the girl, but that will have to wait.

Lina follows behind, still whimpering. 'Because the next time he came, I reminded him about the bear-baiting and he laughed. And he spoke such harsh words to me, I couldn't believe he could be so cruel. As if once he'd got what he wanted, he forgot all his promises.'

'That's men for you.' Sophia is finding it hard to summon much sympathy, but the girl is very young. 'Stay downstairs, Lina, and don't open the door to anyone else, except Ben when he arrives.'

On the first floor she stops in the gallery to lift up the lid of the window seat and take out the case containing her fencing rapiers. She selects her favourite, the lightest and easiest to balance, and removes the small wooden button that covers the tip for practice bouts. Keeping the weapon pressed against the side of her leg, she pushes open the doors at the far end and crosses the landing to the Green Chamber.

Jasper is standing with his back to the door and his hands clasped behind him, his gaze fixed on the painting of his parents' wedding. She has the impression that he has been standing like that for some time, so that she could discover him in this pose. She clears her throat, though he is well aware of her presence; he half-turns, enough to register her clothes.

'Good grief, are you going to a costume party as a beggar?' He looks back at the picture. 'I can see why you would want this painting out of the way. See how beautiful my mother was.'

Sophia leans the rapier silently against the door frame and takes a step closer. It's true that Maud de Wolfe was striking: the pointed face and beady eyes that seem rodent-like on her son sit better on her; she is as delicate as a china doll. But that is not what interests Sophia. Her eye falls on the jewelled brooch Maud is wearing pinned to the front of her elaborate bodice. A background of white stones, with red stones forming a horizontal band, above it three red circles. How had she never noticed it before?

'Very beautiful,' she agrees. 'And high-born too.'

He looks at her narrowly, as if she might be mocking. 'Her great-grandmother was a Devereux,' he says. 'Did Humphrey tell you that? Probably didn't want to make you feel inferior. Not that the Earl of Essex would ever acknowledge me as kin, since my father was a tradesman in his eyes.' The bitterness in his tone suggests that this rejection is not hypothetical. He has approached Essex and been knocked back. 'But still. We are cousins, however distant. Noble blood flowed in my mother's veins, which is more than can be said for you.'

'I had better return this to you, then.' She reaches into the purse at her belt and takes out the brooch. 'It's your mother's, I think – the same one she has on there. You left it in Agnes Lovell's grave, along with a letter intended for me.'

He turns slowly and meets her eye; she doesn't flinch, though she has to clench her teeth to stop them chattering. A number of expressions chase their way across Jasper's face; in the end he opts for amusement.

'That was rather clever, wasn't it? An encrypted warning. I'd originally planned to send the letter anonymously to you at the playhouse, that's why I wrote it in a pastiche of bad verse. But when Edmund dragged me into that mess of his stepmother's making, I saw a better opportunity. A note found with a murdered girl would get far more attention. I thought all the pamphleteers would be speculating about it.' He seems disappointed.

'To what purpose?' Sophia says. 'What did you hope to achieve?'

'To warn you. To let you know that you could not rest safe, in my father's house, with my father's money. To show you that someone knew about your past, and what you were.'

'And what is that?' She has to fight to keep her voice steady.

'I guessed there was something about you from the very beginning,' he says, jabbing a finger towards her. 'When my father came home and announced that he intended to marry a nobody, some governess he'd fallen in love with at first sight, I didn't believe a word of it. Humphrey de Wolfe never did anything on impulse. I reckoned there would be some politicking behind it, but it took me a long while to find out.'

'Politicking?'

'I'm not a fool, Sophia. I always knew what my father did. Alongside his legitimate business, I mean. Men coming and going with letters at all hours of the night, whisperings in corridors, Sir Francis Walsingham dropping by, shutting himself away with my father behind closed doors for hours – I worked it out before I was twelve years old. And I became very skilled at listening and hiding. If I'm honest, I was offended that they never recruited me when I came of age.'

'I imagine they thought you didn't have the temperament for the business,' she says coldly.

'I realised my father had married you as a favour to Walsingham,' he says, ignoring this, 'so I guessed you must have done them some service. Of course, it's well known what methods women spies use to get information, so I've always assumed you were a whore. But I never presumed to confront my father to his face – he'd made his choice, for whatever reason. For six years I tolerated you in my mother's place, I lived in fear that you would give my father a son he could be proud of – thank God that didn't happen – but I never imagined that you would find a way to cozen me so comprehensively out of everything.'

'Not this again. Jasper, I had nothing to do with Humphrey's will. It was as much a surprise to me.'

'But less of a disappointment, eh? After his death, when I saw you had no intention of righting the injustice of a will he made when we were at odds, I swore I would find out all I could about you so that I could expose you. And there was plenty to find, wasn't there, Sophia Underhill?'

'So you thought, with that ciphered rhyme, that you could frighten me into signing everything over to you?'

'Not *everything*.' He gives her a thin smile. 'Just the share of my father's estate that is rightfully due to me as his only son. I'll let you keep a modest widow's portion – I'm not a monster.'

'Or what?'

'Or I will put it about town that you had a Jesuit traitor's bastard and sold it.'

'And I will put it about town that you dumped Agnes Lovell's body at The Theatre.'

'No one will believe that. It's been announced that her uncle killed her. Whereas people will be all too ready to believe the worst about you. All the city wives hate you – you think you're above them because you read Latin and Greek. And a lot of my father's former business associates take my side – they think you must have duped him into disinheriting me. It's even been insinuated – his death being so sudden – that you and your blackamoor witch friend worked on him with poisons.'

This is her breaking point. Jasper himself is the only person who would set that rumour snaking through London. She lunges at him, her arm raised to strike him before she has registered the urge to do so, but this time he is ready for her: with a soft whisper, his sword slides from its scabbard and points at the tender pulse of her throat.

She takes a step back and he matches her, forcing her towards the door. She lets out a wild bark of laughter.

'What will you do – run me through in my own home? How will you explain that away? My servants saw you come in.'

'I'll say you attacked me and I was obliged to defend myself. I should have done this long ago.'

She takes another step back and he follows, closing the distance between them. She can feel the scratch of steel against her skin. It only needs one more step . . .

'If you kill me, you'll lose all hope of getting anything from your father's estate,' she says.

'What?' The tension in his sword arm slackens a fraction.

'I have no official heir at present.' She is speaking at twice her normal speed. 'In the event of my death, under the terms of Humphrey's will, a portion of the estate goes to charitable causes and the rest reverts to the crown. It doesn't come back to you. I suppose you could contest it in the courts, but good luck getting that money back from the queen once she's got her hands on it. Whereas if I live, perhaps this would be a good time for us to discuss how to dispose of your father's assets more equitably. I'm your only chance of improving your situation. As long as you convince your friend Edmund North not to have me murdered and left in a ditch.'

Jasper hesitates; she can see that he is weighing up whether to believe her. In that pause, she takes another step back, reaches behind with her right hand and snatches up her rapier from the doorway. With one smooth stroke she brings it up to clash against his blade; he is so startled that he almost drops his weapon, but he quickly recovers and lunges at her, putting her on the back foot. She parries, allowing him to move forward, keeping her moves defensive to give him a false sense of superiority, until he has pushed her through the door and on to the landing, where she suddenly turns and thrusts in quarte over the arm, forcing him to change direction. Now she is the one on the offensive; he glances over his left shoulder and realises he is in danger of being driven towards the stairs. To avoid that, he shifts to his right and she closes in on him, forcing him backwards through the double doors and into the gallery.

Jasper has no finesse, but he is dogged; what he lacks in grace, he makes up for in aggression, and Sophia, who has only fought elegant display bouts intended to show her fine technique, and never against an opponent who wanted her dead, is obliged to rapidly change her style of attack. They move down the gallery in tandem to the ring of clashing steel, now one gaining ground, now the other; an ornamental table crashes to the floor, a tapestry is ripped from its fastenings, a chair is kicked aside, but neither will give an inch. Grim-faced, Sophia wipes sweat from her brow with her free hand; it hardly seems possible that only moments ago she had thought she might never feel warm again. Jasper too is breathing hard; while he is stronger than her, and younger, his fondness for wine and tobacco go some way to countering that advantage.

'It's not true – is it,' he pants, as he drives her towards the windows at the far end, 'that you – have no heir? What about – your son?'

He is trying to distract her, but she will not be drawn; she feints, then lunges on her left leg; caught off guard, he moves his arm too high and the tip of her rapier catches him under the ribs. He curses, and comes back at her with renewed ferocity.

'I know who he is,' he says, through his teeth. Though the touch wasn't deep, blood begins to soak through the side of his shirt.

'You're wrong,' she hisses back, angry with herself for being drawn in, though she wants to shut down his speculation as quickly as possible, in case he thinks of going after Tobie. 'My son – died – as a baby—' The words feel like stones in her mouth; she is not superstitious, but for a moment she hopes she hasn't taunted the Fates by speaking it aloud.

'Horseshit,' Jasper says, taking advantage of her distraction to drive her back towards the wall. 'It's one – of those – player boys. That's why you're always – hanging around – the theatres—'

'I told you – he's dead!' But she has allowed herself to become emotional; she has lost her calm, and when he makes a false thrust, causing her to lower her blade, she is not quick enough to parry as he lunges over the arm, aiming for her face; she twists away, and the point of his weapon scores along her collarbone. Pain sears through her shoulder, hot blood courses down her arm and chest; she stumbles, but before he can deliver another stroke she surges at him with a roar, no precision but pure fury, striking at his sword arm and catching him a fierce blow that rips along his flesh above the wrist. His weapon falls to the ground with a clatter; he clutches at the wound with his left hand and she kicks his leg from under him so that he falls on his side. She stands over him, her rapier pointed at his throat.

'Jesus, Sophia, you've proved your point.' He twists his head to squint up at her. 'Enough now. This wound needs a surgeon. So does yours, by the look of it.'

She puts a foot on his injured arm until he cries out. His face has turned white; he seems to have realised that she is in earnest. His eyes widen in fear.

'What do you want? You're not seriously going to kill me in my father's house?'

'I'd say it was self-defence.' She jabs the steel tip gently at his skin and he yelps. 'Really, Jasper, who would miss you? No one. Maybe the landlord of the Half-Eagle and a couple of whores over the river, and they'll soon find new customers.

Edmund North only keeps you around in case you can be useful to him. If I cut your throat right now, there's not a soul in London would mourn you. They'd have to pay strangers to go to your funeral.'

She expects him to retaliate with a choice insult, but all the fight drains from him; instead he curls into a ball, silent tears sliding from his eyes. Her words have scored a truer hit than her blade, it seems. But she can't pity him; if the fight had gone differently, she has no doubt that he would have had no hesitation in putting his sword through her neck – and smiling as he did it.

'Oh, get up, I'm not going to kill you. But only for Humphrey's sake, and because you're not worth the trouble.'

Before Jasper can move, the doors at the far end of the gallery are flung open; she turns to see Ben and Hilary standing on the threshold.

'Sophia, no!' Ben hurls himself the length of the gallery; she steps back and drops her rapier. She realises her hands are shaking; there is a quantity of blood on her sleeve, and she can't work out whose it is.

'Blimey, I thought you were going to skewer him,' Ben says, moving her gently to one side so he can lift Jasper to his feet. 'Come on, mate.' He straightens Jasper as if he were a child. 'Got someone who wants to talk to you. *Cecil*,' he mouths to Sophia over his shoulder.

'I think he needs a doctor,' Sophia says. Her voice sounds faint in her ears.

'We'll sort him out on the way,' Ben says, unwinding a scarf from his neck and wrapping it tightly around Jasper's wounded arm. 'You could do with one, too.'

'I'll send for Leila,' Hilary says. 'Come to the kitchen and we'll bathe that cut in the meantime.'

Sophia turns to her steward. She has never been so grateful to see her. 'I thought you'd gone.'

'Some business matters to attend to,' Hilary says briskly.

'I'll explain later. There's something downstairs you should see.'

Ben has Jasper firmly by his good arm; Hilary supports Sophia, who feels increasingly that her legs will not hold her up for much longer. In the hall they find Mick stoically containing Edmund North by pinning both arms behind his back.

'Mistress de Wolfe.' Edmund tries to sound high-handed. 'Tell your ape to let me go – I only wanted to talk to you.'

'Caught him trying to climb over the wall, madam,' Mick says.

'This one should come with me as well,' Ben says. 'If you can spare your man here.'

Sophia nods weakly, and Mick and Ben lead their captives towards the yard. She feels suddenly overwhelmed by exhaustion. She stumbles, and Hilary catches her around her waist; she leans into her steward and realises she is shivering violently.

'I'm sorry I doubted you,' she murmurs, into Hilary's bony shoulder.

'It's forgotten,' Hilary says, though her voice sounds muffled and distant; Sophia feels herself falling, and everything goes dark.

THIRTY-SIX

5th January 1599

The Blackfriars theatre shimmers with the glow of a hundred candles (a hundred and forty, to be precise, as Richard Burbage tells anyone who will listen), and the light refracts and glitters in the facets of jewels and the sheen of expensive fabrics. This is a select audience of invited guests to circumvent the legal restrictions – courtiers and affluent city people, aldermen and guild masters – though they have all been encouraged this evening to make a generous donation towards the building of the Chamberlain's Men's new playhouse south of the river. Burbage is confident that, with their support, it can be operational by the summer – but then Burbage is always confident, that's what makes people reach for their purses. It will rise like a phoenix from the scattered timbers of The Theatre, and it will be called The Globe, because it will offer Londoners the whole world in a wooden O.

But for tonight they play a festive comedy: jigs and crossdressing, mistaken identities and thwarted love – all the crowd-pleasers; the guests, for all their sophistication, show their delight with whoops and stamping feet. After the last applause has died away and the actors have taken their bows,

Tobie steps out on stage into a pool of golden light, alone except for the Italian lute-player who positions himself unobtrusively at the back. The rustling of skirts and chinking of gold chains settles, as the audience sits forward expectantly to see what the angel-faced boy will do.

Tobie closes his eyes and begins to sing. It's a simple arrangement of a sonnet that opens with the line 'Shall I compare thee to a summer's day?' Even now that it has broken, Tobie's voice seems to come from another sphere; it has a quality that transports the listener, that connects directly with all their deepest joys and sorrows. The melody is spare and haunting; it embodies a yearning for something once known, now lost. Throughout the theatre no one moves; you could hear a pin drop. When he sings the line, 'But thy eternal summer shall not fade' to the bare accompaniment of the lute strings, Sophia feels the hairs on her arms and neck stand up.

So long as men can breathe, or eyes can see,
So long lives this, and this gives life to thee.

'For Agnes,' he says, as the final note reverberates around the hall, and bows his head.

Sophia realises that her face is wet with tears. All around her, noblemen and ladies are surreptitiously digging handkerchiefs from their sleeves and dabbing at their eyes, too stunned to applaud. What they have seen is less a performance and closer to a collective act of devotion. She is sitting at the back of the theatre, near the door, and she takes the opportunity to slip out into the cold night. She is still weak from three days of fever that felled her after her escape from Edmund North and her duel with Jasper. Beneath her high-collared dress, her wound itches; Leila stitched it carefully and every day she must change the bandage and bathe it with a special tincture to keep out corruption, but she will have a scar. She will not be able to wear a low bodice in public, unless she is prepared to explain it.

She leans against the balustrade at the top of the stairs and watches her breath rise into the night. There has been no more snowfall; a thaw is beginning, but the weather is still bitter. She has reason to be grateful to the ice, though; if not for the frozen Thames, Tobie might be in Antwerp now, or God knows where. Lost in these thoughts, she doesn't notice that a man in a dark cloak has materialised at her side until he speaks; startled, she leaps back, reaching for the knife in her skirts. Another effect of the past week: she has become nervous, jumping at shadows. The man steps back, alarmed.

'Master Secretary would like a word,' he murmurs, gesturing for her to follow.

He leads her down the stairs and through a door into a vast vaulted space under the theatre: the undercroft of the former Great Hall, where the Chamberlain's Men store their costumes and props. The messenger disappears, and Sophia is left alone with Sir Robert Cecil, who seems incongruous in his black velvet suit among the painted flats, feathered wings and masks hanging from the walls. She had not noticed him in the audience; he must have been lurking in the shadows, as always.

'Good to see you've recovered,' he says, without sentiment.

'It would take more than a fever to break me.'

'So I understand. I thought you might appreciate an update on the business, since you have been ill. Sir Thomas North has agreed to drop all charges against the Strange boy. Given that his wife is so unwell, he will have little time to pursue frivolous lawsuits of any kind.'

'Thank you.'

'But the boy should set his sights more modestly next time. If you are in a position to influence him, make sure he knows that. Meanwhile Edmund North will be going back to Ireland with the Earl of Essex. He already has his commission.'

'*Ireland?*'

'Yes. Her Majesty was so pleased with his service last time that she is giving him the opportunity to prove himself again.'

'Last time he led his men unprepared into a massacre and fled the field,' she says drily.

'Then let us hope he will use this occasion to redeem himself,' Cecil says. He lifts an eyebrow. 'I thought you'd be pleased. His record of incompetence means there's a good chance he won't come back. Either way, he will be where he can't do you any harm.'

His record of incompetence means there's a good chance plenty of innocent men won't come back either, Sophia thinks. It seems a high price to pay for her own safety.

'Edmund North has been made to understand the consequences to his family if any accident should befall you or anyone associated with you,' Cecil continues. 'As for your stepson, Jasper de Wolfe . . .' He shakes his head in irritation, as if even having to speak of Jasper is an imposition on his time. 'There was a lawsuit in the offing against him as well. A young woman he's got with child. Did you know about that?'

'He mentioned a grocer's daughter.'

Cecil smiles faintly. 'Well. Her father is Master of the Worshipful Company of Grocers. A man of some influence. He was very insistent that Jasper make reparation by marrying her. That lawsuit has been made to go away, on certain conditions. Jasper de Wolfe is to retire to his house in Northamptonshire and live quietly. If he comes anywhere near your person or your property, or anyone associated with you, there will be swift and severe repercussions. I hope that puts your mind at rest on that score. In any case,' he adds, turning away, 'I hear his sword arm is badly damaged. Tendons cut, the surgeon says. He's unlikely to be fighting any duels in the near future.'

It won't stop him, she thinks. She feels some guilt over

Jasper's injury, and she has sent him money by way of recompense, but she knows the damage to his arm is nothing compared with the insult to his pride. He may slink away to his country house for a while, but he will not forgive her; in time he will forget that she spared his life and remember only what she has taken from him, and he will crouch there in the dark, nursing his clawed hand and plotting his revenge.

'Thank you again,' she says. 'And Essex?'

'As I said before – justice is imperfect, but it usually finds a way. Essex will bring himself down, trust me. I know that's not the answer you want, but we must have patience. You are free to go home and live quietly now. Should you choose.'

'Should I *choose*?'

He has his back to her; he is taking an intense interest in a rack of costumes. 'I freely admit I underestimated you, Mistress de Wolfe. Your tenacity, your insight. Your courage, I might add. I had heard Walsingham praise your qualities, but I confess I have always been somewhat sceptical about the wisdom of using women as agents in the field. Too volatile.'

It is fortunate that he can't see her expression. She hopes he can feel her eyes boring into his back.

Perhaps so, because he drops the hem of a shimmering fairy gown abruptly and turns to look at her.

'I am rebuilding the Service. It is my ambition to restore it to the force it once was under Francis Walsingham, when the realm was saved multiple times by the work of gifted intelligencers. God knows, we need it more than ever now, with the matter of—' He stops himself judiciously.

'The matter of the succession,' Sophia says.

Cecil inclines his head. It is treason to speak of the queen's death, and yet she is nearing seventy; her ministers cannot pretend she will go on for ever.

'The way you pursued the truth of this girl's murder, and didn't waver. I was impressed. These are skills I could use, if you were minded to lend them to England's service again.'

'I had help.'

'Anthony Munday. Yes, he's good. I would like to bring him back too. What do you say?'

She pauses, looking him square in the eye. Already she can feel the jolt in her pulse, the heat like strong drink spiking through her veins. 'It would be my honour.'

He steps forward to shake her hand with a strong grip, unsmiling; the protection of England is serious business. But then his demeanour softens.

'He has an extraordinary gift,' he says quietly.

'Anthony?'

'Your boy. When he sang, it was as if—' He shakes his head; it will not do for Master Secretary to show too much emotion. 'My William is fond of music, but he lacks discipline. I wonder if Master Strange would be interested in giving him tuition? Alongside his work with the Chamberlain's Men, naturally.'

'I'm sure he would be delighted.' Sophia feels her face burning with pride; she also understands this is a reward to her. Music tutor to Master Secretary's son: Tobie would have some status and security that did not rely on her. It's an offer of protection.

'Good. I'll speak to Burbage. I must go.' He moves towards the door.

'You're not staying for the reception?'

'I'm needed at Whitehall. But this has been a pleasant diversion. Give you good night, Mistress de Wolfe.' Halfway down the undercroft he pauses by a crate and picks up an object. 'What's this?'

He is holding an ass's head, with large pointed ears and a comically downturned mouth, made from canvas over a wire frame and covered with real horsehair.

'It's Bottom's head,' she says. 'You know – from *Midsummer Night's Dream*.'

'Never saw it.' He turns the thing between his hands. Sophia suppresses a smile; she can see that he is dying to try it on, but he wouldn't dream of doing so in front of her. She decides to leave him to it.

'Give you good night, Master Secretary,' she says, climbing the steps. Like Eurydice, she knows she must not look back.

There is a reception for the invited guests in the theatre following the show. Lord Hunsdon has dipped into his purse for once to fund it; servants circulate with trays of hot punch and pastries, while in the pit, the cream of London mingles, sparkling and laughing, showing off their finery. Burbage holds court among them, moving easily through the throng, solicitously ensuring that everyone has enough to eat and drink and have they considered a gift to the new theatre yet, because his man of business will be happy to go through the details . . .

Sophia leans against the panelling at the back of the tiered seats, in the dark, too tired to make conversation but taking pleasure in watching how knights of the realm and their ladies flock around Tobie, eager to shake his hand and shower him with compliments. She becomes aware of a presence at her side and turns her head to see the man from Stratford, arms folded, observing the scene from a distance, as he does.

'A successful night,' she remarks.

'Oh yes. Burbage is raking in donations. And we're going to need them – Giles Allen is preparing his lawsuit for the theft of The Theatre the minute the courts open.' He shifts his weight. 'Talking of lawsuits – Sir Thomas North has decided to stop plaguing me with threats of legal retribution. I understand I have you to thank for that.'

She waves this away. 'I think Sir Thomas has bigger worries than whether someone has copied his work.'

'I didn't copy his work,' he says sharply. 'All writers borrow – we are magpies. North should know that.'

Protesting a bit too much, she thinks, but she nods and says nothing.

'But you're right – terrible business with his ward. And I heard his wife has gone mad with grief – she's had to go into the Bedlam.'

She looks at him from the tail of her eye. 'They said she'd taken to wandering the house at night in her shift, trying to scrub imaginary bloodstains from the walls.'

'Really?' He looks instantly alert. She sees him squirrel that away for later. 'Interesting. Poor woman. Who told you?'

'A servant from the North house.' The stable boy Fred, to be precise, who is now her stable boy. For herself, Sophia can't find much sympathy for Lady North, whose derangement is not born of grief but guilt. And yet, in the moment she had lashed out at Jasper, she understood what Judith had meant about the red mist.

'He stole the show tonight,' Will Shakespeare says, following her gaze to where Tobie stands at the foot of the stage, his hands clasped ardently by an elderly marquess.

'Your words?' she asks.

'My poem, but his music. He made it live. You must be very proud.'

'Me?' She looks at him narrowly.

'Tell me, Mistress de Wolfe. What is he to you? What relation?'

She presses her lips together. She could deny it, but she knows she wouldn't fool him.

'I mean no harm,' he says softly. 'But once you have seen it, you can't unsee. It's the eyes.'

She smiles, despite herself. 'Lynx eyes.'

'Ah. He told you. You know, legend says the lynx has the power to see through stone.'

'I think you have that power, Master Shakespeare.'

'Will, please.'

A silence stretches between them. Eventually she says, 'I'm his mother.'

He nods, unsurprised. 'I guessed as much. Does he know?'

'Not yet.'

'Then he will not hear it from me.' He turns his face away. 'My son would have been almost that age now. You are fortunate.'

'I'm so sorry.' They stand side by side in wordless understanding for a minute or more.

'I'll leave you to it,' he murmurs, as Tobie approaches, bounding up the steps between the seats two at a time. He bows to the boy and slips away.

'Mistress de Wolfe.' Tobie lowers his gaze and shuffles awkwardly from foot to foot. Offstage, he has none of the poise that comes so naturally to him when he sings. 'I have not had a chance to thank you for all your kindness to me during my recent troubles. Truly, I don't know how I can repay you.'

'You don't need to. I'm only glad to see you safe and free. And not in Antwerp.'

He gives a self-conscious laugh. 'Yes, that was foolish. I just wanted to run away from everything. I'm glad Anthony found me in time. He made me see that there are people who care for me in London.'

'He's a good man.'

'He's in love with you.' He says it quite matter-of-factly. 'I suppose you know that.'

'Don't be silly. We're old friends.'

Tobie gives her a look such as only a fifteen-year-old boy can give an adult who is being obtuse. 'If you say so.'

'You sang beautifully tonight,' she says, changing the subject.

'I sang for Agnes.' He falls silent. 'I wish you could have met her. It's not just that she was lovely – she was bold and clever and funny too. She made me laugh. You would have liked her.'

'I am certain of it.' She wants to weep for him. She wonders if there will come a day when he will introduce her to another girl he loves.

'Well, anyway, I just wanted to thank you before I go home,' he says, twisting his hands together.

'Are you still at Anthony's?'

'Yes. They've been very kind, but I should go back to my lodgings. Now that I know I won't be arrested, I have no excuse.'

'May I ride back with you? I need to see Anthony, and I'm done with making polite conversation here.' She nods to the press of glittering dignitaries below them. 'Rich people can be very dull, don't you think?'

He grins at her conspiratorial manner. 'You're a rich person,' he points out.

'I suppose so.' She feigns alarm. 'Oh no. Perhaps I'm dull too, and haven't realised?'

'Nah. But I'll give you fair warning if you are.'

They ride in companionable silence, a link-boy lighting the way. She finds herself suddenly shy with Tobie, unsure what to say, searching for an opening to the conversation that will not alarm him. She may not be given another opportunity like this. Every time she glances sidelong at him, she sees his father in profile.

'Tell me about your parents,' she says, as they pass along Wood Street.

He looks surprised. 'What about them?'

'Well – anything. Were they kind, stern, did they play games with you, did they encourage your music? I'm curious.'

She judges from his expression that no one has ever shown curiosity about his family before. He considers.

'They were just . . . ordinary,' he says eventually. 'My mother was a quiet woman – my father spoke over her most of the time. I suppose you would call him stern, though he never beat me. When I was disobedient – which was quite often' – he darts her a cheeky smile – 'he used to say "Bad blood", and my mother would say "Christopher!" like she was warning him. I always thought that was an odd thing to say about your own son, but then he could be odd. Strange by name, Strange by nature, they used to say at his guild, but he was liked well enough, I think. He worked hard. I don't know what else to tell you. They were not remarkable people.'

'But you loved them?'

'Of course.' He looks confused, as if the question is redundant. 'I miss them – although it feels like another lifetime that I lived with them in Canterbury. Hard to believe it is not even three years. What about you, Mistress de Wolfe – did you never want children?'

He is too young to know there are a hundred reasons not to ask that question of a woman. But here it is: her cue. Her throat dries.

'Well, Tobie – you see, the thing is, I once—'

She is interrupted by a raucous bellowing; two men lurch towards them out of the shadows; Nyx jibs, whinnying, and before you can blink Sophia draws her knife, wheels the horse around and has the blade levelled at them, screaming curses as she does so.

The men – two drunks who have stumbled unwittingly into their path from a nearby tavern while belting out a bawdy song – look briefly terrified and stagger away, yelling over their shoulders for a pox on the mad bitch.

Tobie stares at her in amazement as she tucks her knife away and tries to steady her breathing.

'That was not dull at all,' he says, with a mixture of admiration and fear.

'You were asking me,' she prompts, as the link-boy creeps out sheepishly from the doorway where he hid and they continue on their way, but Tobie has already forgotten the previous conversation; his thoughts are elsewhere.

'Thinking of my mother, I've remembered this song she used to sing when I was a little child,' he says, and launches into a sweet ballad about a shepherd boy which has so many verses it lasts all the way to the Mundays' door. Next time, Sophia promises herself. She will tell him next time.

She is shown into a cosy parlour where Beth Munday sits with her younger daughter, absorbed in a game of cards, identical fair heads bent close together. It gives Sophia a pang to see them, and to think of the years she never had with Tobie. Then she remembers Will Shakespeare's words: *you are fortunate*. She must remember that. She may have missed Tobie's past, but she will have the years ahead. Beth looks up and smiles.

'Run and get ready for bed now, Annie, while I talk to Mistress de Wolfe.'

When the little girl has gone, Beth folds the deck of cards together neatly together. 'Anthony is still at rehearsals, I'm afraid. We expect him back any minute, but they are working all hours these past days – they play before the queen tomorrow. But please stay and wait for him.'

Beth gestures Sophia to a settle opposite. She sees Anthony's wife take in her dark red velvet with borders of gold thread and pearl, her necklace of rubies; without envy, but with an assessing eye, calculating what the dress is worth. She has a vague memory that Beth's father, like Anthony's, was a master draper.

'I'm afraid I'm rather overdressed,' she says. 'There was a special performance tonight at the Blackfriars, to raise money for the Chamberlain's Men.'

'I know. Tobie has been nervous about his solo. Did he do well?'

'Better than well.'

Beth smiles. 'I knew he would. And you are feeling better? We were sorry you could not come for new year. Anthony said you took a fever.'

'My own fault. Too much riding about in the snow.' *And climbing on roofs*, she thinks.

'Yes, I heard you have been busy. Anthony mentions you often.'

A silence falls. There is only the crackle of the fire and, from somewhere upstairs, the distant laughter of children. Neither woman looks at the other; instead, they watch the flames as if rapt. The silence grows increasingly uncomfortable. Sophia thinks of Tobie's remark; if even a fifteen-year-old has guessed at Anthony's feelings for her, then surely his wife sees it too. Does Beth suspect that she returns his affection, or – God forbid – that they are already involved?

'I should probably go,' she says, half-rising.

'My husband has been very preoccupied, this past week,' Beth says, as if Sophia has not spoken. She leans forward to poke a log that needs no attention. She keeps her voice light. 'We have hardly seen him.'

'The Admiral's Men—'

'No, not the play. I know he was back and forth to your house on some business he would not talk to me about.' She sets the poker down and folds her hands in her lap.

'It's not what you think.'

'You have no idea what I think.' Beth looks up and holds her gaze. There is no reproach in her clear blue eyes. 'I know what work my husband did for Secretary Walsingham in the past. Secret work, I mean. I will not ask you if you have that in common, though I can make an educated guess. But Anthony lives quietly now. We have three children. So I am asking you – imploring you, even – as one woman to another, out of your charity, not to lead him into danger. Because I think' – she knots her fingers tighter, so that the knuckles turn white; it is costing her to say this – 'I think that Anthony would do anything you asked of him.'

Sophia hardly knows how to answer. Does Beth imagine she would ask him to leave his family? Is that the implication?

'Beth, I would never—' How do you tell a woman you

don't want her husband? She tries again. 'Anthony loves you and the children.'

'I think,' Beth says slowly, agitating the fire again, 'it's possible to love in different ways at the same time. It is for men, anyway. We married too young, and too quickly, and I am so often ill – if he yearns for something more, I can't blame him.'

Sophia can see that she needs to put an end to this, or none of them will be free of the suspicion. She wants to explain to Beth that Anthony's yearning for her belongs in a courtly tale, far removed from this messy, noisy family home. If he thinks he loves her, it's precisely because she is unattainable; that's the whole appeal. But she is not sure this is what Beth wants to hear.

'A couple of years ago,' she says softly, 'Anthony did me the greatest service anyone has ever done me. For that I will be for ever in his debt, and owe him my friendship. That friendship is no threat to you or your family, Beth, I swear it.'

'Service,' Beth murmurs. After a moment, she nods. 'I understand. Tobie.'

Sophia stares. 'He *told* you?'

'Oh, no. Anthony would not betray a confidence. But I have eyes. I knew as soon as I saw the boy.' She hesitates. 'And his father?'

'Dead.'

'I'm sorry.'

'It was a long time ago. Tobie doesn't know who I am yet. I need time, to—' To what? She doesn't know the answer.

'He's a lovely boy,' Beth says. The tension has gone out of her shoulders; perhaps she feels reassured. 'We've enjoyed having him here. Richie idolises him and, between you and me, Priscilla is quite taken. The other morning, when Tobie was out, she said, "Master Strange is very handsome, is he not?" And Anthony barked at her, "Don't even think about it." She looked terrified, poor child.'

She smiles. Sophia feels a tightness in her chest; Anthony will have been thinking of the last thirteen-year-old girl who liked Tobie's looks.

The fire ripples in a sudden draught; she turns to see Anthony standing in the doorway, bringing the chill of the night on his clothes and hair. His eyes flick from her to his wife with apprehension; he is afraid of what the women might have been saying.

'Sophia brought Tobie back,' Beth says brightly, standing and smoothing her skirt. 'I'll go and see to the children.' She kisses him briefly on the cheek as she passes, and closes the door behind her.

Anthony takes the seat she has vacated and gives Sophia a questioning look.

'I couldn't do it,' she says, defeated. 'He gave me the perfect opportunity to tell him, and I was scared. What if he hates me? What if he ran away again? The river is almost thawed now – you wouldn't stop him this time. Perhaps I should be content to be his benefactor, except that people keep guessing. Sooner or later someone will say it to him.'

'Which people?'

'Your wife, for one. And Will Shakespeare.'

'I wouldn't trust him an inch,' Anthony says forcefully. 'He'll use it in a play, you watch.'

'He said all writers are magpies.'

'He's more like a bloody vulture. Did Beth say anything else?'

'Only that she thinks I'm going to steal you away from her and the children.'

She expects him to laugh. Instead he looks at her with a terrible helpless longing.

'I told her that was ridiculous. Because you love her. Because you are a faithful husband and a good father.'

'Yes. All of that is true.' He presses his hands between his knees and looks at the floor. 'And yet it is not the whole truth.'

'Cecil asked me to work for him,' she says briskly, to steer them away from treacherous waters. 'It seems I have confounded his expectations of what a woman is capable of.'

Anthony lifts his head. 'Is that what you want?'

'I want to be useful. I'm not made for needlework and gossip and spending someone else's money. That life will send me as mad as Lady North before too long.'

'Sounds idyllic to me,' he says, fetching up a smile. 'Beats being shouted at by Henslowe all day, anyway.'

'He wants you back too,' she says, lowering her voice. 'Cecil. Think about it, Anthony. We're in the final year of the century. The queen is – well, let's just say she's not getting any younger. Things are going to become interesting.'

'I don't know that I like Cecil's methods,' he says. 'He's cold. Vincent Lovell, for instance.'

'But Vincent Lovell's death saved your young priest in the Clink. There's always a trade-off, in this business. We want to think Walsingham was different because he had a fatherly manner, but he was no saint.'

'I always felt that Walsingham did what he did because he cared about England, and the queen. I can't see what moves Cecil beyond ambition, and his need to prove himself to his dead father.'

'Well. Aren't we all doing that, in our own ways?' She smiles. 'I must go. Give it some thought, anyway.'

'As long as it won't involve any more dead children. This last week, thinking about Agnes – it makes me want to lock Priscilla in a tower.'

'I'd teach her how to escape.'

He doesn't laugh. 'They're already making ballads and lurid stories about it, the penny pamphleteers. Look – I picked this up on the way home.' He reaches into his jacket and brings out a damp sheet of paper with a woodcut of a female figure in a grave, under a bold title.

Sophia takes it from him and reads the headline aloud.

'"The Traitor's Bloody Legacy".' She curls her lip as she skims the page. 'They haven't missed the chance to turn a child's death into an anti-Catholic rant. They're shameless, these broadsheet writers, the way they hide behind anonymity.'

'We'll see a lot more of that once there's a new round of taxes for the Irish campaign.' Anthony sighs. 'Sometimes I despair of ever seeing peace in our lifetime. Perhaps our children will be more fortunate. Though I suppose that depends on who succeeds Elizabeth.'

'The one thing we must never speak of aloud.' She turns the pamphlet between her hands. 'I had a friend some years ago, an Italian philosopher, who believed it was possible to bridge the divide between religions if you could show people where they had common ground. I found it hard to share his optimism, but I suppose we have to try – otherwise, what's the alternative? We keep handing down the same bloody legacy.'

She crumples the paper and throws it into the fire. As it crackles and curls, the children's laughter carries to them from the room above, while outside, melting snow drips from roofs and trees, and the moon rises over London in a clear sky. It is almost Twelfth Night.